Racing has been a part of Pe̶̶̶̶̶̶̶̶̶̶̶̶̶̶̶̶̶̶̶̶̶̶̶̶̶̶̶̶̶̶ years, as a strapper, trainer and punter. These days he's involved in the media, managing the racing department for Australian Associated Press. He lives with his wife on Victoria's west coast and can be found most weekends either at the track, surfing his local break or fishing from his kayak.

Previous books by Klein include *A Strapper's Tale*, *Punter's Luck* and *Punter's Turf*. *Silk Chaser* is his third novel.

Also by Peter Klein

Punter's Turf

SILK CHASER

PETER KLEIN

MACMILLAN
Pan Macmillan Australia

First published 2010 in Macmillan by Pan Macmillan Australia Pty Limited
1 Market Street, Sydney

National Library of Australia
Cataloguing-in-Publication data:

Klein, Peter Martin, 1959– .

Silk chaser / Peter Klein.

9781405039765 (pbk.)

A823.4

Typeset by Midland Typesetters, Australia
Printed by McPherson's Printing Group

Papers used by Pan Macmillan Australia Pty Ltd are natural, recyclable products
made from wood grown in sustainable forests. The manufacturing processes
conform to the environmental regulations of the country of origin.

For Robin

1

She was trouble and everyone seemed to know it but me.
    Kate was the first to warn me off, but what would she know? Ex-girlfriends never want you to find anyone else after they've finished with you. Big Oakie White said pretty much the same thing. He's my main bookmaker and I respect his opinion, but he should stick to the horses, something he knows more about.

Jim Beering said to 'watch her'. Can you believe the guy? Beering was a cop for twenty-five years before he lucked into his cushy role as racecourse detective, so it's his job to be suspicious. But *watch her*? Made her sound like a suspect, for Christ sake. Even Billy, who manages my restaurant, had a word in my ear. 'Be careful, Punter, she's a ball breaker.'

I mean, what were they getting at? Was she a livewire? Yeah, so what? I wouldn't want to be with someone who agrees with me all the time. Does she flirt like a movie star? Too right. With her looks, I would too. Does she like a drink? Hell, yeah. I'd be suspicious of her if she didn't. Was I going to spend my money on her, buy her things? You bet, I wanted to. Maxine's only 'crime', as far as I could tell, was being the socialite daughter of talkback radio star Russell Henshaw. Henshaw was about the biggest name in radio, and the word was he had an ego to match his ratings, but I didn't much care for Henshaw or his radio show. It was Maxine, his daughter, I was dating.

I was on the tram on the way to meet her, in fact. I got off in town and for the first time I noticed that the city shop windows were all plastered with Christmas decorations and posters urging shoppers to buy their presents. To be expected, I suppose; it was, after all, the first week in December. Not that I'd done any Christmas shopping yet. I resist the buying of any yuletide gifts for as long as possible. I simply can't stand the big department stores and all the hype and useless stuff they try and sell you. I'm sure I'd think of something over the next few weeks, probably right on Christmas Eve, which is when I usually did my shopping.

I walked along to the restaurant, dodging the Friday night shoppers, and worked out how long I'd known Maxine. I met her barely a month ago in the champagne bar at Caulfield races, yet I'd spent almost every night since either staying overnight at her place, or she at mine. I didn't think that could happen to someone like me. Crazy girl had taken over my life. I hadn't studied a formguide or watched a race replay all week, and for someone who makes a living out of betting on the horses like I do, well, that's just insane. Formguides weren't the only thing I was guilty of forsaking. I hadn't kept my regular weekly meeting with my manager Billy. He runs my pizza restaurant, Gino's, and we meet religiously every Monday to go through the books and discuss business. I'd also missed my usual Tuesday night snooker game at the Red Triangle with Tiny and the boys. Don't think they didn't know what was going on. And for the first time ever, Big Oakie had to chase me for my betting markets on Thursday night. Why? Because I was with Maxine. She had me hook, line and sinker. They said she was trouble. Well, I'd never been happier.

Her curious moon eyes peeped at me over the top of the menu, black-studded diamonds that flickered and shone with amusement, and I knew when she lowered the menu she'd be sporting that infectious smile, ready to laugh at anything I said.

'What? What's so funny?' I demanded.

'You. How you take so long to order anything.'

'I don't.'

'You do. You know you do. You've been there ten minutes reading the menu and you still haven't made your mind up, have you?'

'I would have, only the waiter confused me with his specials.'

'Here he comes now. I'm going to order for both of us if you're not ready. I'm starving.'

She did, too. Aged Warrnambool sirloin and a glass each of an inky-purple, five-year-old Coriole shiraz. Bit of a blokey meal, not what you'd expect a woman to order. But as I was finding out, Maxine wasn't exactly a conventional lady.

'I want mine rare,' she told the waiter. She had her chin on a fist, fingers showing off her rings and other assorted jewellery dangling from her wrist. Her other hand played with shiny strands of shoulder-length black hair.

'That's not medium or well done, but rare, okay?'

The waiter promised 'absolutely' it would be rare. He made a special note with a flourish in his notebook. Probably wrote down *Beware of table six*. When we'd got our drinks, Maxine swirled hers around expertly in the big Riedel's Vinum glass and took a deep sniff.

'God, that's good,' she said. 'And you were, too, last night. I can hardly walk.'

I grinned sheepishly at her across the table. There was a guy and a woman sitting next to us and another table of four on the opposite side. The guy must have heard; he turned his head none too subtly to catch our conversation. His partner would have heard too, but she was pretending not to notice.

'Are you always like that?' she persisted. She had a voice that carried, a radio announcer's voice just like her father's. One that demanded to be heard above a crowd. I leant forward, spoke in a whisper.

'Can we, er, keep it down a bit?'

Maxine laughed at me again. Don't know what she found so amusing. She took one of my hands in hers, spoke a little more softly – but not much – and said, 'I'm sorry, Punter. I didn't mean anyone else to hear.'

I was beginning to blush. Felt a red rash flooding my face like a tide that everyone in the restaurant must surely see. Those moon eyes were fighting back laughter again. Playing with me.

'But you *were* good,' she said. She'd taken her shoe off and I felt her foot explore my calf. Outrageous.

'And what you're doing is against regulations.'

'What regulations?'

'Government thingummy regulations. Applies to all restaurants. No funny stuff by patrons before dessert.'

She giggled again. Hadn't actually removed her foot. Mind you, I hadn't shifted my leg either.

'Would you . . . like to go outside for ten minutes?'

I nearly had a coughing fit. God, didn't she ever play by the rules?

She leant forward slowly across the table so that my eyes zeroed in helplessly on her cleavage like she knew they would. And there was a generous portion of that thrusting out of the little black dress she was wearing. Her smile left her mouth slightly ajar, a delicious little trapdoor revealing her tongue caressing the back of her teeth.

'There's a ladies' powder room out the back,' she whispered huskily.

I must have looked like a shocked prude. It set her off on another giggling fit. This time I could feel every eye in the room on us when she spoke. I leant forward and whispered desperately through clenched teeth, 'Will you cut it out!'

'Don't worry, Punter, I'm not going drag to you off and have you in the powder room before my steak arrives.'

'That's good to know,' I said meekly.

She turned and faced the couple staring at us goggle-eyed from the table opposite. They'd abandoned their own conversation. Why wouldn't they; ours was much more interesting.

'I'll wait till after dessert.'

'You're trouble,' I said with a grin.

I tiptoed gingerly out of her apartment at six the next morning and went home to try and get some form study done for that afternoon's races. Who was the one who could hardly walk? This was getting ridiculous. Che, my sixteen-month-old black Burmese cat told me as much as I let myself guiltily into my apartment. He let out a high-pitched yowl designed to let me know that I'd been neglecting him. I fixed him up some dried food, put on the kettle and jumped into the bathroom for a quick shower.

When I came back out into the kitchen, Che had already finished his breakfast but he gave it a try; pulled a face as though I'd only doled out half rations.

'I don't think so, buster, you've had enough,' I said, picking him up and opening the back door. Outside, Mrs Givan, my downstairs neighbour, was already putting out her first load of washing. A day like today, with a hot northerly and the forecast for thirty-two degrees, she'd be good for at least three more loads. It had me beat how much washing an old widow could possibly find to do.

'Here,' I said to Che, setting him down, 'Go out and play with Mrs Givan. Do you good to get an airing.'

Over freshly ground coffee, I did some form and marked out betting prices for the races I wanted to play. After an hour or so I was done. I suppose I'm what you call a lazy sort of punter. For a person who makes his living from the track, I don't usually dedicate myself to hours of form study like some of the pros do. There's a woman punter I know, they call her the Professor, because she's always studying the horses. She spends up to ten hours a day doing the form; I mean, can you believe it? If the winners don't jump out at me inside of ten minutes, I move on to the next race. I've got better things to do than read the *Winning Post* cover to cover.

My mobile rang; it was Billy.

'Punter, you still catching up with me for breakfast at eight?'

'What's on the menu?'

'Poached eggs and mushrooms on rye and fresh juice and coffee.'

5

'I've already left,' I said, hanging up.

Half an hour later, I drove past Gino's looking for a park. You'd think early on a Saturday morning I'd get a space right outside. Not so. The twenty-four/seven supermarket opposite always had people taking the car parks on the road, so I ended up having to find a spot a couple of hundred metres past the railway boom gates. I hardly ever came over this side of the railway tracks, but when I did I was always surprised by how much it had changed since I was a kid. The shops were all different back then. There was a milk bar where my brother and I used to ogle Mrs Vladimoss's daughter, Angie. In the summer when Angie wore those low-cut tank tops, we'd be in there four times a day. I wonder if she realised we didn't just come in solely for her strawberry malted milkshakes. The milk bar was long gone, as were Mrs Vladimoss and her daughter. So too were the haberdashery and the fish and chip shop. In fact, as I thought about it, most of the new shops that had sprung up replacing them were restaurants and cafés, catering for the younger crowd which had shifted in and always seemed too busy to cook for themselves. There was another pizza shop which had recently opened; competition for Gino's, but it was all good for business and kept Billy on his toes. There was also a Vietnamese restaurant and a Chinese noodle shop, plus a Japanese sushi place which only opened at lunchtimes. It looked like this end of the street was starting to prosper.

Most of these shops seemed to have suddenly sprouted Christmas decorations. Ribbons and streamers and fat red Santa Clauses riding sleighs pulled by reindeer had appeared like mushrooms after a shower of rain. It was like an outbreak, a splash of colour that had swept through the street. I was thinking that perhaps I'd better have a word to Billy about us doing something for Gino's or we'd look the odd one out. As I walked past the Vietnamese restaurant, I noticed a panel of tin sheeting covering a broken front window. Perhaps a kid had left a bike leaning against the glass pane and it had fallen through. Either that or some drunken hoon had kicked it in. A few minutes later I walked under the sign that proudly announced

Gino's Pizza. In smaller letters underneath it said: *Licensee, Billy McCarroll.* I'd cut Billy in on a third of the place, with the only stipulation that my name was kept out of the books. A while ago, I'd come into a windfall. I decided a run-down pizza joint might make a good place to park the money, especially during the winter months when the tracks were too wet to bet on and I couldn't get a reliable earn from the horses. Billy knows how to keep his mouth shut and to this day, the only person who knows it's my business is Billy himself.

I'd owned Gino's for a couple of years now and unlike the early days, it was actually starting to pay me a wage, rather than drain my pockets of cash. I'd finished renovating and transformed it from the dark and dingy place it used to be. I'd put in French doors which opened outwards into the street. I'd replaced all the scungy furniture with colourful, funky tables and chairs from Ikea. When we'd got a liquor licence, I put in a new bar at considerable expense. In fact, about the only thing the place had in common with old man Gino who used to own it, was that his name was still on the sign above the door.

Billy let me in when he heard the bell and then closed the door behind us. He led me out to the kitchen, chattering cheerfully away as he always did, asking me questions then answering them himself before I could even open my mouth.

'How's it going, Punter? Found me a winner for today? Course you 'ave. Probably been up half the night doin' form, haven't you.'

I'd been up half the night, that much was true. It must have shown in my eyes and my manner; I was still dead tired.

'Ah,' said Billy, latching on. He didn't miss much. 'Don't tell me, another late one with Miss Troubles, was it?'

I ignored the reference to Maxine. 'This meeting is strictly about business,' I said, reaching for the cup of coffee he'd put down in front of me.

'Oh right, of course. And she's none of my business,' he said, busying himself about the stove.

'Damn right she's not. Hey,' I said, 'did you know the Vietnamese restaurant down the road got its window broken?'

'Tan Tat's?'

'Yeah. Looked recent, maybe last night. Did you hear anything?'

Billy shook his head. 'Not a thing. Musta been some smart-arse kid walking by. Little bastards got nothing better to do. They should make 'em all go on compulsory national service.'

If Billy had his way, the entire youth of Australia would be packed off to boot camp and made to serve out two years of military service. Not that Billy had actually done any time in the army, but he thought it such a good idea that it was obviously the cure for all of our delinquent teenagers' behaviour.

'You wouldn't see a kid in Israel kickin' in a shop window, would you?' he said defiantly.

'I've never been to Israel, Billy.'

'Either have I, but I bet you wouldn't see any kids kickin' in shop windows there. They've all learnt a bit of respect, serving time in the army.'

'It might have been an accident, perhaps a kid leaning his bike against the window and it fell through.'

Billy scoffed. 'Two years in the Nasho,' he said solemnly, 'it's the only way to learn those little bastards.'

He must have been reading my mind, because he changed the topic and asked if we should start putting up some Christmas decorations like the other shops in the strip.

'You know, I was just thinking that,' I said. 'Perhaps we should get into the Christmas spirit.'

'You want me to get a quote for some Christmassy stuff? You know, Santas, angels, the sort of shit everyone puts up?'

'That's the thing though, isn't it? Everyone puts up the same-old same-old.'

'It's Christmas, Punter. People expect to see that crap. Come Christmas they want to see Santas and reindeers and angels and stuff. What else you gonna put up this time of year?'

'I dunno. Leave it with me for a couple of days and I'll get back to you.' I asked him how we'd done for the week.

'Not bad. We're on track for budget for this quarter. I'm drowning at the moment though, since we lost Andrew.

8

Haven't been able to find a replacement for him yet. You'd think some kid would jump at a part-time job like that.'

'You advertised?'

Billy nodded towards the window. 'Put a sign up out front. I've also spread the word we're looking to hire. In the meantime, I'll bat on as best I can.'

I could always trust Billy to do the best he could. I'd known him years ago when he was a battling jockey working for my father. Increasing weight had forced him out of the game and he'd drifted into a succession of hospitality jobs before ending up at Gino's when the old man himself had run the place. There, he'd been chief dishwasher, barman, pizza maker and anything else Gino had asked him to do. It seemed I'd inherited him when the place became mine. And I couldn't have asked for a more loyal and trustworthy employee. Billy lived rent-free in the tiny flat above the shop as part of the deal. He was on a good wicket and he knew it, which is why he took an obvious pride in anything to do with the place.

Over breakfast we spoke about some operational issues. We had a cracked toilet bowl that needed replacing. And our insurance premium was due. Trouble with a restaurant, there's always expenses you've got to put your hand in your pocket for. I gave Billy the green light for both items and then he showed me the summer menu he'd put together. It was essentially a different mix of the same food we offered all year round; a dozen varieties of pizzas, assorted garlic bread. Some pastas and desserts.

'What's changed?' I said. Other than the new-look font and colour, it seemed pretty much the same to me.

'Garlic bread. It's now *gourmet*, made on the premises.'

'Gourmet? What do we do that's different from last week?'

Billy sighed patiently. 'It's not what we do, or don't do to it,' he explained, 'it's the perception in people's minds when they see the menu.'

I looked blankly at him.

'A couple come in and see plain old garlic bread on the menu, right? Hardly gonna excite 'em, is it? For all they know it's just some tasteless frozen shit I've bought across the road at the supermarket.'

'Is that where we get it from?'

'No, we make it up ourselves. But it don't matter where we get it from, Punter, garlic bread is garlic bread, either way you cut and slice it. But, tell 'em it's gourmet, made on the premises garlic bread, and I'll have to fight 'em off the counter with a stick, won't I? Specially if I pan-fry some garlic butter up and leave it wafting through the restaurant all night.'

'I knew there was a reason I hired you as manager.'

'You stick to your horses and leave me to run the show here. You'll see, we'll put Pizza Hut out of business yet.'

After my breakfast meeting with Billy, I drove straight to the races at Caulfield. It's only a five-minute drive and I parked my kombi van in my usual spot under the shade of the two gum trees by the side of the members' entrance. My old bus always looks like an intruder in the members' car park, where gleaming Porsches and BMWs are the usual means of transport. I'd owned my van for over a decade and it was second-hand when I bought it, so naturally it was showing its age. It had telltale signs of rust on the roof and tailgate, and the side door needed an appointment with a panel beater for coming off second best with a trolley in a car park. But I was attached to my van. I'd surfed the entire east coast in it and used it as a sort of pseudo surf room where I kept my wave skis, wetsuits and other assorted surfing gear. I smiled at the driver of a shining Mercedes coupe who pulled in and parked alongside me. The driver got out and turned his nose up disapprovingly at me. Gave me the sort of look that inferred I was parking illegally.

'Good day for it,' I said, nodding appreciatively towards his car. 'Nice motor.'

Mercedes man grunted a reply that left no doubt he didn't converse with tradesmen and hurried off. Yeah, nice motor, mate, but where would you put the surfing gear?

Just outside the entrance area, old George was standing patiently with his white plastic bucket collecting for the Salvos. I tipped him a fiver and he accepted it graciously as always.

'Thanks, Punter, hope you back a winner or two today.'

'You too, George.'

Some gamblers have immutable racetrack habits. They wear the same ties, the same suits. I know one bloke who confesses to wearing the same boxer shorts each time he goes, because he swears they're his lucky undies. Me, I don't have too many superstitions when it comes to clothes, but I've always tipped the Salvos on the way into a meeting. I sometimes tip them on the way out too, if I've had a good day. Other charities won't get a dollar out of me. Maybe it's the way they hound you; stick a tin in your face and ask you for donations. I don't know what they do with the money or where it goes. I'd never stopped to ask George about it. I just gave him my loose change and sometimes I won and sometimes I lost, it didn't seem to matter. But I know I always felt better if I put a dollar or two in George's bucket before the first race.

Daisy was working the till at the café when I went to grab a coffee. She used to cook for me and the rest of Dad's stablehands a lifetime ago, which was why she still treated me like a young nephew. These days she'd ceased preparing meals for strappers and had advanced up the ladder of catering. Daisy managed the restaurant for the caterers at the four metropolitan racetracks, and presided over a large casual staff who turned over hundreds of meals a day and endless afternoon teas.

'Hello, luv,' she greeted me. 'How's your dad, he got anything going today?'

Daisy loved a bet as much as anyone and she always looked out for my father's horses on his home track at Caulfield. I told her his best today was Princess Upstart.

Daisy immediately pulled out a formguide from her apron and circled the horse.

'Thanks, luv. You have a good day now and don't forget to come back for lunch.' She eyed me critically over the top of her glasses. 'I'm sure you're not eating nearly enough. It's roast lamb today. Make sure you see me; I'll slice you up an extra serve.'

I had to suppress a laugh. She remained convinced I was a perennial meal skipper, like I used to be back at the stables. I promised I'd see her later and left her to it.

Later in the afternoon, I saw Maxine again. She was leading in Princess Upstart, owned by her father and trained by my old man. Dad would have been none too happy about it either. The way he saw it, she was a wealthy owner's daughter playing at being a strapper when it suited her. It was all very well dressing up and taking a horse to the races, but what about getting your hands dirty at four in the morning and mucking out the stables like the horse's usual strapper did? It takes around ten to twelve weeks to get a horse ready to race and all strappers look forward to their hard work culminating in leading their charges in on raceday. Maxine's insistence on taking her father's horse to the races may have created friction with the filly's regular handler; just another fire for my father to put out. No, Dad didn't like it one bit, but he went along with Russell Henshaw's wishes anyway. Henshaw did, after all, have a dozen impeccably bred gallopers in Dad's stables, so if his socialite daughter wanted to lead them in on raceday and it kept him happy, well, Dad would grit his teeth and bear it.

I leant against the mounting yard fence and watched Maxine and the other strappers walking their horses around. There's something I love about watching the horses in those few final minutes before a race. Some are flighty and skittish, jumping at shadows and giving the impression that they'd rather be anywhere else but on a racecourse. Others clomp sleepily around as if they were a milk-cart hack. I won't play a race until I see the horses parade in front of me. I want to know how a horse has come on from its last run, or if it's ruined its chances by sweating up nervously in the mounting yard. Some of these horses were actually breaking out in a light sweat now, but it wasn't because they were upset, it was due to the unseasonably hot weather we were getting. Already it was twenty-eight degrees and rising. By late afternoon it would easily get to the predicted top of thirty-two. Since early November we'd been experiencing a spate of thirty degree plus days. Melbourne can cop a heatwave, but you don't normally get the real 'hotties' until January or February, the bushfire season. Must be something to do with global warming; at least that's what everyone was saying. Even the betting agencies were running a book to see if December would be our hottest month on record.

The area around the mounting yard was starting to fill up with punters, eager to check out their fancies before having a bet. You see a lot of people looking at the horses before a race, although most wouldn't know a fit horse from a rocking horse. But they lean against the fence and whisper knowingly that number five can't win because she's trained off or is wearing bandages, or some other nonsense. Truth is, there's only a handful of people I've met over the years who can look at a horse before a race and tell you what it's going to do. I had a good teacher of course, my father, although my betting activities weren't exactly the vocation he'd hoped I'd take up. For me and my brother David, it was always assumed we'd follow in Dad's footsteps and take over the horse-training duties at Parraboo Lodge. David had slotted easily into that role and had been Dad's assistant trainer for over a decade. He'd eventually take over from Dad when the old man retired – if he ever did.

As for myself, I was still the black sheep of the family, because according to Dad I was 'wasting my ability and would end up like all punters; broke'. I'd actually avoided penury for the best part of ten years now, and was quite happy with the comfortable lifestyle that I had. Did I have to get up at the crack of dawn to muck out boxes like other strappers did? No. Did I have to worry about the phone ringing incessantly with owners demanding to know how their horse was going? Forget it. I wasn't cut out for the regimented lifestyle of a trainer's son. So despite my father's pre-ordained edict that I follow him into the training business, I haven't gone back to work for him and I've managed to get by living on the punt. I'm not big-time and I have my ups and downs. But betting on the horses is what I do best. So I guess it's punter by name and punter by trade.

Maxine walked by leading Princess Upstart. An appropriate name, I thought, given the woman who was strapping it.

The filly was rock-hard fit, all bone and muscle. That's the stamp I like to see on my father's horses. Certain trainers turn their gallopers out with a trademark look and my father, David John Punter, certainly put an unmistakable seal on his horses when they were ready to win. DJ knew a bit about winning. Two Melbourne Cups, a swag of Group races and five training premierships in a career spanning forty-odd years were testament to his training prowess.

The other trainers were by now deep in conversation with their connections. Attentive owners were soaking up every word a trainer or jockey uttered, like a verdict being handed down by a High Court judge. Hoppy Baker declared emphatically to half a dozen clients how well their horse had improved since her last run. Hoppy was a trainer who gave instructions like a football coach booming out orders to his players on an oval. It was said he didn't need a telephone, and I could guess why; I could hear him from the other side of the mounting yard. The stewards gave the order for the jockeys to mount up and I swung my attention back to the horses.

Princess Upstart was the logical favourite at evens. She had a touch of class, was on her home track and had run a slashing second at her last start. Sixbefour was about ready to peak after two races and she was value at the fives. The other chance was What About Me, who was trained up Albury way. Her trainer, Tosca Hughes, didn't bring horses to town unless he thought they could win. The bookies were keeping her safe at fours. The rest of the ten-horse field I could safely put a line through. The strappers led them on a final lap around the yard before they made their way out the gate and onto the track. I caught Maxine's eye and gave her a wink and a wave as she walked by. She gave me her infectious laugh, the cheeky smile, and was that an extra wiggle from those shapely jodhpured hips? A couple of guys behind me thought so – I could practically hear them drooling while they were discussing her.

'Maaate, get a load of the chick leading that horse around. That's a crime . . . you can't go paradin' round in them things.'

'Steady, mate. We're here for the betting, not the birds.'

I laughed to myself. Time to hit the betting ring, try and make a quid.

I watch as the horses parade in the mounting yard. Strappers leading their charges around, waiting for the jockeys to mount up. They're mostly female strappers; perhaps eight or nine women and a couple of guys. Years ago you hardly saw a woman in racing stables. Nowadays, it's considered a respectable job. And trainers love employing women. They reckon they're kinder to the horses and don't get as aggro with them as men do. What a con. If only they knew what they are really like. Some of the things I've seen . . .

I mean, look at that one leading number three around. How typical. Is it possible to wear a pair of jodhpurs any tighter around your arse? Stupid little bitch. God, they make me angry. They're all the same. Every single one of them. Dolling themselves up for one reason and one reason only. You watch, I'll bet you anything she tries it on. Here they come, the jockeys. Now, see if I'm wrong. There you go, what'd I tell you? Look at the dirty trollop. She's not even paying the slightest attention to the trainer, or even the horse. No, instead she's giving the jockey a slutty smile. A cute look-at-me laugh. You wouldn't do that for a guy strapper, would you? Bitch. And look at that one with number ten. The one in the red top. How about the way she legged the hoop into the saddle? She's still got her hand on his boot. That's not even subtle. Why don't you just give him your phone number now? Filthy little silk chaser.

After the strappers lead their horses onto the track, they return to the mounting yard. Some make their way up to the area set aside for attendants in the grandstand. A few of them, including number three, elect to watch the race by the fence opposite the winning post. Well, of course she would. That way, she can show off her figure to the whole grandstand. I mean, look at her, sticking her backside out like she's a bloody model. Laughing loudly at some inane joke with a bunch of other girls. Pathetic. Did you see that, the way that guy strapper tried to make conversation with her? And her complete disregard of him. Dismissed by a toss of her hair. Just like Amanda used to do.

2

'Just tell me one thing,' said Tiny, ''cause I never could figure it out. Why do girls stay in a relationship with guys that abuse them?'

We were climbing the stairs of the Red Triangle in Fitzroy. There was me and Tiny, and my brother David. David had also invited Myles Perry, a trainer who rented some boxes from my father, for our regular Tuesday night game of snooker. Tiny took the stairs two at a time. His name belied his size; he was a giant of a man who topped six foot six and could fight like a threshing machine. He earnt a living by standing the door four nights a week at a couple of King Street clubs.

Tonight, there was only one topic that anyone wanted to talk about; how 'Mad' Charlie Dawson had killed his ex-girlfriend. It was juicy racing news. When a half-crazed jumps jockey murders his strapper girlfriend, it's a story guaranteed to sell papers. It had been all over the broadsheets and on the TV and radio for the past couple of days. The story had started to dry up a little now, only because the police had arrested Dawson on Sunday. But the media was still milking it for all it was worth and had switched their focus from who the killer was to why he'd done it.

Mad Charlie Dawson; David and I had known him from years ago when he rode track work for my father. Most people who worked at Caulfield knew him or had a story to tell about him.

As a teenager, I was too afraid to even look him in the eye. The wild, cross-eyed stare, the temper blow-ups that could happen at a moment's notice. I remember he once jumped off his horse during track work and decked an early-morning jogger who'd run across his path and nearly collided with him. A total over-reaction, but that was Charlie. He'd flare up over anything.

'I dunno,' said David. 'I thought she'd broken up with him some time ago. He was a bloody bomb waiting to go off, wasn't he? Remember when he used to ride work for Dad?'

I nodded. 'He'd be about the only bloke the old man wouldn't go crook at if he mucked up a gallop. I don't know how he managed to sack him without causing a scene.'

David snorted sarcastically. 'Because he got *me* to sack him, is what he did. Waited till he was interstate and then told me to get rid of him. Think I wasn't shittin' myself?'

We'd reached the end of the rickety wooden staircase and come out onto the top floor. I held open the door for the others to file inside.

'What did you say to him?' I said.

'I told him the old man was spelling his steeplechasers; didn't need a jumps jockey anymore to ride work. I made sure to sling him an extra five hundred along with his wages and told him the old man would be straight on the phone as soon as we got a jumper in the yard again. You reckon I wasn't laying it on thick.'

We all laughed, commiserating with David.

'All the time he was giving me that crazy punch-drunk look, where you don't know if he's going to have a go at you or go on home.'

'Yeah, I know that look,' said Tiny with empathy. 'I had to throw him out of a club I was bouncing about a year ago. I literally had to pick him up and walk him off the premises. I mean, he's a jockey, right? Half my size. I take him out and tell him it's over for him for the night. Finished. Told him no hard feelings, but he's pissed and being a nuisance and he's barred for a week. You know what the mad prick did? There's a hot-dog vendor outside. He grabs the guy's skewer and comes at me full tilt like a midget attacking a basketball player. Fair dinkum, I didn't want to hurt him, but I ended up having to give him a real belting 'cause he just wouldn't stop. When he's had a drink, he's a certified nutcase. That's why I can't understand that poor girl even hanging around with him anymore.'

'Well, according to the papers,' said Myles, 'she didn't. She split up and moved out on him some months ago. He's been up on assault charges with her before. She even took out an AVO on him. So she did all the right things. But it still didn't stop the bastard.'

I'd read all the grizzly details myself, of course. 'Jumps jockey charged with brutal murder' and 'Strapper slain as she slept' screamed the headlines. Apparently Mad Charlie Dawson, nicknamed for the complete disregard he had for his own life jumping horses over fences, had taken another in a fit of jealous pique. His victim was a former girlfriend, Julie Summers, who had worked as a strapper for Flemington trainer Colin Lovell.

David nodded emphatically. 'He actually rang the cops from her flat. Said he'd found her like that. They reckon he was paranoid about her seeing other guys. He couldn't stand it when she broke off with him. When the police picked him up, they reckon the stupid git was that blind drunk he couldn't even remember what happened.'

'That's his defence, is it? The weak dog,' said Tiny. 'I wished I'd have been there to help out. I can't understand guys who turn on their women like that.'

At the bar I said g'day to Simon. As usual, he was fixing drinks and organising tables while playing blitz chess with some hapless wood pusher. Simon supplemented his income by playing chess with anyone who cared to take him on at five minutes on the clock. They got five minutes, but Simon's handicap was that his clock kept ticking down if customers came to the bar and had to be served. Didn't seem to worry him whether he had five minutes or thirty seconds left on his clock, he always seemed to find the right move to beat his opponent. He clunked a piece confidently down on the board, hit the clock and smiled when he saw me.

'G'day, Punter. Fellas.' He nodded at us. 'The usual table?'

'Unless there's one with more pockets.'

Simon fixed us up with a set of balls, a wooden triangle and cues, served us the obligatory cold beers and went back to his game. As we walked off to our table, I heard him announce checkmate to his opponent. Don't know how he does it.

Tuesday night wasn't what you'd call busy. A smattering of uni students and a few locals sinking balls over a quiet beer in the semi-darkness. It was still stiflingly hot; had been since the weekend. We were on the top floor and the building's tin roof radiated heat like a slow-cooking oven. At least Simon had opened every window in the place to catch the hint of an evening breeze. I wished to hell the wind would make up its mind instead of teasing us. It was easily thirty degrees in this makeshift sauna.

The place had about forty full-sized billiard tables spread out comfortably over its massive wooden floor. We walked over to the corner where table twenty-three held pride of place. It was a beautifully crafted, full-length slate job, over a hundred years old according to its Harry Evans & Sons brass plate. It was the best table in the saloon because of its private location in the corner and the deck of half a dozen chairs on a raised platform looking down onto it. After you took your shot, you could sit back, sip your beer and enjoy the atmosphere. The seats were old and tattered and smelt of mildew, and there was no dress code as such. But we always had a good time shooting the balls and kicking around any racetrack gossip we'd heard during the week.

David racked up the balls as I flipped a dollar coin onto the cloth to pick sides. I chose Myles, leaving David with Tiny for a best of three rounds.

David lined up his cue ready to break, the tip of his tongue poking out of his mouth in concentration. He drew the cue backwards and forwards several times in meticulous preparation that had Tiny chomping at the bit.

'Oh, for gawd's sake, Dave, hit the thing, will you? We'll be here all night!'

Typical David. Methodical and prepared. Took no chances and went by the book. Perhaps that's why he got on so well with Dad. David was only three years older than me, but already looked a middle-aged man. He'd started going bald a while ago. Thank goodness for the shaved look, which was how he wore his hair. He had a perennially worried expression on his face, moulded by the constant strain of running a big stable for my demanding father. Every time he'd look into a horse's box he'd be half expecting to see a swollen joint or a bowed tendon. I'd been with him on his stable rounds often enough and in a perverse sort of a way, he only seemed happy when he found something wrong with the horses. Tiny also knew about this trait of his and we shared a secret delight in winding him up. I caught Tiny's eye and started the ball rolling.

'That filly of Dad's won well on Saturday.'

'Princess Upstart?'

'Yeah. She's won what, two out of three starts now? She's a goer.'

David thought about it while he was lining up the break. 'Trouble is she'll get too much weight from now on. Going to make it difficult to place her.'

I winked at Tiny. Glass half full.

'C'mon!' said Tiny. 'Can you break, for Christ sake? If I came back here next Tuesday I still wouldn't have missed anything.'

David finally drove his cue and bounced the ball softly off the back cushion to just kiss the triangle of red balls and leave me with absolutely nothing to go for.

'Thanks, David.'

'Don't mention it.'

I took my shot, missed. Made way for Tiny. He too was in a stirring mood tonight and it was clear he'd been saving something up for me.

'Tell you what else looked a goer,' he said, leaning over the table and summing up the angle, 'the filly leading Princess Upstart around.'

'Who's that?' asked Myles.

'Punter's new woman, Maxine Henshaw. Surprised you didn't see her photo with Punter in the Sunday gossip columns.'

Tiny walked around to the corner pocket, giving me a look which said he knew he'd scored a point off me without even sinking a ball. 'By the way, nice photo, Punter. Or should that be *mystery beau*?'

The others laughed. Bastards.

I'd been dreading that picture and hoping against hope that none of my racing acquaintances would see it. Fat chance. Maxine had dragged me along to some trendy new bar opening last week where a gossip columnist had taken a photo with her hanging off my arm. The caption in the Sunday paper had read: *Maxine Henshaw with her latest mystery beau.*

I chalked my tip and assumed a nonchalant gaze at the table.

'Is that Henshaw, the radio announcer's daughter?' asked Myles. 'I thought I recognised her leading your father's horse around. She certainly . . . stands out in the crowd.'

'*Stands out?*' said Tiny, sporting a huge grin. 'There weren't too many blokes watching the horses walk around the yard, I can tell you that.'

Tiny winked at me and slammed a red into the corner pocket. 'In fact I'm surprised you've got a leave pass to come here tonight, Punter.'

Maxine was interstate for a couple of days, busy with a new client she was doing some public relations work for. That hadn't stopped us calling each other like a couple of lovesick teenagers. It was the first time apart we'd had since we'd met, but I certainly wasn't going to admit it to this company of bozos.

'I don't need a leave pass to go anywhere,' I said defiantly. 'If I want to go out with my mates, then that's what I'll do,' I added with swaggering bravado.

'Yeah. Is that right?'

'That's right.'

Tiny lined up the pink and put it away just as easily as he had the red ball.

'I hear she's a livewire.'

'That's what people keep telling me.'

Tiny sighed a heavy sigh like a concerned parent. 'It's just that we've never seen you dedicate as much time to a woman as you do to a formguide.'

'I don't.'

'You have been.'

'I haven't.'

'Do, don't. Have, haven't.' He turned to David. 'You're his brother, David, tell 'im he's in denial.'

David nodded dogmatically. 'It's true. I've never seen him under the thumb like this before.'

'See,' said Tiny, potting another red. I wished he'd miss – shut the smug lair up and give us a shot. 'Even your own brother reckons you're gone.'

'I'm not *gone*,' I said exasperatedly. 'I have my own time and space and so does Maxine.'

With uncanny timing my mobile rang. Guess who?

'Hi Maxine . . . No, just out with the boys playing snooker. What? . . . Of course I miss you.' I turned away from Tiny when I said that, but I could feel his smirk burn a gaping hole in my back. 'Yeah, yeah. Uh-huh. Okay, I will. I love you, too.' Last words said in a muffled whisper to avoid the embarrassment of the guys hearing. But judging from the guffaws I could hear behind me, they hadn't missed a thing. '. . . No, course not. You're not causing me any trouble. Okay, I'll see you then.'

I switched my phone off and turned back around to face them. Tiny was shaking his head in a told-you-so way. David was biting his lip trying not to laugh. Even Myles was grinning.

'*Don't* say a word,' I said threateningly. 'Not one word.'

Tiny squinted down his cue, lining up another shot. 'Gone,' he said.

Next morning I was woken up at five thirty by my usual early-morning call. The call is ultra reliable and on the dot every day of the week. The downside is that the time never varies. If ever I want a sleep-in it's too bad, because the wake-up call comes from Che, who has it in his mind that it's time the big cat should get out of bed and feed the little cat his breakfast. And if the big cat doesn't get the message, well then his job is to scratch and meow at the door until I do. It was no use hiding under the blankets and hoping he'd lose interest. I'd tried that. He'd only become more insistent and louder, like he was on this occasion.

Meow. Scratch, scratch.

'All right already. I'm coming.' I turned over and snatched a look at the clock. 5.33 a.m. Che was silent for a moment before he started up his pawing again. Obviously didn't believe me.

'I *said*, I'm coming.'

Meow.

'Oh, for Christ sake. Ridiculous creature.'

I got out of bed cursing, pulled on a dressing gown and gave Che some dried biscuity things for his breakfast. He'd taken a shine to some expensive, gourmet stuff called Fussy Feline, which cost at least twenty per cent more than the home brand equivalent. And I was silly enough to keep buying it for him. While he ate his breakfast, I stumbled around making a pot of coffee and getting myself dressed. That afternoon there was a Mornington race meeting on with a couple of races that looked playable. My plan was to go down for an early surf on the east coast with a mate before heading off to the races in the afternoon.

A little over an hour later I was atop the cliffs overlooking Big Lefts at Flinders. There looked to be a nice little swell running and I could see that Billco was already out in the water along with a couple of other board riders. He's a wave ski rider like me. We sit on a ski about the size of a surfboard, strap ourselves in with a seatbelt and use a paddle to catch waves. There's not many of us around these days; it's easier to learn to ride a mal than master an eskimo roll. And young kids wouldn't be seen dead on anything other than a shortboard. But the few of us who have stubbornly clung to our craft over the years all know one another and try to surf with each other when we can.

Big Lefts always looks smaller until you paddle out the half kilometre or so to the break and realise it's twice the size you thought it was. What looks from atop the cliffs to be friendly lines marching harmlessly in turns into giant grey slabs determined to rear up and crush you on the reefs once you get out there. I pulled into my first wave about twenty minutes later. Billco waved and hollered at me as I took the drop on a curling boomer and surfed past him. That set the pattern for us both. Catch a screamer, work it hard for as long as you could, then drop back over the shoulder and paddle back out to the line-up. Bit of chitchat about this and that while waiting for waves, then do it all again. After two hours I was wet, stoked and sated. I'd had my surfing fix. I was also famished and in need of fuel, another reason to call it a day.

'Going in,' I mouthed at Billco, and pointed with my hand to the cliffs.

He nodded. 'Next wave,' he said.

We caught the next one together, sharing the wave all the way into the shallow waters sheltering the rock pools and kelp beds before picking up our skis and clambering over the seaweed-covered boulders leading to the path up the cliff.

'How did you go with the Christmas thing?' I said. I'd run by him an idea I had about Christmas decorations for Gino's.

'It's done. I played around with the brushes on Sunday afternoon. I don't know if it's what you're after, but you might as well come back for a bite to eat and take a look.'

Billco used to work as a set designer for a TV station. He was about sixty, although you wouldn't have picked it the way he handled himself in the surf. He was around the same height and weight as me, sported a greying beard and had a gentle nature; in fact I couldn't recall him ever losing his temper in all the years I'd known him. He'd taken a redundancy package after his company went through a downsizing and now seemed to have found the perfect retirement: painting and surfing. He lived off one of the main tourist roads heading back towards

Red Hill, his rambling old house and gardens doubling as a gallery on weekends, attracting the tourists who drove down from Melbourne to the peninsula. The sign out the front said: *Flinders Art Gallery – surf art, landscapes and portraits.*

Every time I walked into Billco's house, I was reminded of how talented an artist he was. He took me around the back through his work shed. Dozens of canvasses and paintings were stacked against the walls. A half-finished painting of a surfer catching a wave hung on an easel. It was a beautiful picture and seemed to capture the moment in time perfectly.

'That's where we were surfing. Big Lefts looking back towards the cliffs, isn't it?' I asked.

Billco nodded. 'Mmm, that's right. A longboarder's girl-friend commissioned me to paint it for his birthday. I'm about halfway through.'

We walked into the hallway of his house, where more sketches and drawings hung on the walls.

'What was this done with, Billco? Pencil?'

We stood in front of a sketch of an old man staring at us intently. Intelligence seemed to jump out of his eyes. The wrinkled and lined face, although weathered and spent, fairly dripped with a bright and enquiring mind. It stopped me dead in my tracks, demanding an explanation.

'Charcoal, actually,' said Billco.

'Who is it?'

He looked fondly at it for a moment, gathering his thoughts. 'A client wanted a sketch drawn of her husband who'd recently passed away. He was a professor at Melbourne University.'

'I knew it! I mean, I knew the guy was clever. You've caught the intelligence in his eyes. You really must have copied his likeness.'

'Well, as a matter of fact, I didn't copy anything, I drew him blind.'

'Blind?' I didn't follow and my puzzled look must have been obvious. Billco explained.

'His widow came in and said she wanted me to draw a likeness of her husband as she remembered him. She came in several times and described him to me while I sketched him. I'd ask her about him and from her description, I imagined what he might have been like. He was a professor and not one to suffer fools easily, so I gave him a sharp, probing stare that I think would have reduced his students to instant silence. And his untidy mane of hair, long and unkempt, a nuisance item that I figured he tolerated, but probably never spent time grooming. The widow actually gave me a photo of the old professor after I'd completed my sketches. I ended up doing three for her and kept this one, a sort of mock-up. Here's the photo, I keep it behind the sketch.'

Billco reached up and lifted the sketch off the wall. Behind the frame was a colour photo which he passed to me. I studied it for a moment, looking from the photo to the sketch and back again.

'I can't believe the likeness,' I said. 'You really sketched that from her description?'

Billco nodded modestly. 'I've done others like that too. It used to be a party trick of mine. People describing someone they knew, like their boss, and I'd sketch them.'

'You're amazing.'

Billco laughed. 'No, I just enjoy painting or drawing and hopefully getting a cheque from the client when I've completed the thing. I've still got to eat and pay the bills.'

I looked at the price tags on some of the paintings and sketches hanging in the hallway. Five hundred for this, three hundred for that. I reckoned he was undercharging. But Billco's expenses wouldn't amount to much. I figured he'd probably only have to sell a couple of items each month to keep the wolf from the door. And turning out quality work like he did, I doubt if he'd ever have a shortage of buyers.

'Come out to the garage and have a look at what I've done for your friend.'

Billco led me out to his garage-cum-workshop. In spite of the obvious roominess in the old house and grounds, he seemed to have filled every available space with paintings and works in progress, so much so that he'd had to convert the garage into another studio.

'What do you think?' he said, gesturing to a large drawing. 'I didn't really know what to do, so I just sort of played around. If your friend doesn't like it, I can always try something else.'

I stared with astonishment at the giant poster that Billco had created. I'd called him on the Saturday after speaking with Billy and told him that a friend of mine was looking for something a little different for his pizza shop's Christmas decorations. Could he come up with a poster that would make his shop stand out? Could he ever; the drawing he'd done was absolutely brilliant. It had a huge merry-looking Santa Claus being towed by his reindeer on a giant pizza instead of the usual sleigh. Santa even had a cape with the words *Merry Xmas from Gino's!* on it which fluttered behind him. The flying carpet pizza was headed unmistakably towards Glenhuntly Road; the number 67 tram was parked right out the front. I'd asked for something different and he'd certainly given us a decoration that would make us stand out from the other shops.

'I love it! It's amazing.'

'You think your mate will like it?'

'I can guarantee it.'

'Well, you can roll it up and take it with you. Just be careful you don't crease it when you put it in the car.'

I reached into my pocket and peeled off some bills. 'How much do I owe you?'

'Don't be silly, Punter. I don't want anything, it took me no time at all to knock up.'

'You've earned it. I've got to give you something.'

'Tell you what, if anyone in your friend's restaurant likes it, get him to pass on my number.'

I said goodbye to Billco shortly after lunch, with a pile of his business cards and a promise to call him and let him know what Billy thought of his flying Santa on a pizza. Then I got in my van and drove to the races at Mornington.

My afternoon at the races turned out all right. There were two races I thought I could play, a two-year-old scamper over a thousand metres and a middle-distance handicap for restricted class runners. The three horses that I backed were at least reliable plodders and my second pick won at six dollars, giving me a good result on the race. The two-year-old race had only one horse I liked, but at a dollar seventy, it was well under its odds. So I left the race alone and was secretly pleased to see it get beaten. Take unders, go under.

There was a good-sized crowd in attendance for a Wednesday. A lot of people were already in Christmas holiday mode and what better place to spend an afternoon than at a country race meeting. I walked down the stairs of the grandstand to the mounting yard to have a look at the two-year-olds who'd just raced. I always look them over after they've run. I know it's considered an old-fashioned thing to do, and most punters would argue that if anything's amiss it will show up in the steward's report anyway. But I want to see the horses in the flesh. See the ones whose flanks are heaving and will benefit from the run. Notice the angry trainers who think their jockey butchered the ride. You can pick up some useful information just by watching, if you know what to look for.

"Ullo, is that the *mystery beau*?' said a gruff and officious voice behind me. The voice belonged to Jim Beering, the state's head racecourse detective. He stood tallish and solid, his hands clasped behind his back in the manner that cops have. That's what Beering was for twenty-odd years before he retired from the police force and lucked into this cushy role some time ago. It's the perfect job for a copper who likes a bet. He had on his usual faded sepia-brown suit and a matching well-worn trilby. Must have had the suit for twenty years too, or maybe he had several suits all the same colour. His jacket was unbuttoned as usual, allowing a burgeoning pot belly to hang over his belt. Despite his ballooning waistline, Beering could handle himself when he had to. I'd seen him in action and knew he was a whole lot faster than he looked. I'd first got to know Beering through my father years ago and occasionally passed on anything useful I'd heard around the traps. He was a handy person to know; one phone call from Beering could get you into or out of a squeeze and I preferred the latter, so I made it my business to stay sweet with him. Once in a while, my information had even helped him in some of his cases. So he always made a point of picking my brains if he saw me at the track.

'Not you too, Jim. I didn't think you read the gossip columns.'

'I read the papers cover to cover. And wasn't I surprised to find a picture of you and Miss Troubles arm in arm?'

'She's no trouble, far as I'm concerned.'

He raised his eyebrows disbelievingly at me then changed the topic.

'Terrible thing that strapper, Julie Summers, getting murdered the other day.'

I nodded. 'I see they wasted no time in rounding up Mad Charlie Dawson and charging him.'

Beering grunted cynically. 'He's a crazy bastard, that one. They should lock 'im up and throw away the key.'

'I'd hate you to be judging me in a case. His lawyer's actually pleaded not guilty, hasn't he?'

Beering scoffed. 'Silly bastard rang the cops from her flat, he did. Said he found her like that. Can you buy that? It's an open and shut case. He'd bashed her right through their relationship. Every time he got pissed. Which is most nights for Charlie. Then last Saturday he must have gone around there and just snapped. Finished her off for good.'

'Finished is the word. Stabbing frenzy is what the papers said.'

Beering sniffed and nodded. 'Cut her throat and stabbed her twenty-seven times is what my contact at Homicide told me. That's the signature of a seriously twisted mind.'

As the last of the horses were led out of the mounting yard, Beering dropped the conversation about the Summers murder, pulled out his race book and started flicking through it. I knew what was coming next.

'Eh, your old man got anything running today?' he asked.

I don't know why, but every time Beering saw me at the races he always checked to see if Dad had a runner that had some sort of chance. I may have tipped him the odd winner or two from his stable over the years, but Dad wouldn't tell me if the world was ending and I wouldn't ask him anyway, so the 'inside information' that Beering thought I had was non-existent.

I turned and faced him. 'Yeah, he's got one in the last. But it's twenty to one and the ambulance would probably beat it home.'

'Is that right? Didn't think your old man kept any slow ones.'

'It'll win a race. Look for him a couple of starts from now in something longer, but don't expect any twenty to one about him then.'

Beering sniffed good-naturedly. 'You Punter clan can never give a straight tip, can you? Always gotta have conditions attached. I don't know who's worse; you, your old man or your brother.'

Those freaking police idiots! They don't know jack shit. To think they arrested that ex-boyfriend jumps jockey. Always thinking the bloody obvious. Mind you, it was wonderful timing that Mad Charlie Dawson happened along and muddied the waters. I couldn't have planned it better if I'd tried to frame him. The halfwit. Sometimes you can get lucky. Should I tell them? Hell no, why spoil it! Let the police go on with that bullshit spin they've been spreading to convince the community they've got it all wrapped up. That they've caught the killer and everything is going to be okay.

That Summers tart knew she had it coming. She did. You could see it in her eyes when I woke her. Oh, and it was so easy. Like finding out where she lived. The bloody race book practically gives you their address! How simple. Stalking 101. Select one of the bitches in the racecourse mounting yard. Look at the saddle cloth number of the horse they are leading in and check in the formguide who the trainer is. Then, after the race, wait in your car by the horse float park for the nice driver to take them home. Follow them back in your car, tra la la la la . . . When they get back to the stables, you track the dirty little scag back to her home. How extraordinarily fucking simple.

Sure, there's a bit of casing to do. That's to be expected. Did she live alone? Did her friends drop around? How hard was it going to be to get in? Summers' place only took me one night. It was perfect, from the moment I let myself in through her open laundry window, to creeping silently around her tiny flat. No one steals more silently through the night than I do. No one. Every room told me a story confirming what I already knew about her. That pile of trashy celebrity gossip magazines by the coffee table; typical, weren't they? The obligatory party photos on her fridge door, all posing with a different male partner. They are never satisfied. Always have to be searching for someone better, someone who can offer more.

I left her bedroom to last. It's the room I looked forward to the most, and I felt like I almost couldn't wait, but I forced myself to be patient, show some restraint. After all, if a job's worth doing, it's worth doing properly . . .

The first drawer in her dresser was filled with her carelessly tossed lingerie which I sifted through with my knife. Various bras and panties and a skimpy little G-string. I picked it up with the tip of my blade, trained my pencil torch over it and inspected it. The whore. That merely confirmed it, didn't it? Amanda used to get out in the same sort of slut gear too. And this one? Just like her. Another filthy little silk chaser, same as they all were. She was curled up in the bed, oblivious of my presence, a heavy breather; slept with her mouth agape as she dreamt her dreams. After a little while, when I was ready, I woke her from those dreams and turned them into nightmares.

3

Maxine's text asked if I could pick her up at the airport from her six thirty flight and drive her straight to a function. She certainly liked her text messages. I'd counted thirteen in the four days since Tuesday, when she'd gone away.

Missing u heaps xxx Maxine

Can't wait 2 c u soon

And of course, *U can text me!*

Me, text anyone? I was still in the Dark Ages. Couldn't understand why you didn't just ring someone up and talk to them. And if you couldn't reach them, then you left a message. Besides, my large fingers seemed to struggle with the miniscule keypad on my mobile phone. That was my excuse and I was sticking to it. I did make an exception for Maxine, however, and sent a clumsy reply confirming I'd meet her flight. It seemed to take ages for me to tap out on my phone even though it was only a sentence or two.

I waited at the gate where her flight was due in. There were lots of people around, a typical busy Friday evening with travellers coming and going before the weekend set in. The arrivals monitor said Maxine's flight was on schedule and so it was, the doors opening up a few minutes later to let the passengers come streaming through. Maxine was the fifth passenger out; she must have been travelling up front. She gave an excited wave and a huge smile when she saw me. Then she stopped right in the middle of the aisle and gave me a huge pash which forced the rest of the passengers to walk around us. Someone gave a wolf whistle as I came up for air and one of the ground staff asked us to move on as we were blocking the path. Maxine didn't seem to notice.

'I missed you, Punter.'

'Me too.'

'You could have texted me more and told me you missed me.'

'You know what I'm like with those things. I did leave messages on your voice mail.'

'Pathetic.'

'I know. How was the trip, business go okay?'

'Bloody Winning Way is a pain in the arse.'

Maxine ran her own public relations business. Although it was only a small company, she seemed to have an ever-growing list of clients. Her father was rumoured to have steered a few customers who'd advertised on his radio show her way, but Maxine was obviously very good at what she did to win the business. She'd been in Sydney organising an event and doing the PR work for a racing client, Winning Way Syndications, and was putting on a similar function for them tonight in Melbourne.

I smiled at her. 'A demanding client?'

'You could say that. Kagan Hall, who owns the company, is a bloody perfectionist who wants to micromanage every little detail.'

She pulled a brochure from her handbag as we walked and thrust it into my hand. I read it as Maxine hurried me along to the baggage carousel. It was a glossy publication showing an impossibly good-looking couple cheering their horse past the finishing post. The brochure was full of testimonials from satisfied clients who had bought horses through Winning Way. Pictures of leading jockeys and trainers jumped off the pages to reassure you that this was the only outfit in town you could trust. I had to admit it was extremely well put together.

'Is this your work?' I asked.

'Yeah. That's what I'm getting paid to do.'

'It's very professional. I'd be tempted to buy a share in a horse after reading it. I mean, listen to this: *Mrs Donovan from Hawthorn says, "I invested five thousand dollars in the Winning Way number four syndicate and we struck gold! Duncan's Luck won the Caulfield Guineas and overnight our colt was worth eight million dollars."*'

Maxine gave me a cynical look. 'Yeah, for all the Mrs Donovans I had to track down, there's another hundred who've bought slow ones. You should know better than anyone, they can't all win. Anyway, my job's to paint Winning Way in a positive light. Get as many people as possible along to these sales functions so that they'll buy shares in Hall's syndicates.'

'How's it going; they selling?'

Maxine nodded. 'It's a slog. You've just got to keep the momentum up, which is what this do tonight is all about.'

Forty-five minutes later, I found a park not far from the Rialto building where the event was being held. We walked in together and caught a lift up to the twenty-eighth floor. In the foyer was a rather effeminate-looking concierge who was ticking off attendees on his list and giving out name tags. He checked off another couple ahead of us and then turned his attention towards Maxine and I. He quickly found her name tag but couldn't seem to locate my name on the list.

'It's Punter,' said Maxine with growing impatience. 'I rang up myself yesterday and requested an extra guest ticket.'

The guy fussed around and gave an exaggerated pout as he peered at his computer screen to see if he could find me. No sign; I'd fallen through the cracks, didn't exist. He apologised politely, but told me I couldn't *possibly* go in unless I was on the list.

'Oh, *really*?' said Maxine.

'Yes, unfortunately, he can't. I'm so sorry,' he said, 'but we have a strict allocation for catering purposes and unless you're on my list, I simply can't allow you in.'

I felt like telling him he should apply for a job guarding the members' gate at Flemington. But I didn't have to say anything,

Maxine beat me to the punch. She leant forward and gave him a combative stare.

'Actually, it's *my* company that's organising this event tonight, so as far as catering purposes goes, that's quite all right.'

Mr gatekeeper bit his lip. He knew he was up against formidable opposition, but still had some fight left in him. 'I'll still have to have a name for my list to let him in,' he lisped defiantly.

'A name. You need a name?'

'I'm afraid so.'

Maxine leant over the bench and picked up a bright pink highlighter. Then she snatched the sheet of paper with the list of names on it out of his hand.

'Hey! That's my list, what are you doing?' He sounded shocked.

I knew I was still in the honeymoon discovery stage with Maxine, but I didn't expect her aggressive response and was a bit surprised at how far she went. In giant letters that took up the entire A4 page, Maxine wrote over the top of all the other names: John Punter.

'There you go.' She smiled acridly at him. 'A nice little name for your nice little list. Happy now? C'mon, Punter, let's go, we're running late.'

Maxine escorted me into the room, which was already full of attendees. At a guess, I'd say two hundred people were sipping drinks and mingling with one another; a turn-up that Maxine seemed well pleased with.

'Can I be rude and leave you on your own for a moment?' she said. 'Got to check everything's running smoothly.'

'Sure. I'll be okay. You do what you need to do.'

I grabbed a glass of red from a waiter hovering nearby and stood by to see if I might recognise anyone. It was certainly a racing crowd; you would have to be deaf not to hear the talk of horses and track gossip. The attendees were a mixture of members and owners drawn from the three metropolitan racing clubs and they all seemed younger than myself; single, twenty-somethings, no kids, no mortgage and plenty of cash and credit to throw around. Just the type of prospects to tip into a horse. But there were some older people in amongst the group as well. In fact one walked past, stopped and said hello to me. It was Daisy from the racecourse café.

Daisy looked like a living monument to a 1960s *Women's Weekly* magazine. Normally I saw her in an apron and uniform while she tended the cash register. Tonight she was dressed up with her hair in a bun, a pink floral frock and a white French lace handbag which she clutched firmly with both hands. I leant forward as she gave me a kiss on the cheek.

'Hello, luv. Fancy seeing you here.'

'Hello, Daisy. Could say the same about you. Didn't think you attended this sort of thing. You here with anyone?'

Daisy smiled and nodded her forehead to a similarly dressed crowd of older ladies standing by the side of the room. 'I'm with the girls from the café. We've decided to bite the bullet and buy a share in a horse.'

'No way! Good on you.'

I felt genuinely pleased for her. A little surprised, but thrilled that she could participate in owning a racehorse with her friends. I guess there was no law that said she couldn't; it's just that you don't expect someone nearly eligible for the pension to suddenly buy into a horse. She must have read the look on my face.

'Oh, I know. I probably should save my money. But Keith left me a little bit when he passed on last year and I've always fancied owning a horse. Is that so wicked?'

I laughed. 'Of course not.'

'Me and the girls saw the ads they were running in *Best Bets* and over drinks we decided we'd all chip in and buy a share if it wasn't too expensive. Do you think they're all right, this mob?'

I confessed I didn't know much more than her. 'But my girlfriend is doing the public relations work for Winning Way. She's organised this whole shebang tonight.'

'Where is she? You'll have to introduce me.'

I looked around the room and spotted Maxine over towards

the bar area talking to a group. I pointed her out to Daisy. 'She looks tied up now, but I'll bring her around to meet you when she's free.'

'She looks lovely, Punter. I'd better get back to the girls now. Say hello to your father for me next time you see him.'

'I will. Hey Daisy, I hope you buy into a Melbourne Cup winner.'

Next to me there was a loudish young group throwing down Winning Way's hospitality as quickly as they could. I didn't know who was worse, the guys or the girls. Perhaps it was the free booze or because it was Friday night and the end of the working week, but they were putting it away. I caught one of the guy's eyes, gave him a friendly nod and struck up a conversation with him.

'You here to buy a horse then?' he asked.

'Just tagging along,' I said, shaking my head. 'How about you?'

'I'll see what they're offering in the presentation. But that guy can certainly pick a winner,' he said, pointing his glass towards a man talking to a group of people near the podium. I followed his gaze and recognised a handsome, charismatic-looking man in his late thirties. It was Kagan Hall. Even from twenty metres away you could hear his cultured, very British voice as he effortlessly made conversation with total strangers. There must be an art to that type of thing. To be able to approach people you've never met and work the room making small talk. They say it's a learnt skill. If that was so, then I'd never taken classes.

Hall was talking about some horse he'd just bought. 'One of the nicest colts I've ever seen,' he said to the group, who were hanging off his every word. 'Big girth and shoulders, lovely stride. Just the sort of horse that will mature into a Derby horse by next spring.'

'Are shares in him still for sale?' asked one of the would-be owners.

'Yes, there are a few left, but there's a lot of interest being shown in him. I wouldn't leave it for too long.'

Oh, that was good. *Very* good. A born salesman. Didn't push too hard or sound desperate, just enough to whet the appetite. I saw the bloke who'd been asking about shares now talking earnestly to his mates, perhaps seeing how much of a bank they could rustle up between them. Hall seamlessly excused himself and moved on to the next lot of prospects, joining them like a long-lost friend.

'Hello.' He flashed that ultra-confident smile. 'I'm Kagan Hall. Have you raced a horse before?'

Slick operator. I had to hand it to him. I didn't know how he did it. Day after day, week after week. Buying horses and then having to flog them off to punters. Looked a tough way to make a quid. There were around thirty-odd syndication schemes operating in Australia that I was aware of. Some had been around for decades. They were the real deal, headed by respected judges of horseflesh who picked winners in the sale ring every year. It was a lucrative trade to get into in a bull market. When conditions were right, you simply bought a bunch of yearlings, put a mark-up on them to cover expenses and management fees and offloaded them to eager buyers like I was seeing here tonight. But there must have been difficulties associated with the trade. If you bought big-time like Hall did, then you had to borrow the funds to make the purchases. I figured he'd have to find the payments to make the interest and pay his staff and then for all of this. I looked around the room and did the maths. Upwards of two hundred people at, say, thirty dollars a head for drinks and finger food. No wonder the man at the concierge had given us such a hard time about catering. Then, he'd have to advertise; that would cost a small fortune each month, especially for the exposure he was getting. And of course Maxine wouldn't come cheaply either, promoting the whole box and dice. Sounded like a lot of work and pressure to get an earn out of. Think I'd stick to punting.

I was saved from further thoughts by Maxine, who waved at me through the crowd and then walked over.

'Hi sweetie, sorry to leave you alone. They're just about to start the presentation. Can you save me a seat up front somewhere and I'll come and join you in a tick?'

Ushers herded us towards the seated area of the room, and I selected a couple of chairs near the front, putting my jacket on the spare seat for Maxine. On stage, the lights dimmed as a PowerPoint presentation flicked on and Kagan Hall welcomed us from a podium. Maxine came along and squeezed in next to me.

'All going to plan?' I whispered.

'Yeah, so far so good. He'll launch into his spiel now. You watch him, he's a natural.'

Maxine wasn't telling me anything that I didn't already know. In front of a crowd, Kagan Hall was a born performer. He should have been on TV. From the moment he spoke his first word he had the audience eating out of his hand. A large screen showed a video of an impressive yearling colt being led around the sales by an attendant. It reared up and struck out cheekily with its forelegs before the tap of the auctioneer's gavel confirmed a sale. '*Sold to Kagan Hall! Another successful purchase to Winning Way Syndications.*'

Hall stopped the video and froze the image of the colt in front of us all. He paused for a moment, using the silence to build the suspense. Then he leant forward on the podium, seemingly making eye contact with every person in the room.

'Why do we do it?' he asked the crowd. 'Why do we put our hand up for a horse in the sale ring?'

Hall left the podium and strode confidently forwards to the front of the stage. He held his arms open like a politician, assuring his voters that he had all the answers. There was some nervous coughing and throat-clearing. Finally, someone in the audience called out from the back of the room.

'I dunno, we must all be dreaming. Half the horses never even make it to the track and the ones that do are mostly too slow to win a race!'

The respondent got a few laughs from the rest of the audience before a solemn-faced Hall spoke again.

'You, my friend, have hit the nail right on the head. We're all dreamers, those of us in the racing game. We dream that the horse we've bought will turn out to be a good one. We dare to dream that it will win a Golden Slipper, a Cox Plate, a Melbourne Cup. After all, some horse has to win it every year and why shouldn't it be yours?'

He paused briefly and smiled warmly at his audience.

'Let me tell you some sobering facts. It's true, nearly half the horses sold don't make it to the track. They break down, they have mishaps, they need more time, they're too slow, they're retired for breeding. You've heard all the excuses. At Winning Way we don't have a magic prescription, but we do have a rigorous procedure to ensure that we only select the best credentialed yearlings. We go through all pedigrees with a fine-tooth comb and if they don't meet our selection criteria, we strike them off our list. Other syndication companies will promise you the world and won't even give you an atlas, but our record stacks up against the very best. For those who aren't familiar with our record, here's a brief reminder.'

Hall stood to the side and flicked his remote control. It brought up the next clip showing Winning Way's star gallopers. There had been a few over the last five years. The video started with Time Machine, who'd kick-started Hall's syndication career in Australia. He'd won the Slipper and Sires Produce Stakes before being syndicated for more than what several mansions in Toorak were worth. Then Sarasun galloped into view. They'd bought him in New Zealand for the proverbial song, a tried horse who'd gone on to win the AJC Derby. He'd been a colt too, which meant he would earn far more from the breeding barn than he could at the track. That had led to his early retirement and fattened the wallets of his lucky owners. There were plenty of other horses mentioned in the clip, most of which I'd heard of. All the images had a picture of Hall in the background; at the races accepting a trophy, or at the sale yards making a winning bid, his very presence a reminder to us all of his astute judgement.

Hall froze the clip and took up his position at the podium again.

'Ladies and gentleman, I've given you a small sample of what Winning Way has achieved in five short years, and I want you to share with me in even greater success.'

He stopped, probing the room for any non-believers. It was hard not be a complete convert.

'Winning Way isn't the cheapest syndicator around, and I make no apology for that; it's a costly business. But we get the results. For those of you looking to make an astute purchase, I invite you to join me in my current offerings tonight.'

He hit the remote again and took us through a dozen-odd weanlings which he'd purchased. All very slick and polished. He showed the glossy pedigree charts, positively oozing with winning bloodlines. Then he wheeled in his guest speakers. He had his stable vet talk about how professional Winning Way were to deal with. Then he had two top trainers wax lyrical about the quality of youngsters that they'd received over the years from Hall. Finally, he had the Chairman of the Racehorse Owners Association stand up and waffle on about him for five minutes. For Christ sake, I thought they were going to give him a medal. Eventually Hall wound up the formal part of the function and invited everyone to stay for drinks and see him or his staff about buying shares in any of the horses offered. I couldn't believe the applause he received when he finished. You'd think he was a bloody rock star.

Maxine gave my hand a quick squeeze and whispered to me, 'What did you think, impressive, wasn't he?'

Had to admit he was. If I needed further proof, surely it was in the throng that was swamping him offstage, eager no doubt to wave their credit cards and chequebooks at him to secure a share in one of his horses.

'C'mon, I'll introduce you to Kagan. You can meet my father too, it's about time you did.'

I followed Maxine to the bar area and left her for a moment while I grabbed a couple of drinks. When I walked back to her, we were joined by a petite brunette with her partner in tow.

'Hi Punter. Here on business or with friends?' Her eyes

flickered towards Maxine standing behind me. 'Are you going to introduce me?'

'Oh, hi Kate. Er, this is Maxine.'

I don't know why we males find it difficult to introduce ex-girfriends to the current model. They don't mind at all, seem to find it amusing in fact, a sort of game where they eye each other off and try to score subtle points. Kate and I had known each other for several years. Our problem was we'd gotten to know each other intimately on our first night. Sex on the first date sounds great at the time, but trust me; it's all downhill from there. It didn't cut us off completely, but it put some space between us from that time on. As she's told me often enough, I'm not her type and we're strictly friends. And as far as that night went, we conveniently avoid the subject and haven't talked about it since. Fortunately, Kate's a keen racegoer and I see her most Saturdays at the track. We've shared other bonding experiences together. She works as a crime reporter with *The Age*. You wouldn't pick her for one. Slim, a good looker and a classy dresser. Especially when she did herself up for the races. The girl had style. But she was a tough cookie underneath all the gloss and smarts. She'd done her journalism apprenticeship covering real estate and business before settling on the crime beat, which she found far more interesting. She could smell a breaking story like a blowfly could molasses through a feed-room door. Her editor and peers agreed she had one of the best black books of 'colourful identities' in the country, and she certainly knew how to milk them. Several times I'd helped her out with information on people relating to her stories and likewise, she's helped me if I've ever needed to find something. So we go back, professionally and personally.

'I've heard about you,' said Kate in a voice that could pass for anything between admiration and taking the piss. 'You're Russell Henshaw's daughter, aren't you?'

'And you work for a newspaper or something,' said Maxine, in a manner suggesting a position as a junior receptionist. Touché.

'Journalist, actually. I'm with *The Age*.'

'Oh really? That must be so exciting. Are you here covering this event tonight?'

Kate shook her head, gave a careless little toss of her hair and smiled dismissively. 'Oh no, I don't cover the social pages. Strictly crime.'

Two alpha females playing the bitch game. This could go on all night. I broke the stalemate and offered a handshake to Kate's partner. He seemed the type she'd go for. Good-looking, sporty, well-educated sort of a voice. Nathan, he said his name was. Told me he worked in the media doing something or other with a website. We all laughed politely at a joke he made about fools and their money being parted when it came to buying horses. Then Kate smoothly excused them both.

'Must leave you to it then,' she said, placing a hand on Nathan's shoulder and guiding him away.

Maxine grabbed my arm and said, 'There's Kagan now. Let's go over while he's free.'

We walked over and Maxine introduced me.

'So pleased to meet you,' he said, making it sound like I was the one person in the room he'd been wanting to meet all night. 'Tell me, DJ's your father, right?'

Said that was so. Never hurts to have a famous trainer as a father for a conversation starter. 'It was an interesting presentation tonight.'

'I'm so glad you enjoyed it. We had a wonderful attendance, thanks to Maxine.' He turned and gave Maxine one of his charming smiles and patted her on the shoulder.

'How many of these do you usually put on each year?' I asked.

'Oh, dozens of the damn things. It never really stops. I'm presenting up at the Gold Coast next week, then it's up to Rockhampton and Townsville before we hit Darwin on the return trip. We've got Adelaide and Perth to organise and – Maxine doesn't know this yet –' he said naughtily, pretending Maxine couldn't hear, 'I've just teed up a New Zealand trip that coincides with their national sale.'

'I didn't know about *that*.' Maxine feigned horror.

'Why so many?' I asked.

'Got to keep in front of buyers' faces. Top-of-mind brand awareness, that's what I want. When a potential owner thinks about syndicators, I want them thinking Winning Way and no one else. That's why we do all the PR, the advertising and schmoozing. You have to remind them constantly that you're out there.'

I found myself becoming genuinely interested in the business and was about to ask another question when Maxine's father, Russell Henshaw, burst into our circle.

'Nice talk, Kagan. When you finish with the syndication business, you can always get a job on radio any time,' he said, slapping Hall on the back and laughing at his own joke.

'I might take you up on that, if ever this falls over,' said Hall.

'That's not going to happen any time soon,' said Maxine. 'At least not while I'm running the publicity.'

'You've done a super job, too, my love,' said Henshaw, giving Maxine a kiss on her cheek.

'Dad, I want you to meet John.'

Henshaw wore a loud apricot-coloured striped shirt, no tie, under a navy blazer. An even brighter matching handkerchief was stuffed into his jacket. That was surely proof that money couldn't always buy good taste. I'd seen Henshaw around the track often enough. Once or twice he'd bowled up when I'd been talking to Dad or David and interrupted our conversation just like he'd done now. So he must have known me by sight, just as I did him. But we'd never been formally introduced before and so I offered my hand, gave him my best smile and told him how pleased I was to meet him.

'Yeah,' he said, ignoring my outstretched hand, 'I've got horses with your old man. You're the son that turned his back on the stable, aren't you?'

'I'm not really involved with the stable these days,' I said, withdrawing my hand and putting it awkwardly by my side.

'Oh, that's right,' he said dismissively, 'you weren't *suited* to stable life, were you?' Henshaw didn't wait for my reply, instead turning back to Hall. He pointed his thumb at me like I wasn't there and said, 'His old man's a leading trainer and he's knocked back going into the business.'

I glared at Henshaw, feeling a rush of blood flush through my face. If he was looking to bait me then he was succeeding. Before I could reply, Maxine came to my defence.

'Punter doesn't have to follow his father into training, Dad. If he isn't interested, then that's up to him.'

'Sure, princess. I'm just jokin' around.' He looked at me. 'You know that, don't you? No offence meant.'

'No offence taken.'

'Tell me, are you here to give Maxine a hand tonight?'

'I actually picked Maxine up from the airport,' I said neutrally.

'Oh, playing the taxi driver?' He gave Hall a dig in the ribs with his elbow and smirked at me. 'Well, whatever makes my little princess happy.'

Maxine looked at him patiently. 'I didn't see you at the airport offering to pick me up.'

'Hardly. That's why they invented taxis.' Henshaw winked at Hall, then planted another kiss on Maxine's cheek before he abruptly excused himself and moved off.

There was no doubt Russell Henshaw was a rude bastard. Nor the slightest doubt he disliked me. The way he leered at me, his bullying, provocative face looking for an argument told me all I needed to know. What a pain in the arse. Mental note to self, don't be in a hurry to meet up with Maxine's old man again.

We stayed another forty minutes or so before I took Maxine home. I can't say either of us was in the mood for the other's company. She was tired from the interstate travel and organising the night's event. I was cranky after meeting her father. I didn't understand how he'd got under my skin the way he had, or why. Normally, I don't even register someone having a dig at me. It's not like I'm thin-skinned or can't take criticism. But he seemed to go out of his way to annoy me, to find fault in what I did. Maybe he thought I wasn't good enough for his daughter; whatever.

I didn't raise the subject with Maxine, though perhaps it's what I needed to do. Anyway, between my feelings of being worked over by Maxine's father and her being exhausted, the night was hardly a success. We didn't have any dinner, relying on the finger food we'd had at the function. Instead, I made some tea while Maxine took a shower and when she came out of the bathroom, we sipped our tea and talked for all of five minutes before she said if she didn't get some sleep, she was going to pass out. I took the hint and told her it was probably best if I went home to my place. Truth was, I was secretly glad to go back to my own home. 'You get a good night's sleep,' I said, reaching over and giving her a kiss. 'I'll see you tomorrow when the batteries are recharged.'

'Goodnight, Punter. The batteries will be fired up then, I promise.'

On the way home, I swung by Gino's. The place was closed for the evening and the staff had long since gone home, but I stuffed a couple of invoices that had to be paid under the door for Billy. Then I drove down Glenhuntly Road on my way home. As I passed the Chinese restaurant I was surprised to see it still open. It was late, yet people were standing around talking outside and in the open doorway. I slowed down and had a stickybeak. The restaurant wasn't actually open at all, and the people weren't customers, as I had thought, but a couple of workmen surveying some damage. They had their van parked out the front; Douglas & Son Glaziers. That was appropriate given the job they were looking at. The entire front window was broken and wicked-looking shards of glass littered the footpath. It was just like the Vietnamese restaurant three doors up I'd noticed a week earlier. Only this time I wasn't so sure it was some kid who'd leant his bike clumsily against the window. I pulled over and looked back at the Vietnamese place. They'd put a temporary corrugated-iron security shield up and appeared to be still waiting for the glaziers to put a new window in. It's probably what the Chinese shop would do too. Good business for the security companies and glaziers, not so good for the restaurateurs.

Next morning I woke up to the usual five thirty home invasion. *Scratch, scratch* on the bedroom door. A short silence followed by a head butt, then a strange burrowing sound.

'All right, I'm coming.'

That response bought me approximately thirty seconds of silence before the ruckus started up again. This time there was a sound like a fingernail running down a blackboard.

'Oh for Christ sake, I said I was coming, didn't I?'

The source of the noise meowed loudly, satisfied that appropriate action was under way. I switched on my bedside lamp, threw on a robe and slippers and opened my door. Che marched in, tail held high, and nearly tripped me up as I walked out to the kitchen. I tipped some dried biscuits into his bowl, and he attacked them like he hadn't been fed for two days.

'You're a greedy creature, aren't you?' I gave him a pat on the neck and left him to his breakfast while I jumped into the shower.

Over coffee and breakfast, I scanned through the races at Moonee Valley, which I planned to go to that afternoon. There were several playable races, including race five, in which my father had a horse called Sometimes in with a good chance. In fact the more I looked at her form, the more I liked her. She was fast reaching her peak, stepped up to her right distance and loved the Valley track. The only thing I wasn't sure about was the rider. Dad hadn't declared a jockey in time for the papers to publish it. If he went with Williams, who'd ridden her last start, then that was fine, except it would carry its full weight of fifty-six kilos. If he was going to claim on it and use an apprentice jockey, then that was okay too, provided it was a half-decent rider. I always steer clear of inexperienced kids, who seem to find ways to get a favourite beaten. It was still far too early to get the official riders for the day from the website or the radio. They didn't come through till around 8 a.m., and it was just gone six. But there was another way, straight from the horse's mouth, so to speak. I picked up the phone and called my brother, David.

I figured he'd be busying himself around the stables, doing the hundred and one things that needed doing on a raceday. He'd know who was riding the horse and he could also tell me how she'd gone since her last start. He took a while to answer and when he did, he sounded a little distant.

'Hi David, it's me. I just wanted to find out who's riding Sometimes today. Is Dad going to use Williams or put a kid up on board?'

'Um, she's actually not running today.'

'She's not?'

'No. None of Dad's horses are.'

'What? He's got half a dozen entered, hasn't he?'

David went silent on me for a moment before I got the sense something was wrong.

'You haven't heard, have you?'

'Heard what? David, what's up?'

'It's Carmen, Carmen Leek. She . . . died last night. Dad's scratched all his runners as a mark of respect.'

I had to think for a moment who David was talking about before the penny dropped. 'Young Carmen, who straps for the old man?'

'Yeah, that's her.'

'How did she . . . I mean, was she in an accident or something?'

David's blunt silence told me that wasn't so. 'No, no accident. She was murdered.'

4

I drove out to Moonee Valley around eleven. The radio was
on, but I wasn't paying any attention to the panel on *Turf
Talk*. I was thinking of what had happened to Carmen Leek.
I knew her on a nod-your-head, say g'day basis. She'd been
working at Dad's stables for about five years; rode a bit of track
work, devoted to looking after her horses. She must have been
reliable or else Dad wouldn't have put up with her. And now
she was dead.

Although Carmen's death hadn't yet been reported in the
media, news of what had happened had spread faster than a
bushfire at the track. Nothing, but nothing stays secret on
a racecourse. The first person to give me the mail about her
was Thommo. He joined me in the queue as I lined up at
the cappuccino bar by the betting ring. Thommo dresses just
like your average member. Well groomed, always in a suit and
tie and polished shoes. He had an oversized set of binoculars
hanging off his shoulders. They weren't for watching the races,
by the way. They were to give you an expertly delivered bump
in the side as he brushed past you in the crowded betting ring.
Afterwards, as you reached for your wallet or purse, you'd
discover they were missing and wonder how you'd managed to
drop them. Thommo's a pickpocket. There's not many of them
around nowadays. Everyone uses EFTPOS and people don't
carry around the amounts of cash they used to. But there's still

one area where a pickpocket can ply their trade: at the races. Thommo's what I call a racetrack acquaintance. I accept what he does and we've came to an understanding that any friends of mine are strictly off-limits to him. Occasionally I tip him a winner and once or twice he's repaid the favour by using his special skills in his professional capacity for me.

'Mate, I'm sorry to hear about what happened to that girl who worked for your father,' he said.

I nodded at him. 'I just found out from my brother this morning. Carmen, her name was. Murdered, apparently.'

'How was she killed?' Typical Thommo, cut straight to the chase.

'You know as much as I do. It'll probably come out in tonight's news.'

Thommo gave the girl some money for his coffee and thanked her. 'I see your old man's scratched all his runners today.'

'Yeah. As a sign of respect.'

'Your father always had class, Punter.'

'I think he'd swap all of his class to bring the girl back, if he could.'

Thommo sipped his coffee, thumbed his formguide and changed the topic. 'You got anything for today?'

'I liked the old man's filly, but now that she's not running nothing really stands out for me. Gonna be a slow day at the office, I reckon. How 'bout you, what's it looking like?'

Thommo relied on a packed betting ring to make his day worthwhile. Carnival time when partying racegoers crammed into the track like sardines was when he had his best paydays. He had his own rating system; four-wallet days he used to call his better efforts. Quieter times of the year he'd rate them lower. He swirled his coffee around in his cup and scanned the crowd that was starting to trickle in. It was still early; the first race was another forty minutes away, but Thommo always had a good feel for what the attendance would be.

'Might get a few latecomers for the main race, but the crowd'd be nothing to get excited about.'

'A one-wallet sort of a day?' I enquired.

'Yeah. Dunno how a man's supposed to earn a living. No one comes to the races nowadays. They all stay home and bet on the internet.'

I nodded solemnly. Agreed declining crowds must be a problem in his line of business.

'I gotta go,' I said. 'Might see you for a drink later.'

I walked over to the betting area. Big Oakie White's staff were busy setting up his stand, although there was no sign of Oakie himself as yet. Big Oakie was my main bookie and I also did a nice little side business supplying him with pre-post prices. I said g'day to his daughter, Michelle, who clerked for him on the stand, and then I moved on to the horse stalls to kill a bit of time before the first race started. Trainers were emerging from the mounting yard with saddles for their runners. I did a slow lap of the stalls, letting my feet take me where they fancied. Over at the swabbing stalls the vets were taking samples from some of the horses as they arrived off the floats. Groups of hopeful owners wandered by and proudly showed off their horses to family or friends. Hard-faced punters lounged against the rail with dog-eared formguides, trying to find that elusive winner. I thought about what Thommo had said earlier; no one comes to the races nowadays. That was true; you didn't actually have to go to the races to have a bet. But there's something I love about going to the track. The smell of a sweating horse, or even the ammonia-like stench of a horse staling. A strapper swearing because a horse stood on his foot. The stewards, whispering quietly amongst themselves and wearing their funny-looking hats. Pint-sized jockeys talking in their squeaky voices. I loved it, loved every sight and sound I could take in. Tell me I'm old-fashioned, but I can't get that sitting at home in front of a TV screen.

They called the runners into the mounting yard and I watched them parade. With Dad's horse being scratched, I had no other betting prospects, so it was strictly a watch-and-wait sort of a day. In fact, my routine hardly changed for the next five races; check out the fitness of the horses in the yard before the race. Have a look at the betting. Watch the race. See how they pulled up and then do it all again. And they say the life of a professional punter is glamorous. Days like today, it can be downright boring. By the time the fifth was over, I decided I'd meet up with the gang and have a drink at the bar.

There's a small group of us who've gotten to know each other over the years. We're all keen racegoers and get to meet up most Saturday meetings. We usually get together for a drink after the main race of the day and commiserate with each other if we've lost or congratulate ourselves if we've backed a winner. Thommo was there of course, although his occupation was known only to myself. To the others in the group, he'd passed himself off as 'working in sales'. That was the beauty of a day at the races. You could be an out-of-work alcoholic or a millionaire businessman, it didn't really matter. When you sat at a bar at the track and had a drink with someone, you were just another punter trying to pick a winner. And so it was with our gang. Members of our group came and went. New people were introduced; some stayed and others moved on. I didn't know a lot about most of them and I expect most didn't know a lot about me either, other than that I was the son of a successful trainer and bet for a living.

Thommo was drinking with Tiny and his girlfriend, Louise. Two other regulars from our group, Matt and Ric, were there as well. I went to the bar and got myself a lemon squash and a sandwich and joined them. They'd all heard about Carmen's murder. I think everyone on the course had. Condolences were passed on to me as if I had a personal link to the girl. Nothing against Carmen, but she worked for my father. I barely knew her and I rarely spoke a word to my father. But I accepted it all with graciousness and told them what I'd said to Thommo earlier, that I knew as much as they did about the whole thing. When the conversation about Carmen petered out, Tiny winked at me and asked me how the battle was.

'Tough going today. Can't even find a race to play.'

'Wish I had your trouble,' said Tiny. 'I've found four so far and I'm doin' my arse.'

Louise seemed to find my lack of action a puzzle. 'You mean you've been here all day and haven't even had a bet?' she asked.

I nodded, gave her a smile. She was good company, a real looker and had been with Tiny all of three months. He'd met her pulling beers at a club he was bouncing. A good match, I thought.

'But don't you get bored? I mean, what's the point of coming if you don't bet?'

I shrugged. 'Sometimes you've got to be patient. Patient and disciplined enough to wait till the right race comes along.'

'Punter's right,' echoed Matt. 'You've got to have the patience and discipline to only bet those races you think you can win.'

'My problem's too much discipline,' said Ric. 'I've got too many ground rules and even with those, I still can't make up my mind. Then, when I'm all set to go, I'll talk to someone in the ring and they'll tell me they heard the trainer say the nag had a setback or some other bullshit that'll sway me from my original bet.'

'That's not discipline,' said Matt, 'that's procrastination. At the end of the day, you gotta make your own decision on having a bet or not having a bet. Isn't that right, Punter?'

They all looked at me over their glasses, awaiting my verdict. The thing is, even though they all knew I bet for a living, it didn't matter what I said or how many times I explained something, my advice would be listened to and forgotten by next Saturday.

'Well, you do the form, pick your chances and if the price is right, you make your bets. Unless something drastically changes on raceday, there's no way you should change your mind. If you've come to a conclusion about an outcome for a race, then you should stick with your reasoning.'

'But why come to the races if there's nothing to bet on?' said Louise, genuinely mystified. 'I mean, you could go shopping, or have a long lunch, or –'

'They don't understand, do they, Punter,' said Tiny, cutting in. 'He's still gotta be here, luv, to see what's goin' down. He's gotta look at the horses, work out what's fit and what's not. Watch their runs, check their prices. All that sorta shit. It's like homework. Isn't that right?'

'Kind of.'

'You see,' said Matt, making sure that Ric had got the point, 'you gotta have patience and discipline.'

I smiled at Matt. I'd known him for about a year or so, a regular racegoer who never missed a meeting. He was Ric's mate and the way they carried on chiding each other over punting theory, they were more like an old married couple. Matt had started off sharing a drink with Ric at the races and then he began sitting with us until he became one of the group. He was a few years older than me, tallish, fortyish and looked as if he worked at keeping in shape. He had a boyish face and an outgoing, cheeky personality. It was hard not to laugh along with his sense of humour and he didn't mind telling a joke against his own punting ineptness. He could afford to be happy-go-lucky too, because he didn't have to work. He'd inherited some property from his parents and lived off the investments. He told me once that his wife worked, but he was content to stay at home and play house, look after his kids and dabble in the stock market.

Ric, on the other hand, was the exact opposite. Ten kilos over what he should have been and didn't care. Scruffy hair that always looked like it wanted a cut or a wash. He dressed and acted in the manner of a morose public servant; which indeed had been his occupation for the past sixteen years. Some nondescript job where he was buried in the basement of the Bureau of Statistics. I must admit, I always found it hard work trying to make conversation with him. I'd put it to him once that he must enjoy his job, having been there so long. You know what he told me? That he hated every bloody minute of his work. For Christ sake, talk about gloomy. These days I made sure to just keep the subject to racing with him.

I asked Matt how his week had been.

'I have a confession,' he announced solemnly. 'I played a maiden race at Echuca last Monday. Backed the odds on fave in a six-horse field and it lost its rider in a scrimmage at the turn.'

A clicking of tongues and shaking of heads all round from us know-it-all punters.

'I know. I shouldn't be even looking at the fields for Echuca. But I had a couple of hours to kill in the afternoon until I picked the kids up from school. I got sucked into grabbing the formguide and ducking into the local TAB.'

We all gave him a good-natured roasting about the folly of backing maidens at country meetings. Matt took it in his stride and even bent over the bar and made a pretence of self-flagellation.

'Twenty lashes,' he said, 'as punishment for such an obvious punting misdemeanour.'

The banter went on like it did every Saturday. After another drink, I said I'd call it a day and left them to it. Outside, there were still plenty of punters milling about the betting ring trying to get out on the last race of the day. It always has me beat why the average gambler tries to get square in the last. It's no easier than trying to find the winner of the first. In a lot of cases it's harder. If you want to bet, you've just got to be disciplined and choose the right race. Matt was right about that. And the right race isn't necessarily the last race. Even though I wasn't going to have a bet, I stood and watched the runners in the mounting yard. It was on my way to the car park, which meant I could look at them parade and then make it out to my van in time to listen to the race on the radio, while beating the crowd home. The race was a shocker, one of those anything-can-win mares' races, where ten out of twelve runners could salute the judge.

''Ullo, Punter, surprised you're still here. You should know that betting on mares' races can only lead to ruin.'

Beering. He leant next to me on the rail, both of us watching the horses parade. So much for my early exit. Beering was in his usual wearily worn sepia-brown suit and hat. Fashion pundits said that brown was the 'in' colour this year, but I couldn't imagine Jim winning a fashions on the field contest with his garb.

'G'day, Jim. Yep, you should avoid all mares' races, maidens, highweights, inexperienced apprentices and wet tracks, and don't play a race on Melbourne Cup Day except the Cup itself. Wonder there's any races left to bet on.'

'You seem to find 'em.'

'Not today, I haven't.'

Beering grunted, cleared his throat and spat some phlegm over the rail. Small talk over, time to get serious.

'You'd have heard by now about that girl from your old man's yard last night?'

'Yeah, David told me this morning. But I don't know the details.'

Beering pointed to a wayward horse who was back-pedalling away from its approaching trainer and jockey. Its handler, a young woman, calmed it soothingly with a pat and a kind word.

'A good strapper, that girl,' he said.

I nodded in agreement. 'Most of the girls are. The old man swears by them. Says they're gentler with the horses than any guy is.'

'That so?'

'Yeah, I'd go along with that. Years ago if you saw a girl working in a stable it would be a rarity. Now it's the other way around; they outnumber the guys. They're more reliable too. Don't get on the piss and sleep in like half the strappers did in my day.'

We watched the rest of the jockeys mount up before Beering spoke again.

'They let Mad Charlie out,' he said softly.

'They *what*? I thought he was locked away awaiting trial for killing that Summers girl?'

'He was. The DPP dropped the charges this afternoon at a special court hearing. Entered a *nolle prosequi*.'

'Noel who?'

Beering rolled his eyes at my ignorance and explained. '*Nolle prosequi*. It's a legal term used when they refuse to pursue charges. When evidence comes to light that effectively results in the discontinuance of a prosecution.'

I squinted at him in confusion. 'Can you translate that into English?'

'Okay, let me put it like this. What did you hear about the Summers girl's death?' he asked.

'What everyone else saw in the papers, I guess. Brutally murdered, knifed repeatedly.'

The last of the horses had gone out onto the track and we had the mounting yard fence to ourselves. Even though there was no one within earshot, Beering kept his voice low.

'Let me tell you something, Punter,' he said. 'The stuff you see on a major crime in the papers and on TV, it's always minus a few details. When they issue a statement on a murder, they never reveal the full facts until they've got all their bases covered. With Summers, they had to identify the body, do an autopsy, make contact with her family, get a team to go over the crime scene for prints and –'

'I get the picture, Jim. The public just got the bare bones.'

'Yeah, that's right. There's a lot more to her death than's been mentioned. Like that she'd been raped, for starters.'

'Did Mad Charlie –'

'No, hear me out,' Beering cut me short. 'The autopsy found semen that didn't match Charlie's. They also established that her death was at least four hours earlier than when Charlie was put at the scene of the crime, and his lawyer's rounded up a rock-solid witness who can vouch for him not being anywhere near there at the time. Importantly, they got a sample of skin tissue from under Summers' nails, which they're pretty sure she got from scratching her killer. It wasn't Charlie's.'

'So it's not the open-and-shut case everyone thought it was?'

'No. And I'll admit I was as guilty as everyone else for pointing the finger at Mad Charlie. It's someone different. And there's something else which wasn't handed over to the press. The killer had written something all over Summers' bedroom mirror with her lipstick.'

'What, like an obscenity?'

'He'd written the words *Silk Chaser*. You know what a silk chaser is, Punter?'

I knew what it meant, as would anyone working around stables. 'It's a derogatory stable term. Used to describe a girl trying to romantically attract a jockey. Hence the term; a jockey wears racing silks, so she's a silk chaser.'

Beering turned and nodded at me, loosening the tie from around his neck.

'Is there any chance that Mad Charlie could have written that on Summers' mirror?'

'He could have, but it wouldn't explain what was scribbled on Carmen Leek's bedroom wall. Charlie was still locked up in remand when Carmen was killed last night. The same message was found there.'

'What, the same words, *Silk Chaser*?'

Beering nodded grimly. 'That information wasn't made public, which is why the police are thinking it's probably the same person who killed Summers.'

I thought that through for a moment, considered what he was saying. 'What do you think?'

'Same frenzied knife attack, same message left on the wall. Both victims young, good-looking, female strappers. No apparent motive for either of 'em. I'll tell you what I think – I'm worried.'

5

How delicious! That's the only way I can describe it. The watching and anticipation. The stalking and waiting; so exciting! The preparation. The look in their eye when they know what's going to happen to them. It's hard to say what the best bit is really. Selecting them gives me goose bumps, because they don't realise they're being chosen. Actually, I do admit to getting aroused during the selection process. I find it a turn-on sorting the wheat from the chaff, sifting through all those vacuous brunette lookalikes. There's never a shortage of that type of girl, is there? The way they dress, the way they act. The dirty way they look at the jockeys. When I think about it, stalking gives me a high, too. Following safely at a distance. Invisible to the little trollop's senses. Jesus, even an antelope can sense a lion's presence in the grass. And it's so easy to follow the brainless scags home. They suspect nothing, know nothing.

I never try too hard to conceal my presence, although I've heard tell of others who go to extraordinary lengths to try and hide their DNA evidence. Like using latex gloves and condoms or even vacuuming up their mess afterwards. But all those precautionary measures sound rather silly, really. They say you always leave a trace of something behind, no matter how careful you might be. And I really don't care if they find my prints or my semen. For I have no record, and I never will have. I'm unknown to police. Indeed, I'm unknown to my victims until I make their acquaintance and then, it's all too brief. I'm the invisible man, so do your best, catch me if you can.

What have I covered? Selection, stalking . . . but I can't leave out the waiting. Now that's always exciting. Especially if I've let myself in and have to hang about until they return. And speaking of letting myself in, how easy that has been. With the spate of hot weather, the idiots had virtually put a 'house open' sign up, leaving every window ajar, flimsy flyscreen doors their only security. One slash with a knife through the mesh and you could unsnip any lock in seconds.

My, what a surprise. What a complete, fucking surprise when they find me dressed in my jockey silks and a knife against their throat. That outfit's so clever, isn't it? And so appropriate. Makes perfect sense, really. I mean, they're silk chasers anyway, so why not provide the uniform? Give them what they really want. And what about my other little touch with that Carmen strumpet? Oh my God! That was just massively brilliant, given that it was totally spontaneous. Her trembling fingers, barely gripping the lipstick in fear. But I made her write those words. Letter by letter. She could barely spell, the halfwit. I guess she's not going to learn anytime now.

I should have made Amanda write those words before I killed her. Her of all people; Amanda, the original silk chaser. The filthy two-timer could have written a book about the subject. But I didn't think of it at the time. She was my first kill and it was all a bit of a hurried blur. I should have drawn it out more, taken my time like I've learnt to do now, done the job properly. Still, I'm a bit like an improving racehorse; getting better with each run, aren't I?

Saturday night was like Groundhog Day. I picked up Maxine from her apartment, drove her to yet another function she was organising and dutifully swanned around with a glass of wine trying to mingle with people I neither knew nor particularly cared about. This time it was an opening night for a new art gallery over in Armadale that Maxine was promoting. Even her instructions were the same: 'Do you mind if I leave you for a minute? I've just got to make sure everybody's happy and the show's running smoothly,' she said.

No sweat, I was getting used to the drill by now. At least the subject matter was something I could relate to. The new gallery was called *The Sport of Kings* and like the name suggested, it had an interesting collection of prints and original artworks from the turf. There were also a number of other sports represented. Tennis, football, boxing and swimming's greatest moments had all been painted or photographed for sport devotees. Some of the works were quite good, not that I know anything about art. One caught my eye over on the far wall. It demanded attention and had a small group of admirers surrounding it. The painting was an original Charles Billich, in which he'd captured the essence of Derby Day. Men in morning suits and top hats. Smiling ladies sipping champagne from flute glasses underneath wide brims and fascinators. The mood of a crowd in party mode. A city skyline in the background and the horses transposed against a sea of jockeys' vibrant silk colours. I could imagine how nicely that painting would look hanging above my fireplace.

I found myself drawn to the painting and walked closer to look at it. There was a group in front of me already inspecting it and as I approached them from behind, I recognised Kagan Hall's voice floating over and above everyone else's. See what I mean about Groundhog Day? The same racing A-list was invited to all these gigs. Hall was talking to a man and a woman with the same confidence and authoritative knowledge about art as he had about racing. Was there nothing he didn't know about? I listened to him impressing the pair.

'Well, of course Billich is renowned for painting sport and horse scenes. But he's done some wonderful exotics and then there are his dance paintings. His Bolshoi collection is probably regarded as his best example.'

The woman on his left, a ditzy-sounding redhead, made some ooohing and aaahing noises. Said he knew an *awful* lot about Billich. Her partner seemed impressed too and he took a step forward to inspect the painting more closely.

'Of course, I should know,' Hall said, 'I have two of them in my own collection.'

He held up his catalogue for the woman to see and that entailed standing nice and close; close enough to place a hand on the small of her back and impart some other clever arty fact about Billich. He kept his hand there too, the smooth bastard, even with her partner only a step away. Hall prattled on about texture and light as he lowered his hand to her buttocks. She appeared halfway between squirming politely and not wanting to cause a scene. Must be hard for a woman to know how to react in that situation.

'G'day, Kagan,' I said, pushing between the two of them and pretending to peer at the painting. 'How would you like to get your hands on that?'

He turned around coolly and carefully dropped his arm by his side. If I'd surprised him, he didn't show it.

'Oh hello, Punter,' he said.

'Nice painting. Hi,' I said to the redhead. 'I'm John Punter.'

'I'm . . . we're just going,' she said.

'Friend of yours?' I asked Hall.

Hall took his time answering, watching as the woman grabbed her partner's arm and hustled him across to the safety of the other side of the gallery.

'No, I never met her before in my life. Excuse me, will you. I've just seen some people I need to speak to.'

I ended up doing slow laps of the gallery floor, balancing a glass of red and a catalogue and trying to look like I fitted in. I'd done half a dozen rounds and inspected every painting and print before I thought everyone must surely think I was doing track work. I gratefully accepted some sushi being offered by a waitress and then took myself off to a quiet corner, hoping the night would finish soon and I could go home. Maxine eventually spotted me hiding away and came to my rescue.

'I'm sorry, Punter. I've left you all alone, haven't I? They'll be finished in a minute. Jacki, she's the gallery owner, has just got to make a bit of a speech, and I've got to organise some photos and then we're done. Then you can have me all to yourself.'

Maxine planted an apologetic kiss on my cheek and dashed off again to do whatever she had to do. Her minute grew to half an hour as the gallery owner droned on and on in her speech, thanking anyone and everyone who'd helped her set up shop. Finally she finished, Maxine was happy with the photos the journalists had taken and we left.

We drove home to my place for a change. My idea. The last couple of weeks I'd stayed the night at Maxine's pad over in South Yarra. She owned one of those huge two-storey apartment-cum-townhouses with everything that opened and shut. Her father had bought it for her as a twenty-first birthday present and I could have fitted my entire flat in her entrance hall and lounge area. Nothing wrong with spending the night at Maxine's, but the truth was that over the past couple of nights I'd felt like I was being hijacked. Pick Maxine up, go to one of her functions, go back to her place. Di dah, di dah. So when I made a right-hand turn at Glenferrie Road she said, 'Oh, are we going to your flat, then?'

'Uh-huh. Mr Punter, aka assistant events coordinator, has decided that after dutifully following orders and attending two functions in two days, he has the choice of where we spend tonight.'

Maxine giggled and put a hand on my knee. I felt her relax for the first time all night. 'I guess I have been a bit bossy, haven't I? Do you want to stop off somewhere and get some takeaway?'

'No. I'll cook up something at home for us.'

'Do you want to buy some wine?'

'No. Got a rack full of it.'

'Do you want to pick up a DVD, then?'

I shook my head.

'Is there *anything* you want to do tonight?'

'Uh-huh.'

I felt for her hand and positioned it a little higher up on my thigh.

'Oh,' she said. 'I see.'

I don't know if it was that we'd both been missing each other over the past week or so, but as soon as we got inside my front door we attacked each other like a couple of wild animals. Clawed our clothes off with urgency and had each other on the bed, the floor and on several other items of furniture not really designed for coupling. We grunted, we groaned, we sighed. Laughed at each other when we were finally sated. Then fell asleep together on a battle-strewn bed surrounded by lingerie and carelessly discarded clothes.

The next morning I awoke to Che scratching at my open bedroom door for his breakfast. He was none too pleased about another big cat invading his territory, either. He looked disdainfully at Maxine sleeping in my bed and gave one of his high-pitched yowls, which clearly meant *I don't like this* in cat talk. I slipped out of bed and fixed him a bowl of those obscenely priced top-shelf biscuits he insisted on. Well, let's be honest, I was the sucker who bought them for him.

First light was peeping through the plantation shutters in the lounge room and I debated whether to put some coffee on or go back to bed.

'Punter? Is that you clobbering around out there? For god's sake, it must be midnight, come back to bed.'

An easy decision to make. I slipped back underneath the sheets. 'How come you're so warm?' I said, spooning up to her. She wriggled back into me, seemed to perfectly complement my body shape.

'What were you doing, getting up?' she asked dreamily.

'Feeding Che. It's his breakfast time.'

'What time is it?'

'Five thirty.'

'Oh my God! I'm never awake at this hour. In fact, I'm not awake now.'

I cradled her in my arms. Hands exploring gently, my stubble rubbing on her neck. 'I know how to wake you up.'

When I woke up again, it was nearly ten. I gazed at Maxine, lying asleep and naked next to me. She looked like one of those exotic nudes that someone like Billich might paint. A wave of hair curled over her face. The sheet was drawn back to reveal the small of her back and the glimpse of a breast. Quite stunning really, women's bodies, the way they attracted men. I thought about it for a moment and about our relationship. Last week I'd missed her like crazy when she'd been away. When she'd got back, it had been all work with her and I'd been ignored, which had irritated me. Yep, admit it, Punter, you've had the sulks for the past two days because Maxine left you on your own at those functions. Not the centre of her attention, were you? But that was all forgotten now, as I planned to treat her to a long, lingering breakfast down at Southbank.

Maxine woke up with a start. 'Oh, fuck!' she said, sitting bolt upright in bed. 'I'm going to be late and it's all your fault.'

'My fault?'

She jumped out of bed, talking to me as she dashed for the shower. Che let out a screech; she must have trodden on him in the hallway.

'Oh, you stupid cat! You shouldn't be there. Yes, it's your fault. I've got be at a racing barbeque Winning Way is sponsoring. You should have woken me hours ago.'

So much for the long, lingering breakfast. After her shower, Maxine dashed about with a towel wrapped around her trying to locate various items of clothing discarded from the night before.

'Have you seen my shoes? Oh, why do they always hide on me when I need them most?'

'Try underneath the couch in the lounge room.'

'I didn't think we got that far.'

'Trust me, we did.'

'Can you call me a cab?'

I called up a Silver Top and told the operator that yes, the passenger was ready to go right now.

'Have some toast before it gets cold.'

Maxine took a mouthful of coffee and a snatched bite of toast before running back to the bedroom to get dressed. A pitter-patter of hurried footsteps on my wooden floorboards signified she'd found her high heels. They reverberated around my apartment along with a steady stream of curses about how late she was going to be.

'Are you mad at me?' she said, fiddling with an earring.

'It's just that I thought we were going to spend —'

She cut me off. 'I'm sorry, sweetie, forgot to tell you about this work do thingy. You can come with me if you want.'

I must have looked less than impressed.

'No, I didn't think so. I'm sorry. You'd probably be bored. How about we do dinner tonight instead? Just us, I promise.'

When the cab tooted outside she pecked me on the cheek and apologised again for having to rush off. She hurried down the stairs, flung open the taxi's door and dived inside. Then she wound down the window as it drove off, gave me a frantic wave and a final parting goodbye that all of Hawthorn must have heard. 'Hey, Punter, you were great last night!'

Che joined me on the doorstep as I watched the taxi disappear up Glenferrie Road, a *don't-ever-invite-her-back-again* expression on his face.

A little later my mobile rang. It was Billy.

'Punter, it's me. Some bad news, I'm afraid.'

'Oh yeah?' That'd be unusual for me this morning. 'What's up?'

'It's Gino's. Somebody smashed in the front window.'

I swore.

'Yep, they got us and the milk bar three doors down.'

'Them too?'

'Made a right bloody mess. Glass everywhere. I've called a security company and they'll be out soon to put up some shutters.'

'What about the window, when can they fix that?'

'Dunno. I'm goin' through the phonebook now tryin' to find a glazier who works on a Sunday.'

'Any other damage, anything stolen?'

'Nothin' I can see. Little bastards want a good dose of national service,' said Billy, starting up on his favourite theme. 'Six months of marchin' up and down sand dunes in the outback. That'd fix 'em, guaranteed. They'd learn a bit of respect for other's people's property, I can tell you.'

'Did you see anything?'

'Nah. I heard it, though. And then a moment later another crash of glass. Must have been the milk bar's window, the second one. By the time I rushed downstairs they were gone.'

'Can we still open up for business tonight?'

'I think we'll be okay. It won't look the best, but it'll be safe enough once we sweep up all the glass and the security shutters go up. We'll just have to cope, that's all. Listen, I gotta go, the cops are here.'

'Do what you can, Billy. I'll drop by later and have a look at the damage myself.'

About the only good news I could salvage from Gino's broken window was that I hadn't yet dropped off the poster that Billco had painted. If it had been put up in the window, it may have been damaged. Billy rang off, leaving me out on the verandah with Che. He sensed things weren't going well for me and gave me one of his commiserating *you're-not-happy-I'm-not-happy* chirps. I picked him up and took him back inside.

'I know, I know,' I said, stroking him. 'Girlfriend's bailed. Window's smashed. Not a great way to start the day. Things can only get better.'

6

Things didn't get better, nor did I see Maxine on Sunday night. She sent me a text saying she was caught up with work. A text, for Christ sake. I didn't hear from her on Monday either, and I was damned if I was going to call. I read through all the papers instead. Gloomy news for the start of a week; yet another impassioned plea by some poor teenager's mother for police to clean up the violence surrounding the nightclub precinct. Seems the kid had got himself kicked half to death and his life hung by a thread. Been a lot of bashings happening around King Street lately. Even Tiny had commented that it was getting out of hand, and he should know, he bounces there four nights a week.

My mobile sat silent until late afternoon, when it rang while I was in my study. I snatched at it, half expecting Maxine to call to apologise. Well, she ought to, shouldn't she? Running out on me and cancelling yet *another* date.

It was Billy, wanting to know if we were still on for our regular weekly catch-up.

'Sure Billy, I'll drop by around half past four,' I said.

I looked at my messages again. Fourth time today. You never know, I may have missed a call. Not from Maxine, that's for sure. I pulled up her text from last night and re-read it. Che came in and rubbed against my leg.

'That's right, buddy. I'm officially back in sulk mode. If she wants to make contact then she can call me. There's no way I'm gonna make the first move.'

Che gave me a supportive little chirp.

'Too right. After all, a man's gotta have some pride, right?'

I grabbed my keys, a jacket and my mobile, ready to go to Gino's.

'Well, maybe I'll just send her a text. A little one. Let her know I don't really care one way or the other.'

Che didn't think it was a good idea. But I spent the best part of half an hour composing a non-committal response to Maxine's text from yesterday. I must have drafted a dozen different answers before settling on a reply.

Got your message. Shame about work getting in the way. Let's catch up later in the week when you're free. XXX Punter.

Pathetic, really. I sent it anyway.

Half an hour later, I stood outside Gino's and surveyed the damage from the weekend. The glazier still hadn't got around to putting in a new window and the ugly steel shutters which had been there since midday on Sunday were still in place. Billy had told me he'd gone with a larger company, supposedly a twenty-four/seven service. They must have had more work than they could handle. I walked down a couple of shops to the milk bar. An identical story. Front window smashed in and awaiting a new one. Their shopfront looked even worse than mine, with the security shutters sticking out as if it were an old abandoned building. I walked back to Gino's and rang the bell for Billy to let me in.

'It's a mess, isn't it?' I said.

Billy nodded his head in agreement. He had his hands around a chunk of garlic bread and was chewing a mouthful as I spoke. When he finished, I half expected another diatribe about the little misfits who were probably to blame. Instead he told me about a strange call he'd got earlier that afternoon.

'The guy rang me out of the blue. I didn't know what he was on about. Talking about Glenhuntly not being a safe neighbourhood anymore. That you couldn't expect to watch your business every minute of the day. He told me there was an easier way and said there were a few businesses in the street using his services now.'

I cut Billy short; wasn't quite sure if I was hearing him right.

'Hang on, Billy, what was the guy selling?'

'Well he was just offering to, you know, keep an eye on the shop for us.'

'Keep an eye on it. How?'

'He reckons for a small monthly fee he can look after us. Make sure Gino's doesn't get trashed.'

'Is that right? And how much is this small monthly fee going to cost?'

'That's the good part!' said Billy. He was at his enthusiastic best and must have sensed I was warming to the proposal. 'He only wants a spot a month.'

'Only a spot. How much you reckon the window's going to set us back, two grand?'

'More.' Billy had the quote in his back pocket and pulled it out. 'Twenty-three hundred plus GST.'

'Well there you go, we're already ahead. A spot a month is twelve hundred a year. The window's twenty-three hundred. We'd be eleven hundred up, if he saves us a window a year.'

Billy positively beamed like he was the teacher's pet. 'So I can give him the go-ahead, then?'

I looked fondly at Billy. He was like a younger brother to me in some ways and I could certainly trust him like he was my own blood. But sometimes that trust was a little misguided.

'No, Billy, we're not going to avail ourselves of his services.'

'We're not?'

'No. If he rings up again, you're to tell him to piss off. We're not interested in dealing with him.'

Billy's eyes nearly popped out of his head in genuine surprise. He couldn't follow my logic. 'But . . . why would you wanna do that?'

'Because I'd lay long odds on that he's the one who smashed

our window and everyone else's in the street too. This guy's running a protection racket.'

It took a moment for it to sink in and then when it finally dawned on him, Billy was appalled. 'Shit, he can't go round doin' things like that. We should tell the cops.'

'Billy, the police aren't going to put a twenty-four-hour guard up to watch our windows. Sure, they'll listen to our suspicions about this guy offering his dubious security services and go through the motions of an investigation, but he's too clever to get caught kicking in our window with a divvy van parked across the street. Let's call his bluff. See what happens. Hey, come out to the van with me, I've got something for you.'

Outside, I reached into the back of the van and passed him the rolled-up poster that Billco had painted.

'What's that?"

'A little Christmas surprise for Gino's. God knows it needs some cheering up.'

On Tuesday I'd still not heard from Maxine.

I went out to Sandown in the afternoon. Watched a few races, stayed to see how one of my father's two-year-olds performed and then left early without even having a bet. George was still manning the gates with his plastic Salvation Army collections bucket when I walked out. I put some loose coins in as I passed.

'Thanks, Punter. You calling it quits already?'

'A slow day, George.'

'Sometimes a feast, other times a famine, huh?'

'How they fall, so shall they go.'

'That's poetic.'

I shrugged. 'No sense betting on bad races, George.'

On the way out Billy called me on the mobile.

'Punter, that bloke called.'

'Which bloke?'

'The one you said to tell to piss off.'

'And did you?'

'Fuckin' oath I did.'

'What did he say?'

'He said I shouldn't be too hasty. That Glenhuntly's shopping strip had got a bad name for vandalism and you never knew when to expect trouble. He reckoned he'd touch base again in case I changed my mind.'

'I'll bet he will.'

'Punter, did I handle him good?' asked Billy, a touch apprehensively.

'You did good, Billy, real good.'

'Oh by the way, the window's all fixed now. Good as new. And I gotta tell you, that poster is unbelievable! I've put it up on the new window with a few ribbons and streamers. It's the best Christmas display in Glenhuntly Road by a mile. I've even had people come in and ask who did it. You can tell your artist mate I've passed out a heap of his cards.'

In the evening I met up with the boys for our regular snooker game at the Red Triangle. There were only three of us; myself, Tiny and David. David's news was all about Carmen's murder, but I knew more about her death than anyone from what Beering had told me at the races on the weekend. Tiny reckoned he'd still like to get his hands on Mad Charlie anyway, despite his being released from custody and having all charges against him dropped. I mentioned to Tiny about the teenager who had been bashed outside the nightclub. He reckoned the whole area was going to the dogs.

'Some of the things I've seen . . . fair dinkum, you wouldn't get it happening ten years ago.'

'What's the difference?' David asked. 'Kids'd get up to the same trouble a generation ago, wouldn't they?'

'Uh-uh. It's different now. You'd always get punters comin' into pubs and clubs getting pissed and wanting to fight. Now they're off their faces scoffing pills like smarties. Throwing down ecstasy and Christ knows what other shit. I threw a kid out the other day, must have been half my size, but I'm not kidding, he fought like he was possessed. Fuckin' head full of amphetamines and it's like he's got the strength of five men. And we got hundreds of these amped-up idiots all coming out of the clubs at the same time, in the same area. Jesus, used to be you could count on one hand the number of clubs in the city. Now, there must be thirty or more clubs in the King and Queens street block alone.'

There didn't seem to be a lot of spark from any of us that night. None of the friendly banter and swipes at one another we usually engaged in. There were no jibes about 'Miss Troubles', for which I was glad. In any case, I wasn't exactly in the mood for conversation about Maxine. Maybe it was the talk of nightclub violence or the unresolved deaths of Carmen Leek and Julie Summers that had put a dampener on things. Whatever, none of us seemed to be really enjoying ourselves and we called it a night around ten and went our separate ways.

The following morning Maxine called. About time. I was spoiling to have it out with her, show her who was boss.

'Hi Punter.'

'Hi stranger. What's news?'

'I've been so busy with work you wouldn't believe it.'

'Let me guess, Winning Way Syndications?'

'My favourite client. *Not*. Anyway, I was thinking, you wanna catch up?'

'What, tonight?'

'Can't, I'm booked solid till the end of the week. How's Friday?'

'Sure. Sounds good.'

'Hey, have you missed me?'

One of the deadly trick questions females can throw in at any time. Better get it right.

'Of course I have. Been thinking about you nonstop, actually.'

Brought a giggled response from her. God, I missed hearing that.

'You're fibbing.'

'I'm not. I've been thinking especially about last Saturday night.' Correct answer.

'I'm sorry I had to rush off like that.'

'There's nothing to be sorry about.' Spoken like a smitten teenager.

'I'll make it up to you on Friday, I promise.'

When we rang off, I was glad we were back on the same page again. All is forgiven, so forth. As I put down the phone, Che looked condescendingly at me from atop the kitchen bench where he was perched.

'You've been eavesdropping again, haven't you?'

Didn't deny it.

'Don't look at me like that.'

Che's face suggested that I hadn't exactly 'had it out with her' as I'd threatened to.

'I handled the situation perfectly,' I said defensively. 'Besides, it's absolutely none of your business.'

The rest of the week zoomed by. Perhaps it was because I was 'back in town' with Maxine. Crazy girl. Crazy relationship. Up and down like a yo-yo. You think you know where you stand and then all of a sudden the goalposts move. In the zone one day, on the outer the next. Bloody thing was like a roller-coaster ride.

When Friday morning rolled around, I got stuck into Saturday's form with gusto. I'd logged onto my online form service. I had my racing publications spread out on my desk: *Winning Post*, *Sportsman* and *Best Bets*. Plus the daily newspapers. I like to read through the racing stories first and pick up any late news that might sway my selections before I do any serious form analysis. The papers only had a light sprinkling of racing gossip which was hardly going to change my mind about what I'd be betting on. Down at Cranbourne the trainers were at loggerheads amongst themselves. Half of them wanted an all-weather synthetic track installed at their training centre and the opposing trainers couldn't decide if they wanted to retain the existing grass track. The authorities had given them a month's deadline to sort it out, but you just knew it would drag on for years before anyone made a decision. There was some news on the recovery of a battling jockey who'd been injured in a particularly nasty fall. He'd only just come back from a fall three months ago, poor bastard. You tend to forget about the country riders trying to earn a quid on the bush circuit. They're not good enough to match it in the city against the top hoops like Oliver and Dunn and company, but they take the same risks and earn a lot less money. The *Herald Sun* had a short piece about a strapper's prize being awarded at tomorrow's meeting:

Tomorrow's main race at Caulfield carries a strapper's prize of $250 and a plaque for the best turned out horse. Gary Hogan, principal of Laskers Insurance, said it was fitting that strappers were given some recognition for the important job they do in racing and his company was proud to sponsor such an award. A winner will be selected each week up until New Year's Day, culminating in the final day's winner receiving $1000 and a trophy.

That was good news for strappers. Too often they were the forgotten soldiers of racing, earning a pittance and working longer hours than any trainer or jockey did. Speaking of strappers, there was no further news of Carmen Leek or Julie Summers that I could see. Last week's headlines are today's fish and chips wrapping, I suppose. I put the papers aside and started in earnest on the form. Winners to find and a living to make.

By mid-afternoon I'd worked through all the Caulfield races and done the Sydney form, too. The Caulfield meeting looked okay; three playable races and one of them a standout bet. In Sydney they were racing at Randwick and I thought if I stuck with a horse of Gai's in the mile race, I'd probably be okay. At three o'clock I made myself a cup of tea and stretched out on the couch. Che jumped up immediately and joined me, like I knew he would.

'Nap time is it, little fellow?'

He gave a little chirp and snuggled up next to me. No choice, was there? I couldn't possibly disturb His Royal Highness now. I dozed off for maybe an hour or so and when I woke Che was still stretched out alongside me. They say a cat can sleep for up to eighteen hours a day. Che would just about be pushing the limit some days. I marvelled at how he could fall asleep anywhere, any time. I stood up gently, trying carefully not to interrupt his slumber, but he half opened his eyes and looked at me sleepily before snuggling back down again.

At seven thirty sharp my taxi arrived and drove me into town. I'd thought about driving in to meet Maxine, but I wanted to enjoy a couple of drinks without having to worry about getting breathalysed. She'd rung me earlier to tell me where to meet up: some new seafood restaurant called Snapper Reef at the Docklands end of town. We got caught up in traffic at the west end of Collins Street, but I didn't mind. I quite enjoyed watching the city sights as a passenger, which I didn't get to do too often. Since my last trip into town a couple of weeks back, the shops seemed to be displaying even more Christmas decorations. Every window seemed ablaze with fairy lights and ribbons draped around some likely looking gift. Signage screamed 'Buy now, don't be late! The perfect Xmas gift . . .' I looked at the date on my watch; still over a week to think about shopping yet.

There were lots of bars at this end of town and they were all full of people who spilled outside onto the footpath tables and laneways. They were mostly office workers, some still wearing Santa hats from their office parties. Laughter and conversation; lots of it. Forget about budgets and sales and the P&L. Today was Friday and Christmas was on the doorstep.

I wondered how I would get on working the nine to five. Except it was more like eight to six these days from all accounts. I tried to picture myself sitting at a desk, doing something vaguely useful with a computer. I'd probably get bored, log onto my online form service and start playing the races. There would probably be staff meetings to attend. I'd have to take notes, look interested, contribute as part of the team. I'd have to learn a new language; *Going forward. The bottom line. Strategically speaking.* Corpy talk, I called it. A load of bullshit, wasn't it? No, I didn't think I'd be suited to the corporate lifestyle.

I couldn't play with my cat. I couldn't take a nap during the afternoon. I certainly couldn't go for a surf when I felt like it. It would only end in tears. I pictured the entire staff of an open-plan office watching me being escorted to the door by security, after being sacked for reading the formguide during work hours. 'Not a good cultural fit,' explained the manager. Ridiculous daydream.

The cab pulled up outside the restaurant precinct at the quay and I palmed the driver a note. It didn't take me long to find the place, a twenty-table restaurant which was already about three-quarters full, right beside the docks along with a dozen other bars and cafés. Maxine was waiting for me at the table. She was talking on her mobile and scribbling down notes in her diary. She had a half-empty glass of white wine in front of her and a dish of cashews. She mouthed 'Won't be long' at me as I sat down. Obviously been here for some time.

'Okay, I'm done with work for tonight,' she said as she ended the call. 'See, the mobile is now switched off.'

'Just you and me?'

She smiled. Flashed her black-studded moon eyes. 'Just you and me, Punter.'

'No clients, no functions you've got to dash off to?'

'Scout's honour,' she said, holding up her hand in a salute. 'And, because I've had a good week, this is going to be my treat tonight.'

A waiter came around and took our drink orders. I opened with a Beck's. Maxine threw down the rest of her white and ordered the same again. I asked her about her week.

'Sensational,' she said. 'Got a heap of extra functions confirmed from Winning Way, which should see me through till next Easter. Plus, one of Dad's radio clients wants some PR work done for a residential housing development coming up. Isn't that just the best!'

I told her how pleased I was for her and let her rattle on excitedly for a solid half hour about her PR work in general. Seeing and listening to her now, I could understand that her business would always come ahead of everything else in her life. She lived, breathed and ate it; was passionate about it. So rushing off and leaving me last Sunday for a work function wouldn't have even been a consideration for her. She'd just go, because she was driven by her work. It was clear she had a totally different set of ground rules from those I lived by. That was okay, I could live with that, but tonight was the first time that I truly understood where she was coming from.

A waiter hovered nearby and I caught his eye, grateful to break the one-way conversation.

'We should order,' I said. 'What are you having?'

'You wanna share a seafood basket with me? I saw one brought out before, chock full of absolutely yummy fishy things.'

'I'm there,' I said.

She turned to the waiter, 'One yummy fish basket thing-ummy.'

'Yes, ma'am.'

'And bring over a bottle of whatever I'm drinking here,' she said, holding up her glass. 'Punter, same for you?'

The bottle was actually a boutique Yarra Ranges chardonnay, very expensive and very good. We made some serious inroads into it before the fisherman's basket had even arrived at our table.

Maxine said, 'Do you think we should go another?'

'Don't see why not. It's a top drop.'

'It's a *damn* top drop,' she said, licking her lips.

For the next forty minutes we battled our way through an impossibly large seafood basket. Calamari rings, fresh prawns and crayfish, crumbed scallops, grilled whiting fillets. You name it, they had it piled up and served on our platter, along with lashings of salad, dips of mayonnaise and tartare sauce and wedges of lemon.

'I can't eat anymore,' I protested.

'Either can I. More wine?' She didn't wait for a reply and splashed a top-up into my glass. Spilt a bit onto the tablecloth too, although she didn't seem to notice.

'What about dessert, can you find room for that?'

I'd seen a lemon sorbet on the menu earlier. Funny how you can always fit a sweet in. I nodded a yes, and when the waiter took our order, Maxine asked for a couple of Drambuies as well.

'Jesus, Maxine, I'll be slipping under the table soon.'

'Nonsense, it'll clear your palate. Besides,' she said, teasing a foot against my leg, 'any talk of slipping under the table is premature.'

'It is?'

'Uh-huh. You're gonna take me dancing first.'

'Dancing?'

'That's right. You're gonna take me to a club, spin me around, then take me home and fuck me senseless.'

'Can we skip the middle bit?'

I knew there was a catch somewhere. Dancing. For Christ sake. I was bloody hopeless at the caper, detested it. And night-clubs, they should be banned. Can't hear anyone speak, can't even hear yourself talk. Full of young kids or tragic-looking middle-aged men on the make. And they made you queue, just like we had to when we made it to the club Maxine wanted to go to, a place called The Vault. Ridiculous name. Ridiculous place. We could hear the music thumping through the door as two security guards, a guy and a woman, opened it up every now and then to let someone in or out. Pity it wasn't Tiny manning the door; at least he'd have let us jump the queue. Already, drunks were getting the heave-ho and it wasn't even midnight yet. We watched as a couple of young blokes were escorted out, arms tightly held by three beefy security guys. When they got outside, they were led away from the doorway up to the adjacent laneway and shoved unceremoniously to the ground. One of them gave some lip, looked like he was going to make something of it, but had the sense to back off at the last moment. Smart decision, kid. We shuffled another couple of metres up the line. Maxine was getting impatient and noisy.

'Why can't they let us in? They just keep you here so that passing traffic will see you waiting and think it's a hot venue.'

Agreed it was a bullshit ploy.

'Hey!' she yelled out to the bouncer, 'there's plenty of room inside, how about speeding things up a bit?'

Others waiting in the queue thought it was good idea and egged Maxine on. 'You tell 'em!' they urged.

She didn't need any of their encouragement and singled out the woman security guard. 'Hey! I'm talking to you. Did you hear me? How about lettin' us in? We've been here forever.'

This time her request wasn't ignored and the security guards looked back down the line to where the disturbance was coming from. They talked briefly to one another and then walked down to where Maxine and I were standing.

The woman spoke to us both. She was good, made lots of eye contact and used all the right body language. Obviously an experienced crowd controller.

'It shouldn't be long now, guys, but I'm going to have to ask you to keep it down, okay?'

I gave her a smile and a reassuring nod. Gave the super-sized Maori towering behind her one as well. Not so Maxine. The drink was kicking in and she'd taken an instant dislike to the woman.

'When?' she demanded petulantly. 'When are you gonna let us in?'

'As soon as we can.'

'There's heaps of room inside and you keep us out here like we don't know. You think we're idiots, do you?'

She was starting to get loud and abusive. The security couple looked at each other and nodded; not a good sign. Then they turned around to face us again.

'Look,' said the woman guard, 'I'm going to have to ask you to leave. You're obviously not happy waiting to get in and you're causing a disturbance.'

Maxine wasn't used to being shown the door. 'What, you're throwing *me* out? I haven't even put a foot inside your pissy little club yet.'

'Come on,' I said to Maxine. 'Let's go.' I grabbed her by the arm, went to walk her away.

'Fuckin' door bitch thinks she's God, she does.'

'Right, you two are out of here now!'

We got bundled professionally out of the queue. The woman had done a bit of Aikido or something; she expertly grabbed hold of Maxine's arm and twisted it up her back. Marched her up to the laneway. The Maori bouncer didn't look like he was going to use as much finesse with me. He closed both his huge fists and took a step forward.

'It's okay mate, we're just leaving,' I said, back-pedalling.

I quickly joined Maxine at the corner of the alley. She was seething, looking to go on with it. 'That fucking bitch. I wouldn't go into her club if you paid me! Fuck her. Fuck you!' she yelled back at them. This was getting embarrassing. She wasn't too steady on her feet and lurched against me for support. I was seeing a side to Maxine tonight that I wasn't altogether comfortable with. Hitting the drink; we all do at times, but it doesn't mean we have to get smashed. Or abusive. Giving grief to bouncers isn't what I call clever and I was starting to wonder how many more nights there'd be in our relationship where I'd be hauling her arse out of trouble.

'C'mon, let's get out of here,' I said, putting an arm around her and leading her away. 'I'm taking you home.'

Getting home from King Street at that hour is easier said than done. First, you've got to find a taxi that'll take you. The nightclub precinct is a no-go zone for cabbies after eleven. They don't mind dropping punters off before then, but picking up clubbers spilling out afterwards, amped up on drink and drugs, was strictly for the brave or foolish. We took off up King Street and I suggested we walk up to a cab rank I knew in Collins Street.

'Can't we just hail one?' said Maxine. 'Look, there's one coming now.' She broke away from me and tottered dangerously into the path of one driving towards her, waving her hands. It swerved to miss her. 'It didn't stop . . . it had a light on, they're not supposed to refuse a fare.'

I don't know that I'd pick us up either if I was a cabby. We looked like trouble.

We headed up Collins towards Queens, past seedy bars

and clubs and fluorescent-lit doorways offering the promise of a good time. Groups of young men and women marauded menacingly about us; you could almost smell the aggression and violence in the air. Up ahead, a bunch of guys were spread-eagled over the entire footpath yelling and swearing. One of them deliberately bumped into me, hoping to provoke a fight. I ignored the little prick and guided Maxine across to the other side of the road. More revellers spilled out onto the roadway. One young guy attempted cartwheels at the traffic lights just as the lights turned green. Lucky he wasn't mowed down, the stupid git. I felt uneasy; didn't like our situation one bit. Gone midnight, stuck in the badlands, couldn't get a cab for love or money. Maxine's drunken behaviour wasn't exactly helping. I should never have allowed her to drag me here in the first place.

We walked two blocks up to the cab rank on Williams Street. There were three taxis when we started crossing at the lights, but by the time we got there only one remained.

Luckily we were next in line and Maxine opened the back door for us. As she did, a bunch of three guys and a couple of women pushed past her and jumped into the cab.

'Thanks, luv,' mouthed one of the guys at Maxine, as if she were a concierge.

'Hey!' she yelled indignantly. 'That's ours, we were here first.'

The cheeky bastards had claimed it, and possession's nine-tenths of the law.

'I don't think so. We booked this one.'

'Bullshit. This is a rank. It's whoever's first in line.' Maxine still had a hand on the door, and wasn't going to let it go.

'It's ours, you stupid bitch. Now piss off!' The guy on the back seat passenger side rammed the door open on her. It hit her hard in the stomach and she staggered back into my arms. I couldn't believe it; nor the total over-reaction that followed. He got out of the car and let fly with a big-fisted haymaker, and if I hadn't stepped in and blocked it, he would have knocked Maxine for a six. I gave him a couple of quick punches to the head, but he was a solid brute, or maybe too drunk to feel them. I grabbed the car door and slammed it back on his knee. Bastard felt that all right. He doubled over in pain and I shoved a foot into his side, which bundled him back in with his mates. Then I quickly swung the door shut and yelled at the driver to take off. He should have. Just driven away to avoid any hassles. But the cretin sat there waiting like he didn't know what to do, the engine running and the passengers spilling out of the doors: three angry young men and a couple of tarts intent on giving it to us.

The first one came at me again, but he was vulnerable, coming at me from the very side I'd kicked him back in from before. He howled like a child as I slammed the door shut on his hand. The other two guys came at me with a rush from the driver's side. One of them was so keen to get at me that he half tripped and stumbled over his mate. He lurched towards me, throwing a wild fist which didn't connect with anything. His face did, though. I rammed a knee into it as he spilled forwards, and followed up with another to his groin as the third guy fronted up.

'You want some of that? You wanna go a round?' I yelled at him. We circled each other. One on one he wasn't so sure, especially with his mates groaning about on all fours. As I jockeyed around him, I caught sight of Maxine punching on with one of the women. I didn't know where the other had got to for the moment, until I saw her come running up behind Maxine with a beer bottle clutched in her hand.

'Maxine! Behind you!' I yelled, and sprinted over to lend a hand. Maxine spun around just as the bottle smashed into her, sending shards of amber glass all over the pavement. She fell heavily, her head hitting the gutter like a dropped watermelon.

7

The Alfred Hospital emergency department was not a pleasant place to be early on a Saturday morning. It was full of paler-than-zombie druggies who'd overdosed and drunken youths with blood-caked faces and ripped shirts caused by mindless, alcohol-fuelled fighting. In the waiting room, bewildered friends and partners, some crying, wondered how loved ones had ended up there; how a night had gone so horribly wrong. I was one of those left wondering; had been thinking about it for three hours, while trying to extract some comfort from the stiff plastic chair that I'd been slouching on.

Fortunately for Maxine, they'd taken her straight into the ops room. Unlike half the mob in here, groaning and bleeding all over the floor waiting to see a medic, the ambulance officers who'd brought her in had insisted on immediate attention. I didn't yet know what the extent of her injuries was, only that she was in a coma. I'd left a message for her father at his radio station. I didn't know who else to call. Since then, I'd received little information on her condition, so like everyone else I sat and waited.

We'd been lucky that a police patrol had been close by when Maxine had been hit. They'd come roaring up, lights ablaze, and called an ambulance. The taxi driver had panicked and driven off; I can't say I blamed him. And the guys and the

85

girls who had attacked us had disappeared as quickly as they'd come. Just another Friday night in clubland.

I went up and fed a coin into the machine for yet another cup of hot chocolate. It was preferable to the dishwater slop they passed off as instant coffee. I sat back and sipped it, trying to think through what had happened. She'd been pissed, I knew that; was well on her way at the restaurant. I hadn't seen Maxine like that before. I mean, I knew she drank, but this was different. I should never have gone out from there, should have taken her straight home. It hadn't helped that she'd been loud and aggressive. She didn't exactly help her case. I mean, you don't give lip to bouncers, it's just not on. And fighting over that frigging taxi, for Christ sake. Maybe I could have done something more to help her. If I'd been closer to her when she'd reached the taxi, perhaps I could have made her walk away before that guy slammed the door into her. He was brave, wasn't he? A drunken idiot with the build of a footballer and he tries to punch a woman half his size over a cab ride he pinched off her. And what about those stupid women joining in? The ambulance guy had told me that was the norm for this part of town. 'As far as glassing goes,' he'd said, 'any girl hanging around here on a weekend could get a job as a glazier.'

'What the hell happened to my daughter?'

Russell Henshaw, striding into the hospital waiting room like he owned the place. I tried to tell him she was in a coma and that's all I knew, but he stormed off to reception and demanded to speak to the doctor in charge. The woman at the counter told him the doctor was still busy, but that she'd come out and see him as soon as she could. In the meantime, he was welcome to take a seat. He gave the waiting room a dismissive glance. Not used to marking time.

'Do you know who I am?' he demanded.

The receptionist looked at him through the security window with tired, unimpressed eyes. She'd been up half the night dealing with abusive drunks and drug addicts and now this bozo of a prima donna was trying to pull rank.

'Yeah,' she said, 'I recognise you. You're the radio guy; I've heard your show. But I'm the woman who runs the front desk and right now, you can take a seat like everyone else or come back some other time.'

Henshaw's glaring response was completely lost on her. Well, could he see his daughter then? No, not yet. Still being tended to. He came back over to where I was sitting, bristling with indignation.

'Incompetent bastards,' he said.

Henshaw looked like he'd only had a few hours' sleep before my message had roused him. Shadowed, hooded eyes protested against being awoken at that hour. He'd obviously dressed hurriedly, thrown on some old jeans and runners, a complete mismatch to his top half which consisted of a suit jacket and business shirt he might have been wearing the night before.

'Well, what happened?' he asked me again.

'We were coming home from a night out when she got into an argument over a cab. One of the women in their group hit her on the head with a beer bottle.'

'That's just utterly appalling. Where were you?' he asked accusingly.

'I was with her.'

'If you'd been *with her*, protecting her, this might never have happened.'

I let that pass.

'Where did this altercation take place?'

When I told him he hit the roof.

'You bloody fool! Walking around there at that time of night with my daughter! Don't you listen to the radio, read the papers? In case you've been living under a rock for the past ten years, it's dangerous out there.'

What was I supposed to do, apologise for Maxine's behaviour? Obviously it was entirely my fault. 'Look, it just happened. Okay? It's one of those things.'

'Did the police catch them?'

'No.'

'I won't rest until I find out who was responsible for assaulting my daughter.'

I'd given a brief statement to the two police officers who'd shown up, describing our attackers. Could have been any of ten thousand clubbers. Good luck to him.

'Mr Henshaw?'

We looked up to see a woman dressed in a white lab coat peering at us through slim-framed glasses. She introduced herself as Doctor Karen Southby. She was tallish, her head still covered in a hair mesh, and she had a no-nonsense manner which suggested she'd tell you exactly how it was.

'Yes. I'm Maxine's father.'

No mention of me, of course. Had to introduce myself.

'You can come and see her now if you like. But I have to warn you, she's in a comatose state.'

'How bad is she, is she going to be all right?' said Henshaw.

The doctor talked to us as she walked, probably a matter of necessity; she simply had too many patients to attend and couldn't stand around and chat like a local family doctor could. She led us through some fold-back doors and we followed her into a ward.

'I won't beat about the bush, Mr Henshaw. Anyone in her state is at risk.'

The doctor kept up a brisk pace, pushing through corridors and doors with us trailing along in her wake. Henshaw put a hand on her elbow to anchor her and when she stopped he said, 'What sort of risk are you talking about?'

She shrugged matter-of-factly and looked Henshaw straight in the eye. 'Sometimes the patient recovers completely. Other times, it can involve lifelong brain damage or even death.'

Henshaw swallowed and took a deep breath.

I asked the obvious. 'What category does Maxine fit into right now?'

'We won't really know until we can diagnose her properly. She may need surgery, she may not. I can tell you we've taken some blood tests which indicate she had an extremely high alcohol level.'

Henshaw shot me an accusatory glance. My fault, of course, that she was tanked.

'How long is she likely to stay in a coma?' I asked.

'A day, a week. Perhaps more. The longer it is, the slimmer her chances of recovery.'

Jesus; optimistic sort, wasn't she.

We came to Maxine's ward and the doctor led us over to her bed. A nurse was fussing around adjusting an intravenous drip. I hardly recognised her. Poor girl had an oxygen mask on and what seemed like a dozen different tubes attaching her to a monitor.

'Can she hear us?' I asked.

The doctor shook her head. 'I doubt it. She's in a state of deep sleep.'

The nurse took her temperature as we looked on. 'Stable,' she said to the doctor. Only bit of good news I'd heard so far.

We only stayed for a little while; both of us were awkward in each other's company. Just he and I looking at Maxine's unconscious body. Nothing to say to each other, or to Maxine.

'Well, there's not much we can do at the moment,' I said, making leaving noises.

'Yes, you're right. Why don't you go? Leave her alone, like you did last night.'

Ignorant fool was playing the blame game. Hardly the time or place, both of us standing over her in bed.

'Russell, I'm not responsible for what happened to Maxine.'

'Aren't you? You heard the doctor; the blood test showed she was full of booze. You took her out, got her drunk and ended up in Queen Street at that hour. Of course it's your fault.'

I shook my head. 'It wasn't like that.'

'No? Let me tell you something,' he said with an aggressive sneer. 'I've never liked you. I picked you straightaway as a gold-digging, two-bob gambler who'll end up with the arse out of your pants.'

'Is that right?'

'You're no good and I don't want you seeing Maxine again.'

'Shouldn't she be the one who decides that?'

He took a step closer to me, ferocious, spiteful eyes blaming me for what had happened to his daughter.

'You stay away from her.'

I shouldn't have come to the races today. I was sluggish, making mistakes. Tired from the lack of sleep and too much wine, which was still washing around in my head from last night. But of course Maxine was the real reason I couldn't concentrate. I'd called the hospital earlier to see if there'd been any change in her condition. Nothing. Stable, but still in a coma. I didn't know quite what to do. Should I go back to the hospital, sit by her bed? Send flowers, a card? Damn it, I'm bloody hopeless in these types of situations; what was I supposed to do? I ended up calling my brother David. I told him what had happened, including Henshaw warning me off his daughter.

'Listen, don't worry about Henshaw,' he said. 'He's always been a control freak. He's just spinning out about Maxine.'

'You think so?'

'Course he is.'

I could hear David's mind ticking over at the other end of the phone. Always methodical, planning the best option even in a crisis, just like he did with the horses.

'There's nothing you can do, for now. Maxine's in hospital where she needs to be. You said they'd notify you as soon as anything changes.'

'I guess so. I was worried about Henshaw blaming me for the whole thing and taking his horses away from Dad.'

'Don't be an idiot. That's not going to happen, and even if it did, you think the old man gives a shit about Russell Henshaw? You know what a massive effort he is to train for?'

I thought back to last night at the hospital, at Henshaw's impossibly rude behaviour at the hospital's reception and the grilling he'd given me.

'I can imagine.'

'Believe me, he's not worth it. All his unannounced visits, his constant phone calls wanting to know about the horses. If he wants to walk away from Parraboo Lodge, then that's his problem, not ours. But I'll talk to the old man about it if it makes you feel better.'

'Thanks, David.'

'And don't let Henshaw put you off Maxine. If you want be with her, that's for you and her to decide.'

As always, my brother's reassuring voice cheered me up and left me feeling a bit more optimistic about things. But even after talking with David, things weren't working out at the track. I kept bumping into people I didn't want to meet. Trader Bill pestered me at the edge of the betting ring. He lies in wait like a flathead buried in the sand, and when some likely prey passes by, he pounces as if from nowhere. Even though it was December and nudging a warm twenty-eight degrees, Trader still wore a tatty old overcoat. How else would he cover the armful of watches he was trying to sell me? Told him I still had his watch from last year and no, I didn't have a lazy spot I could lend him.

When I managed to ditch Trader, I walked straight into Russell Henshaw, who was with his usual entourage of hangers-on. He was the last person I wanted to meet today and probably me, him. He sized me up; his quarrelsome face looked as if he was readying himself for another argument. I got in first; no harm in being civil.

'Any news on Maxine?' I asked.

'None,' he said brusquely and kept walking. Royalty don't fraternise with riffraff, especially gold-digging boyfriends who'd so obviously been responsible for their daughter's injuries. The next person on my didn't-want-to-meet list was Kagan Hall. Thankfully I heard him before I saw him, so I was able to make a successful detour around where he was standing. He was yakking away to some group of would-be racehorse owners in front of the horse stalls. Carrying on about some new colt he'd bought and they'd better be quick, because the shares were selling fast. He was ogling some strapper in the stalls while he was talking; didn't he ever stop?

In the betting ring I wasn't switched on like I should have been. I'd taken evens about a horse I'd sworn was set to start in the red. Damn thing had drifted out to two dollars forty. I'd missed the fives about a filly I'd played in race three and ended up getting no better than four fifty. When a horse I backed in the main race missed the start and flew home to be beaten by a nose, I closed up shop and called it a day. No sense in throwing good money after bad. I rang the hospital again, but after hearing there was still no change in Maxine's condition, I decided to go to the bar and catch up with the gang over afternoon tea.

There were a few of the regular crew I could see in the corner, so I bought a salad sandwich and a cup of coffee and went over to join them. It turned out that David had run into Tiny earlier and had passed on what had happened to Maxine. So they all knew about her; saved me having to break the news.

Everyone was genuinely sorry for her. Tiny, for all his prior harping on about clubland and how dangerous a place it was, didn't once say I told you so. Instead, he was quite sympathetic, as indeed they all were. There were no barbs about my 'Miss Troubles' today.

'Mate, it's a shithole, that place,' said Tiny. 'They oughta fair dinkum send the army in there on a weekend and barricade it. It's about the only way to stop the fightin'. How many of 'em were there?'

'Five. Three guys and two girls. At least the guys fought clean. More than I can say for the two girls.'

'Everyone wants to fight with a weapon nowadays. Women especially. It's like glassin' someone's the "in" thing.'

'I can't understand it; you know, the mindless, unprovoked violence,' said Louise.

I shrugged. I didn't understand either.

Matt had a theory; he always had a theory. 'I think it's got something to do with Generation Y. They want something and they want it now. So when they're under the influence and a bouncer says no, or they're told to wait, or someone beats them to a cab, they just hit out, you know.'

As expected Ric thought Matt's theory was a crock of shit. 'That's crap, mate. Wanting something now doesn't necessarily turn you violent. If I go up to the bar and I've gotta wait five minutes to get served, am I gonna throw a tantrum and glass the barman?'

'No,' said Matt. 'But you're not Generation Y and not under the influence of any booze or drugs.'

Louise thought it was a sign of the way our society was headed. 'I mean, when I was at school, you'd never see girls physically fighting.' She looked at Tiny for a comment. 'Did you ever see that growing up at school, luv?'

'I never saw much school,' admitted Tiny, 'but yeah, you're right. Women are getting wilder. World's gettin' a meaner place.'

Hearing the gang's banter was uplifting; they were a good tonic. After another cup of coffee I decided I'd look at the horses in the mounting yard before the next race. I excused myself and walked through to the members' side fence where I leant up comfortably against the railing. The first runners were just starting to appear in the yard when Kate sidled up to me.

'Hi Punter. I'm sorry to hear about Maxine.'

'Yeah, well, just one of those things.'

'Has there been any news from the hospital?'

I shook my head glumly. Kate laid a hand on my arm, gave it a squeeze. 'Don't worry, she'll be okay.'

'Thanks. By the way, how's Ned?'

'Nathan.'

Really should make more of an effort to remember names, especially ex-girfriend's partner's names.

'Nathan's fine.'

'Not here today?'

'No, he's not what you call an avid racegoer.'

Kate didn't seem overly eager to talk about him and she swung the conversation back to neutral ground.

'You winning?'

'Doing my arse. I've pulled up stumps today. Just going to watch this and head home.'

'I don't know how you do it. Front up meeting after meeting, week after week. Especially if you lose. Doesn't it worry you, when you have bad days?'

I thought about it. 'No, it doesn't worry me. Around thirty per cent of the races I play each year will end up losers.'

'Well, can't you try to improve your run rate or something?'

I laughed. She sounded like a teacher scolding a pupil. 'Believe me, I've tried. I've had years where I've played fewer races, been more selective. Same result. I've tried going the other way, betting on more races. Two years ago I went crazy, upped the ante and started betting on the interstates and all the Sunday races.'

'Same again?'

'Uh-huh. You'd think more bets would increase the hit rate or playing less races would improve the profitability. It doesn't work out like that. Or maybe it's just my betting. But that's what it is and that's as good as it's going to get. As long as it provides me with a living.'

We stood and watched the horses parading for a few moments in companionable silence. The horses seemed especially well presented. One had a blue and red ribbon in her mane. Another had little heart brush marks stencilled across her hind quarters. It was as if they'd made a special effort to show them at their best. The strappers, too, were well turned out, the girls in spotless jodhpurs and polished boots, guys in suits and ties. You'd have thought this was Derby Day the way they were dressed.

'Smartly done up, aren't they?' I said.

Kate put her race book in front of me, her thumb pointing to the sponsor's name: *Laskers Insurance, proudly sponsoring today's strapper's prize.* 'This race is for the strapper's award.'

'Oh, of course.' I remembered seeing the article earlier in the week.

'Who do you think will win?'

I watched them walking around the ring. Every strapper had made a special effort. Stablehands don't earn a lot of money, so when an opportunity comes along where they can snaffle a few extra dollars, they usually grasp it with both hands. I saw one guy who presented head and shoulders above the rest. He was wearing a dark suit and a matching hat, looked as if he'd bought it especially for the occasion. Even had a feather in his brim. His horse looked a treat, groomed to a sheen and its four white socks brightly shampooed. Kate thought he was the standout. I wasn't so sure. I watched the guy from Laskers Insurance in the middle of the ring, inspecting every horse and strapper walking around him. He was a solemn-looking, middle-aged chap who was standing alongside a chubby-faced committeeman from the race club. They both seemed to be taking their task seriously. The committeeman had a clipboard and seemed to be making notes from the other man's comments as the strappers and their charges paraded. It looked like they were well organised and had some sort of scoring system in place. But Laskers' man hardly gave the guy strapper we'd been watching a glance. He only had eyes for the fillies. One in particular he seemed to watch intently; a pretty girl wearing an old-time groom's cap and a matching red ribbon in her hair and in her horse's mane. When she passed by, she doffed her cap ever so femininely and gave him a smile. That settled it as far as I was concerned.

'Odds on, the girl with the cap,' I said.

'No, the guy's much better turned out. Have a look at the trouble he's gone to,' argued Kate.

As we waited for the jockeys to mount up, I provided Kate with an imaginary market on each strapper's chances.

'A dollar eighty red-ribbon-girl, three's the guy with the hat and fives for the blonde leading in number seven. Tens the rest of the field.'

'I'll have ten on the guy with the hat, then.'

'Done,' I said.

We didn't have to wait long. As soon as the jockeys were mounting up, Mr Chubby Face made a special announcement over the microphone that the strapper's prize was being judged. Shortly after, he and Laskers' man conferred with one another and seemed to come to a decision.

'The winner of the strapper's prize for the best turned out horse goes to number four, Melissa Jordan, and her horse, City Sights. Melissa, as soon as the jockeys have ridden onto the track, we ask that you come forward and collect your prize.'

I wriggled my thumb and fingers in front of Kate's nose. 'Um, a matter of a tenner?'

'I was dudded. He only had eyes for that girl. He didn't bother looking at anyone else.'

What a fantastic idea, a strapper's prize! Of course, there can only be one real judge of that contest. Someone who knows and under-stands what those little strumpets are really up to. Namely, yours truely.

I make sure to get right up close against the mounting yard fence where I can watch them clearly. And from where I'm standing I notice the sponsor and a fat committeeman jotting down points on a clipboard. Now that's very professional. Perhaps I should do some-thing similar? Formalise things a bit more, maybe work out a scoring system myself. But no. There's no need. I know instinctively which of those trollops will get my vote. They virtually pick themselves, don't they?

But this is wonderful entertainment! They've dressed up for today; I like to think especially for me, but of course I know it's because of the contest. Even the guy strappers have taken the trouble to wear suits and ties. But with two men judging, I doubt they'll go for the male strappers. Not unless they're faggots. Now then, time for business. Which harlot will it be today, who's going to get my vote, hmmm?

Number one's a bit on the podgy side. She shouldn't really be wearing jodhpurs owning a backside like that. She appears to be a simple country girl and I smile smugly to myself when I see that the horse is in fact trained up bush at Bendigo. Next. Horse numbers two and eight both have male strappers, so moving right along . . .

. . Number seven has possibilities. She's youngish, still perfecting the slutty looks she's trying to palm off to anyone stupid enough to pay

attention. *In a year or two she'll be ripe. Number ten's as ugly as sin; an old brood mare. I watch intently as the last of the stragglers comes into the ring. They are all there now, all the strappers and their horses.*

Have a close look at number four, will you. Tight jodhpurs around her arse. Blouse buttons open for all the world to see. The only thing stopping a decent peek down there is the ridiculous pinafore with the horse number on it that strappers are required to wear. Now then, did you see that; the way she flicked her plait? Amanda used to flick her hair like that too. This one's got a black plait with a red ribbon in it and a matching one in her horse's mane. But wait, did I just see what I think I saw? Did she really tip her cap to the judges? I can't believe it. And he's fallen for it too, that sponsor fellow. So has the fat committeeman. Fallen for her treacherous little ways, each of them thinking they're half a chance with her. She knows that. She knows the power she has over men. Just like Amanda.

By the way the two judges zero in on her, I can tell the competition is as good as over. And so it proves to be. After the jockeys ride their horses out onto the track, they announce the winner on the PA and, shock horror, it's number four. Melissa, Sweet Melissa. She steps forward to collect her prize. Holds a hand to her face in an 'Oh-my-god-I-can't-believe-I've-won' sort of way, and responds briefly with some insincere words of thanks for the sponsor. I check her trainer in the race book. Some local battler. The horse has some form though. I might even back it; it's got half a chance. Now, wouldn't that be a nice double for Melissa, picking up the strapper's prize and her horse winning the race. And even better would be the trifecta; my little rendezvous with her later tonight. But she doesn't know anything about that yet, so let's not spoil it for her.

8

I'd only just gone to bed when the hospital rang me.

'Is this John Punter?'

'Yes.'

'We have some news about Maxine Henshaw. She's come out of her coma and she's going to be okay.'

Thank god for that. The four words I most wanted to hear: *going to be okay.* I'd been Googling anything I could find about brain trauma on the internet and the more I looked, the more convinced I was that Maxine was a goner. It seemed that cyberspace was full of gloomy predictions and case histories of coma patients, with such cheerful information as: . . . *It's not uncommon for victims to be comatose for weeks or months at a time . . . the longer they are, the greater their chances for permanent brain damage.*

Maxine had been out for just under twenty-four hours, so she'd been lucky, the doctor said. Apart from some cuts to the back of her head caused by the beer bottle, she was relatively unscathed. They were keeping her in for observation for a couple more days, but I could come and visit her tomorrow if I wanted to.

The next morning after breakfast, I drove over to the Alfred Hospital. On the way, I stopped off at a florist and bought a big bunch of something colourful and fragrant. Can't remember what exactly, just pointed them out and the girl wrapped them for me and sold me a card as well. At reception, they gave me directions to where I could find Maxine. They'd shifted her out of Emergency and put her into a private room. As I trooped through the various wards, there didn't seem to be many visitors around; still a bit early yet. I thought I may have even been the first. But as I walked through J Ward and into Maxine's room, I saw that I'd been beaten to the post. Russell Henshaw was there ahead of me, sitting in a chair next to Maxine, who looked to be sleeping peacefully.

I nodded at him. 'You been here long?' I said civilly.

'Hours,' he replied gruffly. 'More than I can say for you.'

I doubted he'd been here for very long. They'd told me last night; strictly no visitors before eight thirty, so don't think I was buying any of his father-keeps-all-night-bedside-vigil story.

'I bought these,' I said, holding my bunch of flowers awkwardly in my hands.

Henshaw grunted and jerked his head towards the window. There, on a table, was the largest bunch of flowers I'd ever seen. Bought by Daddy, obviously. Must have cost a packet; they made mine seem pathetic. I placed my humble offering next to them and looked at Maxine. She still had tubes sticking out of her arms and attached to monitoring machines. A nurse came in and checked her; smiled at us as she fussed around Maxine.

'How is she?' I asked.

'I don't know why you'd be interested,' butted in Henshaw.

I ignored him. 'Nurse, can you tell me the latest?'

'She's going to be fine, a very lucky girl. She's very drowsy, we've got her on medication, so it's best if you don't stay too long.'

The nurse fluffed up her pillows a little and checked the monitors. Maxine looked pale and childlike lying there. I watched her a moment, unsure whether I should try to talk to her, maybe wake her up. Felt a prat sitting there with her bully-boy father.

'I thought I made myself quite clear yesterday,' said Henshaw. 'I don't want you seeing my daughter again.'

'When I started going out with Maxine, I didn't sign up for the package,' I said.

'What do you mean?'

'The father-comes-with-daughter deal.'

'You impertinent little fool. No one speaks to me like that.'

This was getting loud and nasty and the nurse was doing her diplomatic best to pretend not to notice. But I couldn't help myself, I finally lost my temper.

'Oh fuck off, Russell. Wake up to yourself. If I hadn't been there looking out for Maxine, she may not even be here with us now.'

'It's your fault she's here at all!'

'Yeah, is that right? You believe what you want to believe. I don't give a shit what you think.'

'I don't want you seeing her, I tell you. I won't put up with it. I've got horses with your father,' he said, a nasty black-mailer's edge entering his voice. 'Don't think I won't hesitate to take them somewhere else.' He let the threat hang.

'Look, you can give them to the pope to train for all I care. Your horses aren't my problem. And like I've told you before, as far as not seeing Maxine again, that's something I'd want to hear from her, not you.'

The silly bastard went for me, can you believe it? In the same hospital room where his daughter lay before us, a victim of violence herself, and a nurse was trying to do her job. He came at me like a windmill blowing in a gale, swinging a wild succession of haymakers that I easily dodged. Then he grabbed me by the shirt front and I thought, for Christ sake, enough is enough. I gave him a cuff on the bridge of his nose, not hard, but enough to make him drop his hands.

The nurse yelled at us, 'Stop it! I'm calling security.'

Henshaw came at me again and this time I let him have it, gave him a decent right-hander under the eye. He fell to the side, bringing the stand carrying Maxine's tubes and bottles crashing down beside him.

'Sit down, you bloody fool!' I told him.

'Stop it, the pair of you!' shouted the nurse.

A big gorilla of a security guard came rushing in from the corridor, not quite believing what he was seeing. Henshaw glared at me from the floor where he'd fallen. This time he wasn't in such a hurry to get up.

'Right, you two. You're out of here now!' barked the security guard at us.

'He started it,' said Henshaw, pointing a threatening finger at me. 'I want him arrested for assault.'

'*I started it?* You've got to be kidding. I was defending myself.'

A meek little voice broke the silence.

'Can't you two stop arguing?' Maxine said, drawing herself up weakly on her pillow. 'You woke me up,' she said. 'Both of you, with your stupid fighting.'

I muttered an apology; suggested it might be better if I left. Henshaw, for once, agreed with me.

'You want them both to leave, miss?' said the security guard.

'I think that's *definitely* a good idea,' said the nurse, starting to clean up the mess.

Maxine spoke again, softly, almost to herself. 'I'm afraid I'm going to have to get some more sleep. You'll have to come back later. I'm so . . . tired.'

Poor girl looked exhausted, like she was going to collapse back onto the bed as she spoke.

That was enough as far as the nurse was concerned. She shooed us both out, forbidding us to see Maxine again before the afternoon's visiting session, and with the explicit instruction that we weren't to visit her together. The security guard marched us all the way to the foyer, determined we wouldn't cause any more trouble. Outside, Henshaw stormed off ahead of me. I got to the entrance steps and waited there, giving him time to get into his car. I didn't particularly want another scene with him in the car park. His car was in the first bay, something loud and yellow, a Maserati I think. He got in, slammed the door, threw the thing into reverse and then straightened it up and roared past the entrance, giving me a glare as he sped by. An absolute psycho. I really didn't fancy having him for a father-in-law.

As his car disappeared out through the gates, my mobile rang. It was Kate.

'Hi Punter, I'm at work. There was a police report that came in earlier I thought I should tell you about.'

Kate is usually either pretty jovial or deadpan on the phone. This morning it was the latter, so I figured the news couldn't be good.

'What's up?'

'There was a girl murdered last night. You and I sort of know her.' Kate paused a moment before continuing. 'She was the girl who won the strapper's prize yesterday.'

An hour later I was sitting in a café opposite Great Southern Station sipping a cappuccino and waiting for Kate. Her workplace at *The Age* was only a short stroll away. She didn't keep me waiting long. Five minutes after I'd arrived she eased her petite figure into the chair next to me, a coffee in her hand.

'Hi Punter.'

'Hi.'

'My editor's just assigned me this story I called you about. I'm gonna be tied up solid on it for a couple of days.'

'Tell me what happened.'

'Another raceday, another female strapper murdered. Melissa Jordan was her name.'

'The girl you and I saw win the strapper's prize yesterday?'

'Uh-huh. And she was done just like the others. They've all been killed in their homes. All showing signs of multiple stab wounds and sexual assault. They found Melissa this morning the same way, although they're still completing an autopsy on her. That makes three in the past month. There's someone out there killing female strappers.'

I thought back to the first killing. 'Everyone thought Julie Summers was killed by Mad Charlie until the police let him go,' I said. I was thinking about what Beering had told me, the reasoning behind dropping the charges. 'Beering used some fancy legal jargon for describing why the DPP didn't go ahead. *Noel* something or other.'

'*Nolle prosequi.* It's when they refuse to pursue charges because of certain evidence coming to light. I know all about Mad Charlie's alibi and the other bits and pieces ruling him out, including the scribble on the wall of the victims' bedrooms.'

'The girl killed last night, was . . .?'

Kate nodded matter-of-factly. 'Same writing on her bedroom wall: *Silk Chaser.* I saw the police photos, although we've been requested by police not to mention that in the papers.'

'Can they do that?'

'Up to a point, but I think it's gonna be hard to keep a lid on this one.'

'What do the cops think? They got any ideas?'

'You want my opinion? They haven't got a clue.'

I thought about that for a moment while taking a sip of coffee. 'Why do you think he's killing them?'

Kate drained her cup, set it down again and wiped her mouth with a paper napkin.

'Beats me. Find his motive, you probably find the killer.'

I realised we'd both jumped in with a *he* as the killer. 'There's no possibility he could be a she?'

'It's true, there have been female serial killers, so you can't discount it. But in the first two cases, the victims were raped and semen samples were found. It's the same MO with Melissa Jordan, which suggests a similar finding.'

'She'd been dealt with the same way?'

'Poor girl. Her apartment was broken into while she slept. He attacked her in her bed. She never had a chance.'

I thought back to yesterday afternoon when I'd been standing next to the mounting yard with Kate. Melissa Jordan had been leading her horse around, pretty as a model, wearing that groom's cap and the red ribbon in her hair. Dressed to impress for the strapper's prize. She had, too; caught the judges' eye and won the thing. But that was yesterday, and now she was gone. A pale corpse lying in the coroner's morgue.

'Listen, I'd better get going,' said Kate, 'but if you hear anything at the track, and it doesn't matter how insignificant, can you give me the heads up? This story's not going to go away quickly.'

'Sure. Anything I hear, you'll know about.'

Kate got up to leave. 'Hey, I nearly forgot to ask, any news about Maxine?'

'She's okay. Came out of her coma last night with no complications.'

Kate laid a hand on mine. 'I'm so pleased.'

When I got back to my flat, I didn't quite know what to do with myself for the rest of the day. Che suggested a lunchtime feed was probably a good starting point. He rubbed against my leg and let out one of his not-before-time meows.

'Oh for goodness' sake, anyone would think you hadn't been fed for a week.'

I spooned a handful of dry biscuits into his feed bowl and he hoed into it like a greedy pony who'd found the door to the oat bin open. Ridiculous creature.

Outside, Mrs Givan was putting out her first load of washing for the day. Colours this time, but there was every chance of another wash later on. Maybe the whites would come out then. I mean, I know she had method, unlike myself who chucked everything in together once a week when I realised I'd run out of clothes. I waved at her through the window when she looked up at me. Nice old dear. Shouldn't complain about her as a neighbour if doing lots of washing was her worst crime. She fed Che for me too, if I was away overnight. In fact, I'm sure that feline was double-dipping during the day and getting an extra feed from her when he shouldn't.

Mrs Givan had picked a good day to hang out her washing. It was a brilliant December afternoon with the promise of a warm northerly. It occured to me that perhaps I, too, should do some chores around my flat, maybe even some washing of my own. I looked into my laundry basket, which was badly overflowing.

It was crying out for an empty, but when I checked my tallboy, it still had three days' supply of undies and T-shirts in it. I had a quick peek at the flag tower across the road at Scotch College. Yep, definitely offshore. Stuff it. Never do today what can be put off till tomorrow. I was going surfing.

Nothing like the first smack of a wave as it breaks over your head. I was at Gunnamatta, way down the beach towards Cape Schanck, where I'd found a nice isolated bank. There were little lefts and rights forming off an A-frame; an easy rip to paddle out in and, even better, all the stand-ups were surfing at the first car park, too far for them to venture down, so I had the wave all to myself. And today conditions were just right. Clean waters, a warm offshore breeze; just what I needed to clear my mind and get some exercise. I caught a couple of sets in quick succession, then enjoyed a leisurely wait in between waves dangling my legs over the sides of the ski. When it got too warm, I flipped over and eskimo-rolled back up, enjoying the sensation of the refreshing water dripping down my hair. A school of whiting skipped by; don't know what they made of me splashing about like a whale. A flock of gulls hovered overhead, ever watchful for possible food scraps.

They don't miss much, whether it's fish and chips from tourists or baitfish getting rounded up by predators. Between the sets I thought about the girl who had been killed yesterday. She was the third in about a month. Bloody scary stuff. Some nutter out there picking off young girls. But strappers; he was targeting female strappers. Kate said the police thought it was the same person, but didn't have a clue who it was. And what else had she said? That's right, find his motive and you find the killer. But why would someone kill three young strappers?

After a couple of hours I'd had my fill of waves, so I came back in and showered off in the car park. When I'd changed and packed my ski and things into my van, I called the hospital and asked if they could put me through to Maxine's room. The receptionist let it ring half a dozen times before it switched back to her phone.

'Not answering, I'm afraid,' she said. Would I like to leave a message?

'Just tell her I called, please, and I'll try her again later.'

I thought I might drop by the hospital on the way back into town if Maxine was feeling up to it, but I didn't want to if her old man was around. Not that I was taking his warning off seriously; I just wanted some time alone with her without her father's aggro.

My stomach said 'feed me' as it always did after a surf, so I figured I may as well head to Gino's. I could get some dinner there and catch up with Billy, then afterwards swing by the hospital and see Maxine on the way home. It was a bitch driving back into town. It had been a hot day, everyone had hit the beaches and now they were returning home at crawling speed. By the time I made Glenhuntly Road, it was almost seven.

Gino's was humming when I walked in the door. The big poster of Santa and his flying pizza held pride of place on the front window. People outside were looking at it while waiting for their tram. I smiled to myself; it was a hit. There were a couple of casuals manning the ovens and making pizzas and some new waitress Billy had put on was busily running drinks from the bar to customers' tables. I stole a quick look at the orders; always a good indication of how we were travelling. There were twenty-odd yellow post-it notes queued up on the counter and Jason, the young guy on cook's duty, was picking them up and laying them down about as fast he could possibly go. Billy chipped in to help in between manning the cash register and together they were a formidable team, making up a pizza in thirty seconds flat. They had a good system and were coping with the rush, but even so, I sometimes felt tempted to roll up my sleeves and get behind the counter to help out on a busy night like tonight. I'd seriously thought about it, dropping the silent partner bit and going public that I owned the place. But Gino's was my bolthole. Nobody but Billy knew it was mine and I didn't want to be a slave to the business like I knew I surely would if I became actively involved.

Billy looked up over the counter and gave me a grin.

'G'day, Punter. Usual table? Usual pizza?'

The place was full but there's always a little table down the back that Billy keeps reserved for me in the evenings. It's the only extravagance I afford myself; after all, what's the point of owning a restaurant if you can't get a table?

'You got it, Billy. A coldie wouldn't go astray either.'

'One Seafood Delight and a Beck's to table seventeen,' he said, writing down the order and putting it at the front of the pile. Jumping the queue was another advantage that came your way when you owned your own joint. Billy brought over my beer and a lemon squash for himself and joined me.

'Don't let me stop you if you're busy,' I said.

'Nah, we've stemmed the tide. It'll ease off now till about eight before it starts picking up again. I may as well take a break now, while I can.'

Billy took a gulp of his squash and wiped his mouth with his hand. 'Hey, guess who called me back yesterday?'

'Let me guess. Mr Protector?'

Billy nodded. 'He asked if I'd had a chance to think through his proposal.'

'No kidding. What did you tell him?'

'I gave him the same answer as before. Told him to piss off.'

'Good.'

We chewed the fat while waiting for my pizza. Billy and I are careful not to talk business openly in front of staff if I drop by during working hours, so we usually confine our conversation to the horses. To them, I'm just a regular customer and a punting mate of Billy's.

'Hey, did you hear about that other strapper who got murdered?' he said. 'That's the third one. What the hell's goin' on out there?'

I shook my head. 'Some crazy, that's for sure.'

'The second one worked for your old man, didn't she?'

'Yeah. Carmen Leek.'

'She just lived around the corner. Used to drop by here regularly. A lovely kid; she didn't deserve to die like that.'

'None of them did, Billy.'

When I got back to my van I called the hospital again and asked to be put through to Maxine. There was a short delay, then the receptionist apologised.

'I'm afraid Ms Henshaw has checked out,' she said. Made it sound like a hotel.

'She's left?' I must have sounded like the none-too-well-informed boyfriend, which indeed I was.

'I'm sorry . . . you're family, a friend of hers?'

'Friend. I was going to drop around and visit her tonight.'

'Yes, well, she signed out earlier this evening. Her father took her home, I believe.'

Her father, for Christ sake.

'So she's quite okay then?'

'We wouldn't release her unless she was.'

I thanked the receptionist and hung up. Bloody Henshaw, whisking his daughter home before I could see her again. Cantankerous old fool. I sank back into my seat. Hadn't started the engine up yet, just sulked over the way he was getting on my goat. Hang on a minute, why was he shitting me? Why was I letting him? Put aside the fact I'd decked him; he'd started that himself. But he was Maxine's father, and he was entitled to take her home and make sure she was okay. I thought about it for a moment before it materialised. *Why hadn't I been told?* That was the real reason, wasn't it? Maxine hadn't told me she was leaving the hospital and I felt I was the one who should have been there to take her home, not her overbearing, protective wanker of a father. Stuff him, I'd call her at home, let her know I was there for her.

I tried her mobile number, but it switched to her voice mail, so I left a message. Then I sent a follow-up text message, too. It was the longest text that clumsy-fingers me had ever sent her. Was there any more I could do tonight? Perhaps drop around to her apartment? If Henshaw was still there, then I definitely didn't want another run-in with him. But I had her home number and I decided to call that and see if I could reach her. It was a no-go. All I got was her businesslike voice on the recorder inviting me to leave my name and number and she would return my call as soon as she was able. I pictured her as she spoke. Even if you'd never seen Maxine, you'd imagine her as pretty, vibrant and sexy, just from her voice.

I started to leave a message, but as soon as I mentioned my name the phone picked up at the other end. 'Maxine, is that you? It's Punter.'

'No, it's not.'

I didn't need an introduction to know whose voice was on the other end of the line.

'Oh goody, my favourite pa.'

'Don't you dare talk to me like that. You've caused enough trouble for today. What do you want?'

'What, are you Maxine's PA?'

'Don't be so bloody impertinent.'

'I didn't realise Maxine was checking out of the hospital today.'

'Well, why would you? You've hardly been sighted the entire time she's been there. Do you think we're going to ask your permission?'

Ignore. 'I want to speak to her.'

'You can't, she's not available.'

'Bullshit, put her on.'

'She's sleeping. I'm not going to disturb her. The doctor says she still needs plenty of rest to get over her ordeal.'

'Is she okay?'

'She'll be all right. No thanks to you.'

'Is it any use asking you to tell her I called?'

A churlish snort was my response.

It was almost a dead heat to see who hung up first, but I think I won by a short half head. Jammed my thumb on the button and cut the stubborn bastard off before I had to endure another word. It was bloody hopeless, wasn't it.

Next morning's headlines just about screamed at me to read them immediately. The *Herald Sun* went for the sensational: 'Strapper slaughter – serial killer runs amok'. It ran stories and photos over several pages, including the sports section, with commentary from several leading trainers, jockeys and administrators. They'd even asked my father what he thought:

Leading trainer David Punter, whose employee Carmen Leek was one of the recent murder victims said, 'The police need to catch this madman and catch him quickly.' Meanwhile Adrian Nicholls, Secretary of the Australian Workers Union, said he wanted to see some immediate action by the racing clubs to improve security, or else he'd have to consider recommending that stablehands take strike action. 'You can't expect our female strappers to work in an environment where a killer seems to be able to pick them off at will. The clubs need to get off their arses and do something before it's too late. These are human lives we're talking about.' Melbourne Racing Club CEO, Morris Wilby, agreed that security needed to be improved, but added that talk of strikes by the union was premature. 'Of course we're working closely with police in all of this, but how far do you go, what exactly do you protect? You can't just throw a cordon around every stable and every strapper working at the races. And talk of strikes is nonsense, you can't just shut down an entire industry.' Police have told the *Herald Sun* that they are currently investigating the murders of three female stablehands over the past month, and while they are pursuing several lines of inquiry, they would appreciate any information that the public may be able to provide.

The Age's story, written by Kate and another reporter, covered similar ground. They'd interviewed some female strappers from around Caulfield stables and asked them what they thought. The response was predictable:

'I'm scared to walk to work in the morning,' said Jessica Railings, who works for local trainer Mick Price. 'We've all arranged to car pool until this is over.' Another strapper, who didn't want to be named or photographed, had this to say: 'It's like someone's hunting us. Am I scared? Of course I am, we all are. You'd be a fool not to be thinking about it.'

Kate had also interviewed a criminal psychologist, a professor Andrea Rose, and got her slant on who the killer might be.

'It's always interesting to speculate in these cases as to what sort of profile a killer may have. The public expect them to be readily identifiable monsters. But they're not always the people we imagine them to be. The stereotype we have of them – bullied as kids, cruel to animals and pulled the wings off flies – doesn't always apply. But they're usually single, uneducated males who have had trouble forming long-term relationships. There are so many other factors and in this case, there's simply not enough known at this point to make an accurate guess about the killer's profile.'

Over breakfast, I read through all the articles again. Jesus, talk about media hype. I wondered if there would be the same coverage if three homeless people had been found stabbed to death by the river. Probably not, but then again they weren't young and female and didn't work in an industry which is constantly in the public eye.

My mobile rang. Maxine.

'Hello stranger,' she said.

'Hi luv. You okay?'

'I'm fine. Feels like I haven't seen you for weeks, though.'

'Yesterday morning, actually. But it hasn't been from want of trying. That father of yours set up a cordon around you tighter than security at the White House.'

'It's about time you two learnt to get on.'

'I must admit I've never dated a girl whose father I had to fight off.'

'You two are like a cat and dog.'

'I think we need a mediator.'

'You'll have to sort it out. You're both adults.'

'I thought we did.'

'Yes, using my hospital room as a boxing ring. I heard you both got thrown out. Probably a good thing too. Dad's got a black eye, you know; did you have to hit him so hard?'

I let it pass. 'What are you doing today? How about I take you out for a nice long lunch?'

'No, I'm working. Gotta get on top of things.'

'You're mad; you've only just come back from being knocked out.'

'It was only concussion. Won't stop me if I take things easy.'

I snorted. Maxine take things easy? That'll be the day.

'I promise I will,' she said. 'Why don't you come over for dinner tonight and afterwards you can show me how much you missed me.'

'*Growwwl.*'

'I take it that's a yes, then?'

I got another call shortly after, this time from Jim Beering.

'Punter, I need to see you.'

Typical Beering. He expected a lot from his friends and associates. No 'Would you mind?' or 'Are you available?' Just an abrupt order barked out, taking it for granted you'd comply whenever or wherever you were. A throwback to his cop days.

'I might be busy, Jim, have to check the diary first.'

Beering scoffed. 'You, busy on a Monday morning! All you'll be doin' is going through last Saturday's results for about the fifth time. Drop around my office. I'll expect you at nine sharp.'

'You want to tell me what's up?'

'I'll explain when you get here,' he said, and hung up.

9

On the way over to Beering's office at Caulfield racecourse, I switched on the radio in my van. It's tuned in to the racing station, of course, but after five minutes of listening to scratchings and track conditions from around Australia, I starting pushing the buttons, roaming around for something different. The first station I changed to was the Russell Henshaw show and, as usual, he was right in the middle of applying the blow-torch to someone.

'Two things I want to raise this morning,' said Henshaw in a commanding preacher's tone, his voice proclaiming a fervent gospel to his multitude of listeners. 'One is an issue that is spreading like a cancer across our community. I refer, of course, to the ever-growing wave of violence in our city. Nightclub revellers, intoxicated by alcohol and drugs, fighting amongst themselves and innocent citizens as police stand by, seemingly powerless to stop them. This isn't an isolated incident. It's happening each and every night. Young drunken packs of hoons choosing to drink until they drop. They're holding this city to ransom with their reprehensible behaviour while the rest of us have to put up with it. The senseless assaults on the public, police and even ambulance officers. The filthy language and offensive behaviour. The robberies and damage to property. I tell you, it has to stop.'

Henshaw paused for a moment before continuing.

'I have to declare a personal interest in this matter,' he said solemnly. 'My own daughter was the victim of a savage attack only last Friday night.'

Henshaw stopped speaking again for effect and I could imagine his legions of fans gasping in shock.

'She was lucky to get out of that situation alive. Obviously the police aren't able to do anything and the city council seems to have washed its hands of the whole affair. Mind you, they don't knock back the licence fees for the liquor permits they issue to the bars and clubs that are opening in endless numbers. I tell you, listeners, it's out of control and it's got to stop. And another thing . . .'

Henshaw could sure waffle on, but he was only getting warmed up. The nightclub tirade was only an appetiser to what was coming.

'Over the past month, we've witnessed no fewer than three murders, three vicious murders of young female stablehands. It seems the police are no closer to finding the killer than they were a month ago when the killings first started. It's obvious we've got a lunatic out there, but what are the police doing apart from making excuses and shuffling paperwork? Well, we're going to find out. I have the police commissioner here with me and in a moment I'm going to ask him exactly what is being done. We have a right to safety and peace in our community, and I tell you we're not getting it. This city is falling apart at the seams. It's disintegrating into a cesspit of drunkenness, violence and flagrant disregard of the law. I'm going to open the lines for some calls before we go to the police commissioner. We've got Trevor from Ringwood on the line. Trevor, let me ask you this, do you feel safe at night?'

What did Trevor think? What the hell else was Trevor, or any other of Henshaw's pre-conditioned listeners going to say after being whipped into a frenzy by his right-wing diatribe? For Christ sake. I listened to three callers in rapid succession, all of whom would have gladly agreed to the army marching in and declaring martial law if Henshaw had decreed it. He finally put the police commissioner on and to the man's credit,

I thought he did a half-reasonable job of defending himself. But every time he looked like answering a question and wriggling off the hook, Henshaw would cut him off and try to trip him up again.

'So you say you're no closer to catching this killer?'

'I didn't say that,' said the police commissioner. 'I said that we were following several lines of enquiry.'

'But you've had to appeal to the public for help?'

'That's true. If the public can help us in any way we've set up a hotline which they can call –'

'So I put it to you that in effect you've no idea who this strapper killer is, have you?'

'Those words are yours, not mine. We don't know enough about this person to classify them, nor will I, or my department, use sensational descriptions in referring to the killer.'

'So you've got no description, no motive and no suspect, is that correct, Commissioner?'

'As I said, we are following several lines of enquiry.'

'But in the meantime these killings could well continue unabated?'

'I hardly think you need to exaggerate the situation.'

'Commissioner, I want to put aside the serial killer for the moment and talk about the extraordinary nightclub violence that seems to be taking over the city. It's quite apparent that the police are powerless to do anything about it. We're going to throw the lines open to our listeners again, so they can ask you themselves why no action is being taken . . .'

And so it went on. I wouldn't have swapped positions with the police commissioner for tomorrow's racing results given to me today. That poor sod was copping an absolute caning from Henshaw. But I guess that's how the top shock jocks operated; they didn't win ratings points by being nice to people. I switched the radio off in disgust as I turned my van into the red-brick gateway of Caulfield racecourse.

Beering's office is located under the escalator of the members' grandstand. You wouldn't know there's an office there except for the tinted glass window by the side wall. There was no one manning the reception area yet, but his door was open so I walked through and found him sitting at his desk. He looked like he'd been at work for a few hours already. The coffee in the percolator was half empty and he was surrounded by scrunched-up newspapers. His tie was at half mast and he wore the frown of a man whose problems were not going away.

'Morning, Jim.'

He nodded at me then jerked his head towards the percolator. 'Coffee, if you want one.'

I grabbed a mug off the sideboard, helped myself, then sat down in the chair in front of his desk.

'Do you know why I asked you here this morning?' he said, folding his fingers church-steeple style under his chin.

I looked at the newspapers on his desk, all of them opened to the very stories I'd been reading myself earlier that morning. 'Let me guess, you're looking for a good thing in the third at Swan Hill today?'

'I didn't call you in to tip me a winner, Punter.'

'I didn't think so.'

He pushed one of the papers forward. 'You read the news this morning, all this stuff about the strapper killer?'

'Read it. Heard it. They had the police commissioner on the radio being made to jump through hoops by Mr Shock Jock himself, Russell Henshaw.'

'Yeah, well, I'm not surprised he's jumpin' through hoops. We all are. The police, the race clubs, management, trainers and strappers – *especially* strappers. We're all feeling the heat.'

Beering got up and started pacing the room, his hands behind his back like he was on patrol. 'I've been instructed by upstairs to drop everything and give this absolute priority. Do whatever it takes to help the police find this bloke and put a stop to it.'

I turned my chair around so I could see him without straining my neck. Damn pacing habit of his would send me to a chiropractor yet.

'This is going to have a real impact on the racing industry if we don't put an end to it. We've got young girls too afraid to walk to work in the morning. The clubs have been put on notice by the union, so there could be industrial stoppages. If they call off the races it's going to affect betting turnover and if they do that, it's going to impact on prize money and if –'

'Oh for Christ sake, Jim, I don't need a bloody economics lecture. I get the picture. I'd like to see the killer caught as much as the next bloke.'

'I'm glad to hear that because I need your help to catch him.'

'Me? Oh right, I'll just pull out my black book and look up "S" for serial killers and give you his details.'

'Get serious, Punter. You know a lot of people on and off the track, talk to people I wouldn't know existed.'

'So I mix in certain circles. I don't see how that's going to help you.'

Beering sat down again and leant forward over his desk, his fingers resuming the church-steeple impersonation. 'Listen, every piece of information helps and at the moment, the police have hardly got a scrap. I know you a whole lot better than you know yourself. You see things others don't notice. People open up and talk to you about stuff they wouldn't say to others.'

'Yeah, they talk about borrowing a lazy spot to tide them over until next week's pay, is what my contacts discuss.'

'Don't sell yourself short, son. Remember that insurance scam with that dodgy Kiwi trainer? Or what about when O'Reilly's horses were getting nobbled? You were like a dog with a bone, wouldn't let it go. Even I told you to leave it alone. But you found out who it was. And that drug trafficker, Carvill-Smyth. It was your sniffing around that put him away.'

Beering was playing to my ego. It was true, I had helped by passing on bits of information here and there in the past. But I'd also had my own reasons to stick my beak in where it wasn't wanted. Family or friends had been involved in those cases and I'd gladly helped out. This was different. I had no direct involvement. No compelling motivation to volunteer for a job that wasn't mine to do.

'What's this, an episode of *This is Your Life*?'

He blinked at me patiently. 'Look, all I want you to do is

keep your eyes and ears open, and if you pick up anything, let me know about it. You'd be doing me a favour, and god knows you owe me plenty.'

'That's all?'

'That's all.'

I shrugged. What the heck, it wouldn't hurt, and the track would be full of gossip this week anyway. 'All right, I'll do what I can, Jim,' I said, standing up.

'Good man,' he said. It was the first time he'd smiled all morning.

How about the papers this morning, can you believe the shit they write? 'Psycho serial killer'. 'Sadistic strapper slayer'. 'Strapper killer strikes again'. Why is it that papers always try to use matching-lettered words in a headline? At least those lazy reporters have finally started to get their act together; have actually woken up to the fact that, hello, three strappers murdered in a month just may be related. The idiots. Still, I have to admit I get a certain satisfaction from reading about my deeds and I'm careful to cut out all the clippings no matter how badly they're written.

I re-read all of the articles about Melissa Jordan. They left out any mention of sexual assault, although I thought that would have been obvious given the state that I'd left her in. The other two, Julie Summers and Carmen Leek, had been reported as being sexually assaulted. Perhaps it has something to do with the process of the official autopsy. Or maybe it's just the cops holding back information. Not wanting to scare the public any more than they have to. But there are other details they're sitting on, too. Things that matter, like the lipstick message I made those harlots write. Doesn't the public have the right to know why they died? I flick through my clippings again and think about it some more. The police don't necessarily release all information from a crime scene. Everyone knows they hide certain bits and pieces away in their back pocket, just like on TV. So maybe the press haven't been fully informed. Or maybe the police requested they leave it out.

The skin on the back of my neck is tender where she scratched me. The filthy bitch, she fought like a tiger. The first one I've struck who really put up a fight, though Julie might have got a scratch in before she realised how pointless it was. Reminds me a bit of that stray cat I trapped when I was a kid. Remember . . . I cornered it in the garage and threw bits of red-gum firewood at it. The first one copped it a beauty, knocked it arse over. It tried to hide, find cover amongst the shelves and boxes, but the firewood was heavy and my aim was good. After the fourth or fifth hit the cat had nowhere to run. It knew it, too. Made a strange high-pitched growling sound like I'd never heard a cat make. As if to say, I'm afraid of you, but if I can't escape I'm not going down without a fight. Didn't do it any good, just like it didn't do sweet Melissa Jordan any good either. But what if she'd scratched my face or my eyes? Left some telltale visible evidence for someone to start asking questions about? I'll just have to be a bit more careful in the future. Do a proper job right from the start.

I got an interesting call around lunchtime from Chas Bannon. Chas is a wonderful old trainer, but he's actually wheelchair-bound these days and just pokes along with a few horses in his stables. But he's been an astute horseman in his time, a 'money trainer' with a reputation for bringing off a plunge. Now and then he'd call me if he had something he was setting up. Get me to put a commission on for him and make sure he got the right odds. Five or six times he'd done that and he wasn't often wrong either. But today he wasn't calling up about any plunge he was setting up.

'How are you, son, you still backin' a winner?' he said. Everyone was 'son' to Chas, easier than trying to remember names at his age. Women were simply addressed as 'lass'.

'Trying to, Chas. What about you? Been a while since that last horse you set up at Seymour. You've probably still got money left from that stashed in a chaff bag under your bed.'

Chas laughed. An old man's chuckle; honest and hearty. 'Yeah, we got plenty that day, didn't we, son? Twenties into threes. Horses like Mystic don't come along too often, do they?'

'You got another one like him; that why you calling?'

'No, no business like that. I was wondering, you want to go to the sales for me on Friday? Put your hand up for a horse I'm keen on.'

'Where, Oaklands?'

'Yeah, they got a clearing sale this week. There's a half sister to that good mare Frollick I trained, up for sale. The breeder knows I'd be a sucker to buy her if I turn up. I stand out like a sore thumb in my wheelchair at the sales. I was thinking if you went along and bid, it wouldn't drive the price up nearly as much as if I was there.'

'You think you can steal her, getting me to bid for you?'

'No, but I won't get ripped off by that greedy vendor putting in dummy bids. I know the tricks that sly dog gets up to. There's a drink in it for you.'

The sales; I hadn't been to the horse sales since last autumn. Next Friday would only have the usual ho–hum sub-standard bush meeting. Might make a nice diversion. Why not.

'I'd be glad to go out for you, Chas. And don't worry about the drink either. Just remember me when you've got another Mystic going around.'

Chas gave another warm chuckle. 'Thanks, son. I'll call you later in the week and let you know what's going on.'

Later that evening at Maxine's she said, 'I've got a little some-thing for you.'

'Oooh, I like presents,' I said.

She giggled, stood up in her dressing gown in front of the couch where we'd both been sitting eating takeaway for dinner. She disappeared for a moment to one of the back rooms. It might have been her bedroom or one of the guest rooms. You could get lost in her apartment, the size of the thing. When she came back, she was carrying a bright pink gift bag with a small parcel wrapped up in tissue paper inside it.

'For me, what is it?' I said, holding it up and inspecting it.

'Go on, open it, slow coach!'

I did. Inside the tissue paper was a little velvet jeweller's box with the promise of unknown baubles inside. I opened the lid.

'Well, what do you think?'

Bit lost for words, really. Well, wasn't quite expecting it; didn't know that I actually wanted it.

'God, Punter. Don't look so excited!'

'No, I am. *Really.*'

I held the key out in front of me and forced a smile. 'It's just that I wasn't expecting you to, you know, commit to anything with me.'

'Oh, for heaven's sake. It's just the key to my apartment. It means you can come and go without having to worry if I'm here or not. I thought it was a nice little way to say thank you for everything.'

'It's a beautiful way to say thank you.'

'You mean it?'

'Uh-huh.'

She placed a hand on my thigh, gave it a bit of squeeze. 'I know another way to say thank you.'

'Didn't we just do that?'

She slowly undid the belt of her gown, let it fall open. 'That was hours ago.'

I took a peek. Magnificent. Then looked down at the key I held in my hand. Maybe this wasn't going to be such a bad arrangement.

'You're right. Hours ago.'

The next morning after breakfast, I left Maxine's place with a kiss and a promise that we'd talk again soon, then jumped in my van to drive home. Before I turned the key, I switched on my phone and saw that Billy had sent me a text early that morning. Really early; two twenty-seven, to be exact. The text said: *Gino's window smashed AGAIN. Call me.*

I did. Billy picked up the phone almost straightaway.

'What happened?'

'That bastard's been at it again. And to think, we only just got the window fixed last week! I can't believe this is happening.'

'Whoa, slow down, Billy. Tell me what's going on.'

'The window, it was smashed again last night. I'd only been in bed for an hour before I heard the sound of smashing glass. I looked down from my window upstairs and heard a car drive away, but I didn't see anything. When I got downstairs it was like a bomb had gone off. Glass everywhere. I've already had the security firm come around and put up shutters. And I've called the glaziers again; Christ, they may as well camp over if this keeps up. 'Bout the only thing that escaped any serious damage was that Santa poster. Just copped a couple of small tears, nothing that can't be sticky-taped back together.'

'At least that's something.'

I took in what Billy had just told me. The guy had called our bluff and the problem wasn't going to go away.

'Okay, Billy, here's what's going to happen. The guy offering to protect Gino's from vandalism is going to ring you.'

'He is?'

I sighed. 'Trust me, Billy, he's going to call. And when he does, I want you to tell him you've changed your mind, that maybe you hadn't thought this through properly.'

'I haven't?'

'Billy, listen. Just set up a meeting at Gino's with this guy, anytime in the afternoon while we're closed. Can you do that?'

'Okay, I'll do what you ask. Are you going to pay this guy to get him off our backs?'

'I just want to talk to the guy.'

When I finally got back to my apartment, Che gave me a hard time.

'Reeeeeooooow.'

'I know, I'm late for your breakfast.'

Another yowl. Where had I been? Very disappointed with my behaviour, so forth.

'Well, yes, I stayed over at Maxine's, but that's none of your business.'

I gave him a bowl of his Fussy Feline, then I made myself a pot of freshly ground coffee and loaded up the toaster with a couple of thick slabs of rye. I'd already had breakfast at Maxine's earlier that morning. She'd fixed me one of her healthy meals – yoghurt and fruit – which hadn't exactly filled me up, and she only had herbal tea for liquid refreshments. If I was going to become a more permanent boarder at her lodgings, then I could see some changes would need to be made to our grocery arrangements. I thought about her giving me the spare key. Did that mean I'd have to reciprocate, give her a key to my place? Shit, this was starting to get complicated. What was the etiquette here? Did I want Maxine popping in and out of my place unannounced? I liked my privacy, my little castle. What had I got myself into?

'Che, how would you feel if Maxine came to stay, like on a regular basis?'

A sullen look, then he turned his back on me. Not the most encouraging response.

'Yeah, well, it's not up to you anyway, buster.'

Maybe I should call Kate; she'd know what to do in a situation like this. Then I thought better of it. You never discuss something like that with an ex. Jesus, I could get myself into a pickle. I pondered my 'problem' and decided that overall it wasn't such a bad deal. Plenty of guys I know would be glad to swap places with me, have Maxine Henshaw's key in their pockets. Speaking of Henshaw, I flicked on the radio, realising that his show would be on. God, did this mean I was becoming a fan?

It took me a little time to realise who he was talking to this morning, then the penny dropped: some Yank expert on serial killers.

'. . . And tell me, Doctor Lamare, from your experience, what makes them the sort of person they are? What turns a perfectly normal human being into a monster? Because that's what they are, aren't they?'

Lead the witness, why don't you? Typical Henshaw.

'Well,' said Lamare, 'most people would certainly describe them that way. But a serial killer wouldn't necessarily see themselves as a monster. Indeed, many would be adamant they are doing good. For example, there was a guy they caught killing prostitutes not long ago in DC. He was convinced he was carrying out God's work and cleansing the streets of temptation for mankind. You see, in many cases it's about their ability to hold the power of life and death. It's probably the only real power they've been able to exert in their lives, which is why they go on killing.'

'Tell us about their lives,' said Henshaw. 'What sort of people they are.'

'At the risk of sounding as though I'm stereotyping all serial killers, most do share certain common traits. For example, an average profile would probably be a white male in his twenties or thirties. He would possibly target strangers near his home or place of work and importantly, there is usually no relationship between the killer and victim, or maybe just a slight acquaintance. The other factor that studies have shown is the apparent lack of motive for killing, which –'

'But hang on a minute, this guy's killing young, female stablehands. There must be a motive. He must have a grudge or something.'

'Well, as I was saying, although there often seems to be a lack of motivation and the killings appear to be random, it's usually the case that the motivations are simply shrouded. It's only when they're caught that the true reasons come out as to why they kill.'

'Like what? What sort of things would make this person a killer?'

I had to hand it to Henshaw, he was persistent. He knew what to seize on; what his listening audience wanted to hear.

'Usually their past holds the key. They may have come from a dysfunctional family background involving physical or sexual abuse. Their parents may have been drug addicts or alcoholics. Common is a feeling of resentment towards society which is brought on by their own feelings of failure. These can include sexual frustrations, an inability to be socially accepted or to form normal relationships with the opposite sex. They may have had overbearing parents, or they may have experienced some form of betrayal or abandonment, often from the mother, which seems to be a common element with a lot of serial killers. Other traits include aggressive daydreaming and, of course, isolation. Who knows, maybe this guy was left alone for long periods as a child. I'm only speculating here, you understand, but we have had serial killers who as children were actually kept locked up in cellars or their rooms for days at a time by their parents.'

'You mentioned that they daydream. These dreams, do the fantasies become reality?'

'Sometimes the daydreams continue to develop and expand from about the age of eight, right through to adolescence and into manhood and the killer escapes by following or enacting their dreams.'

'That's a chilling thought, Doctor. For those listeners who have just joined us, we're talking with Doctor Mike Lamare about the profile of serial killers and in particular, what the makeup of the strapper killer might be. Doctor, this might sound a silly question, but you've mentioned some factors such as an overbearing mother who may have been the cause of setting a killer on their path. Why don't they just kill the cause of their problem and stop there? Why do they go on killing strangers?'

'It's not that simple. It's an interesting fact that serial killers rarely kill the source of their resentment such as a repressive mother, for example. However, they may kill those who have a likeness to, or remind them of that person.'

'So he's killing them, through others?'

'It's complicated, but yes, something like that.'

'They must be absolutely psychotic nutcases,' said Henshaw, handing down his verdict.

'Actually, most aren't psychotics. They'd be technically

classed as psychopaths who are suffering from chronic mental disorders or abnormal social behaviour.'

'You sound like you're making a case for excusing them; that it's not their fault they've become what they have.'

'No, not at all. No one can be excused for mass murder. I'm merely pointing out that the past usually holds the key to what they have become.'

'Doctor, we're going to throw the lines open now to our listeners . . .'

What a conceited fool. What pretence of knowledge does he have that makes him an expert on killing? Does he think his fancy qualifications give him an understanding of what I do? And that Russell Henshaw, what a self-righteous fuckwit he is. I feel like ringing in to the radio station and setting him straight on a few things. Maybe they could let me take some calls from those moronic listeners. Wouldn't that be a thrill . . .

'Hi, I'm Bill. I'm a pensioner from Mentone. I just wondered if there's any danger to someone like me from a guy like you?'

'Unfortunately, no Bill. It should be quite obvious that I'm not going out of my way to kill males. Although I should kill you for asking such a stupid question.'

'Okay, thanks. Sorry about that.'

'Not at all. Next please.'

'Hello, this is Tracey. I was reading about all your victims having certain characteristics and –'

'That's a big word, Tracey.'

'Um, thanks. And anyway, as I'm eighteen and a brunette, I wondered if I was a likely target?'

'Are you a slutty-looking strapper? Always got an eye out for the jockeys?'

'No. I mean, I try to dress to impress, but I work in a shoe shop. I don't know anything about racing.'

'Then I'm not going to kill you, Tracey.'

'Oh, I'm so relieved!'

'You have a nice day now.'

A wonderful fantasy, isn't it? I could go on for hours imagining all sorts of silly things. Perhaps that quack was right about one thing; I've always been a bit of a daydreamer. But daydreams are infinitely better than nightmares. Like Father's visits, creeping into my room every night to 'tuck me in' . . . Then later, when I moved out into the flat at the back of our house. Perhaps that's why he built it. To muffle my cries. He knew all about inflicting pain, the cunt. Taught me all he knew about that since I was five years old. I learned good off him, real good. And Mother's constant whoring around with those jockeys. Think I didn't know, even at my age, what she was up to? A regular stream of silks paying her visits. She fucked jockeys and he fucked me and we all pretended nothing happened. One happy family. Now that's dreaming . . .

10

The protection guy had rung Billy back just like I figured he would, and Billy had organised the meeting for Thursday afternoon at three. I got to Gino's at about a quarter to and went in by the back laneway so I wouldn't be seen if the guy was watching the front of the shop.

'Everything all set up?' I asked Billy.

'Just like you wanted.'

I had Billy fix a table directly opposite the entrance to the kitchen so my back was to the wall, and Billy slotted in to sit next to me. It was quite dim inside with the security shutters blocking out the daylight where the front window used to be. Billy asked if I wanted any more lights switched on.

'No, the one over the counter and this one above the table is perfect.'

'Is there anything else I can do?'

'No. When he gets here, just bring him in and introduce me as your friend, that's all you have to say,' I said.

Right on three the front doorbell rang. Billy looked at me and I nodded at him to go and answer it. I heard two voices greeting Billy and then they followed him inside. One of them belonged to a fit and gym-chiselled Italian-looking guy in his mid-twenties.

'I'm Lorenzo,' he announced.

He was flashily dressed, a dark suit jacket and pants and a

crisp white T-shirt under his jacket. He sported a carefully grown three-day stubble, the sort you'd have to spend an hour a day manicuring to get just right, like the movie stars do. He wore a pair of god-awful, exaggerated square-toed shoes that made his feet look like a clown's. In his hand he twirled a pair of designer sunglasses, which drew attention to the big-name watch hanging loosely on his wrist. A wannabe gangster if ever I'd seen one.

He introduced his friend who stood alongside him; 'My associate, Angelo.' The muscle. Angelo wasn't flash, just big. Not overly tall, but he was solid and built like a wrestler. He too wore a suit, with a button-up knitted top underneath the jacket. At a guess, I'd put him at ten years older than Lorenzo. Billy led them through to where I was sitting at the table and presented me. 'A friend of mine, Punter,' he said, sitting down next to me.

Lorenzo gave me the once over, nodded at me as if it didn't really matter to him whether I was there or not, and then gestured towards the darkened shutters, getting straight down to business.

'You guys have got a problem,' he said, walking a couple of steps back towards the front counter and inspecting the damage. 'See, you just can't go on getting your window broken every week, it's bad for business. Isn't it, Angelo?'

Angelo nodded solemnly; thought that was so.

Lorenzo prodded a finger at the shutters and shook his head distastefully. 'Yeah, it's bad for business. A customer sees that and he says to himself, "I'm not gonna go in there. I'm gonna go to the shop across the street instead." Where's he gonna go, Angelo?'

'To the shop across the street.'

For Christ sake, talk about a Laurel and Hardy act. I was nearly drumming my fingers on the table waiting for him to get to the punchline. Lorenzo walked back by the counter and spotted the fridge behind the bar. He made a detour and helped himself to two Crown Lagers. He gave one of the beers to Angelo, who remained standing watching us, then sat down to join me and Billy at the table.

'Why don't you help yourself to a beer, fellas,' said Billy. I could sense him smarting at Lorenzo's arrogance and I pressed my knee to his thigh to shut him up. Lorenzo ignored his comment; got on with his game plan. It was a script he had down pat, and I could imagine him walking into a hundred little restaurants like this all over town, reciting the same lines.

'Yeah,' he continued, 'you fix a window and it gets broken again, then you start up all over, but in the meantime the customers've gone walkabout and so have your takings. So, you got a problem.'

He only had to look at Angelo this time for the parrot-like response. 'Yeah, they got a problem,' he echoed.

'And unless you got someone like me and Angelo to protect your place –' he looked about the room as if it could disappear at any moment '– then, you ain't gonna have no place left.'

Not bad. I'd heard better, but still, reasonably polished.

'So, let me see if I've got this right,' I said. 'If Gino's pays you guys a hundred a month, you'll make sure that we never get another broken window again?'

Lorenzo shook his head quickly. 'No, it's gone up since the last time we spoke. It's a hundred and fifty a month now.' He turned around and looked at Angelo.

'Inflation, eh, Angelo?'

Angelo nodded dumbly back.

'I see, a hundred and fifty. That's a lot of money for a small business like this to pay every month,' I said. 'What if Gino's can't afford it?'

A dark cloud was brewing over Lorenzo's face. I was expecting it; knew the fireworks would have to start sooner or later. He stood up suddenly, the chair falling to the ground behind him. Then he grabbed his bottle of beer and, turning around, made a big show of smashing it over the counter, and then hurled what was left of the bottle at the bar. That seemed to be the signal for Angelo to get in on the act too. He picked up a tray of china coffee cups from the sideboard and threw them after the beer bottle with a terrific crash. Billy tensed. I could feel him ready to spring up, but I checked him, made him sit still.

'If you don't fucking pay,' Lorenzo said angrily, 'who knows what accidents might happen at Gino's? Broken windows, graffiti, vandalism. Fires can start up in these places too, can't they, Angelo?'

'Fires been known to happen,' said the parrot.

Lorenzo turned and faced me. 'So what's it gonna be, then?'

I looked at Billy and gave a resigned shrug, and then I turned back to Lorenzo. 'I don't think you leave us a lot of choice. All right,' I said, gesturing with my hands for him to take a seat, 'let's talk business.'

Lorenzo smiled and sat down. 'I thought you guys would be reasonable about things.'

I pulled out a roll from my shirt pocket and laid it on the table in front of him, let the greedy bastard see I was carrying plenty.

'How about I give you six months in advance?'

He snatched at the bundle. Even greedier than I thought.

'Might as well make it a year, then you won't have to see us around so often.'

No one had noticed Tiny come out of the kitchen until he walked up behind Angelo and poked the shotgun into his back. He'd timed it just as we'd planned; to stay hidden and not make an appearance until I showed them the money.

'You know what this is, big fella?' said Tiny.

Angelo knew; had probably felt the cold of a steel barrel before in his line of work. He nodded his head and raised his hands voluntarily as Lorenzo's head whipped around to see who had spoken.

'Tell us what it is, Angelo,' said Tiny.

'It's a shotgun.'

'That's right, Angelo. And they make a helluva mess to a man's guts at this close range. Whatta they do to a man's guts?'

Angelo knew the drill; 'Make a helluva mess.'

Lorenzo appeared lost for words, astonished that the tide had turned so quickly against him. Tiny shoved Angelo forwards with the gun's barrel and told him to sit down next to Lorenzo, then he stepped into the light where we could see him.

Tiny is an intimidating sort of a bloke close up. He seems as tall as the ghost gums he once chopped for a living, a veritable mountain of a man. A big, raw-boned country brawler with fists the size of a council worker's shovel. Today he wore a bib and brace overalls, no shirt; his lanky tattooed arms left you in no doubt that if he ever let rip with a punch, you'd be out for the count.

'Lorenzo, what the fuck are you doing here?'

'Tiny?' said Lorenzo.

'You two know each other?' I asked incredulously.

'I bounce for his old man at the Grainstore Club,' said Tiny. 'What the hell are you doing? If your father knew what you've been up to he'd kick your arse till yer nose bleeds.'

'Oh shit, don't go tellin' him. Please don't do that, I didn't mean youse any harm. I wouldn't have come around if I'd known it was your place.'

'You oughta be afuckin' shamed of yourself,' said Tiny, getting stuck into him.

Lorenzo had suddenly lost all of his wannabe gangster confidence; he looked more like a student getting an earful from his headmaster.

'Tryin' to fleece these poor bastards out of an honest quid. You, workin' a protection scam! After all your father's taught you. You oughta hang your head in shame, boy.'

'I'm sorry, I didn't mean to –'

'Shut up! I gotta think what the fuck I'm gonna do with you now.'

Billy suggested he get us a beer from the fridge to help us with the thinking process. We thought that was a good idea.

'Can I put my hands down?' asked Angelo.

'No!' said Tiny out of sheer annoyance. 'Keep 'em where I can see 'em.'

'Okay, I keep 'em where I can see 'em,' mumbled Angelo.

'I'm gonna have to ring his old man,' said Tiny, 'explain the situation.'

'No, you can't! He'll kill me,' pleaded Lorenzo.

'And I fuckin' shouldn't?' yelled Tiny, moving menacingly close to the table. He had the shotgun cradled in one arm and a stubby in the other.

I intervened. 'How many others have you done in the Glenhuntly strip?'

'What, shops?'

'Yes, shops like ours. Smashed their windows and put it on them for protection money?'

He owned up to the other three I'd known about. I wiggled my fingers. 'Let's have it back, then.'

'What?'

Tiny prompted him. 'The money, you git.'

'Oh sure, I was gonna give you that back, of course.'

Lorenzo pulled out a wad, the size of which suggested we hadn't been the only restaurant on his collection list today.

'Here's your money back,' he said almost apologetically, stuffing the rest of the cash back into his jacket pocket. I wiggled the fingers again.

'What?'

'There's also the cost of the windows.'

'But you'd be insured for those, wouldn't you?'

I shook my head. 'A small business can't afford to pay the premiums these days.' I looked at Angelo, ridiculous, with his hands still in the air. 'Can they, Angelo?'

'No,' he agreed, 'small business can't afford premiums.'

Lorenzo pulled out the wad again, though not as quickly as last time. 'How much?'

I looked across at Billy. 'How much?'

'Twenty-three hundred a piece plus GST,' he said with relish.

Lorenzo peeled off the notes from his fast-diminishing bankroll.

'There's the matter of the security shutters, too.'

'Security shutters? *Fuck!*'

'Oi!' butted in Tiny. 'Show some fuckin' respect.'

'Sorry. Security shutters.' He winced when Billy told him how much.

'I'm in the wrong fuckin' game, those blokes got a racket goin'.' He shelled out for the shutters and asked if he was square.

'Uh-uh,' I said pointing to the smashed coffee cups. 'There's the tray of cups and the two beers you helped yourself to.'

Lorenzo gritted his teeth when Billy figured it out at around twenty broken cups at five dollars a cup. He half looked like he was going to say something, but a fierce glare from Tiny saw him hand over the last of his notes.

'Is that it, then?'

'Correct weight,' I said.

'Hang on,' said Tiny. 'We're not done. I don't ever want to see you around here again playing your standover game. Not at Gino's or any other restaurant or shop on the Glenhuntly strip. You're barred from around here, you understand?'

Lorenzo looked down guiltily, wouldn't meet Tiny's eyes.

'I hear you, Tiny. I won't. You . . . won't tell the old man, will you?'

'Go on, fuck off out of here before I change my mind.'

Lorenzo didn't need to be told twice. He was out of there quicker than a horse jumping from the outside gate in the Oakleigh Plate. There was silence for a moment after we heard the door close, then Angelo spoke.

'Um, can I put my hands down now?'

On Friday morning I dropped around to Terry the Greek's for a haircut and shave. I'd been going there since I was kid. Despite the ever-growing number of unisex saloons in the Glenhuntly Road strip, I stubbornly resisted the free cappuccinos, the gimmicky massage chairs or the expensive product I'd probably be suckered into buying if I ever did go into one. Instead I stuck to Terry's. It was a bit like stepping into a time warp. He actually owned his shop, which was only three doors down from Gino's. It was an identical building to Gino's, with an upstairs apartment where Terry and his wife and two daughters lived. Downstairs, as you walked in, he had an old glass shop cabinet filled with smokes and lighters and pipes and the sort of smoking paraphernalia you only see at trash and treasure stalls these days. He had other odds and ends in the cabinet as well, mainly hair and shaving products that belonged to another era, and bottles of Brylcreem and mysterious Greek shaving potions with exotic smells. He was lathering me up with some of the stuff now, to the ever-present sound of the racing station playing on the radio. In between lathers I could see him stealing glances at his formguide. I hoped he'd pay a bit more attention when he started on me with the cut-throat razor.

'You got one today, Terry?' I asked him.

'I tell you,' he said, his eyes lighting up excitedly, 'is a bush horse in race four that was a tragedy beaten last start. She's a moral today, you should have something on her yourself.'

A tragedy beaten. I wish I had a dollar for every time I'd heard that line.

'My day off today, Terry.'

I had no intention of playing the races today. I was heading out to the sales after my haircut to bid on the horse for Chas Bannon.

'How's your father?'

Terry always asked after Dad. Years ago he'd been involved in a syndicate of a moderately successful horse trained by him. He still had the winning photo proudly displayed on the back wall of the shop, along with a dozen other ageing racing photographs.

'He's fine,' I said. 'Still training winners.'

'You know he trained my besta ever horse, Fright. I had lotsa horses with trainers over the years, but your old man, he the best.'

I almost laughed, which wouldn't have been wise, considering Terry was slicing delicately away at my chin with the razor. It was just that Terry made out like he was a big-time operator with two hundred horses in work. True, he'd raced a dozen horses, but he'd be lucky if he'd owned more than a hair in their tail. He walked to the back wall and proudly pointed his razor at the photos. I watched him from the mirror as he gave me the 'owner's tour', as he did every once in a while, just in case I'd forgotten.

'Here, dis is Fright winning at Sandown,' he said with reverence.

You'd have thought it was Kingston Town winning a Cox Plate, the way he was talking about it.

'That day, your father say he a good thing and he win like one too. I get the eight to one and thankayou very much.'

I guess that was Terry's way of saying he'd cleaned up. He pointed other horses out to me too. Gallopers from long ago, their photos faded with age.

'And Precise, you woulda remember her, no?'

It was kind of hard to hurry Terry when he got into one of his racehorse reminiscing moods, but I dropped a hint that I had to get out to the sales and promised I'd look at the photos on the way out.

'Of course, of course, I sorry. I talk too much and forget everyone in a hurry, got things to do. Me, I not gotta lot to do except cut people's hair. If no people come, I no cut hair. In between, I sell smokes, listen to races, try and betta a winner.'

'You've got a good life, Terry. No stress.'

He smiled contentedly and recommenced the attack on my stubble. 'Is not a bad life,' he agreed. 'Hey,' he said, changing the subject, 'you see all the broken windows in the shops lately? Gino's down the street, they gotta smashed twice in the past week and down past the railway, other restaurants they gotta windows smashed too.'

'I noticed.'

'Bada business. Is probably kids, you know? Nothing better to do.'

'I got a feeling they won't be around anymore, Terry.'

Terry finished up with my shave and haircut in just over an hour. It would have been a lot quicker if he hadn't darted back and forth to look at his formguide or serve customers in between snips. But I didn't mind, I sort of liked the way he fiddled around and got things done in his own time. Besides, where the hell else would I go to get my monthly treat of a shave? Terry was just applying the final touches, wiping my face with a hot hand towel, when a guy came in wanting some smokes. While Terry served him, I swung down out of the barber's chair and took a look at the photos on his wall. Aside from Fright and Precise, which were both city winners, most of the horses were country gallopers I'd never heard of. Some of the photos dated back to the sixties and seventies, the horses ridden by jockeys who had long since vanished or given the game away. I looked closely at the photo of Precise. There were three photos actually, a larger centre shot of her passing the post, a smaller shot of her returning to scale and another of the happy connections being presented with a trophy. Jockeys seemed to ride much longer then; they almost looked comical with their legs hanging way down and their feet jammed in the stirrups. Not like today where they ride super-short, with only their toes in the irons. The jockey colours, too, seemed simpler. Back then, there seemed to be a lot more silks in just the one, or at most two colour combinations. Nowadays, owners had four or five colours, with stripes or motifs and any combination of checks and bands. I suppose with twenty thousand new horses registered each year in Australia, perhaps all the older colours had been taken. There was even a horse I'd seen the other day that went around with a yacht and a dollar sign on its silks. You'd never have seen that in years gone by.

I slipped Terry a fifty and told him to keep the change. He complained it was 'too mucha tip'. Way I figured, I was getting the haircut cheap and the shave for nothing, compared to any other fancy Glenhuntly salon I cared to go to.

'Okay, Punter, I taka your tip, but I give you one of mine. You backa number two in race four at Moe. She a tragedy beaten last start.'

'See you next time, Terry,' I said. A tragedy beaten, for Christ sake.

The Oaklands sale yards weren't exactly bristling with buyers. This was, after all, the last sale before Christmas, a modest affair of tried horses and broodmares. Most of the serious players weren't to be seen; they'd be saving their money for the annual round of yearling sales beginning in January. Today's attendees were mainly a sprinkling of stud masters trying to offload disappointing breeding stock and battling trainers trying to find a bargain tried horse. Although there weren't many people about, the atmosphere was relaxed and welcoming. Christmas greetings and best wishes for the new year were exchanged among clients as they slapped each on the back and shook hands. I picked up a catalogue from the main counter and wandered over towards the horse barns, flicking through the pages as I walked.

Chas Bannon wanted me to bid on lot forty-three. There wasn't much I had to do. He'd inspected the horse himself a month ago in the paddock and had it vetted. He'd arranged finance with the auctioneer to a certain limit and had also organised for me to act as his agent. All I had to do was bid for the horse and, hopefully, buy it. I decided to have a look at the horse anyway. I found her in block B, not far from the main parade ring.

The catalogue said she was an unraced three-year-old filly, sired by Storm Halo out of More Than Enough. The dam may well have had enough too, judging by her produce record. She was getting on in years, eighteen by my reckoning, and had had seven foals for just two winners. Frollick was by far her best daughter, but that was two foals ago. Since then she'd thrown yet another maiden galloper and this horse, Lotsoflaughs, whom Chas wanted to buy. On paper, it didn't make me suddenly want to talk to my bank manager. When you buy a horse, the dam's produce records don't lie and a two out of eight strike rate wasn't what you'd call brilliant. But Chas had seen all the progeny from the mare over the years and he said the only ones that fired were the bay-coloured ones with a likeness to the mother. Frollick had been a bay and Chas liked the fact that Lotsoflaughs was a dead ringer to her. I'd pointed out warily to Chas that she'd had several unsuccessful trials and had never even made it to the track, but he wasn't deterred from buying her.

'Never mind she hasn't raced yet,' he'd told me. 'That stock don't mature until they're three or older.'

I walked past the filly's box door and feigned a look of bored interest at her. That was all her vendor needed to jump off his stool and greet me like a long-lost relative. He asked me if I wanted to see the filly paraded.

'She's a lovely filly, a half sister to Frollick, you know.'

I told him I was just passing the time, but hoped he got a good price for her anyway. 'What do you think she'll fetch?'

'Hard to say,' he said. 'Depends on the interest level.' He didn't know if I was a tyre-kicker or a genuine buyer, but he certainly wasn't naïve enough to let me know what his reserve was. I nodded a smile at him and walked on.

Over by the fast-food stand, I bought a coffee and took it inside the auditorium, where I picked a seat in one of the back rows. It was a good position, giving me a front-on view of the horses as they came into the auctioneer's ring and also allowed me to see anyone else bidding. I looked around the sparsely filled sales ring. There were only a handful of people sitting there at the moment, but they were beginning to trickle in as the starting time drew closer. The auctioneer started reading out loud the usual legal rigmarole of the conditions of the sale. I don't know why they bother; no one pays them the slightest attention.

The first hundred or so lots were all tried racehorses. Some were two-year-olds which had already demonstrated they were too slow to make the grade, their owners keen to cut their losses while they could. Then you got into the older horses, a mixed bag at best. Most were chaff bandits, coasting along with the odd win or placing. Others hadn't even graduated to the track yet for one reason or another; they were too fractious and scatty, or just unsound, or maybe they couldn't run a thousand metres down a well. Lots of reasons a horse doesn't make it, and you really needed to know their history or you'd end up blowing your money. One thing's for sure, an owner rarely parted company with a horse if it had any ability.

I watched about a dozen horses go under the hammer. Despite the 'caveat emptor' tag that goes with a tried horse, there didn't seem to be any shortage of buyers prepared to take the risk. I heard a trainer in the row in front of me talking to an owner about a horse they were planning to bid on.

'I know the bloke that had him before. Couldn't train a dog to bark. If I can't improve him, I'll give the game away. If the worst comes to the worst, we can put him over the jumps.' Bragging and urging; racing's standard fare. One man's trash, another man's treasure.

In between sales, I looked around the auditorium and noticed that Kagan Hall had come in and was standing by the chute where they brought the horses in from the parade ring. I didn't think he'd bother with a sale like this, but he was talking intently to a group of people, another of his syndicates, perhaps. I flicked over the page in my book to the lot coming up. That had actually been withdrawn, as had the one after that. Lot twenty-four was the one I reckoned he'd be bidding on. A lightly raced, well-bred three-year-old entire. If it came good and won a race or two, he could sell it as a stallion prospect. It was the sort of horse that had Hall's name all over it. Sure enough, when it entered the ring, Hall ceased talking and turned around. While its handler circled the ring, the auction-eer praised the horse's virtues.

'Unluckily struck down by a virus as a two-year-old . . . The victim of an ownership dispute . . . Now here to be sold today. Don't miss this opportunity, ladies and gentleman. Well, start me off. What am I bid? Two hundred thousand, two fifty for starters? You tell me, what's he worth?'

Hall put his hand up for fifty. There was a counter bid from some breeder standing up the back and they traded small, tentative bids against each other until the horse was eventu-ally knocked down to Hall for a hundred and thirty thousand. He appeared pleased, smiling and nodding with the other members of his syndicate as he signed the buyer's chit from the auctioneer's spotter. Obviously another successful Winning Way purchase.

Hall and his syndicate left the ring shortly after, and I forgot about him as the countdown to Chas Bannon's filly grew closer. I ducked over to the cafeteria and bought another coffee which I took back inside to my seat. Then I watched another dozen or so horses sold before my lot was led into the ring.

She was a nice enough type, a dark bay just like her half sister. A bit leggy, but she had a strong and long body which suggested she'd grow into those gawky pins of hers, once she matured. Maybe Chas was right; she just needed a bit of time to grow and develop. The auctioneer started her off at some stupid gambit price and quickly dropped back in increments of ten thousand at a time.

'All right then, fifty, I'll take fifty. Forty, forty thousand, she's got to be worth that at least.'

No response. Not a single bid.

'Well, give me thirty then, and she's cheap as chips at that price. Go on, who'll give me thirty for the unraced half sister to Frollick.'

Silence.

'You're making it hard for me, ladies and gentleman. All right, let's make it twenty then, and I'll meet the market. Somebody start me off with twenty.'

Someone did and I looked around closely to see who it might be. Sometimes the vendor or one of his friends throws in a dummy bid to get the sale started; just one of the tricks they get up to. Whoever it was, it brought a counter bid of five thousand from a bloke sitting down near the front row. He looked tentatively back to where the original bid had come from. No further response from there. The auctioneer held his gavel solemnly to the crowd, appealing for another bid, but no one seemed interested. I kept still; no sense in showing my hand too early.

'Going once, going twice for twenty-five thousand . . .'

As he swung the hammer down I raised my hand to a spotter for another thousand. My bid raised the stakes and the guy came back for another thousand. I saw him again and he came back with the same. We could go back and forth like this all day. I'd never know what his budget was, but I knew what Chas Bannon had drawn a line at. Time to change strategy and let him know we meant business. I held up my hand with five fingers clearly stuck out.

'Thirty-two thousand, I have. It's against you up the front,' the auctioneer said, challenging the guy to another bid. He came back with a counter of two thousand and I immediately held up my hand for another five. The guy threw me a dirty look, then shook his head at the auctioneer. He'd bowed out and the horse was mine.

After I signed for it, I called Chas on my mobile and passed on the good news.

'Well done, son! Well done,' he said excitedly down the phone. You'd think from his response he was a first-time buyer rather than an experienced old hand. It was good to see he still had the enthusiasm for getting his hands on a new horse at his age.

'Can you arrange to put her on a float and send over to my stables?'

'Good as done, Chas,' I said.

When I'd finished with Chas, I went straight over to the general office and organised some transport for the filly. That was my official duties completed for the day, but as I had nothing else to do, I thought I'd stretch my legs, stroll around and look at some more horses. I walked up barns A and B, but most of the horses there had already been sold. Across the paddock were two more barns I hadn't been to yet. I sauntered up and down the aisles, poking my head over a stall here and there if anything caught my interest. If a horse was being paraded, I'd stop and have a look at it and check its record. I probably inspected half a dozen horses before I felt I'd exhausted those two barns.

At the end of the quadrangle was one more barn, a solitary line of twenty boxes all by themselves. It looked like they'd tacked them on as an afterthought; an overflow stable for the busy yearling sales. As I got nearer, I could hear the *clip-clop* of a horse being led about on the bitumen pathway. Then a voice which I recognised.

'That's right, turn her around and face her up to me. No, not like that, make her stand properly.'

Kagan Hall. Inspecting a horse and, by the sound of things, giving the attendant a hard time. They couldn't see me yet, because I was on the opposite side of the barn looking at them through the wire mesh of an empty stall.

'What's that scar from, the one on her off-side hock?' said Hall.

'Um, I don't really know,' said the attendant. She was young-ish, probably in her early twenties, pretty in a tomboy sort of way; thin and wiry, with hair that could have done with a good combing.

'Where's your boss?' asked Hall brusquely.

'He must be in the sales ring,' she said, almost apologetically.

'Well, walk her up and back again for me.'

The girl did as she was asked and I stood and watched from the cover of my stall. I checked the catalogue against the sticker on the horse's rump. Number seventy-eight, some poorly performed, ill-bred thing, which I couldn't imagine Hall buying for an instant. Hall watched as the girl led the horse up and down. She was smartly dressed in a pink cotton polo shirt which had the stud's logo emblazoned on the chest. She wore riding boots and cream jodhpurs which hugged her skinny hips as she walked the horse up the pathway and back for Hall.

'You say your boss is somewhere in the sales ring?'

'Yes, I'm sorry. He'll be a while yet, he's got a filly he's selling that comes up in another twenty minutes or so.'

'Are there any other staff around who can tell me about that scar?'

I looked up and down the aisles. The barn was deserted apart from the girl and several horses, a bit of a lonely spot to have to tend your horses all day without any company.

'There's just me,' she said.

'Well, I want to have a proper look at that scar. Take her back in her box where I can inspect her thoroughly.'

'You want to look at her inside the box?'

'That's right,' said Hall smoothly.

The girl looked a little put out. Normally a prospect was happy to just see a horse walk up and down and run a hand over its legs. And here was this guy making her jump through hoops and taking up all her time. But she did as she was told; it was, after all, her job.

Out of curiosity, I followed along the opposite aisle, still invisible to the pair of them. When I got to the box behind where they'd gone into, I couldn't see them because the wire mesh had been replaced by wooden panels. That was probably a good thing, because then they would also have been able to see me. There was silence for a moment; presumably Hall was inspecting the horse's scar. Then I could hear their voices floating faintly over the wall. Hall said something to the girl; I couldn't quite make out what. But I clearly heard her reply.

'Please . . . *no.*'

Another silence, then; '*No!* Stop it.' She sounded urgent, scared.

'Your boss wouldn't like it if he found out you weren't pleasing clients,' said Hall in a bullying tone.

I heard her shout, 'No!'

'You dirty little bitch! Scratch me like that, will you? I'll show you.'

I ran around the end of the barn to the stable where they were. Hall had the girl pinned in the corner of the box, one hand gripping the back of her hair, trying to hold her still. With the other, he'd succeeded in tugging her jodhpurs down to her knees. Her polo shirt had a rip down the front of it, showing the white of her bra, and she was fighting a losing battle to stave Hall off. Meanwhile, the horse stood nervously, eyeing the pair of them while tied to its chain.

'For Christ sake, Hall,' I said, throwing open the stable door with a loud bang. 'Didn't you ever learn that when a girl says no, she means no?'

Both of them wheeled around in surprise at my entrance. Hall looked astonished that anyone had been able to creep up on him. When he saw it was me, his face turned from astonishment to pure loathing.

'*You*, you damn pervert!' he said.

I ignored him for the moment and faced the girl. 'You okay, luv?'

The girl seemed embarrassed, half ashamed of her semi-naked state. She hoiked her jodhpurs up, crossed her arms around her breasts and ran past me, out of the box.

'It's okay,' I called after her, but she'd sprinted to safety and was gone.

'Look what you've done, you idiot,' said Hall. 'The little trollop was begging for it and you've gone and scared her off.'

'Excuse me, *begging* for it? She didn't look like she was begging for anything from where I was standing.'

'How long had you been spying on us?' Hall demanded.

I couldn't believe what I was hearing. He'd regained his composure a little by now and was even dusting some of the straw from his trousers. The suave bastard. 'Long enough to know she didn't want any part of you.'

'Don't be ridiculous,' he said dismissively, trying to push past me and out into the yard.

I grabbed him by the lapels and thrust him back hard against the wooden wall of the box. He didn't like that and for a moment I thought he was going to do something about it, too. I grabbed him harder, my fists tightly holding his shirt buttons under his chin and jamming him against the wall.

'You're a fucking low-life, Hall, aren't you?'

'I don't know what you mean.'

'If I hadn't shown up, you'd have had her, wouldn't you?'

'There was nothing to it. You're imagining things.'

'I know your form.'

'You don't know what you're talking about.'

'Don't I?' I looked at him, deciding where exactly to hit him. Probably the mouth to start with, to shut him up. God knows he deserved it.

'Look, it was just a harmless bit of fun, that's all,' he said, changing to a more conciliatory manner with me. I felt him relax against my grip, give up the struggle. 'So, no hard feelings then,' he said cheerily as if nothing had happened. 'But I really must get going. Got some more horses to look at.'

I loosened my fingers and felt myself let go of him. He left me shaking my head as he strode off quickly and purposefully, making his way back towards the main ring area and brushing himself down and tucking in his shirt as he walked.

When he'd gone, I walked back along the line of boxes past a feedroom. Inside, I heard muffled sobbing. It was the girl who'd been with Hall a moment ago. I stuck my head inside and gave a warning cough so as not to alarm her.

'Are you all right?' I asked her gently.

She was sitting on the feedroom floor, her hands wrapped protectively around her knees. She looked up, a little startled when I spoke.

'Thanks. I'm fine.' She nodded at me, dropping her head shyly down again as soon as she did.

'I just happened to be walking past and heard you shout. Did he harm you?'

She shook her head straightaway and stifled another sob. 'I should have known better than to be alone with 'im.'

'You know him?'

'Kagan Hall? Everyone knows that prick; what he gets up to. He can't keep his hands to himself, he can't. Thinks every girl who works in a stable is his for the taking. The bastard.' She gave a little sniff and I offered her a tissue which she took gratefully.

'Do you want to do anything more about it, I mean, press charges with the police or something?'

She shook her head slowly, gave me a despairing look. 'It wouldn't be worth the bother,' she said. 'Giving statements to the police, having to explain to my boss what happened. The stigma I'd cop once it got out. My name would be mud; the tramp that tried to have it off with Kagan Hall at the sales.'

'That's not true. You know it didn't happen that way.'

146

'No,' she said, shaking her head resolutely. She'd made up her mind. 'I'd never get another job in a stable again.'

'Of course you would.'

'You don't understand. Guys like Hall . . . they think they can walk on water. They get away with murder.'

11

When I got home from the sales, I fed Che, cracked open a coldie and made myself some tuna pasta. After dinner I sat down on the lounge, nursing my drink, and thought about Kagan Hall. Jesus, he was something, wasn't he? Had I seen what I thought I'd seen? Of course I had. The prick would have just about raped that girl if I hadn't come along. But the arrogance, the sheer arrogance of Hall in denying anything had happened was beyond belief. He'd just shrugged it off like it was a game.

There was another thing that came to me; that art gallery opening I'd gone to with Maxine. Hall had been true to form then as well, groping that woman behind her husband's back. In fact, just about every time I'd see him, he was touching or feeling or ogling someone. Even that night at the Rialto when Maxine had put on the special Winning Way presentation, he'd been all touchy-feely with her. Although he was Maxine's client, I wondered if he'd ever tried his luck with her.

I had a bit of a think about his nationality. He was a Brit; his English background was hardly a secret, but I wondered where he had come from to be where he was now. I'd never heard of him till about five years ago, when he'd seemed to suddenly arrive on the scene like a whirlwind. He'd certainly made an immediate impression, with his smooth presentations and wall-to-wall advertising. And the guy could pick winners; his track record attested to that. I was curious about what he'd done before. He must have worked in the industry, perhaps for one of the big bloodstock agencies in the UK or overseas before coming to Australia. I took my beer into the office and fired up my computer. It's not the quickest machine in the world, but after several minutes I had online access and Googled Hall's name. He certainly had a web presence. Virtually all of the recent references to him were connected to Winning Way Syndications. There were direct links to his website, newspaper stories about his winning horses, references back to sale results and other assorted bits and pieces relating to horse syndicates and the like. I had to trawl through three pages of semi-promotional material before I could find anything other than his Australian connection. It wasn't much, just a brief UK story from one of the international breeding magazines which mentioned Hall winding up his syndication business there – the Winning Star Syndicate – and that Kagan Hall and his partner, Paul Mead, would go their separate ways to pursue new opportunities in racing.

I looked at the date; just over six years ago. Probably not long before he'd surfaced in Australia. I scanned down the page for any other relevant items about Hall but couldn't see any. Perhaps it went back too far; I didn't know how these things worked. I thought about his syndication business in the UK and wondered if it had been as accomplished as his Australian venture. I noted he'd taken a similar name for his current operation, swapping the Winning Star name for Winning Way in Australia. Perhaps there were legal restrictions in using the same name? If it had been successful, why wind it up? Good syndicators usually stayed around forever; at least, the Australian ones I knew did. My old mate Vern from Classic Bloodstock must have been in the business for decades, and there were others I could think of with similar longevity in the trade. So why had Hall left? Maybe he'd had a dispute with his partner. Going their separate ways *to pursue new opportunities* covered a lot of ground. But I was curious to find out. I searched Winning Star Syndications, but all I got was a notice telling me the page was no longer available.

I tried Googling Hall's ex-partner, Paul Mead, but this time I encountered so many references beginning with *Paul* and *Mead* that I didn't know where to begin. I tried cutting the search down to Mead, but that wasn't any easier. I was looking for a bloodstock syndicator, but all I could find out about Mead was that it was an ancient alcoholic beverage. I spent another hour trawling through UK bloodstock syndicate websites hoping to find Mead in the management of any of those companies. No-go; it was as if he'd vanished. You'd think there'd have been something more in the racing papers about Hall or Mead and why they dissolved their partnership. Perhaps I just didn't have access to the right papers going back far enough. But I knew someone who did. I reached for my mobile and called Kate.

She was working at her computer, I could tell, talking into the phone as it nestled between cheek and shoulder while she continued tapping away at the keyboard.

'Hi Kate, it's me.'

'Hi Punter. What's happening?'

'You still at work? It's gone seven.'

'Yep, never stops. Listen, I'm kinda busy at the moment, got a story to finish.' Kate always had a deadline to meet.

'I won't hold you up. I just wondered if you have anything in your UK archives on Kagan Hall going back, say, five to ten years.'

I could hear the typing stop at her end.

'Kagan Hall. *The* Kagan Hall from Winning Way Syndications?'

'That's the one. Apparently he ran a syndicate in the UK known as Winning Star before he came out to Australia. Had a partner in it called Paul Mead, but they dissolved it a few years back. I'm trying to find out why.'

I heard someone asking her 'How long would it be?' and she replied five minutes.

'Look, I really gotta go. Can this wait till sometime next week? You know I'm always good for a favour, but business comes first.'

'Oh, sure. I understand. It can wait, I'll let you go. It's just that you did say to call you if anything came up about the strapper killings.'

That got her attention.

'Hang on, what's Hall got to do with any of that?'

'I don't know. Probably nothing.'

'Punter, you can't just ring up and expect me to cop that as an explanation. What have you got, what do you know about Hall?'

The trouble with Kate; you can quickly find yourself at the wrong end of an interrogation.

'I told you, I don't know. I've got nothing but a hunch, that's why I'm calling you. How about you dig up what you can find out and we swap notes next week?'

'Next week nothing. I know you and your hunches. I'll run a search tonight.'

'I thought you had a story to finish?'

'I'll kill that in two minutes flat. What exactly am I supposed to be looking for?'

'I don't quite know. But if you can check out any articles relating to Hall or his partner's business in the UK, it may help. I thought you might have access to more papers and magazines than what's available over the net.'

'Sure, we've got PA, TNS Media Monitors, Reuters and every major UK paper online. If he's appeared in the media, I can find him.'

'That's great. You at the races tomorrow?'

'I'll be there.'

'Good. Let's have a show and tell then.'

The following morning I drove to Flemington racecourse an hour before the first. It was going to be a busy day at the office.

Four races to play, maybe five if things fell into place. It's rare that I bet on two or more races in a day and lately there had been several days where I hadn't seen a race worth tackling. But today was the last weekend's racing before Christmas and a number of good-quality fields had accepted. I tipped George at the gate as I went in; put a fiver into his plastic collections bucket. He peered at me between the bridge of his Salvation Army cap and his goggle-like glasses; thanked me and wished me luck. I walked past the horse stall area first, looking for David. Dad had a two-year-old in the first race and I didn't think it would hurt to ask my brother if it had trained on since its last start. I ducked into the stalls where Dad's runners were stabled, but was brought to an abrupt stop by a burly security officer who stood in my way.

'Have you got a pass, mate? You need to be a licensed person to get into the horse stalls.'

I had to admit that I wasn't a licensed person. I just wanted to see my foreman brother; usually just walked in, so forth. But today I was politely but firmly told I'd have to stay outside the fenced-off section of the horse stalls.

'What's with all the protection?' I asked him.

The guy jerked his head towards the horse stalls opposite. There were two security men guarding the entrances there as well. 'It's the strapper killings. Our company's been hired to guard all stalls at the main meetings until further notice.'

'No kidding?'

'Nuh. The race clubs have hit the panic buttons. Still, not complainin', good overtime for us for Christmas.'

I walked around the outside of the fence and located David about three-quarters of the way along. He was fumbling around inside the leather raceday bag, probably checking to see that everything he'd packed meticulously a couple of hours earlier was still there in readiness for today.

'Come in,' he said when he saw me.

'Can't. They've got this security thing happening. Strictly licensed persons only. Extra protection for the strapper killings.'

'Oh, of course. Forgotten you haven't got a stablehand's ticket any longer.'

'Mine expired about ten years ago. The horse okay for today?'

He nodded. 'Cherry Ripe. The old man thinks she's well suited. Reckons she's trained on well since her last start placing.'

'That's what I wanted to hear.'

'What about you, you got anything that stands out today?'

I gave David a couple of horses for later in the day and told him what price I thought they should be. Then I left him to it and walked over to the members' entrance.

There's a little café up on the second floor which serves the best crab sandwiches I've ever tasted. I could eat them all day if they kept dishing them up to me. I bought a plate of them and a coffee and when I'd paid, I spotted Kate already sitting by a corner table waiting for me.

'Kate. Get you anything, a coffee, a sandwich? They make the best crab sandwiches here known to mankind.'

'I'm sure they do, but no thanks, I've already got a drink.'

She was playing with the straw in her lemon squash and took a little sip from it after she spoke. She was wearing lipstick, makeup, a designer dress and jacket. A set of petite baby Zeiss binoculars were slung across the back of her chair. She knew how to dress up and looked every bit the seasoned racegoer, which indeed she was. I sat down next to her and started on a sandwich.

'I had a look through our online archives last night for anything on Kagan Hall and his partner Mead,' she said.

'Any luck?'

'Uh-huh. In fact I found several articles, mostly about Hall.' Kate reached into her handbag and pulled out an envelope.

'Great. Want to give me a look?'

Instead of giving me the envelope she waved it in front of me. 'I thought this was supposed to be a show and tell,' she said. 'I want you to tell me why you asked me to look into Hall's background first.'

I was still chewing on a mouthful, so I couldn't reply straight-away. Kate eyed my plate with increasing interest. 'Mmm, actually they don't look too bad,' she said, helping herself to one.

'Hall's a groper,' I said, swallowing. 'Can't keep his hands off the women. I caught him the other day out at the sales trying to have his way with some poor stablegirl in a barn. He'd have raped her for sure if I hadn't happened to be there. In fact, I've noticed him a few times trying it on with different women.'

'Figures,' she said thoughtfully.

'You don't seem surprised.'

Kate helped herself to another sandwich.

'Addictive, aren't they?'

'I'm converted,' she said, licking her lips. 'My shout for another round. Here, read these while I buy us another plate. It might explain.'

I opened the envelope Kate had left me and pulled out six photocopied articles from various UK publications. She had them sorted in chronological date order. Three were from the daily city newspapers, two from specialist racing formguides and the other was some local suburban paper at Newmarket. I started reading the first article which was from seven years ago.

WINNING STAR SYNDICATOR ON RAPE CHARGE

Albrights solicitors representing Horse Syndicator, Kagan Hall, said their client would vigorously defend a charge of rape brought against him by an eighteen-year-old woman. The woman, a former stablehand, alleged the sexual assault took place on her seventeenth birthday last year at a party held at her employer's stables. Hall is a director of the successful racehorse syndication company Winning Star.

There were several more articles like the first one, short on detail and long on 'alleged' this and thats. But the one that caught my eye appeared to have been written a couple of months after the rape charge was first mentioned. It was written by one of the sex, sport and scandal racing guides, so I don't know how much of it was fact.

SYNDICATOR'S STAR HAS FALLEN

It will come as no surprise to readers of *The Tout* that racehorse syndicator, Winning Star, has wound up its business. As first reported by this paper, sales of shares in racehorses by investors slowed to a trickle as news of director Kagan Hall's pending rape charges first came to light. There have been whispers of overdue bills from several auction houses both in the UK and abroad as buyers shy away from the adverse publicity attributed to Hall and his syndicate.

The charges against Hall appear likely to be dropped, although this is yet to be officially confirmed by police. This follows the disappearance of the plaintiff, Sonia Lockwood, whose untimely vanishing act has effectively ended the case against Hall. Despite a wide-ranging search, police have found no clues as to her whereabouts.

It does appear the unwanted publicity has impacted severely on Winning Star's business. Neither Hall nor his solicitors were available for comment last night, however it is believed that Hall intends taking an extended vacation abroad. Co-director Paul Mead was asked if going into business with Hall as a partner had been a mistake. 'No comment,' was his reply.

'Have his actions ruined what was once a thriving business?'

'No comment.'

It is understood that arrangements have been made with two rival syndication companies to take over the management of Winning Star's horses. Investors will be notified by the administrators as soon as possible.

Kate came back with another plate of crab sandwiches as I finished reading. One of them was already gone, a little gap missing from the neatly arranged pile.

'Sorry,' said Kate, sporting a guilty smile. 'Had to have a nibble while I waited in the queue to pay.'

'Told you they were good.' I helped myself to one of the remaining sandwiches, which were fast disappearing in Kate's hands.

'That's interesting what you found out about Hall.'

Kate gave her mouth a dab with the serviette and wriggled into a more comfortable position on her stool. 'Yeah well, it's certainly a background he'd probably not want to advertise. But it depends on where you're coming from,' she said, shrugging. 'Like, last night you hinted that Hall might be a possible strapper killer suspect. I mean, okay, it's interesting about his past in the UK, the dropped rape charge and his failed business over there. And your observations about him groping some stablegirl at the sales is all very well, but . . .'

'It would have been a lot more than that if I hadn't happened along. Trust me.'

'I'm not disputing what you saw. It's just that you'd need a lot more to implicate him with any of the strapper killings. Do you have anything else that ties him in?'

'Hell, I don't know. He's at the races every Saturday. He's out to get his hand on every bit of skirt at the track that he can. He's been up on a rape charge before.'

'Alleged rape charge. A case that's gone nowhere.'

'Only because the girl conveniently disappeared.'

Kate frowned and considered, conceded the point. 'Perhaps a little too conveniently.'

'I'd say it's more than just a coincidence,' I said. 'The girl disappeared shortly before the trial. The case collapsed and the police had no choice but to let Hall walk.'

'Okay, I agree. His form in the UK and your observations of him over here don't exactly make him look an angel.'

'Another thing; I remember seeing Hall at the races ogling the third strapper who was killed. He was standing outside her stall. Melissa Jordan, who won the strapper's prize.'

'Can you put him anywhere near her later that night when she was killed?'

I gave Kate a blank look.

'What about the others who were killed, was he anywhere near them?'

'I don't know, Kate. It's not as if I've asked him or been tailing him around.'

'Punter, don't take this the wrong way. I'm just trying to put the same slant on it as the police would. I mean, I don't want to appear cynical, but despite the connection we think we're making between Hall and the missing Sonia and the strapper killings, all you've really got is a randy con who goes to the races every Saturday. That description could fit a lot of blokes.'

'Could be me.'

'Exactly. You never miss a meeting. Probably watched every one of those strappers parade in the mounting yard. In fact I saw you watching Melissa Jordan leading her horse around.'

'It must be me.'

'Yep. You were there. Can you account for your actions the night Melissa Jordan was killed?'

'No, I went home, had an early one.'

'You got any witnesses?'

'Tell me you're winding me up?'

She put a hand on my arm and smiled. 'I'm just demonstrating how easy it is to jump to conclusions.'

'So you don't think it's worth digging up any more about him?'

'I didn't say that. What I've got is a boss, something you wouldn't know about, who actually decides what my priorities are. I can't just go off on a tangent and investigate some story that takes my fancy. It's got to have legs, be newsworthy.'

'If it ties in with the strapper killings it would make the headlines.'

'Yeah, but all you've got at the moment is a suspect in your mind. You need a lot more facts before I could take it any further. You know what I'd do, I'd hand it over as a quiet tip to police and let them decide what to make of him.'

'I was actually thinking of passing it on to Beering,' I said.

Kate nodded. 'Do it. It's a good idea. Let him and the police check him out. At least that way you've done what you can.'

She took another sip of her squash and frowned as if thinking of something else. 'Have you discussed this with anyone else?'

'No. Just you.'

'Not even Maxine?'

I shook my head. 'I thought of asking Maxine about Hall, but it's a tricky one because he's her client. I can imagine how she'd react if I rocked up and told her that her main client was the strapper killer. "Don't want to alarm you, sweetie, and this shouldn't affect your working relationship with him, but Hall's a killer and you shouldn't spend time alone with him".'

Kate wasn't as flippant as I was. 'What if he did turn out to be the killer? Wouldn't you have wanted to warn her as early as possible?'

I was late getting to the mounting yard. My meeting with Kate had eaten into my punting time and the jockeys had already been legged up for the first race and were making their way out. Inside the enclosure, I was taken aback by all the extra security. It was quite noticeable; two armed security guards patrolling the inner sanctum of the lawn area and another standing by the gate to the members' area. The one by the gate was staring intently at the crowd, as if daring any potential murderer to try their best. The other two stationed inside walked slowly around the ring like huge apes, doing laps next to horses led by female strappers. I don't know if it made the girls feel any safer, but it certainly made a statement. When the horses went out onto the track and the strappers filed back, the security guards formed a protective cordon around the women and followed them inside to the grandstand.

Out in the betting ring, most bookmakers were giving threes about one of Dad's horses, Hideaway Island. Most bookies, that is, except Big Oakie White, who kept her safe at two dollars eighty. The big fella stood on his stand like an old bull walrus, leaning comfortably against the railing, his huge pumpkin face wearing a contented smile.

'Whadda ya know, Punter?' he asked me.

'I know you're giving two points under everyone else for the fave.'

Oakie scanned the ring with his owl-like eyes and grinned. 'Don't mean I have to. Don't mean you have to back her with me, either.'

'True, but I thought we could do some business on account of me backing two horses as savers with you, if you give me the threes.'

Oakie made a show of worriedly looking at his board and then scanning the ring again before telling me, as he always did, that it was punters like me who were sending him broke. I told him my bets and he called them out to his clerk who printed out three tickets for me as I gave him my cash.

'Thanks, Oakie. Hey, good crowd here today.'

Oakie nodded slowly and looked away into the public section. 'Yeah, but not all of 'em here for the betting, though,' he said, jerking his head towards a couple of guards patrolling the outer ring. 'Bloody security here today, you reckon they had a royal visit or something going on.'

Up in the stand, I swept the lawns with my binoculars to bring them into focus and the first person I picked up on was Jim Beering. Hard to miss in his brown suit and hat leaning against the outer course rail. He was facing the grandstand and watching, always watching the crowd for trouble. Drunks, pickpockets, warned-off licensees. *Serial killers.* Seeing him reminded me to catch up with him later. I didn't want to see him too early in the day as it would interfere with my punting, so I sent him a text asking if I could meet him by the mounting yard before the main race. From where I was sitting, I could see him pull out his phone and read my message. He replied with a simple 'OK' then added, 'Got a winner?'

I texted him back, saying 'Hideaway Island in the first.'

I could almost imagine him swearing with frustration from the realisation he wouldn't have time to back it.

There were only two horses to be loaded into the starting gates and I watched the barrier attendants lead them up and close the gates. Dad's horse had drawn the extreme outside, but in races down the straight, that's been an advantage in recent years, as horses on the grandstand side seem to have a faster lane than those on the flat side. When the barriers opened, two packs formed and went their separate ways, one making a beeline for the grandstand rail and the other for the inside fence. Watching them head on, it was impossible to tell who was leading who. I don't know how the race callers do it; calling straight races must be a nightmare for them. I kept my glasses on Hideaway Island.

Her jockey was in a good position running third and close to the leaders in his pack. Over on the rails there were a couple of horses vying for the lead and I still couldn't tell if they were in front or behind the group on the grandstand side. When they got to the clock tower I knew we were home. The jockey still had a stranglehold on the filly and she'd booted a half length in front. I put my glasses down. Nice feeling, starting the day with a winner.

Hideaway Island wasn't the only winner I backed that afternoon. I played the next race as well. It looked a contest between the top two, and that's exactly how it panned out. No fancy prices, two seventy the pair. I backed both of them and didn't care which won. Race three was a cup of tea race and race four I couldn't get the price I wanted about my top pick. I didn't want to bet against it so I sat the race out. The horse won anyway, despite its price. Race five looked a bit of a gamble; a race restricted to apprentice riders only. They'd made some horse a ridiculously short-priced favourite. I never take the shorts about a horse unless it's a champion, and I certainly don't take odds on about some pimply faced apprentice who's likely to miss the start or get caught wide. I did a quick check of the percentages. If I backed every other runner in the race bar the fave and two no-hopers, I'd win regardless of which horse saluted. Not a bad speculation for a race I hadn't planned to play. That's how it worked out, too. The odds-on pop found itself pocketed at the turn; stupid kid was half asleep and should have got out a furlong before he was caught napping. An eight to one chance scored and I was happy to have made wages for the day.

'Fuckin' kid couldn't ride the ghost train at Luna Park,' spat out one disgruntled punter next to me.

I nodded in commiseration. 'Should have won by the length of the straight,' I said. Rule number one, never admit you've just won to a punter who's just done their money. They'll only be dark on you for bettering them, or worse, put the hard word on you for a bite. With half an hour to go before the main race,

I decided I'd have a quick afternoon tea with the gang before my catch-up chat with Beering.

I thought I must have been one of the first to arrive as I couldn't see any of the others at our usual spot. But then I saw Ric coming back from the bar with a drink. I bought a squash and joined him at the table where he was sitting.

'Looks like just you and me today, Ric,' I said, sitting down alongside him.

'Nah, Matt's floating around somewhere,' he said. 'Gone to bet on some no-hoper in Adelaide. But I haven't seen any of the others yet.'

I nodded and took a sip of my squash. Laid my *Best Bets* on the table and placed my binoculars on top of them. Ric was sorting through his formguide, circling numbers here and there, a studious look on his face.

'How's the battle?' I asked him.

He shrugged. 'Up and down. Be more up if that useless kid hadn't slaughtered the fave in the last.'

I laughed and agreed with him.

'How 'bout you?'

I sighed like a loser. Best policy, I find. 'It's a hard game the punt, son.'

Ric grunted and went back to his form study. We sank into a mini silence; both of us checking our formguides and watching the TV monitors. A couple of minutes went by and I looked at Ric over the top of my glass. Mostly when I'd seen him at the track, he'd been with Matt or the rest of the gang. Alone with him, I felt a little awkward in his company and decided I should probably make more of an effort to get to know him.

'How's work?' I asked him.

'Huh? Oh, same old shit, just a different day.'

'I don't know how you stick at it.'

Got another grunt by way of response. He looked up at some interstate race playing on the TV.

'You married, Ric, any kids?'

Shook his head.

'A partner?'

Another shake.

'You got any hobbies?'

He looked at me blankly.

'Sorry, wasn't meaning to pry, but you know, something to pass the time. Like me, I go surfing whenever I get a chance. Or play some snooker every now and then for a bit of fun.'

'Just horseracing.'

I'm not the world's greatest conversationalist, but it felt like one-way traffic trying to engage him. He didn't seem to want to elaborate on anything I asked him and he didn't seem particularly interested in anything I did. I didn't think he was secretive or rude. He was just indifferent, didn't want to connect with me. Still, I persevered to avoid an uncomfortable silence.

'You done any Christmas shopping yet?'

Parents dead. There was no one he had to buy for.

'Follow the tennis? The Open's coming up in January.'

He told me he couldn't stand tennis. The players all grunted too much.

In the end, I plain ran out of things to talk about and gave up. Maybe we just didn't have anything in common. So we fell back to studying our formguides in silence and I was sort of glad when Matt showed up a few minutes later, chattering away as he usually did. Made for easier conversation with the three of us there.

'G'day Matt,' I said. 'How's the wife?'

'She's great.'

'We ever going to see her at the track someday?'

'You kidding! Drag her away from the malls. This is my Saturday afternoon therapy and shopping's hers.'

I laughed. 'What about your kids? They'd be on Christmas holidays now, wouldn't they?'

'Yeah. The little buggers are at home right through till New Year.'

'Is that right? Then I reckon schools short-change children now. I can remember we never went back until February.'

'January, February – It's never soon enough when you're a parent, trust me,' he laughed.

'Reckon I'd know to the day,' said Ric glumly.

'You winning?'

Matt had bet on some horse at Morphettville which he reckoned they'd have to send out a search party for. Said he'd never backed a slower galloper in all his life. Ric immediately needled him about being stupid enough to back anything in Adelaide in the first place. I left them to it, sniping and point-scoring off each other as usual like an old married couple.

I went out to my usual place by the mounting yard fence for the next race, looking about for Beering. I spotted him walking over with a hot-dog in his hand. 'If I knew you were eating that fast food rubbish, I'd have invited you to lunch in the members',' I said.

Beering sniffed good-naturedly. 'You think I've got time to mix with the hoi polloi? Workers like me got to take their meals on the run.'

He took a bite of his hot-dog. It looked revolting; doused with French mustard to either disguise or enhance the rubbery flavour. The horses started to trickle into the yard and as they did, one of the race club staff erected a couple of sandwich boards inside the grass ring near the presentation table announcing that this race was for the strapper's prize.

I nodded towards the sign. 'Had any luck finding the strapper killer?'

Beering swallowed another mouthful and wiped a dribble of mustard off his chin with his hand.

'I wish. Papers have been giving us hell, my department's had all leave cancelled and now we've got to put up with these hired clowns,' he said, nodding to the three security guards. They'd marched into the ring like an SAS battalion, strutting around as if they owned the place. Earlier in the day, they'd been a little unsure of their routine, the movements of the horses and strappers, but after a few races it seemed like their confidence had grown and now they were almost directing the mounting yard traffic.

'They going to make any difference?'

'Bloody goons. Our chairman and the board have shit 'emselves, they have, just trying to appease the union. They're convinced they have to be seen to be doing more to provide protection for strappers until this killer's caught.'

'So they brought in the hired guns?'

'Yep. If you ask me, all it will do is drive the killer underground, make it even harder to catch him.'

We watched as the final horses and strappers entered the ring. It was a large field, eighteen horses, and I could see the judges with their clipboards busily making notes and trying to select the winner. I thought it would prove a difficult task today as there were so many well turned out strappers and horses. A tallish, wafer-thin strapper walked by leading her horse, its mane plaited like it was entered for the Royal Show. She wore riding boots and whiter-than-white vanilla ice cream—coloured jodhpurs. It was clear she'd gone to a lot of trouble. But they all had. Number eight was an eye-catcher: a cheeky young blonde whom I half knew from the track. She donned a pair of designer sunglasses, the brand name emblazoned on the side in huge letters. She was flirting with one of the security guards, who had taken it upon himself to walk laps of the mounting yard alongside her as if he were her personal protector. Number ten seemed to wiggle around with a beaming smile etched onto her face. If they were giving out happy awards, she'd win for sure.

'Like the bloomin' Royal Melbourne Show, ain't it?' said Beering cynically.

'Give them a break, Jim. Only chance some strappers have of picking up some extra cash. Half the trainers don't sling anymore and they work all day for a pittance.'

Beering grunted. 'S'pose you're right.'

We watched for a few more minutes as the strappers led their charges around. They were already running late because of the large field and only half the jockeys had mounted up.

'You wanted to see me?' he asked.

'I've got a name for you to check out,' I said.

'Pertaining to what?' Amazing how quickly Beering could revert back to cop talk.

'You said to keep my eyes and ears open and pass anything on, no matter how silly it sounds.'

'The strapper killer? You've heard something?'

'It's probably nothing. But you and the police would be able to check him out, make certain.'

'Who is it, do I know him?'

I looked over to the side of the mounting yard steps, which were still packed with punters watching the horses being led around. The strapper's prize was about to be announced and people were milling about to see who had won. In a group by the steps stood a man I was beginning to think I knew better than he knew himself. He was talking to another guy, making small talk about the horses. I could hear his suave, upper-class British accent from where I was standing. He was staring lasciviously at every female strapper who passed by, undressing them with his leering eyes. No doubt imagining what he'd do to them if he caught them alone in a stable. I turned back to Beering. 'It's a spruiker with a shady past who can't keep his hands off the ladies. Goes by the name of Kagan Hall.'

12

After the races I dropped back to my flat, fed Che, changed out of my raceday suit and had a shower. Then I drove over to Maxine's. When I buzzed her on the intercom, she chided me for not using the key she'd given me.

'Sorry,' I said, 'force of habit.'

I still hadn't used her key in the short time that I'd had it. I probably wouldn't have needed a key to get into her place tonight anyway. A guy had left a telephone book jammed in the entrance door, and was ferrying groceries back and forth from his car out the front. I nodded at him as I walked in and he didn't seem too concerned when I made my way up the stairs to Maxine's. I'd rented an apartment once with a similar intercom system; pain in the arse they were too. People would come home late or drunk and forget their key, then buzz every intercom in the block until finally someone opened the door for them.

Maxine had left the door ajar for me. I called out to her and her head appeared like a jack-in-the-box from the bathroom down the hallway. She had a towel draped around her, obviously still getting ready to go out.

'Hi sweetie. Fix yourself a drink and I'll be out in a min. We still eating out at that seafood place in Middle Park?'

'There's a John Dory reserved with your name on it.'

'Oh goody! Won't be long, I promise.'

I helped myself to a light beer from her fridge. There was plenty to drink inside of it. Wine, a dozen or so chilled bottles; all premium brands. Tonic water, juices. Soy milk – yuck. Not a lot of food to be seen, though. I think Maxine preferred to eat out with the hours she kept. It probably explained the spotless kitchen. The sparkling European stove didn't look as if it had ever been used, and I pulled the oven open to have a stickybeak. Sure enough, a couple of expensive-looking frying pans were stacked neatly on the oven racks. Costly sort of a cupboard if that's all it was used for. I sipped my beer and took in the view from the back of her place. I hadn't really noticed it before. All my previous trips to Maxine's seemed to have been hit-and-run missions made in the dark. Both of us home late, the inevitable wild scramble in the bedroom, and then I'd scurry off at the crack of dawn back to my place. Her kitchen and lounge opened up to a smaller patio area which overlooked a communal garden down below. It was very peaceful; green manicured lawns lit by gentle spotlights. Attractive shrubs and bushes surrounded a feature waterfall and rock pool. I hated to think what the strata title fees in this place would be. Maxine had her own stairway leading into the garden and I took a couple of steps down, admiring the greenery. It was very pleasant, a warm night, gentle breeze. I could get used to this place; perhaps I should make more use of it.

'I'm nearly ready. How do I look?' she said.

She had on a sexy white skirt. Not quite a mini, but damn near. A red scooped top with a plunging neckline. Lots of bling. Perfume; don't know which brand, but it made me want to stop and investigate. I gave a suggestive growl. She squirmed playfully, avoiding my clutches.

'Not now! We're late as it is. Can you lock the back door and I'll get my purse.'

Later, at the restaurant, Maxine was bubbling over with enthusiasm for some new law firm client she'd picked up. Over dinner, I let her gush on about them while nursing a glass of something very good the waitress had recommended. Quite enjoyable; sipping a cold wine, listening to Maxine and casting the occasional discreet glance at her barely covered neckline.

'Punter, are you listening?'

'What? Of course I've heard of them. Freedales. Didn't they act for a jockey or trainer recently who was warned off for life?'

'It was a trainer. They get a lot of racing and sporting cases. Rodney Ellis, he's one of Freedales' top QCs, he got it reduced to just a twelve-month suspension. Can you believe that, from life to just twelve months?'

'He must be terribly clever.'

'He *is*. I got to meet him and some of the other senior partners. But the beauty of the whole deal is that they've outsourced the entire in-house marketing and they're giving me the lot.'

'The lot?'

'Uh-huh. Advertising, PR, media releases, newsletters, corporate events. The whole box and dice. I'll probably have to put on staff to cope.'

'Sounds like you're the clever one. Are you going to be able to handle all the extra work? I mean, with Winning Way's business.'

Maxine nodded her head enthusiastically as if she'd already gone through the schedule.

'It'll be fine. I've done virtually all of the planning and bookings for Winning Way's functions. I just have to turn up and see that everything's all right. But Freedales,' she said, getting back to her favourite new client, 'are great, *so* professional. And I only have to report through to one chain of command, Rodney Ellis. He's such a nice guy.'

Thought I'd better try to steer the conversation back to something other than law firms.

'How's your head feel now?'

'Apart from a lump and the stitches, it's fine. The doctor said I was lucky. Wanted me to take it easy for a while. They're always too cautious.'

'I must admit I was a bit concerned when you launched straight back into work. You were knocked out, after all.'

'I can't sit around, I've got a business to run. Hey, you know the other thing I'm really looking forward to doing?'

'What?'

'Leading in Dad's horse, Princess Upstart, on New Year's Day.'

'As if you haven't got enough on your plate.'

'It just so happens she's entered for the race with the strapper's prize. And you know what?' she said, with a determined look in her eye, 'I'm gonna win it.'

I frowned; wasn't sure it sounded such a great idea. 'You know, there was a lot of security around the track today with this strapper killer still on the loose. It's got a lot of people very worried.'

'I know, I read the papers. It's just some crazy. They'll catch him soon. Besides, even though that girl from your dad's stables was killed, I always feel safe enough at Parraboo Lodge. Anyway, I'm not a full-time strapper and I don't live in the stables. I'm not really part of their world; it's just something I do for fun.'

'Do you ever think that maybe her regular strapper should lead her in?'

'Why?'

'Well, this is sorta getting into a philosophical argument, but most strappers really look forward to leading in their own horses come raceday.'

'Oh, I get it. And I'm cutting them out because I just turn up on raceday and claim the glory?'

'Well, I'm not saying that. But they don't get paid much, so a chance to win something extra from a strapper's prize would be something to look forward to.'

Maxine pretended to cry. 'Oh, *please*. Can I have a handkerchief? For heaven's sake. Dad owns the horse and if I want to lead it in, then that's just tough titties for the strapper. Anyway, have you seen Belinda, the girl who normally looks after Princess Upstart?'

I knew Belinda. A big girl who wouldn't look out of place in a football team. 'I know her.'

'Well, could you ever see her winning a strapper's prize? Not unless she spent the next three months at Jenny Craig.'

I shrugged. Not an argument I was going to win. And obviously wasn't worth mentioning that Belinda was very good at her job.

'Well if you are going to take her, I'll ask David to watch out at the stables for you. I know the old man's taking extra precautions as it is, but you can't be too careful until this guy's caught.'

'Okay.'

I swung the conversation back to Winning Way.

'How long have you been doing work for Kagan Hall?'

'About two months.'

'And you've known him for about the same time?'

'No, be longer than that. A year or so. I met him through Dad at the races. They're race track buddies. It's how I got his business.'

'I see. Have you always, like, got on with him?'

'Oh, he's a pain in the arse. I've told you before what a demanding client he can be, always changing his mind. But it's a prestigious account to have and even though he's a nightmare to work with, I put up with him.'

'Ever had any . . . you know, trouble with him?'

Maxine put her glass down, finally sensing I was struggling for the right words. 'Trouble? What sort of trouble?'

'I don't know. Has he ever . . .'

'Has he ever put the hard word on me?'

'Well, yes.'

'Oh, for heaven's sake, Punter.' She placed a hand in mine over the table. 'Are you jealous?'

'No, of course not.'

'My baby's jealous!'

'I'm not.'

'Then why the interest in Kagan Hall?'

I shrugged. Didn't really know if I should tell her my real reason for asking. 'I just wondered, that's all.'

'Look, sweetie, he's never touched me and I have a golden rule; I never fuck with my clients.'

'Phew, glad we got that sorted,' I said, pretending to mop the sweat from my forehead. She smiled, leant forward and let me have a glimpse of what was inside her top.

'And as you're not a client and I don't have to worry about rules, I think we should go on home, don't you?'

I'm sitting in a little café in Brunswick Street eating pasta carbonara. Brunelli's, or some woggy-sounding name, it's called. It's one thirty in the morning and I'm feeling very clever. I've done two tonight. Two! I'm definitely getting better. Stacey and her flatmate Catrina. I hadn't intended to do Catrina, but she was there and it was neces- sary and what good's a job unless it's done properly?

Stacey was a dead ringer for Amanda. I suppose that's why I picked her, why I pick any of them. The jet-black hair, the tarty way she dressed. The sly-looking eyes. Looking, she was always looking to see if men were watching her. She knew that I watched her, was attracted to her. Was it a coincidence that Amanda closely resembled my mother? Is that why I was drawn to her? She certainly had the same features and deceitful ways as my mother did.

I went out with Amanda for a while, if you can call a few awkward dates and an occasional, snatched kiss a relationship. She always insisted I take her to nightclubs. I can see now why she frequented those places; I must have been blind not to notice her eyes always shopping around for talent, for someone better. I was just a handbag, a toy boy to buy her drinks. Me, holding her glass while she danced with that jockey. Writhing away and willing her body to him. And then the two of them, kissing and groping on the dance floor like I wasn't even there. I walked out on Amanda that night without saying a word to her. But I never forgot, and my patience is infinite.

Amanda was my first kill and I waited for nearly two years after that night before I did her. I wanted to be sure that I wouldn't be implicated in her death, and so it turned out. But there have been several others since her and I certainly didn't wait two years for the next one. It's peculiar how this urge to kill becomes stronger with each new killing. The next one after Amanda was eight months later and then only a month went by before I felt the urge again. Lately it's been every week or so, but I would go out every night if I could.

I guess it takes some of us a while before the penny drops on what our purpose in life should be. I now realise I'm on a path I should have followed years ago. Preventing a silk chaser's treachery is what I do. It's a good deed, the correct thing to do. I, with my expert knowledge of how they think and act. It is a gift, this knowledge, and one which I must use wisely to track down every last one of them, before they grow into jockey-fucking whores like my mother was . . .

13

He woke me promptly at five thirty on Monday morning for his breakfast. I got up, fed him and went straight back to bed. Didn't get to sleep in much longer; my mobile rang at six forty-seven. It was Jim Beering calling to tell me the strapper killer had struck again some time on Sunday night. According to Beering, there were two girls this time, both employees of a small-time Flemington trainer, Toby Devon.

'I just thought I'd let you know,' said Beering. 'It'll be all over the news by breakfast time.'

'Jesus,' I said, 'he's never done two before. How many's that now, five?'

'That we know about.'

I caught the double meaning in Beering's answer. 'What are you saying?'

'Homicide have been sifting through some cold cases. There was a woman who was raped and stabbed to death in her flat about a year ago they'd written off as a break-and-enter gone wrong.'

'There's a connection?'

'Uh-huh. The deceased's occupation. Amanda Kaisha was an ex-strapper.'

'Why didn't the police pick up on that straightaway?'

'Sometimes you don't always know what to look for until a pattern emerges. In Amanda's case, she'd quit racing eighteen months before she was killed and had gone back to studying at TAFE. So all police could tag her with at the time was as a full-time student.'

'Jesus. So this guy may have started his killing much earlier than what we thought.'

'He might have. The police are digging up every similar unsolved case in their files. There may be others we don't know about yet.'

I sat up properly in bed, still not yet fully awake, but starting to think through what Beering had told me.

'What about that guy I gave you on Saturday, Kagan Hall; you checked him out?'

'I gave him straight-up to Homicide after you and I spoke at the races. They're making inquiries in the UK about him. And in light of last night's discovery, I'm sure they'll be speaking to him.'

I brought Beering back to the two girls. 'You said the two he killed yesterday both worked for Toby Devon. He had a runner on Saturday, didn't he?'

'Yeah. And one of the murdered girls, Stacey Marshall, was leading in a horse for him. Her room-mate, Catrina, also worked for Devon, although she wasn't working at the races on Saturday. That didn't stop him from killing her, though.'

'Was Stacey in the main race, the one with the strapper's prize?'

'Yeah.'

'Did she win it? I didn't pay any attention after I left you.'

'No, in fact they gave it to one of the guy strappers.'

'And the others who were killed, were they all in the strapper's prize or had perhaps won it?'

'Punter, I know where you're going with this, but trust me, the crew from Homicide are two steps ahead. They've looked at all that. Julie Summers and the girl who worked for your father, Carmen Leek, were both killed before this stupid strapper's prize even started. Melissa Jordan won the strapper's prize and she was victim number three. Then Stacey competed in it, but didn't win, and she was murdered, as was her flatmate who wasn't even there. So there doesn't necessarily appear to be any connection between the strapper's prize and those killed.'

I let that sink in. 'What about the location of where the girls worked? There's been a couple now from Caulfield, haven't there?'

'True. Two from there, but now three from Flemington. The sequence is a Flemington kill first, followed by two in a row at Caulfield and now these two at Flemington. If he did that cold-case girl, Amanda, well, she lived all the way down at Frankston. None of them knew each other, except the two who worked for Devon and roomed together. There's no apparent rhyme or reason apart from the fact they were all strappers.'

'Have you just come from there?' I asked.

'I have, but I wasn't allowed inside the crime scene. Although I can tell you that from what I heard, it wasn't a pretty sight.'

Beering described it: all the familiar trademarks of the strapper killer, including the now infamous words scribbled in lipstick on Stacey's mirror and walls.

'I'll tell you two weird things about that writing,' said Beering. 'The first is that the message was slightly longer than it usually is. This time it said: *I'm a Silk Chaser*. Every other time, just *Silk Chaser* has been written up. The second thing, which has been confirmed by police, is that all the messages except for the one at Julie Summers' crime scene, have been written by the victim.'

'Seriously? They can tell that from just scribble on a wall?'

'Punter, they got forensic handwriting experts who can tell you about the curves and the slants and the slope of writing. They can tell how much pressure's been used to write a word, and all sorts of stuff about the shape of the strokes. Even the spacing between letters. All that shit. They know enough from what they've seen to confirm that the last three murder scenes have all been written up by their victims. All of them probably under frightening duress,' he said soberly.

'So we can assume it was the killer himself who wrote the message for the Summers murder, then got the girls to write their own epitaphs for every killing that followed. It's like he keeps developing his act, keeps trying to bring new tricks to the party.'

Later in the week David rang to remind me about arrangements for Boxing Day. As if anything ever changed. Ever since David and I were young strappers working for my father, the routine had never varied. First, there was the quiet family Christmas Day luncheon at my parents' house. Then, that was followed by the annual Christmas party thrown for all of Dad's stable clients after the Boxing Day meeting at Caulfield. I told David I'd be there to lend a hand, as always, straight after the races.

Christmas Day came and went. My mother prepared a roast chicken, even though the temperature hovered around the high thirties. Cold seafood would have been more appropriate, but Mum was a traditionalist and so we got what she deemed to be authentic Christmas fare. Afterwards, we sat down in the lounge room and exchanged presents and pleasantries. David had brought along Dianne, his perennial fiancée. They'd been together eight years, engaged for at least three. When they were going to tie the knot was anyone's guess. Still, they seemed happy enough in their perpetual state of readiness. They were still my mother's best bet for a grandchild, although she hadn't completely given up on me.

'How's that lovely girl you've been seeing?' she asked me. 'Why didn't you invite her over as well?'

'Maxine will be at the party tomorrow,' I said. 'Besides, she was spending Christmas with her father today.'

'Such a pretty thing . . .' mused mother. She was already in babyland, dreaming of the little booties she could knit. 'You two make such a nice couple.'

We made polite family small talk for the rest of the afternoon. The women carried the conversation as they usually did. David and I and the old man talked racing.

I can't say it was relaxing; my father getting up to answer the phone every five minutes to owners demanding to know something about their horse. A trainer's life doesn't change just because it's Christmas, although you'd think some owners could hold off pestering him for at least one day of the year.

The next day was the annual Parraboo Lodge Christmas party. Even though the party was always professionally catered, it was an unspoken tradition that David and I circulated with the drink trays and mingled with Dad's clients. Of course, I hadn't been involved with the stable in an official capacity for years, but I didn't mind mixing with the predominantly racing crowd, so I played the dutiful son every year and never complained. I'd been at the Caulfield races all day and after the last I drove back and parked my van outside the stables in Booran Road. There was already a fair-sized collection of distinctive-looking owners' cars in attendance. Sounds of laughter and conversation drifted from across the marquees which had been erected between the lawns and pathways surrounding the stables. The party appeared to be well under way.

I walked under the archway sign that said 'Parraboo Lodge'. Most top trainers end up calling their stables after one of their champions. Tommy Smith called his Randwick stables Tulloch Lodge after that great old campaigner who still holds race records decades after his death. But you won't ever see mention of Parraboo in *This Racing Year*. He only ever won three races, but his first win enabled my father to land a plunge which had paid for the building of the stables. They say he had to stuff the cash in chaff bags in the back of his car to get it all home from the track. I asked him about it once; if it was true. A faraway look came into his eye as he travelled back fifty years or more in his mind to that day. 'A good horse that, son,' and then a twinkle and a smile. 'A nice day's work.' That's about as good an admission as you're likely to get off Dad that he's had a winning day. He's trained a lot of quality horses since then, picking up a couple of Melbourne Cups and most of the major Group races, but he's never been tempted to change the stable's name to one of his better-known gallopers.

David was at the first marquee with Dianne, fussing around with some drinks at the bar. They both lived in the foreman's house at the front of the stables which meant David was on call twenty-four/seven. It could easily have been me who ended up in that house; taking phone calls from rude owners. Sorting out staff squabbles. Feeding the horses, mucking out boxes, getting things shipshape, just the way my father demanded them. I was so glad I'd gone my own way all those years ago.

David and Dianne were having a stressful conversation. He was in a flap that they didn't have enough cold champagne on ice.

'Those bloody caterers,' he fumed.

'Can I help?' I said.

'Oh, would you,' said Dianne. 'If you can grab a tray of drinks off the bar and offer them around to the guests, that would be great.'

'Consider it done,' I said. 'Is Maxine here yet?'

'She arrived about twenty minutes ago. She's out the back somewhere with her father.'

The trouble with other people's parties; you couldn't exclude undesirables from the guest list.

I picked up a tray of mixed drinks and carried them out into the back section of the stable block, past boxes one and two, which I used to muck out as a kid. They'd seemed much bigger back then, especially when you'd slept in and were trying to get finished before Dad turned up and caught you out. DJ was there now, with a group of owners including Maxine and her father. They were outside the stable door of Henshaw's horse, Princess Upstart. Maxine was holding court, as usual, chattering away nineteen to the dozen. I caught the tail end of the discussion as I walked up behind them like a waiter with my tray.

'Drinks, anybody?' I asked.

Maxine wheeled around, smiling as she heard my voice, and planted a kiss on the side of my cheek. Henshaw glared coldly at me, a face that would guarantee him a movie role as Dracula.

'Hello, sweetie,' said Maxine.

'I see the hired help's arrived,' said Henshaw sarcastically.

I ignored him, giving out some drinks and collecting empty glasses from my father and one of the other guests.

'DJ's going to run Princess Upstart on New Year's Day at Flemington, aren't you?' said Maxine.

My father said it was one of three meetings he was considering. 'Depends what weight she gets,' he answered.

'Oh no, you *have* to run her at Flemington, she's in the strapper's prize and I'm going to win it. Please say you'll run her?' Maxine played the helpless owner's daughter to perfection, applying not-so-subtle pressure to both my father and Henshaw.

'Dad, please say we can run her in the strapper's prize. I *so* want to win it. I've already bought new riding boots and jodhpurs especially.'

'I don't know, Maxine,' said Henshaw. 'I'm uneasy about you strapping at the races with this madman on the loose. I'd prefer you stayed away until they catch him, just to be on the safe side.'

Henshaw's comment started an instant discussion – it seemed everybody had a view about it.

'There was that shocking killing last weekend; two of them who shared a room at the back of the stables. The police don't seem to have a clue who's done it,' said someone.

'Could be anybody,' said another.

How many times had I heard this talk at the races over the past few weeks?

'Aren't you afraid that he could be out there, watching you as you lead your horse around?' said one of the women.

Maxine was defiant, as I knew she would be. 'Are you kidding? Have you seen the extra security they've got at the races now? They're patrolling the mounting yard every race, the stripping stalls, the float park. You can't walk two steps without being asked for your ID in the restricted areas.'

'I'd feel more comfortable if they actually escorted all female strappers to and from the track,' said Henshaw.

'Oh, don't be ridiculous, Dad, there's far too many strappers to watch them all around the clock.'

'Well, the extra security didn't stop those two girls getting killed the other day,' said Henshaw, 'nor poor Carmen who worked here.'

'They were full-time strappers living at the stables, I'm not. Besides, you can't just stop women strappers leading in horses, I mean where does it end? Are you going to forbid them from walking horses around the stables for exercise? This killer could be anywhere, not just at the races. He might be watching strappers at track work for all anyone knows. Anyway, he's certainly not going to stop me from doing what I've always done.'

It wasn't a bad argument, actually. The killer could indeed be anywhere, stalking the women from any vantage point. Not attending a race meeting wouldn't necessarily protect them.

'Well, if you are that determined to go,' said Henshaw, 'then I insist on arranging your own personal bodyguard to accompany you at all times.'

'Oh, don't be absurd. I'm not going to be seen dead with some uniformed knucklehead following two steps behind me. It takes away all the pleasure of strapping. Besides, Punter's going to look after me on raceday. We've already talked about it, haven't we?'

Henshaw glared at me.

'Well, we've all seen how effective *that* protection has been in the past, haven't we?'

I ignored Henshaw, instead pushing the case for Maxine. 'I think Maxine will be fine as long as we make sure staff are around when she gets the horse ready and when she brings it back from the races to the stables.' I turned and looked at her. 'I can even go in the float with you to and from the races, just to be on the safe side. That way, you'll never be alone.'

Everyone thought it was a good suggestion except Henshaw.

'I still think you need a professional security guard to go with you,' he said.

'Well, if you want to come along in the back of the float with Punter and me, you're welcome to,' said Maxine.

Touché. Somehow I couldn't envisage Henshaw with his expensive suit and shoes travelling in the back of a dirty horse truck like some common stableboy. Especially with me.

'Hey, that'd be fun,' I said, rubbing it in. 'We could share a few tinnies in the float. Be a real bonding session for us.'

Henshaw glowered at me and took a half step forward. I thought for just a moment he might have wanted to take up where he'd left off at the hospital. Maxine neatly avoided any trouble.

'Oh stop it, you two,' she said, putting her arm through mine. 'It's settled then. Punter can come along as a strapper with me on New Year's Day.'

The days following Christmas were eerily quiet. It was still unbearably hot; yet another run of thirty-five degree plus days accompanied by the threatening northerlies that firefighters dread. Those lucky enough had escaped the city's heat by making their annual summer holiday trek to the coastal resorts of Torquay or Portsea. People like me, stuck at home, were driven indoors seeking the shelter of air conditioning and drawn blinds. Glenferrie Road was like a ghost track. Scotch College had shut down for the summer holiday break and unlike the usual endless procession of Camberwell wives dropping their kids off to school in oversized four-wheel drives, there wasn't a car or child to be seen anywhere. I watched from the cool of my balcony as an empty tram rattled up the road.

Kate was with me. She'd dropped by to give me the latest news on the case.

I offered her a chilled glass of champagne and we sat outside with our drinks, trying to catch the promise of an evening sea breeze.

'That's refreshing,' she said.

'Mmm. I don't usually drink the stuff except at Christmas or weddings. Someone gave me a couple of bottles. Goes down well on a night like this.'

Kate gave Che a pat between the ears. He'd wasted no time in jumping up onto her lap and arranging a cuddle.

'He seems to have made himself at home,' she said, juggling her glass in one hand and stroking Che's ears with the other.

'He deserted me as soon as he saw you coming. I've never seen that cat approve of a stranger like he does of you.'

'I'm hardly a stranger. Besides, I've seen him purring around your neighbour, Mrs Givan. And I'm sure he's just as friendly with other regulars who drop by the Punter penthouse.'

Meaning Maxine, of course. Ex-girlfriends; they're black belts in the art of subtle barbs. I thought for a moment of Che hissing at Maxine as she trod on his tail rushing to the bathroom.

'Hmm, he's not as friendly with everyone as you think. Consider yourself one of the lucky few.'

Kate laughed and I laughed at the pair of them; Kate, with her feet propped up on the railing and Che, with his legs flopping down either side of her lap.

'He knows I'm good for a spoil,' she said.

I topped up our glasses and waited for Kate to fill me in on what had been happening.

'Been no sign of him over the Christmas period,' I said. Like every other racegoer, I'd been half expecting the strapper killer to strike again after the Boxing Day meeting. But it seemed as if the killer had taken a break himself over Christmas. Since the two girls at Flemington had been murdered, there had been no further killings.

'No, thank god. But it's only been, what, a week or so since the last two were killed.'

'When you say it like that, it sounds like he's overdue for another.'

'I didn't mean it like that.'

'No, I know what you mean.'

Kate took another sip and played with the stem of the glass in her fingers. 'There're some more details starting to come through about the killings,' she said. 'You're bound to see a bit more about it in the papers over the next few days.'

'Oh, like what?'

'You probably know that not everything gets released to the press by the police at a murder. They don't like to panic people, so they just feed us journos the bare bones and hope we'll go away. However, things are starting to surface now that simply can't be suppressed any longer.'

'Like what?'

Kate thought about it for a moment. 'Well, for example, all the victims had been reported as dying of injuries inflicted by a knife. Now, what's that tell you?'

'That they'd all been stabbed to death?'

'Right, but there's stabbing and then there's *stabbing*. I've seen the official police photographs; those girls had their throats slit and their bodies mutilated. It was a frenzy of rips and slashes that beggars belief. I've never seen anything like it.'

Kate's seen plenty of spilt blood and bodies in her line of work. And I know she's not one to bullshit. It sounded bad.

'I've got some pretty good contacts down at St Kilda Road, as you know.'

That was no bullshit either. You didn't write the stories Kate did without a network of police and underworld contacts. She had both.

'Well,' she continued, 'I'm milking them for all they're worth. A guy I know in forensics confirmed that all of the girls, with the exception of one of the double murders at Flemington, had been raped. They've completed the DNA analysis of the semen samples, all of which have been identified as belonging to the one, as yet unidentified offender.'

'The strapper killer, obviously,' I said.

Kate nodded and continued on. 'Well, that will now become public knowledge. As will the killer's trademark signature, *Silk Chaser*.'

'Wow, you really are in the loop.'

'It's my job, remember? There's one other thing. Forensics has detected traces of an unusual clothing fibre left by the killer on each of the victims.'

I made a face. '*Unusual*, what's that supposed to mean?'

'It could mean they haven't identified it yet, or they're not letting on yet what it is. Either way, the killer's left his tracks on each of the women he's killed.'

We'd polished off the champagne and I looked at the empty bottle and then at Kate.

'I'd better go,' she said, standing up slowly to let Che slide off her lap. He jumped down with a little chirping protest and then milled around, brushing against her legs.

'There's no hurry. At least Che doesn't think so.'

'I've got to be somewhere in half an hour,' she said.

'Oh. Noel?' I said. Not so subtle.

'Nathan, actually.'

Really should try to remember names. 'Of course. Sorry. Nathan's . . . well?'

Kate nodded quickly. 'Mmm, he's fine. And Maxine?'

'She's completely over the knock to her head. Busy with work and things. She's fine, too.'

'Well then, I guess we're all just . . . fine.'

Bit awkward, the parting moment. Both of us putting up imaginary fences that we knew we shouldn't jump. I wished I could say something more meaningful to her; ask her if she was happy with the guy or something. But the fence stayed in place and Kate said goodnight and turned around and left.

It was only seven thirtyish and I was at a bit of a loose end. I hadn't had dinner yet and I felt like eating out, but I also felt like a bit of company. Who to call up at short notice? Maxine was a no-go tonight, at least till nine thirty, she'd said. Yet another bloody meeting with that new law firm she was doing work for. I don't know why they couldn't meet during regular working hours. I suppose that clever partner Ellis, who Maxine was forever going on about, was so busy coining it during the day he could only meet at night. I thought about going over to Maxine's later after dinner, spending the night at her place. But she'd only be tired and grumpy after working, so I decided I was better off seeing her on the weekend. I thought about phoning Tiny, but remembered that he'd be bouncing on a Wednesday night. Besides I'd already played some snooker with him and David the night before. On my fridge door there was a flyer

I had stuck up from a new Chinese takeaway that had opened down the road. Maybe I'd order in.

Che looked at me pathetically from his empty feeding bowl on the kitchen floor.

'No, Che. I think you'll find you've actually *had* dinner tonight.'

A hopeful purr of denial.

'As evidenced by the empty Fussy Feline box in the bin.'

Meow. Could be yesterday's?

'Nice try, but I don't think so, buster. If you're good,' I continued, 'I'll bring you back some of my Seafood Delight.'

Why order in when I owned a restaurant? I was off to Gino's.

The boom gates at the Kooyong level crossing had just swung shut to let a train through. I was cursing them because they take forever to open and I knew if I'd left ten minutes earlier I'd be at Gino's by now and digging into a pizza.

My mobile rang; it was Beering.

'Where are you?' he said gruffly.

'And hello to you, too,' I said.

'Never mind the niceties, I need to see you. Are you at home?'

'I'm at Gino's, or I will be in five minutes.'

'You bloody well live at that place. Good. I'll meet you there, then.'

'Are you chasing tips for Saturday or you want to share a pizza with me?'

'There's a girl they've found. In Newmarket.'

'Newmarket, Flemington? Christ, another strapper killing?'

'It's a strapper killing all right, but I'm talkin' Newmarket in *England.*'

'That's a long way from here.'

'It's the girl who brought a rape charge against Kagan Hall and then went missing.'

'I remember her. She did a disappearing act and Hall's charges were dropped.'

'Yeah, well, she's not the only one to pull a disappearing act. Kagan Hall's gone too, vanished.'

Beering was waiting for me in his car parked out the front of Gino's. He got out when he saw me, and we walked in together. The place was full except for the one small table I keep permanently reserved down the back. Billy winked at me from over the counter and greeted me like a long-lost friend. 'How's it goin', Punter? Table for two, is it?'

'Hi Billy. Can you fit us in?'

'Always find room for a regular like you.'

Billy showed us to my table and then returned promptly to plant a couple of ice-cold Beck's down in front of us without even asking.

'Compliments of the house, fellas,' said Billy cheerfully. 'Usual pizza?' he asked me. I nodded.

'I'll have what he's having,' said Beering.

'Two Seafood Delights it is, then,' said Billy, leaving us to it.

'I dunno how you do it, Punter,' said Beering enviously. 'Score a table on a night when the place is chockers. Don't even have to order drinks; they're comped. Fair dinkum, you must have shares in this joint.'

'I'm a good customer,' I protested. 'They look after me here.'

Beering scoffed and thrust his chin towards the front window. 'Hey, didn't this place have trouble with a broken window a week or so ago? I remember driving past and saw some shutters up.'

'I believe so. Probably some bored teenager with nothing better to do. Billy reckons they all ought to do compulsory national service to keep 'em off the streets.'

'I'd vote to that.'

Beering took a swig of his beer, set it down in front of him and clasped it with his fingers. 'They found the body of that girl in the UK who pressed rape charges against Kagan Hall. He heard about it and now it looks like he's done a runner. We need to find him as soon as we can.'

'Hang on, Jim, bit too fast for me. You want to start from scratch?'

Beering seemed impatient to get on with it, but he obligingly went back to the beginning.

'Sonia Lockwood, the girl who disappeared five years ago after laying rape charges against Hall, was found in a thicket near the Newmarket training tracks.'

'I'm tipping she didn't die of natural causes.'

'No, she didn't,' said Beering, his face serious. 'She died from multiple stab wounds, a similar method used by the strapper killer over here.'

'Are you saying it's the same guy – Hall?'

'You'll make a copper yet, son. The killings are certainly comparable. Hall had a motive to kill Lockwood. He also had the perfect defence; no dead body for police to take the charges any further, until now. And the strapper killings here and the one in the UK are suspiciously alike.'

'What about other signs of his handiwork, like the lipstick messages on their bedroom walls and mirrors?'

'Dunno yet. But I'll tell you something for nothin', the cops in the UK are looking closely at any unsolved murders or disappearances involving female stablehands that Hall could possibly be connected to. His travel itinerary also happens to fit in all too conveniently, with Hall leaving England after Sonia Lockwood disappeared and then resettling in Australia. Hall might have flown under the radar if you hadn't passed on your observations about him, Punter.'

That was probably the closest to a thank you that I'd ever receive from Beering.

'Did they manage to question Hall about those two girls killed at Flemington last week before he shot through?'

'They did. He was supposedly up-country looking at some horses at the time they were killed. In the context of what's happened since, I think they'll re-check that story. Think they'll re-check a lot of things about Kagan Hall.'

'How did Hall get to hear about the UK girl's body being found from over here?'

'Their local police reopened the case, put out an APB for Hall and contacted his London solicitor for his last known where-abouts. The solicitor made contact with Hall and suggested it would go better for him if he voluntarily gave himself up for questioning in a lawyer's presence. They could probably smell another earn in it; Hall's last legal bill must have lined their pockets. In the meantime, Interpol have been swapping notes about him with our Homicide boys. They went around to his house to pick him up for questioning late this afternoon.'

'And?'

'And no Hall. He'd pissed off. Looks like they just missed him.'

Billy brought out our pizzas and another round of beers and we continued on while tucking into our Seafood Delights.

'Jesus, they make a top pizza, this joint,' said Beering, mopping a hand over his chin. 'I used to think old man Gino was the best, but the young bloke who runs it now is pretty good. Is he the owner?'

'One of them. I believe there's a couple of blokes involved.'

Beering nodded, swallowed, got back down to business. 'Anyway, Hall; we gotta find him. You got any ideas where he might be?'

I shook my head. 'But unless he's got a bolthole somewhere, he's got nowhere to hide. He can't go to a horse sale or a race meeting anywhere in the country. He's too well known. I mean, he's plastered his face in ads across every formguide in the country. He may as well have put up his own wanted posters.'

'What about Maxine? He was her client; perhaps he may have let something slip to her?'

'Yeah, worth a try, or even her father; Hall and him were pals at the track. Jesus, to think how closely Maxine worked with that creep over the past few weeks.'

'Might have been the very thing that protected her. The fact he was too well known to her and her father.'

'It looks like you've finally found your man,' I said.

'Well, he's a suspect on the run, is what he is. But now that we know who he is, it's only a matter of time before he's picked up.'

14

They found Hall the very next morning.

Witnesses said they saw a car pull up on the Westgate Bridge. A guy got out, walked to the railing and stood for a moment before placing his hands on the rail and launching himself over the side. There was no suicide note found. No final confession as to what he'd done or why. But some of the missing pieces were starting to emerge. A police search of Hall's house revealed an incriminating pile of clippings about the strapper killings. Every article, every paper's story had been cut out and stored neatly in a folder in his desk. That evidence alone wouldn't convict the man, but it sure as hell didn't do him any favours, and neither would the large collection of pornography they found on his computer.

The media had a tricky one to report. They didn't have all the facts yet, but it wasn't hard to fill in the gaps. Some went straight for the blazing headlines. *The Sun* had 'Suspected strapper killer takes own life' and *The Post*'s was guaranteed to sell copies: 'Strapper killer cheats the noose'. Capital punishment had been abolished in this state after Ronald Ryan was hanged in the sixties, but that wasn't going to stop a gruesome headline as far as they were concerned. I thought Kate's piece was as good as any I'd read; it was certainly more balanced.

RACEHORSE SYNDICATOR FOUND DEAD

Kagan Hall, director of Winning Ways racehorse syndications, has been found dead in the waters by the pylons of the Westgate Bridge. Police believe there were no suspicious circumstances surrounding his death. Hall, a resident of Australia for the past five years, recently had a warrant issued for his arrest for the alleged murder of Sonia Lockwood in England. Ms Lockwood had pressed rape charges against Hall several years ago, but then vanished in mysterious circumstances which eventually caused police to drop the charges against Hall. It is believed that police reopened the case after the recent discovery of her body near Newmarket heath. The cause and nature of Lockwood's death and Hall's alleged involvement have drawn comparisons with the murders perpetrated by Melbourne's notorious strapper killer. Police investigating the recent strapper killings have refused to comment on the case until further lines of inquiry have been completed. It is believed that detectives from Scotland Yard will fly into Melbourne later this week to discuss further aspects of the UK case with local police.

Although the police hadn't confirmed it yet, it was looking like Hall was the one. Maxine was convinced. I'd dropped around to her place on Friday night to tee up arrangements for the races the next day.

'I can't believe I actually worked for a psycho like that,' she said. 'I mean, shit, I could have been one of his victims.'

'I've talked about this with Beering; it's probably because you knew him so well as a client that he was never tempted to try it with you. Any attempt on your life by him would lead a trail straight to his door. His go was stalking strangers.'

Maxine let out a shudder of revulsion. 'You never really know someone, do you? Something like this happens and you find out they're leading a double life. I tell you what I am going to do, though.'

'What?'

'Delete any reference to Winning Way and Kagan Hall from my portfolio of clients. There's no way I'm having a serial killer on my résumé.'

'Yeah, maybe it wouldn't hurt to leave him out,' I said,

stretching back on her sofa. 'I once had a mate who worked as an HR consultant. Said he got a résumé sent to him by a Middle Eastern mechanical engineer trying to find a job in Australia. The bloke was highly qualified, the sort of contractor that consultants can hawk around the big companies at a hundred dollars an hour. Anyway, this guy couldn't pick up a job for love or money. And this was in the middle of the resources boom when skilled contractors were really hard to find.'

'What was his problem?'

'His résumé. My mate went over it, trying to trim it into shape, when he came across what he called the "Never-to-be-hired" info. Turns out this guy had worked for a construction company in India for six years that specialised in large civil engineering projects.'

'Sounds a pretty stable work history to me. What was wrong?'

'The company. He was working for Bin Laden Constructions. Bit awkward trying to get a reference from his previous boss, don't you think? Especially after the Twin Towers came down. I think most prospective employees sort of put it in the too-hard basket.'

'More information supplied than was necessary.'

'Exactly.'

'That settles it. The last three months of work I've done is going to appear on my résumé as *consultancy work*.'

Maxine got up from the sofa and helped herself to another glass of wine from the fridge. 'Want a refill, sweetie?' she asked me.

'No, I'm fine. I was heading home after this anyway, still got some form to do. Just dropped around to see about arrangements for tomorrow.'

Maxine was taking Princess Upstart to Flemington for the New Year's Day meeting. The filly's race was the strapper's prize and knowing Maxine like I did, I knew she'd probably gone to a lot of trouble to make both her and the horse stand out.

'Wait till you see what my outfit is!' she said excitedly. 'I've been out shopping today. You want to see what I'm going to wear?'

I laughed. 'I do, but you can surprise me tomorrow. I'm sure you'll look stunning. What about the horse, what are you going to do to make her catch the judge's eye?'

'Don't worry about the Princess,' she said confidently. 'Your brother and I have got it all organised. David's going to shampoo her up after she works tomorrow and wash her mane and tail and make sure her two white socks come up extra bright and shiny.'

'Sounds like an ad for Omo,' I said.

'I know; whiter than white. And I've got some lovely tartan ribbon I'm going to tie into her mane and bridle. It's the same colour as Dad's silks. It'll look stunning on her at the track.'

'Now, speaking of the track; shall I still meet you at the stables and go with you in the float to the races and back?'

Maxine shrugged. 'There's no need to bother with the security thing, now that Hall's topped himself. But why don't you come with me anyway, be a bit of fun.'

'I can play at being an assistant to the strapper,' I said cheekily. 'Who knows what we might get up to in the back of the float?'

'Is that what happened in your strapping days?'

'You'd be surprised what you can do in the back of a float.'

'You're lucky my father didn't decide to travel with us, the way he carried on at the Christmas party. My god, you bait him.'

'Me? I'm only giving him back what he dishes out to me. Hey, speaking of your old man, I heard him on the radio this morning. He was strangely quiet about the strapper killings compared to what he's been like the past couple of weeks.'

'What did he say?'

'It's what he didn't say. For the past month, he's been getting stuck into the police commissioner, the VRC chairman, criminal psychologists and anyone else he could find with a remote interest in the case. I thought this morning he'd be all over Hall's death. Especially with the body in the UK turning up and the stuff they found in Hall's house. But he was like, "The police have still got a lot of work ahead of them before it can be proven conclusively that Hall was the strapper killer . . . Let's give them the space and time they need to examine the evidence, di dah, di dah." It just struck me as a bit out of character. Usually he goes for the jugular.'

Maxine put a thoughtful finger to her lips. 'You know what it is? Dad and Hall were pretty chummy at the track. He'd be feeling pretty down about it. I think he probably feels betrayed that he gave his friendship to someone who turned out to be a nutter. He did a lot for Kagan in business, put a lot of leads his way. I haven't really spoken to him since the Christmas party. I might give him a call now, see how he's feeling.'

I took that as my exit cue and stood up. 'You don't want me around while you're talking to your father.'

'And you don't really want to be here when I do,' she said, reaching for the phone. She blew me a kiss. 'I'll see you at the stables tomorrow.'

Next morning I drove around to Parraboo Lodge. I parked my van inside the owner's car park right next to Maxine's sporty little coupe. David was in the office at the back of his house; I could see him talking on the phone through the window. He waved at me to come inside.

'I've got something for you,' he said, finishing his call and putting the phone down. 'You'll need this.'

He passed me an official stablehand registration card. I picked it up and checked it over. Something like a cross between a credit card and a driver's licence; very official looking.

'Back when I was strapping, they didn't have these things. It was bring your own pay and a cut lunch.'

David grinned at me. 'Back in the day, eh? Shows how long you've been out of the saddle. Things have changed. These days you can't lead a racehorse out of its box without one of these.'

'This says I'm registered until the end of July? I only need a day pass to go with Maxine.'

'They don't issue these like ski lift tickets. It costs the same to register you for the year as it does for a meeting.'

'Oh. I thought perhaps I was going to get press-ganged into working at the stables again. Chained up and have to do hard labour mucking out the boxes.'

He laughed. 'It was never that bad, was it?'

'Felt like a sentence to me.'

'Your problem was the chief warden.'

'Dad? Yeah, maybe. He's softened a bit since those days, but I was glad to break out, when I did.'

'And now you're back in the nick.'

'Just for old times' sake.'

There was a sharp rap on the window and David waved at someone outside. 'The farrier. I'd better go. The filly's in box eighteen. Maxine's already been here for half an hour getting her ready. I'll see you out there.'

I strolled under the archway opposite the tack room. Neat rows of stables lined the yard overlooking a freshly hosed-down bitumen courtyard. Box eighteen was just along the line and I could see the door ajar and hear Maxine talking to her horse as she went about getting it ready. I walked up to find her busily grooming Princess Upstart.

'If you shine that horse up any more, I'm going to need sunglasses to look at her.'

Maxine turned around in surprise. 'Oh, hello sweetie, I didn't hear you. What do you think, have I missed anything? I'll put the finishing touches on her at the track, of course.'

Maxine had pulled and plaited Princess Upstart's mane into half a dozen little rosettes. It must have taken her a good deal of time and effort. It was the sort of thing you see in Europe; wasn't very often strappers bothered with dressing their horses up to that degree in Australia.

'She looks a proper princess. And so do you.'

On reflection, Maxine's outfit had me puzzled; a set of tatty, grey tradesman's overalls. Not something I figured would catch a judge's eye in the strapper's contest. 'Er, that what you're wearing today?'

'No, silly! Of course not. It's what I've got on *under* these that I'll be parading. I'm not going to risk getting my gear dirty before the event.'

I might have known Maxine would plan for that. She was taking this seriously, all right. A horn like a cargo ship's sounded out the front of the stables.

'Float's here,' she said. 'Can you grab the race bag outside the door?'

We loaded Princess Upstart onto Garrett's big nine-horse float and she walked straight on board without any fuss. Dad only had the one runner entered for today, so there was just me and Maxine sitting in the compartment behind the driver to begin with. Then the driver stopped around the corner at the community stables and picked up another seven horses from the trainers there. One other horse had joined ours in the front, handled by a cheeky-faced, gum-chewing apprentice who told us with absolute certainty that his horse 'was a moral' today.

'Governor's Orders, mate. Race six. Can't be beat. It worked the place down on Thursday.'

'Is that right?' I said. I knew the horse, a perennial 'morning glory', a horse who'd always put in a star-studded track gallop, but never produce in a race.

'Yep. You wanna have something on her, you know.' He patted his shirt pocket; 'I'm havin' me wages on her, I am.'

The kid had made an effort to dress up, as far as apprentice jockeys go; an orange shirt with sleeves that came to his knuckles. A flashy cartoon-character tie at half-mast. His shoes were badly in need of a polish and he was wearing a black suit jacket that was a size too big. When he saw me looking, he proudly straightened it up by the lapels.

'Bag of fruit, today,' he said. 'Classy, eh? Boss said I gotta look me best for the strapper's comp. Reckon I can win it, too. Crack the big double.'

Maxine gave me a dig in the ribs. 'We're in that race, too,' she said to him, nodding to the horse box behind her. 'Princess Upstart.'

He gave Maxine a cursory glance and then looked back at Princess Upstart's head poking through the compartment. 'Nah,' he said, resuming his gum-chewing, 'you may as well have stayed at home. I'm a certainty.'

When we arrived at the track I carried in the raceday bag and the light rug and Maxine led her horse into the stalls. We passed through security; they still had the guards in place at the horse stalls, although with the news about Hall jumping off the Westgate, the tension and the wariness seemed to have eased. Unlike last week, they just waved me through without bothering to inspect my pass. I must have looked official carrying the rug and bag. I helped Maxine hose and scrape the filly down, and when we came back to the stalls, she tied the tartan ribbons into the filly's mane.

'How does she look?'

Very showy, I had to admit. She was a flashy liver chestnut and that colour stood out anyway. But her two white socks, the star on her forehead and the tartan ribbons would almost guarantee she'd draw attention. There was something else that wouldn't go unnoticed either.

'That's not Dad's usual race bridle is it?'

'No, it's not,' said Maxine nonchalantly. 'I bought a white plastic one from the saddlers yesterday. DJ's plain old leather bridles are *so* boring. I've got to make her stand out from the crowd. I bought some matching reins too.'

God knew what my father was going to think of this latest intrusion into his training procedures. I supposed he'd handle it in his usual diplomatic way.

'Now, can you do me a favour,' she said, 'just mind her a moment while I go and get changed?'

I'd forgotten about that. Maxine would want to slip out of her overalls and into whatever it was she was wearing.

'That's fine, go. I'll look after her.'

'Don't go letting her rub against the stalls and dirty herself, will you?'

'No, I'll watch her. I *have* done this before,' I said.

Maxine took off with her tote bag to the ladies' room and I played at being strapper. Been a while since I'd done that; ten years or so. You never forget; it's like riding a bike. Princess Upstart started pawing at the straw on the stall floor and I pulled up her head collar gently and gave her a friendly rebuke. 'Hey, don't go doing that. You'll spring a shoe.'

'Yeah, you wouldn't want that to happen, would you?' said Tiny. He was with Louise, and Ric and Matt were also in tow. They'd spotted me from the other side of the fence and I hadn't noticed them walk up.

'You must be travelling bad, mate,' said Tiny with a grin, 'havin' to take horses to the races for your old man.'

'G'day guys,' I said. 'I'm actually helping out Maxine. She's strapping her father's horse today.'

'Looks like she's gone off for a bet and left you doing all the work,' joked Matt.

'She's actually getting changed for the strapper's competition.'

'She's going in that?' said Ric.

'Yep, been her plan since the prize was announced.'

Louise immediately offered her support. 'Oh, we'll have to barrack for her. I'll bet she does well, she always dresses like a million dollars.'

''Bout what she's spent on this damn thing.'

Louise scolded me, 'Go on, you'll be proud of her if she wins. We'll all look out for her in the parade ring. Are you going to be lending a hand to help her lead it around?'

'God, no. I'll be relinquishing my duties as soon as she comes back. I'll see you all out by the mounting yard before her race.'

I met them all there on the lawn by the mounting yard about forty minutes later as the first of the horses was due to appear. Tiny was leaning over the rail, his timber-tall frame towering over Louise, who was checking her race book. Ric, as usual, was lecturing Matt on some flaw in his betting strategies. When I joined them, Louise was genuinely excited about Maxine's chances in the strapper's prize.

'What's she wearing, tell us?'

I had to admit I honestly didn't know.

'How could you not notice what she's wearing?'

I explained, 'She wore overalls on the way over to stop herself getting dirty. Then, she went and changed when I saw you guys. David came by shortly after and offered to mind the horse until Maxine returned, so I haven't seen what she's got on. Knowing her, she won't do things by half.'

The two judges for the competition had walked out and were standing in the middle of the yard next to a podium with the name 'Laskers Insurance' on it. They were joined by a roly-poly committeeman, who waddled up and stood alongside them. In a moment, the horses started to file in and the committeeman made an announcement.

'Ladies and gentleman, in the following race a prize and trophy will be awarded by our sponsors, Laskers Insurance, for the best turned out horse and strapper. The winner will be announced as the horses are parading before they go out on to the track.'

'What do they get if they win?' asked Matt.

'A grand plus the silverware,' I said, pointing to a trophy sitting on a small table to the side of the podium.

'For that prizemoney, I should have entered myself,' said Matt. 'Only I'm afraid of horses if I get too close. Like to keep this between me and them,' he said, patting the fence.

The first of the horses had wound their way around the yard and were now walking past us. The cheeky apprentice with the cartoon-character tie was leading the top weight, Governor's Orders, around.

'He'll get noticed,' said Tiny.

'I rode with him on the float over,' I said. 'Told me he was a certainty to win the strapper's prize and the race.'

'I dunno about him. What about the horse, can it win?'

'I like the old man's horse better. He's set it for this race and she loves the Flemington mile.'

A few more horses and strappers went by. A couple of guys wore suits and ties. But overall, the girls seemed to have their measure. They were obviously prettier, seemed to be having more fun and they also appeared to have taken that little bit of extra time in doing something special for their horses. A smiling redhead led a horse past us. Louise said, 'She's easily the best so far.'

It was hard to disagree. She wore crisp white jodhpurs, highly polished riding boots and a bright red skivvy that showed off her figure. She'd put some serious time into her horse, too: diamond brush marks on the horse's flanks, and she'd put a single red ribbon which matched her top in her horse's mane. Some other horses passed us. Tiny dug me in the ribs when the apprentice walked by again.

'Have a go at that kid, the cheeky little bastard,' he said, pointing. I hadn't noticed before, but he was wearing a notice pinned onto his back which said *Vote for me*. It got a laugh from the crowd, but I don't know if it would endear him to the judges. Other strappers and their horses were better presented, and far easier on the eye. Especially Maxine.

She walked into the mounting yard like a model strutting a catwalk, sporting a smile that every male thought was for them and them alone. She could do that, turn on the shine button. Clothes? I don't know how much she'd spent, but the knee-high leather show-jumping boots alone would have cost a strapper a month's wages. You just don't see stablehands wear boots that high, except if they're competing in the Garyowen. But Maxine wore them and carried it off magnificently. She wore the oblig-atory jodhpurs, white, tight and figure-hugging, showing off those long shapely legs of hers before they disappeared into the calves of her boots. Her top, like everyone else's, was hard to see, because they made them all wear a pinafore with their horse number on it. It was something short-sleeved and simple. But when you're stacked like she is, you're going to be noticed. The thing that got everyone talking, though, was the hat. I don't know how she did it; she'd certainly kept it a secret from me. It was a men's style fedora with an exaggerated crown and a turned-up back brim, and she had it covered with the same tartan-coloured silks that her rider would wear. Just for effect, she had a huge peacock feather sticking out the side. I could see the judges busily nodding amongst themselves and taking notes. When the jockeys came out and mounted their horses, you could see how well Maxine's hat combined with the jockey's silks. And she'd been right about the snow-white bridle, too. It drew your eye to the horse's head and neck where its carefully plaited mane with the tartan ribbons sewn into the rosettes stood out like a show horse. Tiny let out a long, low wolf whistle.

'Mate,' he said, turning to me, 'just give her the trophy now.'

'She deserves to win, Punter,' said Louise. 'The work she must have put in.'

Not everyone was as complimentary. I overheard a couple of women standing to the side of me jealously bitching about her.

'That's Russell Henshaw's daughter. She must have spent a fortune on that outfit and she's not even a real strapper. Just leads her father's horses in when she thinks they can win.'

'I know, the spoilt bitch. Look at the photographers grovelling around her. I hear she's on with one of DJ's sons.'

'Yeah, which one?'

'Does it matter? She'll drop him as soon as the next big thing comes around.'

Is that how others thought of Maxine? Did she provoke those sorts of feelings in total strangers? Was it just petty jealousy, gossip columnist tripe? I hate hearing people canning someone behind their back. It's not something I care to listen to and I moved closer towards Ric and Matt where I couldn't hear the two women slagging off about her. There was a scrum of photographers clicking away at Maxine as she led her horse by. That hat sure was causing some commotion. The attendants walked around for another few laps, letting everyone get a good look at them. Then when the roly-poly committeeman called for everyone's attention, a hush came over the mounting yard.

'Ladies and gentleman, the judges have selected the winner of the strapper's prize: Maxine Henshaw and her horse Princess

Upstart. Can you please show your appreciation for Maxine and all of the contestants with a big round of applause.'

There was some polite clapping from the crowd. A few cheers and some wolf whistles greeted Maxine as she accepted her trophy and the prize money cheque. Her father appeared out of nowhere and gave her a hug. More photos by the press of the Henshaw family. I could just about see the headlines in tomorrow morning's papers now.

It got even better. Princess Upstart hung on to beat the favourite in a tight finish. I watched the race in the stand and walked back down as the runners returned to the mounting yard. It looked like round two had commenced for the photographers, as they jostled amongst themselves for still more shots of Maxine in *that* hat. They snapped her as she waited for her horse to come back to scale. Then they encircled her after the jockey had unsaddled, a battery of lenses and flashing lights. It was one of the few times I'd seen a horse's jockey or trainer go unnoticed. Finally my old man had had enough.

'For God's sake, David,' he said to my brother, 'get that damn horse out of here and take her back to her stalls. Bloody place has turned into a fashion show.'

15

Late on Tuesday afternoon, I dropped by Maxine's place with a surprise seafood package. Tasmanian oysters and a King Island crayfish, fresh from the Prahran market where I'd stopped on the way back from the races. Totally spontaneous, of course. I didn't feel like cooking and I knew Maxine never did; she usually ate out or ordered in so I thought I'd treat us both to an easy-fix meal. I rang her from the markets and told her not to worry about dinner, it was all taken care of. She told me she'd be another hour by the time she finished up her work with Freedales in the city and said not to worry about buying wine, there was plenty in the fridge. That was true. I couldn't see much food inside – par for the course – but there were a dozen bottles to choose from, none of them cheap labels. I placed the oysters and the cray inside the fridge, then selected a bottle with a skite list of medals as long as your arm. I poured myself a glass and then sat down on the couch with my feet up on the cushion to wait for her.

On her lounge-room table was the silver strapper's trophy she'd won on Saturday with the now-famous hat casually hanging over it. What a wild night that had been. Celebrations on a grand scale, of course, and that had meant sharing the night with both Maxine and her father. At least Henshaw had invited an entourage along to the restaurant to share in the festivities. Joining us were my father and mother, David and his fiancée and the winning jockey, which meant I didn't have to spar with Henshaw all night. Maxine had plonked her trophy in the middle of the table and, despite changing into another outfit for dinner, was still wearing her hat. I think one of the waiters must have tipped off the papers. With a celebrity like Henshaw and his daughter dining in, a bit of publicity never hurt. Within half an hour of us being there, a couple of photographers appeared and started snapping away. They took shots of Maxine and her father and I even consented to put up with her sitting in my lap with her arm around me while she modelled the damn hat. *Flash, flash, flash.* Caught on camera, buddy, whether you like it or not. Yeah; a big night out and some more photos from the gossip columns to add to my collection.

I took another sip of wine. Went down a treat after a long day at the track. Bloody Sandown, hot as a sauna in the summer. Didn't help that I'd done my arse on an afternoon when I probably should have gone surfing instead. But in Maxine's lounge room it was lovely and cool. The evening sea breeze was just starting to blow in through the flyscreen door, which led onto the deck out the back. I got up and unsnipped the lock, slid open the door and took in the view of the city skyline.

'Hi sweetie. I'll join you there. Just get myself a drink.'

I hadn't heard Maxine let herself in, but as I turned around to greet her, I could hear her sounding off enthusiastically about my seafood package in the fridge.

'Yum, what a great idea! Let's eat out on the deck.'

I walked back into the kitchen to give her a hand and gave her a kiss on the cheek as she loaded herself up with the wine and seafood.

'Can you grab a couple of plates and large bowl for the shells?'

'I got it,' I said.

Within minutes we'd put away the oysters. A dozen each don't go far, especially when you're as hungry as we both were. Then we started on the crayfish. I cracked the shell open on top of the spread of newspapers they'd been wrapped in. It's the easiest way to get to the white, succulent flesh and you can make as much mess as you like without having to worry about the juices squirting all over you.

'Mmm,' said Maxine.

I licked my lips. 'Should have bought two, the way we're getting through this.'

'I can make you dessert, if you like. Crepes?'

I must have looked doubtful.

'What? I can make dessert. I can cook; I can.'

'I'm not saying you can't. It's just that I've never seen you cook anything.'

'I did you poached eggs last week.'

'As I recall, you walked down to the bakery for a loaf of bread and I ended up making the eggs.'

She winked at me. 'A mere technicality. The intention was there.'

'Anyway, I'll have to pass on the dessert. It's Tuesday night, snooker with the guys at the Triangle.'

'Sounds like fun.'

'You want to come?'

'Nah, it's a guy thing. I'll soak myself in a hot bath and put on lotions and potions and make myself beautiful for you on your return. You are coming back tonight, aren't you?'

'Three hours, tops. By then, I'll have had enough of Tiny's cracks about that photo of you and me last Saturday.'

She made a face at me. 'I bet Tiny's just jealous.'

Tiny wasn't jealous, but he was in one of his stirring moods.

'Mate,' he said, lining up the blue ball, 'we didn't figure you'd be playin' tonight. Did we fellas?' he said to the others. David and Myles grinned knowingly.

'And why wouldn't I make it along tonight?' I asked.

Tiny hit the cue ball low. Lots of bottom spin; it potted the blue ball in the bottom left pocket and rolled back obediently for another shot at the cluster of reds.

'We thought you'd still be at the optometrist.'

Could see where he was going with this, played along anyway. 'The optometrist?'

'Yeah. We figured he'd still be tryin' to pull that feather out of your eye.'

The photo. Maxine sitting on my lap at the restaurant with the damn hat feather nearly spearing my pupil. 'Ha, ha. That's very funny.'

They thought it was a hoot. Broke out into loud guffaws all around.

'Hey, it won her the strapper's prize, that hat,' said David. 'Don't knock it.'

'I wouldn't mind a good sort getting photographed sittin' on my lap,' said Myles.

'Yeah, well, Maxine's spoken for,' I said.

'Hey, speakin' of Maxine, she did all the PR work for that Kagan Hall guy, didn't she?' said Myles.

I nodded. 'Yep. Least she did up until last week when he took the big drop.'

Tiny stopped sizing up his cue for a moment and stood upright. 'It didn't surprise me, him being the strapper killer. Especially when they found that girl in the UK he'd killed.'

'Supposedly killed.'

'Ah, don't talk like a fuckin' lawyer, Punter. He raped her and killed her, just like he did all these poor girls over here.'

David joined in. 'You gotta admit, all that stuff they found when they searched his place – newspaper clippings of all the strappers killed, the porn on his computer. Scotland Yard wouldn't send a man all the way over here unless they were sure. I bet Maxine must have been pretty shocked to find out her client was a killer?'

'Well, she wasn't exactly impressed,' I said. 'But she reckoned she never felt uncomfortable around him. Maybe because he was her client he kept his distance. It's pretty chilling though, to think what he'd been getting up to.'

'Bet the racing clubs are glad it's all over,' said David. 'The security guards must have cost a packet.'

'And the cops, too. They must be relieved,' said Myles.

'Not half as relieved as the strappers,' said Tiny. 'They'll sleep easier at night from now on.'

After a few games of doubles, we called it quits about eleven and trooped down the wooden stairs. Tiny suggested a coffee in Brunswick Street, like we usually did.

'What about you, Punter, or you wanna get home?'

'No, I'm not in any hurry. I could go a coffee and something to eat.'

We found a little café about a block's walk from the Triangle. I had a short black and got suckered into a Danish pastry. They have all these cakes sitting in those rotating glass displays; too much of a temptation for me. We ended up staying another forty minutes or so talking and eating and sipping our coffees before finally calling it a night.

Half an hour later, I drove back and parked my van outside Maxine's apartment. The block's got an over-the-top security system if you ask me. Anything more than one lock and you've lost me; this place had three. You needed to get through an outside gate, then the foyer door, before finally having to unlock the apartment door. Thankfully they'd made the one key fit all entrances. I let myself in and walked up the stairwell to Maxine's apartment on the second level. When I got to her door, I opened it and then shut it softly, not wanting to wake her. She'd left a light on and the flyscreen door was slightly ajar. Her backpack was on the floor next to the door; must have left it there when she came home. I poured myself a glass of water from the kitchen tap and stood for a moment sipping it next to the sink. I felt a bit sweaty after playing snooker and tossed up whether or not to take a shower. Maxine had an ensuite in her bedroom, but there was also a separate shower and bathroom in the guest room at the end of the hallway. I decided I'd use that so as not to disturb her. Her strapper's trophy was still on the table, but minus the hat, which was no longer hanging off it. As I walked past the table I saw a soft light on in her room. The door was open so I called out gently to her.

'Maxine, are you awake?'

No answer. Must have fallen asleep reading one of her trashy fashion magazines, like I'd seen her do before.

I called out again. 'Maxine? It's me. Just going to take a quick shower.'

Still no answer. I smiled to myself, imagining how I'd find her, flat on her back, sound asleep, with her magazine fallen by her side. I was about to take a quick peek in her room on the way to the guest shower when her bedside light suddenly switched off.

'Maxine?'

I stood still, halfway between her room and the dining-room table. Called her name once more, a bit louder this time. Nothing. I glanced back to the open flyscreen door and to her backpack by the door. I'd never seen her with a backpack before.

I trust my antenna; never known it to be wrong yet. And it was sending me signals, like *Something's wrong here; get out now.* I grabbed the strapper's trophy off the table. Then I walked slowly back down the hallway, clutching the thing like a club. I paused just outside Maxine's bedroom and stood silent, listening very hard.

Nothing.

Not a breath, not a snore. Unnaturally quiet.

I stood absolutely still. Strained my ears for the slightest noise for what seemed a few minutes at least. Then she screamed.

I burst into her room as the door rammed into my face. It copped me right on the side of the jaw and I dropped to the ground like I'd been king-hit. Maxine screamed again and I caught sight of hands slashing wildly down at me. The assailant had a knife and all I had was a damn trophy which I held out desperately in front of me for some protection. Then he hurtled over me and raced up the hallway. I caught a glimpse of the back of him as he leapt out the door onto the patio and made his escape down the outside stairs. I picked myself up, still holding the trophy tightly in my hand, and gave chase. When I got to the door, I saw a shape racing across the backyard. Then came the sound of fleeing footsteps as he clambered over the neighbouring back fence and disappeared.

Maxine yelled out. 'Punter!'

I ran back to her room and scrambled for the light switch, my fingernails madly scratching the wall until I located it and flicked it on. Maxine was cowering in the corner of the room on the floor, her hands tied in front of her. She had some duct tape wrapped around her mouth, which she'd somehow managed to pull down. Thank god she had or we'd both be dead. All she was wearing was her birthday suit and that stupid hat.

'Are you hurt, are you all right?' I squeezed my hands around her arms, not knowing what the crazy bastard had done to her. She shook her head in a trembling reply and I helped her up.

'If you hadn't come back when you did,' she said, 'he would have . . . he was about to . . .' She burst into tears and I held her to me. 'I was sure I was going to be raped and killed, just like the others. Are you sure he's gone?'

'Don't worry, he's pissed off, the gutless bastard. Let me get your hands untied.' Much as I tried, I couldn't free her. It felt like he'd bound her with some sort of heavy cord.

'Come into the kitchen and I'll cut through this with a knife. Here, put this on.' I slipped a robe around her shoulders, put an arm around her and walked her into the kitchen. I found a bread knife and sawed through the cord. When her hands were free, she buried her head against my chest and hugged me tightly, shaking and sobbing uncontrollably.

'You've hurt yourself,' she said, disengaging from me.

'Don't worry about me. I'm okay, it's you we've got to worry about.'

'No, look,' she said, holding up my right hand, which had some puncture marks in it. Blood was seeping down through my fingers.

'And your shoulder, you're cut. He's stabbed you.'

I could see the cut marks now that the shock was wearing off. Could feel it too. His knife must have cut my hand as I'd tried to defend myself with the trophy and he'd ripped into the flesh of my shoulder as well.

'It's not serious,' I said.

'I'm going to call triple 0; you grab a towel from the linen press in the hall to stop the bleeding.'

I found a couple of snow-white face washers in the cupboard. Seemed a shame to stain them with my blood, but I wrapped one around my right hand and held one under my shirt against my shoulder. I walked back along the hallway and paused outside Maxine's bedroom. I was vaguely aware that I shouldn't touch anything, that the police would probably treat it as a crime scene. The door was open, so I stood just outside and looked in. There weren't a lot of signs of a scuffle that were obvious. My guess was the guy had let himself in the back door, crept into her bedroom and pulled a knife on her as she slept. There was absolutely nothing she could have done to try to defend herself. It was just a fluke I'd come back when I had. Five minutes later and I may have been too late. Come home to her bloodied and naked corpse. I shuddered thinking about it and looked up at something that caught my eye; a flame-red message scribbled all over her mirror. It was written in a lipstick which was lying on the dresser underneath the mirror. The writing said: *I'm a filthy silk chaser. That's why I died.*

The police arrived within minutes, an ambulance close behind. When the police got the story from Maxine and me about what had happened and who the likely intruder was, they notified the Homicide team who'd been working on the strapper killer cases. Meanwhile the paramedics examined Maxine and me and told me I was a stitch job, that I needed to get to a hospital and be attended to. I didn't want to leave Maxine alone, but the police told me she'd be looked after by them and that her father had been notified and was on his way over. They also wanted to get her description of her attacker's face while it was fresh in her mind.

Later, at the hospital, a young nurse and an even younger-looking medic put the finishing touches to some sutures in my shoulder.

'You were extremely lucky,' the doctor said, not for the first time. 'No deep penetration wounds. Usually the defending hands take the brunt of it in knife attacks.'

'I had a sort of shield to fend him off with,' I said.

'Your shoulder, too, escaped largely unscathed. A minor flesh cut that could easily have found an artery. But you'll still need to take things easy and give it time to heal properly. In other words, no physical activity for at least a week.'

'No surfing?'

'Absolutely not.'

Two guys walked in as the doctor and nurse were finishing up.

'You should listen to your doctor, Punter,' said Beering. 'If he says no surfin' then that's what he means.' He jerked his head towards the other guy and introduced him. 'Detective Senior Sergeant Gordon Wells.'

Wells, like Beering, was wearing a suit. Except his was a dark grey. Didn't matter what time of day or night, plain-clothes cops always wore suits. I instinctively put my hand out, winced and immediately regretted it. Nodded at him instead.

'Stuck you with his knife, eh?' said Wells.

'The doctor says it's nothing serious,' I said. 'I'd hate to be treated for something that was.'

The doctor smiled at me as he and the nurse excused themselves from the room. 'Don't keep him up too long, he'll probably fall asleep on you anyway with the sedatives he's been given.'

When they'd gone, Wells grabbed one of the visitor chairs and pulled it closer to my bed. He sat down and looked me over professionally. He'd probably seen a few stabbing victims in his time.

'Should I start by telling you how lucky you and your girl-friend are to be alive?'

I nodded. 'Seems to be the word everyone's using tonight. It was him, wasn't it; the strapper killer? When everyone thought it must have been Hall.'

Beering sucked in a deep breath and let it out. 'Yeah, unfor-tunately that seems to be the case. I think everyone assumed that Hall would be the peg that fitted the hole. Now, after Hall's death and this new attack, we think different.'

'In fact,' said Wells, taking up where Beering had left off, 'Forensics hasn't found a trace of Hall's DNA on any of the victims so far. They've still got some testing to complete, but I can tell you there's not so much as a hair of Hall's anywhere near those girls. We've been barking up the wrong tree.'

'What about the girl they found in the UK, did he kill her?'

Wells sat with his arms crossed, leaning against one armrest. He gave a shrug. 'Probably. We may never know for sure. His suicide implies that he thought the game was up when they found her body. So now we're back to square one. Well, not quite. You and Maxine are the only ones who have had an encounter with the strapper killer and lived. It's the first break-through we've had. I know you're probably feeling a bit groggy, but we thought we'd get your version of what happened as soon as possible.'

I readjusted myself on the pillow and rubbed my eyes. The sedatives were starting to kick in, but sleep would have to wait.

'Anything to help catch him. What do you want to know?'

'Take us through the whole thing,' said Wells. 'I understand you walked in on him?'

'That's right. I'd had dinner with Maxine earlier in the night, and then went out for my regular Tuesday night snooker game with some pals. I got back a little after midnight and walked in to find him there.'

'You saw him as soon as you walked in?'

'No. I opened the door and there was a light on in the kitchen. I thought Maxine had gone to bed. The place was quiet; I didn't hear anything at first. I noticed the flyscreen door was ajar, but I just thought that Maxine must have forgotten to close it. There was a backpack lying on the floor by the door. I thought it was hers at first, until I realised I'd never seen her with one.'

Wells glanced sharply at Beering, then back at me. 'We didn't note any backpack in there. Must have been his little bag of goodies that he grabbed when he took off. What happened then?'

'I went to take a shower and could see from the hallway that Maxine had the bedside light on. I assumed she'd fallen asleep reading. I called out to her a couple of times. Just softly, you know, so as not to wake her if she was asleep. Then her light clicked off.'

'She didn't answer you?'

'No. No answer, no sound. I just stood there in the hallway and I sort of got a feeling that something wasn't right. I walked back to the lounge room and grabbed her trophy off the table; only thing I could think of as a weapon.'

Wells nodded. 'That trophy probably saved your life. I'll show it to you after we've finished with it at the lab. Got some pretty ugly slash marks on it.'

I grimaced. I hadn't escaped entirely unscathed. 'When I went back to her room, I stood at the doorway for a minute, listening. Then Maxine screamed out. I raced in, he slammed the door on me, then let fly with his knife. I think what helped me was that I'd fallen to the ground and was thrashing around with the trophy held out in front of me, so he couldn't get a clean go at me. Then he leapt over me and made a bolt for the back door. I got up and chased him as far as the door and I saw him climbing over the neighbour's back fence. Then Maxine yelled out and I went back to her.'

'Did you get a look at him?'

'I never actually saw his face. It was dark in the bedroom when I went in. But Maxine would have seen him for sure.'

Wells nodded. 'She says she did. He made no attempt to cover up. She didn't recognise him; we'll get her to go through our photo files and sit down with our facial imaging experts. But you're sure you couldn't identify him if you saw him again?'

I shook my head, trying to remember. It was all a blur. Serpent-like shadows clawing at me in the dark. Then, the outline of a man clambering over a fence. Like a bad black and white movie, really. Except it wasn't all black and white . . .

'There is another thing I remember. Not his face or anything.'

'No, please go on.'

213

'When he jumped over me and bolted to the back door, I was lying on the ground and could see the back of him disappearing in the light from the kitchen.'

'Yes.'

'He was wearing a funny-coloured stripy top and cap.'

Wells exchanged glances with Beering. 'Same as what Maxine described,' said Beering. 'When you say funny-coloured top, you mean what, like a pyjama top?'

I thought about it for a moment, trying to recall exactly what I'd seen. He'd been scrambling, panicking to get out the back door, and I'd been trying to get up off the floor, my head halfway out in the hallway watching him flee.

'No, not pyjamas,' I said. 'Silks. He was wearing jockey silks.'

16

They kept me at the hospital overnight for observation. I probably could have gone home if I'd pushed it, but it was three in the morning when Beering and Wells left and I was quite happy to snatch some sleep where I was. Normally shared hospital wards aren't my idea of a peaceful night's sleep, but Tuesday nights aren't overly busy apparently, and my room only had one elderly pensioner who'd fallen at a tram stop and broken his hip. Even his snores didn't keep me awake.

Early next morning I received an unexpected visitor when Maxine dropped by my bed. That wasn't a surprise. It was the person she'd brought with her who was: her father. He marched in sullenly behind Maxine and I couldn't tell from the scowl on his face whether I was going to get the elevator or the shaft. I half expected another outburst like when Maxine had been caught up in that taxi incident; that it was entirely my fault, what had happened last night. Maxine leant over and gave me a kiss on the cheek, then sat on my bed looking over the bandages on my hand and shoulder.

'You've been in the wars, sweetie.'

'We both have. You all right?'

Maxine looked tired and drained and although I'd never tell her to her face, she seemed to have aged ten years since last night. She attempted a smile but it couldn't hide all the trauma that I knew she'd been through, the shock of someone who knew they'd escaped certain death. She fidgeted for a moment with her hands, then dropped the pretence of the smile for a frown.

'What I got was a fright, the biggest scare in my life. If you hadn't come back when you did, I wouldn't be standing here now. Isn't that right, Dad?'

Henshaw made a clearing-his-throat noise. It was obvious he'd been dragged along to acknowledge the fact that I may have actually done his daughter a favour for once.

'If you hadn't fended him off with my trophy,' said Maxine, 'he'd have killed us both.' She put her hand in mine, my good one, thankfully, as there was a bit of a squeeze in it. I could see her reliving the nightmare of that moment. 'I can't tell you how frightened I was. You just . . . never think it can happen to you. When you're woken like that, a stranger holding a knife to your throat, your body just goes numb. I was in total shock. I couldn't think, couldn't do anything. And when he made me write that horrible message on my mirror, I knew with absolute certainty I was going to die.'

I squeezed her hand back gently. 'When I walked in,' I said, 'I saw the back door open and his backpack on the floor, which I thought was yours at the time. Seriously, you might want to look at getting some security grilles put over the outside patio.'

Maxine shook her head. 'I'm not going back there. I can't go back, *ever*. I'm going to sell the place, aren't I, Dad?'

Henshaw nodded. 'She's staying with me for the time being until we can sort it all out.'

Felt a pang of jealousy. Daddy always riding in like a white knight. I would have offered to put her up at my place and thought she may have at least run it by me first, but no sense in discussing it here and now. It was understandable, of course; her not wanting to set foot in a place where she was nearly killed and the perpetrator still at large.

'I don't think I'd go back there if I was in your shoes either. Let me know if you want a hand to move anything. Did the police speak to you last night?'

'I had to go down to the station and give a description of the guy and a statement after the medics had done with me. It seemed to take half the night. Dad's taking me down again now to go through some more identikit images with them. We just popped through to see you on the way over.'

'I'm going over myself later in the morning. Beering's calling by to pick me up.'

Maxine looked across at her father, standing to the side of my bed. He didn't seem very comfortable being there. Glanced down at his watch when he caught me looking at him.

'Well, it's nice of you to drop by. Bit of a role reversal isn't it, me being in hospital?'

She smiled and then looked at her father. 'Dad's got something he wants to tell you,' she said.

Oh, here it comes, another official warning-off, this time in front of his daughter.

'Dad, haven't you?'

'Yes. Maxine . . . that is, Maxine and I wanted to thank you for saving her life last night.' He looked down at his shoes, squinted at an imaginary scuff mark.

'*And?* Come on, Dad, the rest of it.'

Wait, there's more. I was starting to enjoy this. Not every day I got to see Henshaw thanking me, especially in front of Maxine.

He looked up from his shoes and met my eyes properly for the first time.

'As a token of my appreciation, er, our appreciation, I felt I should offer you a thank-you gift.'

'You don't have to do that.'

'No. I've made up my mind. I insist.'

Who was I to disagree?

'Tell him what you're giving him, Dad.'

'I'm giving you a half share in Princess Upstart.'

It must have hurt him. Not in the hip pocket. Because he could afford it. The thought of having to share a horse with his daughter's loser boyfriend. A most unlikely partnership. I smiled, thinking about it.

'Well?' said Henshaw.

I don't know what he expected me to do; grovel at his feet proclaiming his generosity? 'A half share, eh. No strings attached?'

'You could sound a bit more grateful.'

'Oh, don't get me wrong, I am. It's a very generous offer. I just like to know where I stand with these things, that's all.'

'No strings. A half share to do what you want with. I'll send you around the registration papers for signing.'

Business transacted, Henshaw started tugging at his cufflinks like it was time to leave. 'Well we'd better get you over to the police station then, if I'm to make my radio show on time,' he said to Maxine.

Maxine reached over and kissed me as she stood up. 'Might see you down there. Call you later, okay?'

As they walked out, I couldn't help myself. 'Bye, Pops. Gonna be fun racing a horse with you.'

It stopped Henshaw in his stride, but he didn't turn around. I heard him give a loud cough and another exaggerated clearing of his throat, and then he kept walking.

Around mid-morning, after the doctor had changed my dressings, Beering picked me up from the hospital and drove me down to the City West police station. Wells, the detective with Beering at the hospital last night, greeted me with a knowing nod at my bandaged hand.

'Bet you're feeling that this morning,' he said.

'Feels like someone poked me with a knife.'

'Come through,' he said, leading us past the front counter to the back of house squad room. He showed us into an interview room and before we went in, he called out to another of his staff to join us.

'Tony, you'd better sit in on this one too.'

We were joined by a fit-looking guy in his mid-thirties whom Wells introduced as Detective Sergeant Tony Norris.

'We just finished interviewing Maxine half an hour ago,' said Wells. 'She's been able to give us a likeness of the guy's face and we're hoping you can shed a bit of light on him as well.'

'I don't know,' I said. 'I told you guys last night I didn't get a look at his face. I only saw the back of him as he bolted out the door.'

'How about as a starting point, we show you the image and see if you recognise him?'

'All right.'

'Hey, and while you're at it,' said Beering, 'any chance of a decent coffee? And I don't mean that instant muck you keep in the kitchen, either.'

'Jesus, we shoulda had this interview in Lygon Street. My apologies,' grinned Norris. 'How about I order some up from the deli downstairs?'

Beering thought it a good idea, so did I. Ten minutes later we were sipping our cappuccinos while huddled around a laptop computer that Norris had set up.

'That's the image we came up with from Maxine,' said Wells. 'Recognise him?'

I studied the picture. The face in front of me had fairly unremarkable eyes. His nose looked a bit thinnish for the dimensions of his face. The lips were pursed and bore a neutral expression. No hint of a smile or aggression. His head was covered by a cap, so I couldn't see any hair. There was no beard or earring or other distinguishing facial features. In fact, there was nothing about him at all that stood out to me. He could have been any one of a hundred other guys.

Norris prompted me. 'Do anything for you?'

I shook me head. 'Can't say whether I've ever seen him or not.'

'Or *not*?' Wells seized on my indecision.

I looked at the image again and pointed at it. 'It's just that the image looks like it could be anybody. It reminds me of one of those animated characters on a computer game; not really lifelike.'

'It's the best we could come up with,' Wells said a little defensively. 'We've had our best artist from the facial identification team work that up using the very latest in computer-imaging techniques.'

'I'm sorry, I don't mean to be critical,' I shrugged. 'I guess it's who Maxine saw. That's the important thing.'

'Tell us again about what you remember him wearing,' said Wells.

'That's easier,' I said. 'Silks, he was wearing jockey silks.'

'That's all?'

'Just the silks and a cap and some sneakers. No trousers or anything. What sort of weirdo goes around wearing that sort of get-up?'

'One who's not intending to ride horses,' said Beering.

'It means something to this guy,' Wells said. 'You and Maxine are the only two who have actually seen him wearing his outfit. She's given us a description of the silks too, although it's a little hazy; she seems to have focused on his face more than what he was wearing. So anything you can remember would help.'

'Well, I don't know if I can add much to what she's already told you. I saw them briefly in the light of the patio door. They were a two-tone colour. Red stripes and white sleeves.'

'What kind of red?' said Norris.

'A bright red. Like a fire engine.'

'And the stripes, were they diagonal, horizontal, vertical? I can get our artist to come in if you like.'

I shook my head. 'No need. If you've got an internet connection, go straight to the Mitty's website. They make the racing silks. You can design a set of colours online.'

He Googled up Mitty's and in no time we had a blank template of a jockey's silks ready to fill in. I took over the mouse and clicked on the different shades of colour and styles. Then I checked out the sleeves and the cap variations. I clicked on the options and a set of colours took shape before our eyes. Silks with three thick red horizontal bands on a white vest and sleeves and two red bands on the cap.

'They the colours?' asked Norris.

I tapped the table undecidedly with my fingers. 'They sort of look like them.'

'But you're not sure?'

'The colours are right, but the combination . . . I don't know, it's still a bit of jumble in my mind. Don't know if there were more stripes, or skinnier stripes or if they were at a different angle. It all happened so fast.'

'That's okay. We understand. It may come to you yet. I'm gonna print this out anyway,' said Norris, getting up. 'I'm impressed with that software program they got. How long's that been available?'

'Ever since they got sick of owners trying to describe colours over the phone to them. This way, there's no mistake. You design them online and if they're available for registration, you go ahead and pay for the order over the web.'

'This registration of colours,' said Wells thoughtfully, 'how does it work? Can we identify who owns those colours from a database somewhere?'

Beering answered him. 'All colours, and there's thousands of 'em, are registered by the governing racing authority. But if they're registered, we can find out who owns 'em.'

'You said *if* they're registered?' Wells didn't miss much and I was beginning to admire his ear for detail.

'If the registration's lapsed, they become available to anyone else who wants them. If the next person who comes along likes the colours, they can claim them. Unless they're famous silks like Phar Lap had.'

I could see Wells playing around with this in his head. Trying to grasp what he had. 'Do either of you recognise these colours?'

Beering shook his head and looked at me. 'Punter's the expert. You seen 'em before?'

I couldn't place them belonging to any horse that I knew and I've got a pretty good head for remembering which silks are associated with a trainer or horse or owner. There was something vaguely familiar about them which I couldn't quite put a finger on. The trouble with jockey silks; they all merge into one giant kaleidoscope of colour after a while.

'No. At least, not any horses that I've backed lately, that's for sure. One thing though, the two-colour combination. There's so many horses and silks registered these days, that all the single and two-colour combinations were taken years ago.'

'How do you mean?' said Wells.

'Like, you'd never be able to register a set of all-black or all-blue colours nowadays. They were snapped up, probably at the turn of the century. And the same goes for popular two-tone combinations. Green and gold stripes. Black and red hoops.'

'How about red and white bands?' chipped in Norris.

'Right,' I agreed. 'The killer's two-coloured silks look old school. Something that might have been first worn in the fifties or sixties.'

Norris shot a satisfied look at Wells.

'Is that good?' I asked.

'It confirms one thing that forensics knows,' said Wells. 'You see, all the victims had traces of the same silk particles that have been picked up by forensics. It had us puzzled at first, not knowing exactly what they were. Now we know for sure they come from the jockey silks he was wearing. And we also know the particles found on the victims are dated around forty years old.'

That fucking nosy prick, Punter. He bloody well nearly blew it for me, didn't he? I know Punter. A smart-arse; always has an answer for everything. Never confesses to a losing day – never owns up to it when he wins. Always sticking his nose into other people's business. The fuck. The more I think about it, the angrier it makes me. He cost me his dirty little trollop girlfriend when I was just minutes, no, seconds away from having her. Punter's trollop, the spoilt brat daughter of that radio celebrity, Russell Henshaw. She's just as bad as the others, worse, in fact; a rich bitch playing at being a strapper, leading in Daddy's horses. That didn't change what she really was though, did it? Deep down she was like all the others. Just another filthy silk chaser.

It wasn't from lack of planning; I'd cased the place patiently and waited out the front until I'd seen Punter drive off. I'd found the weakest link and bypassed the security. Gone in by the flyscreen door at the rear patio. She'd been easy to see from her upstairs window. Stood out like a lighthouse on a cliff. I'd been tempted to take her then, just steal up the stairs and burst in on her. But hadn't I been careful? Given her time to go to bed. And when she turned the lights off, I even gave her another hour before I made my move. She would have been the best so far . . .

So close. I woke her with the knife under her chin. Standard operating procedure. They never quite believe what's happening to them at first. That's why I have to spell it out for them. Well, not everything. That just sends them into a situation-hopeless scenario which totally freaks them out. What works best is little steps and instructions, with the glimmer of hope that if they do as they are told, they won't get hurt. It worked on Maxine. That face of sheer terror when she knew she was totally in my control. But she was smart. Didn't do anything stupid. Just listened and nodded when I told her what I was going to do. Pleaded with me, as they all did, not to harm her. I mean, what did they really think, I was going to tickle them to death?

I disrobed her, of course, not that the slut was wearing anything much. Tied her hands, wrapped some tape around her mouth. No struggles there. Almost like she'd accepted her fate. The fancy hat was a bonus; I honestly hadn't expected to find it sitting on the trophy like it was. I was going to make her wear the boots too; she showed me where they were in the wardrobe. But by the time I'd got her to write the lipstick message, Punter had come back. Jesus, that was close. Just had time to flick off the light. He was such a suspicious bastard, wasn't he? The way he called out to her, paused at the door and wouldn't come in – almost like he knew I was in there.

Did he see me? No, not in that darkened bedroom, he couldn't have. I'm certain of that. Best he would have got was a glimpse of my back as he chased me out. She saw me of course, as indeed all the others did. I was wearing the jockey's cap, although that hardly disguised my face. I'd never bothered with a mask; there was no need because that was the last time any of them would ever see me again. But she's still alive and there is a possibility she may be *able to describe me to the police, or maybe recognise me again at the track.*

What if . . . wait a minute, be cool. She doesn't hang out where I go. Doesn't mix in the circles I do. And even if she does describe me to the cops, she still doesn't know me from a bar of soap. I could be anyone and, let's face it, I dress differently at the races from what I do for my night job. Even so, it's cutting it close. It was below par, a sloppy piece of business. And sloppy business is unfinished business. You'll have to make amends, son. Pay her another visit. And as for her smart-arse boyfriend, he's a fucking liability. Who says the strapper killer should confine his work only to women?

17

Three days had passed since the attack.

Maxine and I were looking at a police identikit image in the *Herald Sun*'s crimebeat section. We had the paper spread out on my regular table at Gino's and we were studying the photo over a couple of drinks while waiting for our order. The press had wasted no time in reporting the latest strapper attack and splashed out the headlines with gusto. The fact that it involved Russell Henshaw's daughter certainly didn't hurt paper sales, and it rekindled the strapper killer mania which had gone quiet since Kagan Hall's death.

The police had withheld a lot of what had actually happened that night. That included mention of my name. I was referred to as the 'friend' who had come back and disturbed the intruder. They'd also kept silent about the chilling lipstick message he'd made Maxine write on her mirror, and also about the jockey silks he was wearing. But the one thing they did plaster up was images of the strapper killer in newspapers, on the TV and various websites. Disappointingly, no one had come forward with a positive identification. Beering had told me that one lady rang in convinced it was her husband. The likeness was uncanny, but the husband had been working on an oil rig in Bass Strait at the time. Other than that, the only leads that police had received was their list of regular confessors, ringing in and admitting to a crime they couldn't possibly have committed.

They all had to be checked out, though, which took precious time and resources.

'So that's him then?' I said.

'Of course it's him,' she said, a touch defensively. 'Do we really have to eat here?'

'Huh, why? What's wrong?'

She eyed the walls critically and settled back to the menu. 'I don't know. It feels kind of cheap.'

'*Cheap?* It's a pizza joint. It's not the Hyatt.'

'I know. I guess I just don't like pizza that much.'

'You can get other stuff here besides pizza, you know.' Now it was my turn to be a little miffed. Knocking my restaurant, so forth. 'There's pasta and they'll do you up a nice salad if you want.'

'I don't want a salad, Punter. I'm not hungry.'

I looked at the image again. The strapper killer's eyes peered out at us from underneath the headline. The caption read: *Do you know this man? Police ask that anyone recognising this person please contact Crimestoppers immediately. On no account should the public approach this person directly.*

'So that's what he really looks like?'

'I just said that, didn't I? You sound like one of those detectives back at the station.' A pause, then, 'Well, it's the closest picture the police could come up with.'

'I'm sorry,' I said. 'It's just that his picture hasn't drawn a single lead.'

'You think I don't know that? That I don't want him caught? You make it sound like it's my fault the photo's not working.'

Prickly. Very prickly.

She picked up the paper, scrutinised the picture again and then let it drop to the table in obvious frustration.

'Oh shit, I don't know if it's him or not,' she said. 'You sit down with the police and you feel like you're under so much pressure to supply an exact description. They give you so many options; eyebrows thick, eyebrows skinny. Wide eyes, wicked eyes. Noses; they've got nose shapes I've never even seen before. They ask you; darker or lighter, smaller or bigger. It's all so confusing. I really don't know if it's the guy I saw or not. But it's the closest I can come up with, even if he does look a bit, I dunno, lifeless.'

'That's the thing, isn't it?'

'It's lacking something. Missing something. It's his likeness, but it hasn't got . . .'

'Soul?'

'Yeah, that's what it's missing. It needs some soul to bring it alive.'

Billy brought my pizza over. A sizzling Seafood Delight straight from the oven. He's got a way of melting the cheese over the anchovies and marinara mix that's to die for.

'Sure you don't want some?'

Maxine turned her nose up at it, but her eyes wouldn't leave the plate. 'Maybe just a bite then.'

'What we need to do,' I said, chewing a mouthful, 'is try another way to bring him to life.'

'I don't think I can do any better describing it to that police artist. She's got all the latest software and imaging gear and I've had two sessions with her already. There comes a point you just start confusing them and yourself.'

'I wasn't thinking of going back to the police.'

The following Saturday's races were at Caulfield. I walked through the members' entrance and tipped George his usual 'fee'. He thanked me with a polite doff of his Salvation Army cap and wished me a good day's punting.

'Hope it all works out,' he said.

I wished he was right, because according to Beering, the search for the strapper killer was doing anything but working out. I dropped into his office under the grandstand and found him leafing through some files at his desk.

'Those colours you saw, Punter, they can't find hide or hair of 'em.'

'What do you mean? Someone must have registered them. They've got to be tucked away in a database somewhere.'

'No, you don't understand. It's not that simple.'

'What could be so hard? All they're doing is looking for red and white striped colours, for Christ sake. Surely there can't be too many of those around.'

Beering got up from his desk and started pacing the room with his hands behind his back; a sure sign things weren't going well. I swivelled around in my chair to face him.

'Problem is, there's no sign of those colours in the database. They've checked it over thoroughly with the racing club. There've been a few similar variations of white and red patterns, but nothing quite like what you described.'

'But there must be. They just can't have found them yet.'

Beering stopped his pacing and sat on the ledge of the tinted window which overlooked the betting ring. Outside, punters were busying themselves for the next race, studying their formguides and scanning the bookmakers' betting boards for the latest prices.

'The club's database only goes back twenty years or so. Anything earlier is in the archives at the Australian Racing Museum.'

'Archives?'

'Yeah, old racebooks and racing calendars, to be precise. Anything prior to setting up their computer database is still in those. They've got books from every meeting from way back to when Archer won the Cup. They reckon that if these are colours from the sixties, they'll be in the archives somewhere. Only trouble is, you've got to look through I dunno how many old race books and calendars to try and find a description of 'em. You got any idea how many races they have to sift through?'

'When did they start up the database?'

'Late eighties.'

'So to be thorough, they've got to go all through that decade plus the race books from the seventies and sixties manually to try and find a description of these colours?'

'Yep, and maybe even earlier if we don't get lucky first.'

I did the maths. We've got fifty-odd race meetings a week now Australia-wide. Probably a quarter as many back then. At least thirty or forty years of race books to get through. My face must have said it all.

'A bloody shitload,' said Beering. 'The bloody books are all listed as of historical interest too, so the museum won't accept a team of hamfisted detectives thumbing through the pages and damaging the things.'

'How else are they going to get through it?'

'They've got a couple of the museum's researchers going through them as a matter of priority.'

I pictured a couple of elderly librarians, methodically sifting through each page at a snail's pace.

'Christ, that'll take forever.'

Beering nodded. 'Welcome to police life, son. Investigations are rarely easy. Meanwhile, we're back to security measures till this prick's caught.'

'I didn't seem to notice any extra security when I walked in.'

'Change of tack,' he said, tapping his nose. 'The blanket coverage hasn't worked and the clubs can't afford to pay for it indefinitely, so they've accepted my recommendations.'

'Which are?'

'Smaller and smarter. We're going covert. Rather than have a dozen security guards traipsing around the mounting yard, we're going to watch the yard with undercover staff. See if we can spot anyone with a likeness to this guy watching from the mounting yard. We'll be up in the stands too, looking down and trying to pick out anyone suspicious. Eh, you could lend a hand there yourself. 'Stead of gazin' at horses tryin' to work out why they got beat, you could put those glasses to good work and see if you can spot him in the crowd.'

'I can do that.'

'The other thing we're going to try,' said Beering, giving up his window position and sitting back at his desk, 'is a decoy. We've got a policewoman from the mounted division playing at being a strapper. She's going to lead horses around just as if she was a real stablehand. Obviously, she'll have a team of detectives ready to call in if she sees anything suspicious. Your old man's kindly offered to participate in the plan and let the police strapper lead in any of his horses on raceday, starting from today. We think it's a long shot, but you never know, it may pay off.'

I thought Beering's plan of watching for the killer secretly was a far better option than blanket security coverage. At least they had a rough description of what he looked like and a slim chance of picking him out in the crowd. And the undercover cop pretending to be a strapper might not be such a silly idea either. It was certainly worth a try.

'What about Maxine? He's still out there; you think he might make another attempt on her?' I said.

'Who knows with this creep. At least she's given herself peace of mind by quitting that place she was in and moving in with her father. Given Homicide some peace of mind too; her old man's St Kilda Road penthouse has got better security than the Reserve Bank.' He gave it some thought. 'Eh, I'm surprised she didn't move in with you, Punter.'

'Yeah, well, perhaps it's best she didn't. Besides, she and my cat don't get on.'

Beering chuckled. 'Can only be one boss in each household. And as far as her workplace goes, she uses a busy serviced office which the police are going to keep an eye on. She's agreed not to do anything silly either, like work back late when no one's around. And between you and her old man looking out for her, she should be okay. She's got a direct line to police if she needs someone in a hurry.'

I stood up to leave and told him I'd keep an eye out for anyone in the crowd who looked remotely like the strapper killer.

'Cheers, Punter. And I know it mightn't sound like it, but believe me, we're closing in.'

'I hope so, Jim.'

I was halfway out the door when he called out.

'Eh, you gonna tip me anything today?'

When I left Beering's office, I went over to the café where I knew I'd find Daisy working. As usual, she was manning the till and she greeted me like a grandson who hasn't had a decent feed in ages.

'You're definitely getting thinner, luv,' she told me. 'What you need is a decent roast. Let me serve you up some lamb from the carvery myself, before you waste away in front of me.'

Good old Daisy, her cure-all for everything was an old-fashioned roast. I don't know what her husband died from, but I'm guessing it wasn't starvation.

'If you don't mind, Daisy, I'll pass on the roast and just grab a cup of tea. But I was hoping to have a quiet word with you. Can you take a break for five minutes? Something I wanted to ask you about.'

'Of course, luv, let me get one of the girls to mind the till and I'll join you for a cuppa.'

After I'd spoken to Daisy, I walked back out into the mounting yard. Time to do some business. Pricey had a horse, Save Us, that I gave a chance in the fourth. A big strong chestnut that had obviously thrived since his last run. I watched him stride around the mounting yard; a big ball of muscle just waiting to be unleashed. My father also had a runner in the race, although I didn't rate it a chance. I didn't recognise the strapper leading it around until I realised that it must be the policewoman Beering had talked about. She was dressed like all the other strappers; wore the standard jodhpurs and riding boots as they all did. To all intents and purposes she was just another stablehand. Yet if you watched closely, she didn't quite seem to blend in. Most strappers know each other from around the traps. It's a tight-knit industry and the camaraderie is evident as they nod and chat amongst themselves. This woman was a little too stand-offish, suggesting she was new to the game or a little aloof. Another thing; although she handled her horse competently enough, she looked just a little bit apprehensive leading it around. She was probably a pretty good horsewoman, but leading a racehorse around the mounting yard if you're not used to it can be a daunting task. They're not like the placid horses she was probably used to and although my father's horses are pretty quiet, her charge was starting to walk circles around her and show up her lack of racetrack experience. Fortunately the stewards called for the jockeys to mount up and she was saved any further embarrassment when my brother legged the rider up and he took control.

I checked out another couple of chances, then went out to the betting ring. Big Oakie had posted Save Us at two fifty and a horse of Col Little's at threes. Then it was fives the field. Alfy Swan was being more generous. He'd eased out Save Us to two seventy and I claimed him for my main bet and a saver on Little's horse. Up in the stand, I pulled my Zeiss 10 × 40s out and swept the crowd down below. He could be there, the strapper killer. Could be any one of the punters mingling innocently on the lawns, a formguide in his hand and a knife in his pocket. He could be up here in the stands too, watching the races like I was. I looked briefly at the guy sitting next to me. He was about the right age and size. He sensed my stare and looked up at me and I immediately turned away again. What about the bloke two rows down? He had a similar build to the guy I'd chased from Maxine's place. It was bloody hopeless. Every man in the crowd looked like a character in a John Bracks painting. All the same and yet not one of them the man I was looking for.

The race started and I swung my glasses to the field. On the railway side Norwegian Raider was making the running. In fact it was pulling hard and the apprentice jockey was stupidly fighting it, trying to force it to settle rather than let it slide along and come back underneath him. It made the favourite's job a lot easier. Save Us stalked the leader from about the five-hundred-metre mark, when it ranged up to second place. As they swung for home, Froggy Newitt gave it full rein and it booted clear of the tiring Norwegian Raider to win easily. I sometimes wonder why I bother saving on the other horse, especially when it looks obvious, but if I backed the fave outright you could almost guarantee Norwegian Raider would have led all the way. There's four thousand ways to get beaten; you might as well play the percentages.

When the horses came back to scale, I stayed longer than I normally do up in the stand. Usually I run the glasses over the beaten brigade looking for signs of future improvement or anything amiss. Today I ignored the horses and scanned the crowd in the public section by the mounting yard fence. Some were politely clapping Newitt as he rode back to the yard. It was a popular win and most punters would have backed it. Some of the regulars in the crowd I recognised. There was a guy called Bundles, so called for the great bundle of formguides he carried around with him at every meeting in a plastic shopping bag. Someone should tell him that the form's gone online now, then he could just take a laptop to the races. Trader Bill was in the thick of things, keeping his eyes and ears open for anyone boasting about a win. If he found someone who'd backed a winner, he'd be all over them trying to sell them one of his armful of watches. Other vaguely familiar faces stood by watching. I saw Beering shuffling around the yard too. He blended in well, that old brown suit and craggy face had horse player written all over him. Amazing what you could pick out in the stand with a decent pair of binoculars. But the one thing I couldn't see was someone with a likeness to the killer. No one staring with murderous intent at the strappers as they collected their charges. What did I expect, a crazed punter dressed in silks holding a sign saying 'strapper killer'? Ridiculous.

After collecting my winnings, I dropped in at the café and caught up with the gang over afternoon tea. Myles Perry was walking back from the bar with my brother and Dianne, carrying a tray of drinks. Tiny and Louise were there with Ric, Matt and Thommo. Looked like a full house today. I grabbed a pot of tea and some sandwiches and joined them.

'Jesus, you can't stay outta the news, can you?' said Tiny. 'That was you, wasn't it, the "friend" who saved Maxine?' He nodded at my hand. 'Looks like you've seen a bit of action, too.'

I raised my eyebrows at Tiny. I still had a bandage running over the palm of my right hand. I suppose I could claim the wound as a surfing injury, but I doubt I'd fool Tiny. The others stopped talking immediately, waiting expectantly to hear my version of what had happened.

'That must have been scary shit,' said Matt. 'I don't know what I would have done if I walked in on something like that.'

'Will you shut up and let him tell us what happened?' said Ric.

'Well, firstly,' I said, 'Maxine's okay. She got off virtually without a scratch. But if I hadn't come back and surprised him when I did . . .' I let the obvious outcome trail off.

'I can't believe it,' said Louise. 'It's like a horror movie. Maxine . . . both of you are just so lucky to have survived. Is she here today?'

'No, she only goes to the track if she's strapping one of her father's horses or on Oaks Day.'

'Did ya get a look at the bastard?' said Tiny. 'I saw his mug shot in the papers.'

'That was all Maxine's description. I really didn't get a good look at him. Just walked back into her apartment and he jumped me and ran off.'

'Wish I'd been there,' said Tiny, glaring longingly into space. 'I'd have given my eye teeth to have walked in there with old trusty.'

'His favourite shotgun,' explained Louise sweetly to the rest of us.

'Be no need for a manhunt or a costly court trial, I can guarantee that,' said Tiny.

'That photo they're showing pull any leads?' asked Thommo.

'Zilch so far. The problem is, it looks too constructed. Too much of somebody and a little bit of nobody. But it's the best likeness Maxine and the police artist could come up with.'

'Do you think you'd recognise him if you ever saw him again?' said Matt.

'Christ,' said Ric, 'didn't he just say he never saw the guy properly? You sound like a cop making out he should know more.'

'Well, I don't know. Maybe he saw what the guy was wearing or remembers something about him that he couldn't think of then. Happens all the time on TV. Sometimes they even hypnotise them and they get flashbacks and remember vital clues and stuff.'

'Have a listen to yourself, will yer? You're a fucking idiot.'

'Well, it makes sense; think about it.'

I broke up the Punch and Judy act and shook my head. 'No. Like I said, he jumped me and bolted. It was all over in a few seconds. He slammed the door on me as I walked in. I was seeing stars after that.'

'Wow, that's heavy,' said Myles. 'But the way the papers had been talking about Kagan Hall, you'd reckon he was a certainty for the wrap. That dead girl they found in England; and then he goes and tops himself. All looked like the chase was up.'

'I'm with you,' said David, 'he had us all fooled. Do you know they're stepping up security again?'

'Didn't seem to do much good last time,' said Louise. 'Those big goons patrolling all around the mounting yard. They can't possibly protect every single female strapper. It's just for show.'

'I can tell you for a fact they've changed their game plan,' said David, lowering his voice knowingly.

'Yeah, how?' said Louise.

'The cops have got a policewoman workin' undercover as a strapper. They've got her planted with one of Dad's horses.' David looked pleased with himself for being the purveyor of prized information. He can be a bit too free with his knowledge sometimes and I didn't think he should be spruiking it around where someone might overhear us at the bar. I wished he'd kept his trap shut and tried to catch his eye, but Louise was all over him by now, demanding to know the details.

'Gee, that's real detective stuff, isn't it? Like, using her as a decoy and then the cops are waiting for him.'

David finally caught the look I'd been giving him.

'*What?*' he said innocently.

'What David was going to add,' I said, 'is that what he just told you stays right here. Wouldn't do to spread that around the track.'

'No, course not,' said Tiny. 'We all know each other well enough to keep our mouths shut. Ain't that right?' Tiny eyeballed everyone in the gang and they all seemed compelled to mutter various sounds of agreement. Most people agreed with Tiny when he asked them to.

Maxine had called me earlier in the day and said she was staying up at Yarra Glen for the weekend at some five-star winery and resort. Freedales had a corporate planning session on and she'd been invited to participate. She asked if I wanted to come up and stay; said I could chill out during the day and we could catch up at night. I could just see myself getting white-line fever in my hotel room on Saturday away from the races. And I could almost guarantee that Saturday night would involve dinner with Rodney Ellis, QC and a table full of those *terribly clever* senior partners who would bore me shitless. Thanks, but no thanks. I'd declined. The working weekend would probably be good for her, though, I thought. Take her mind off what had happened and keep her occupied. After all, Maxine did like to be busy.

On Saturday night I rang Billco. His son answered the phone and told me he was up in Byron Bay at an art show displaying some of his work. He wouldn't be home for another five days; was it urgent? No, nothing that couldn't wait. I said I'd catch up with him when he got back.

On Monday morning after I read the papers, I looked at myself in the mirror and decided I was in need of some serious maintenance. Che thought so too. He'd followed me into the bathroom and jumped up onto the bath where he watched me studying my face. I hadn't shaved since Saturday morning and it felt like I was sporting a week's growth.

'What do you think, little fella, I'm a bit overdue, aren't I?'

Che licked his paws as if the answer was obvious.

'And while I'm at, when was the last time I had a haircut? Be at least a month.'

Che begged to differ, thought it was longer. Chirped at me for my puzzling big cat behaviour.

'I know, strange creatures, we humans. But I'm off to Terry's for a makeover. Can you mind the office while I'm gone?'

Terry was perched on a stool reading the formguide when I walked into his shop. He had the paper spread over the glass counter which haphazardly housed all his smoking and hair products. I don't think Terry would ever be a candidate to make a David Jones window dresser. It was doubtful that the collection of jars and packages in that cabinet had ever been rearranged in the fifteen years I'd known him. A tin of Zippo lighter fluid had been knocked over at the front of the shelf; too fiddly to reach in and stand it up on its end, I suppose. It lay there gathering dust alongside jars of Brylcreem. What cigarette lighter fuel and hair cream had in common I could never work out, but Terry obviously thought there was synergy in displaying them all together. He had cigarettes and pipes and pipe cleaners and cut-throat razors thrown in for good measure. They were all in that cabinet along with unpronounceable Greek shaving creams and tonics which guaranteed to grow your hair back within thirty days.

'Punter,' he greeted me with a smile, 'I'm glad you come. I bin trying to work out who gonna win the seventh at Terang. Is not easy, you know. So many runners.'

Gotta love the way Terry does business. He's glad to see me, but not for a haircut. No, perish the thought I might put money in his pocket for the service he claims to provide. He'd rather talk about finding a winner at Terang. *Terang*, for Christ sake.

'Terry, Monday meetings at Terang aren't what you call very good betting mediums.'

'They not?'

'Bit risky, really. Not the sort of horses who graduate to running at Flemington on a Saturday.'

He looked disappointed with my assessment, but wasn't going to give it up so easily. 'Because I bin following this horse, you see. Him was unlucky last start. He shoulda won . . .'

'Terry, can you fit me in for a cut?' I ran a hand over my chin. 'I might get a shave, too, if you have time.' Bit brutal the butting in, but if you don't cut to the chase with Terry, it's lunchtime by the time he's even got you seated in the chair.

I knew he was a dinosaur, but no one gave a better shave with a cut-throat razor than Terry. They don't teach the apprentices how to do it now and I think there's only a handful of old Greek and Italian barbers like Terry who know how to give a proper shave. He put a hot hand towel over my face and let it steam away while he got his shaving gear ready.

'Hey,' he said, 'is bad business this strapper killer. He still on the loose. Everybody think they catch him, the other fella. You know, the one that jump offa the bridge.'

'Kagan Hall.'

'That's him. He kill strapper girl in England and everyone think he must have killed girls here too.'

'I think everyone was wrong about that.'

Terry took the hot towel off and lathered me up in something that reeked of lanolin. He looked me over from left to right, then deciding I didn't have enough on, gave me a second layer.

'Is gooda stuff,' he said by way of explanation, 'is better when it's more.'

He kicked the pedal beneath the barber's chair and laid me back at an angle. I couldn't see the mirror, was forced to gaze upwards at the years of smoke which had stained the ceiling a dirty mustard yellow. I can remember when Terry used to actually smoke while he cut your hair. Thank god he doesn't do that anymore, but the evidence still remains. Terry scraped away precisely and delicately. This way and that, following the contours of my chin. He pinched my nose to get into the tricky bits under my nostrils. Pulled and stretched at my cheek to make sure he hadn't missed anything. Then he towelled my face dry and lathered me up again. He always did you twice over. It didn't matter if you were happy with his first cut. It was just Terry's way of giving you a close shave. When he'd finished with the shaving, he kicked the pedal and tilted my seat back to a sitting position.

'Is gooda shave?' he asked.

'As always, Terry.'

'Good, I start on your hair then. I give you wash first.'

Terry started fussing around the basin getting his gear ready and I inspected my chin in the mirror. No nicks or cuts and my skin still tingled with the luxury of a cut-throat razor shave. A guy came in and Terry excused himself. My eyes followed him lazily from the mirror as he went across to the counter and served the customer. I relaxed in Terry's old-fashioned barber's chair and took in the back wall of his shop. His old racing photos were there as always. There was Fright, whose red, white and blue colours I easily identified as my father's. I recognised another of Terry's favourites, a horse called Precise in bright orange and black checked colours. Then I sat bolt upright at what I saw.

When Terry had finished serving, he came back surprised to find me staring at his photos with the barber's gown draped around my feet like an altar boy.

'Oh, let me tell you about them horses,' he said. 'Fright, now she was the best. Your old man used to train her, you know? One day, he say to me . . .'

I cut him short. 'Terry, I know all about Fright.'

I pointed to an ageing photo a little smaller than the others mounted to the side of the collection. I'd never heard of the horse; some forgettable hack that had won a maiden race years ago. But I knew the trainer and I'd seen the colours before.

'I want to know about this one. The one with the red horizontal bands on the white vest and sleeves.'

18

'This horse?' Terry said in disbelief. 'Him not much good. Win a bush maiden is all he do.'

'May I?' I said, taking the photo off the wall.

Terry shrugged, still mystified as to why I'd want to look at a photo of some rocking horse when he could be taking me through Fright's glittering career. I placed the photo on the arm of the barber's chair where we could see it better in the light. The photo was a shot of a horse called Think I Can passing the winning post in a race way back in 1966. It had an old Gothic-style italic font proudly describing the occasion. The horse's breeding and the trainer were listed, as were the owners and the winning jockey.

'Chas Bannon trained the horse for you?'

'Yeah. It musta bin the second horse I ever had. Chas used to come in for a haircut and I got talking to him and next thing I ended up in a horse with him. Old Chas, he still drops by now and then. But he no have much hair these days. No getta cut as much as he used to.'

'I know Chas. He's a marvel; still training from a wheel-chair. Tell me, who else was in it?'

Terry picked up the photo carefully and wiped it over with a hand towel from the basin. The writing was fading badly, but you could still make out the owners' names: C Bannon, T Papadopoulis, C Whittle.

'Chas kept a share himself. I had a quarter and Col Whittle and his wife had the other half.'

'The jockey colours, whose were they?'

Terry scratched his head, thinking about it. 'They not mine,' he said, nodding back to the wall where the other photos were. 'I never had my own colours. And when Fright come along, I always used your father's. They must be Chas' colours or belong to the Whittles.'

'Were the Whittles friends of yours?'

Terry shook his head while studying the photo in his hands. 'No. They were clients of Chas. He just put us together when the horse became available.'

'Did you race any other horses with them?'

'No, only this slowpoke. We got rid of it shortly after it won. Chas found a buyer up in Queensland and we sold it. It never won another race.'

'Do they still race horses?'

'The Whittles? I haven't seen them for must be over thirty years. Maybe Chas know where they are.'

'You mind if I borrow this photo, Terry? I'll take good care of it, I promise.'

'Sure, but hey, where you going? You don't wanta I finish cutting your hair?'

I'd pulled the barber's gown over my head and draped it on the back of the chair.

'Might give it a miss today. Got a trainer I need to see.'

Chas Bannon's stables were like a little oasis in the middle of a suburban desert. He had a house and a dozen stables out in the back of his yard down in a side street across from the track. There seemed to be stables in the back of every second house when I was a kid growing up at Caulfield. But then people realised they could build townhouses on their blocks and get a better return rather than renting out stables to battling trainers. Chas' stables were one of the few remaining which hadn't been bulldozed down. He'd bought the place back in the fifties and once you entered through his ivy-covered gate, it was like stepping into a neat little barnyard. A couple of chooks pecked about happily on a flowerbed to the side of the driveway. He had a goat tied to a fence outside the stables, a scruffy brown thing which was down on its knees chewing contentedly at a patch of grass it could just reach at the end of its tether. Chas always kept a goat at his stables. Swore they calmed down fractious horses. Sometimes he even let them share a box with a racehorse if he thought the horse was fretting too much. I reckon the goat always got the better deal. It ate half the straw bedding and most of the lucerne hay net which was meant for the thoroughbred.

Old Chas was sitting in his wheelchair on the porch, dozing in the sun. He was surrounded by a menagerie of cats and dogs sharing a kip on the couch next to him. Three of the dogs, little Jack Russell terriers, sprang to life when they heard me walking up. They jumped down protectively from the verandah and started yipping away at me and their barking woke up Chas.

He put a hand to his brow and squinted to see who it was. 'Oh, it's you, Punter.'

'Hi Chas. Sorry to interrupt.'

'You're not stoppin' me doin' anything important. Come up and join me, I was just having my lunchtime nap.'

I stepped up onto the porch and sat down on one of the weathered cane chairs next to him.

'You could be miles away in the country here, couldn't you?' I said. 'Reminds me of a farmyard when you walk in and see all the animals.'

Chas smiled contentedly. 'I know. I love it and so do the horses. Those idiots over there,' he said, waving a dismissive hand at the racecourse, 'would like nothing better than to sell me up and see me pensioned off with half a dozen boxes on the course. But I own this place and I'll train here till they cart me out in a box. And that won't be any time soon, touch wood. Now then, son,' he said, eying Terry's photograph which I had tucked under my arm, 'what can I do for you?'

I showed Chas the photo and he put on his glasses to inspect it. A hint of a smile broke over the old man's face as his mind trawled back through the years. 'Think I Can. Gee, that's going back awhiles. Where on earth did you dig this up from?'

'I was at Terry's, the barber, and saw it on his shop wall along with all his other racing photos.'

'Ah, figures. Terry'd be the only person who'd bother keeping a photo of a horse so slow.'

'I gathered it wasn't much good from what he told me. He said you'd sold it to someone in Queensland and it never won another race.'

Chas nodded thoughtfully. 'Yeah, I could probably have beaten it home in this thing,' he said, slapping the side of his wheelchair.

'The horse's silks; I'm trying to find out who they were registered to. Were they yours or the owners'?'

'Not mine, son. I've used the grey and yellow stripes ever since I started training fifty-seven years ago. They must have been Terry's or the other owner.'

'No, they weren't Terry's. So they must have belonged to Mr Whittle.'

'Col Whittle,' said Chas, nursing the photo on his lap. 'Now there's an owner I haven't thought about for a long time.'

'He still in the game?'

'Lord, no. That was the last horse he ever owned. His interest waned after that and I heard he died in a car accident. Must be thirty years or so ago.'

'Did you know him well?'

'Not really. Let me think. My memory's not what it used to be . . .' Chas adjusted his glasses and peered at the photo, trying to remember. 'Yeah, it was a long time ago but Col, he was a local builder if I remember correctly,' he said, nodding with more certainty. 'That's right, it's coming to me now. He was a good tradesman, always did a proper job. I got to know him when he put a new roof up over the stables for me. He was a keen racegoer and he ended up taking a share in a few horses I had over a couple of years. One of 'em won a couple of races, that's what got him hooked. But Think I Can was his last horse with me.'

'Would you know what happened to the colours?'

'Jesus, son, I can't even remember what won the last at Caulfield on Saturday, let alone what happened to a set of silks over forty years ago! I probably gave 'em back to Col when the horse was sold. But like I said, he's long gone so they could be anywhere. Most likely buried in a tip by now. You can always get another set made up with the same colours if you want 'em so bad, you know.'

'Tell me, was he married, have any family you knew about? I'm just wondering if they've been sitting in a garage somewhere hidden away all these years.'

Chas stroked his chin, let his eyes wander over to the row of stables opposite. A couple of horses had their heads over the top of their boxes and were munching contentedly away at their feed bins while looking at us. The goat had stretched out to the very end of its tether rope and could just reach a patch of weeds in the garden bed which it was chewing at.

'Col had a wife, Lillian, but I heard she passed away a few years ago.' He frowned, a thought occuring to him. 'Funny couple they made, her and Col.'

'Funny?'

'Funny *strange*. Something not quite right. You'd hear rumours at the track about her having it off with jockeys while Col was out working.'

'Was it true?'

Chas shrugged. 'Dunno for sure. But where there's smoke . . .'

'Did you know where they lived?'

'Col was a local, but I never went to his house.'

'What about when you sent him a training bill, wouldn't his address be in your records?'

'Nah, I don't keep any records going back more than a few years, let alone forty.'

A phone rang from inside the house and his wife called out to him. 'Chas, it's for you.'

'All right, I'm comin',' he said. 'I don't think I can tell you much more about the owner or those colours, son.'

'Of course,' I said, standing up to go. 'It was a long time ago.'

'Would you mind doing something for me on the way out?' He smiled at me. 'Tie that goat a bit closer to that weed patch. He's only done half the job.'

'You're a hard taskmaster, Chas. I'm glad I never strapped for you.'

He winked at me as he wheeled past in his wheelchair. 'If a job's worth doing, it's worth doing properly.'

I dropped by Beering's office on the way back from Chas' stables. He was out at lunch, so I left the photo with his receptionist and asked if she'd get Beering to call me when he got back. Mention of lunch made me think of getting a bite to eat myself, so I drove over to the main shopping strip and bought some sushi rolls which I sat down in my van to eat. Beering rang me just as I ripped the plastic wrapper off.

'Good timing, Jim, as always.'

'My PA said you called and left a race photo for me.'

'Uh-huh.'

'We'll, what's the story?'

'Something that might save you guys a bit of legwork. Those colours in that photo, they're the same as the strapper killer wore the night he attacked Maxine.'

Beering went quiet for a moment, obviously taking in what I'd discovered. 'You sure about that?'

'I am now after seeing them in the photo. They're a spitting image.'

'Where did you get the photo?'

I told him how I'd come across it and also what I'd found out from my visit to Chas Bannon's stables earlier.

'You've been busy.'

'Yep. So your friends in Homicide can wrap up their search

for the missing colours,' I said. 'They belonged to Col Whittle, who died about thirty-odd years ago according to Chas.'

'I'll let Homicide know about it,' said Beering. 'They might want to ask Chas some more questions. But I gotta say that even though you've traced whose colours they were, it sounds a bit of a dead end with both the Whittles dead.'

'It's a lead, isn't it?'

Beering sniffed down the phone. I'd heard that sniff before. It conveyed a cynical disinterest in pursuing something that he knew would be a timewaster.

'*What*, stands to reason, doesn't it?' I said. 'Find where the silks are and the last person holding them may be your killer.'

A patient sigh followed a second cynical sniff. 'Punter, you've done a good job finding that old race photo, even if it was a fluke. But let me tell you something for nothin'. Those colours could be anywhere. You said Chas thought he'd probably sent 'em back to Whittle when he sold his horse years ago.'

'Yeah.'

'Okay, what if he didn't? What if he left 'em at the dry-cleaners and they threw 'em out when they got sick of waiting around for someone to collect 'em?'

'I don't think he would have done that.'

'All right, what if he did send 'em back. Let's suppose Whittle puts 'em in the garbage, or took 'em down to a charity bin. Either way, someone else such as the real strapper killer – and let's face it; we know it's not Whittle or his equally deceased missus – could have got their hands on 'em and we wouldn't have a clue.'

'Maybe his wife kept them and passed them on to one of their kids or something.'

'Did Chas know if they had any children or not?'

'I dunno. He didn't say.'

'Well, let's run with that one, then. Maybe the wife kept the silks in a box in his wardrobe. But when she died, the kids fought over who gets what and cleaned out all the junk before the house was sold. We're back to my garbage theory again.'

I let off my own sigh of disappointment down the phone. 'Jesus, do all investigations have to hit a brick wall?'

'All I'm sayin' is that even though you've found out who they belonged to, there's lots of places those colours could be now after forty-odd years.'

'Yeah, you've just about given me the complete list.'

'Punter, I haven't even started. They could have been taken home by the jockey who rode the horse in his last race. Maybe he gave 'em to *his* kids.'

'So he's got kids, has he?'

'Okay, let's say he hasn't. They could have been left in the jockeys' room and been sitting in lost property since 1966. A strapper might have left them sitting in a float. Yada yada, you want me to go on?'

'I think I get the picture, Jim.'

'You know what I reckon? Forget who might or might not have the colours. There's too many variables. We've got Maxine's likeness of the killer and someone will recognise him sooner or later.'

Beering's take on things soured the rest of my day. I thought I'd done good. Found some missing pieces in the jigsaw. Particularly in finding out who the colours belonged to. Trouble was, I was thinking like a mug gambler who thinks he's found the only chance in a race. Beering thought like a cop; his training taught him there were many possibilities. Even so, I felt a bit of an emotional let-down after all my hard work. My feelings didn't improve when I called Maxine later in the afternoon. She'd only just got back from her corporate planning weekend at Yarra Glen with that legal mob. Now she was telling me they wanted to send her away for three days to Sydney.

'Jesus, honey, you've only just got back. I never see you,' I blurted out. Didn't mean to, but there it was. That was the problem, wasn't it? She was always away on a business trip or working crazy hours for a client.

'I'm sorry, sweetie. But it's more work from Freedales and it's worth a stack. Rodney Ellis has gone out of his way to pass work on to me, so I can't really knock it back, can I?'

'You've just spent all weekend working for them and I haven't seen you since Phar Lap won the Cup.'

'Oh, don't be silly, you're exaggerating. I'll be back on Thursday. I'll see you then, I promise.'

Maxine cut the call short and rang off. Wisely, I thought. I'd have liked to tell her what she ought to do with Freedales and that toffy-sounding QC, Rodney Ellis. I ended up getting stuck into the form for the following day's Sandown meeting. It wasn't bad as far as a summer mid-week card went. Three of the eight races looked playable, including one of my father's horses whom I'd been waiting to see step out. I was halfway through the program when the phone rang with Chas Bannon on the line.

'G'day, son,' he said. 'I got to thinking about Col Whittle and that horse I trained for him after you left.'

'The horse wouldn't bear a lot of thinking about, Chas. Could do its form in about three seconds flat.'

'True, he was no good. But something about Col buzzed about in my mind all afternoon and I couldn't quite remember what it was. But then it came back to me, so I thought I'd give you a call before it slipped away again.'

I pushed my formguide to the side of my desk and sat to attention. 'What is it about Whittle you remembered?'

'It's not really Whittle, it's his son.'

'He had a kid?'

'Well, a stepson. His wife Lillian already had a young boy from a previous marriage. Meggsy, his name was. Least that's all I remember him by.'

'Ginger Meggs. Let me guess, on account of his red hair?'

'Biggest mop you've ever seen. I didn't think of him at first; was trying to remember about the horse and the colours. But here's the funny thing. After Col died, I heard from his wife. Hadn't heard from her in years; no reason she'd keep in touch with me, I s'pose. But then out of the blue, I got this call from Lillian in the early eighties. Seems the kid, who'd grown into a teenager by then, was at a bit of a loose end. Wasn't doing well in school. Didn't have any friends or hobbies and his mother was getting worried about him. He was only a small chap, so Lillian asked if I'd give him a go as an apprentice jockey.'

'Did you take him on?'

'I didn't want to. Bloody kids are a pain in the arse as far as I'm concerned. But Lillian really pleaded with me, said she was desperate to find him something and thought if I could just give him a chance, he'd turn out all right. I wished I'd listened to my better judgement. But I was short of a strapper at the time and the kid wouldn't cost me nearly as much in wages, so I gave him a start.'

'How did he work out?'

'When he first started he'd hardly say boo to me or anyone else. Like he had withdrawn into his own little shell. Green, of course, because he'd never touched a horse till he set foot in my yard. But he seemed to learn quick enough. Within a month he was mucking out stables and leading 'em around. I even put him up on a couple of quiet 'uns and let him walk exercise. He seemed to gain confidence every day he was there. But after about six months, he put on a growth spurt and shot up. Happens all the time with kids. One day an aspiring jock, the next they're playing ruck for a league team. I let him stay on as a strapper, but I had to let him go a couple of months after.'

'Why was that?'

Chas paused a moment as if reluctant to go on. 'He was a bit of a sly bugger and I always had my suspicions; dogs cowering behind me when he walked into the yard or the cats running off whenever they saw him. I sprung him one day belting a young horse of mine with the handle of a pitchfork and fired him on the spot.'

I asked Chas a few more questions, but there wasn't anything else he could tell me. No, he didn't remember the kid's proper name. And no, he had no idea where he might be now. When he hung up, I rang Beering. He wasn't picking up, so I left a message on his answering service anyway telling him about Whittle having a stepson called Meggsy, who once worked for Chas.

The rest of the week passed by pretty quickly. On Tuesday I went to Sandown and had an all right day. I backed Dad's horse at fours and it never looked like losing. I went to the Triangle in the evening and met up with the guys. We played snooker till around eleven and then I came home and went to bed. On Wednesday I seemed to spend half the day answering texts and playing catch-up with messages. I don't know how I could miss so many calls; it was like everyone waited for me to go out of the house and then rang to catch me out.

Maxine had left a couple of texts for me. I don't mind reading them, but I hate trying to respond to the damn things. I called Maxine but she wasn't answering so I left a message on her phone and sure enough, an hour later another text came back from her saying she'd missed my call. Well, of course she had, that's why she wasn't there to take it in the first place. I'm sure Telstra's making a fortune out of everyone who feels compelled to respond every time someone rings or texts.

Kate had left a message on my home answering machine. At least she used the phone in the way it was supposed to be used. She wanted to know if there were any new developments about the strapper killer. Beering had also rung and left yet another message, a one-sentence question which sounded less than enthusiastic. He said, 'Does Meggsy have a real name and a current address?'

I could have predicted his response. Maybe he was right, and all this running around was just a waste of time. I called Billco later in the morning. I didn't get him either, but at least I got hold of his son, who said he still wasn't home from his art exhibition at Byron Bay. He said he'd let Billco know to call me. Another win for Telstra.

On Thursday I went to Ballarat races. I should have stayed home. I got a speeding ticket just as I came over the hill near the tourist castle. Bloody cops had a radar set up just over the dip. An oncoming car flashed its lights at me but it was too late, I'd been zapped. Wasn't over by much, but no one likes starting the day a hundred and ten dollars in the red. I slipped further into deficit as the day wore on. My first horse got beaten in a photo by a sixteen-to-one outsider. I almost willed the jockey to protest, find some excuse that might turn around the result, but it was beaten fair and square and the judge wasn't going to change his mind. I had some luck in the two-thousand-metre race when the favourite won at skinny odds. Then I gave it back in the last when my top two picks ran third and fourth respectively.

I consoled myself with a cup of coffee in the members' café, thinking about how I couldn't take a trick. Away from the track, things weren't exactly humming along either. The search for the strapper killer seemed to have slowed somewhat since the flurry of activity last weekend. Maybe that was just my perception because things weren't falling into place, but that was the story of my life at the moment. Even things with Maxine didn't feel quite right. I'd hardly sighted her since last weekend, since she'd been staying at her old man's penthouse. And it didn't help that she was doing all that bloody work for the legal firm. She was either interstate or attending some damn conference they were putting on. Mental note to self: never engage Freedales for any legal work – they're too busy running in-house seminars to represent you properly. On the drive home my spirits lifted when my mobile rang and Billco answered. He told me he'd had a successful showing in Byron Bay and managed to sell four paintings and take another two orders. Plus, he'd scored a surf, dawn and evening, every day he'd been there. He asked me what I'd been up to and when I told him why I'd rung, he agreed on the spot to my request.

On Friday night, much against Maxine's wishes, I drove her down to Billco's place on the peninsula. She'd got back the day before from interstate, but she was still tired from the trip and couldn't see much point in what I was proposing.

'Look,' I said. 'What have you got to lose? You want to catch this guy, right?'

'Of course I do. I just don't see how one of your surfy mates can improve on what the police have already done.'

'Billco's got other talents apart from surfing.'

When we got there, Maxine changed her tune almost imme-diately Billco greeted us and showed us down the hallway. It was covered in watercolours, small landscapes mainly, and it took Maxine a good five minutes or so to get past looking at those.

'Punter never told me you were a *real* artist,' she said to Billco. 'I mean, these are fabulous.'

Billco grinned modestly. 'There's more inside. Come through and I'll show you around.'

He led us into the large studio-cum-display room I knew from my previous visits. It had probably been the lounge at one time, but it looked like he'd knocked down a wall to make it big enough for his purposes. He had an easel set up in the corner with a half-finished watercolour on it. A variety of paintings and sketches hung on the walls. Maxine dived in straightaway and went into raptures.

'Oh, that's striking! Punter, have a look at this. And this seascape,' she said, looking at the next one, 'is this for sale? It's absolutely stunning.'

After another ten minutes of oohing and aahing at his work, Billco just about had her eating out of his hand. We joined him in the kitchen while he made us some coffee, sitting at his island bench and looking at still more sketches and paintings which covered the walls.

'Punter says he thinks it's worth you having a crack at drawing the killer,' she said. 'Is it something you can do?'

'Shouldn't be too hard,' said Billco nonchalantly, getting some milk from the fridge.

'I've bought along the police sketch for you to see what they came up with,' said Maxine.

'Not necessary,' said Billco, pouring us both a cup.

'But you'll want to see the image they've done, won't you?'

'No. I'd rather not,' he said. 'The way I work is to sketch it out in my mind from your description. If I see someone else's interpretation, it might influence my perception of what this person looks like. Shall we get started?'

Billco led us out to another smaller studio at the back of his house. It had a small couch and a work table with chairs in the corner. We sat down at the table and Billco picked up his tools of trade and went to work. He had an A3 size artist's pad of lightly textured paper which he opened up and flicked through, looking for a clean page. He was sitting opposite me, so all I could make out was the upside-down sketches of previous drawings he'd done. Maxine, who was next to him, made him stop turning the pages to look at a couple that she liked. She'd have walked out with a bundle of his work if they'd been for sale. Billco grabbed an ice-cream container full of pastels. He picked one out and fingered it. Its label said *Rembrandt*, and I fancy Billco had a slight resemblance to the Dutch master as he leant forward, deciding where to start.

'Now, I know you've done all this before with the police artist, but I want you to try to describe this guy again.'

Maxine's response was to reach for her handbag. 'Let me just look at the police image again and I'll remember better.'

'No, don't do that,' said Billco. 'Just close your eyes and think back to what you saw. Keep them closed, don't look at me or what I'm drawing. I'll ask you some questions along the way to help prompt you. You okay with that?'

Maxine had already shut her eyes and nodded. 'Yep, let's do it.'

Billco cradled the pad on the table with one hand and twirled the pastel around in his fingers with the other. 'What's the first thing you remember about this man?'

Maxine stayed silent for a few seconds, concentrating. 'I woke up and he was there on my bed . . . with a hand over my mouth and a knife against my throat. I've never felt so sure I was going to die. It was just terrifying. I . . .' Maxine raised a hand to her mouth and opened her eyes again. I reached across the table and laid a palm on her arm, gave her a comforting squeeze.

'I know it must be hard for you to relive the moment,' said Billco.

Maxine put her hand down by her side and closed her eyes again. 'No, keep going. Keep asking me stuff,' she said resolutely.

'Okay. Was he Australian? Asian? From somewhere else, maybe?'

'No, he looked local and sounded it too. It was dark when he woke me up, but then he switched the bedside lamp on and I could see him clearly.'

'The size and shape of his head; was it big, small, in between?'

'He was wearing that stupid jockey cap and silks, so I couldn't really tell. The cap made it all the more frightening. Made his head look more oversized than maybe it really is. He wore it with the peak on its side,' she said, putting the palm of her hand out in front of her forehead to demonstrate.

'Could you see his hair under the cap?'

'Not really; it must have been fairly short if the cap covered it.'

'Tell me about his eyes. Think about it. Did they speak to you?'

Maxine went silent again and you could tell she was really concentrating hard.

Seconds ticked by. I glanced at Billco. He held a hand up to shoosh me.

'Did they . . . speak to me?' she said, sounding a little puzzled, her eyes still squeezed tightly shut.

'Were they menacing, cruel? Cavalier? Tell me what they said to you.'

She put her elbows on the table and rested her head in her hands, her fingers covering her face. Her two pointer fingers squeezed her temple, seeming to will her mind to remember something, anything that would help.

'Think of when you locked eyes for the first time. It's usually the lasting impression,' said Billco.

When she spoke again, it was like we were sharing that same chilling moment in the room with her and the killer.

'He tied me up with my hands to the front. Then he made me write that message on my mirror with some lipstick. It's hard writing like that . . . with two hands bound together. But what you just said, about locking eyes, I remember now. I'd written those horrible words he told me to write and I sort of kept staring at the writing once I'd done it, because I just knew then that it was all over for me. When I finally looked up from the writing, his face was leering at me from the mirror.'

Maxine dropped her hands to the table now, her eyes still closed, but a more certain and somewhat satisfied expression on her face.

'Yeah, his eyes spoke to me all right, the prick. They said, I own you. Me; I have the power of life and death over you. And there's absolutely nothing you can do about it. They were sorta fervent, you know, like one of those southern gospel preachers. Yet at the same time they had a . . .' she trailed off again, searching for the right choice of words, 'rage, an intensity behind them.'

Billco had started to sketch. 'Go on,' he said, 'this is good, very good.'

'They were mocking eyes, smug in the knowledge that I was completely at his mercy.'

I watched, fascinated, as Billco's sketch came to life. He asked more questions as he drew, coaxing details out of Maxine that I hadn't heard her describe before. Every so often he'd stop and use his fingers to soften edges, or knead his rubber to make a correction. He asked Maxine about the colours, but she deferred to me and Terry's racing photo. We'd bought it along with the police image and I pulled it out of Maxine's tote bag and placed it on the table for him to look at. He studied it for a moment before he went back to work again. He sketched on for a little longer and then put his pastels down. The whole thing took no more than twenty minutes.

'You can open your eyes now,' he said to Maxine. 'Have a look and let me know what you think. It'll probably need a few corrections once you see it.'

He passed the pad across to Maxine, who grabbed at it eagerly. She only looked at it for what seemed a second.

'Oh my god, that is so like him.'

'It is?' said Billco, sounding somewhat relieved.

'The eyes, you've caught the eyes perfectly. In the police shot, he's sorta staring straight at you with lifeless, featureless eyes. But you've somehow brought them to life, given them soul.'

'The police have good systems which usually give a good front-on view of the face. But I've drawn him from a bit of a side angle, the way you must have seen him from the reflection in the mirror. And of course I've probably interpreted what you've described a little differently from how a police artist may have.'

'Can I show you the police image now that you've finished?'

'Sure, be interesting to see the difference.'

Maxine pulled the police image out of her bag and laid it next to Billco's sketch on the table. They both looked at the drawings, curiously noting the differences.

I walked around to their side of the table and joined them, the first time I'd seen the drawing right side up.

Maxine chattered away excitedly to Billco. 'The nose could be a bit thinner. And maybe the chin, too. The police picture is probably a better likeness for that. I'm sorry, I should have described it better.'

'No, it's quite okay,' said Billco. He'd picked up the pad again and was already making corrections to his sketch. 'There's some facial parts you remember better than others.'

He rubbed out some of his drawing in little circles here and there and then used his pastels to add some more lines in.

'The nose thin enough now?'

'That's better, but his nostrils were more . . . flared.'

He made some changes, poked and moulded it with his fingers a bit more before he seemed happy with it. 'Like that?'

'Perfect.'

'What about the eyes, you happy with them?'

'Don't change anything about the eyes!' barked Maxine. It sounded like an order and brought a smile to Billco's face. Finally, he put his pastels and his rubber back into the ice-cream container and put the drawing back alongside the police image.

'Then I guess it's done,' he said.

'What do you think, Punter?' said Maxine. 'Isn't that far more realistic than the one the police did?'

I looked at the police image and saw what I'd already seen several times before; an unremarkable face who could be anybody. Then I looked at Billco's drawing. As different as chalk and cheese. He'd captured it just as Maxine must have seen him in all his horror. The jockey's cap provided a grotesque mask effect and he'd instilled a cruelness in the leering smile of his lips. But it was his eyes that caught my attention. Billco had captured a certain intensity, a life-like fervour that Maxine had described which had been missing from the police picture. They were creepy eyes that repulsed, yet compelled you to stare back at them.

'Punter?' Maxine nudged me. 'What do you reckon?'

I didn't answer, just stood staring at the drawing. I turned it away from me at more of an angle. Then I tried it again from the opposite side. The eyes stared back at me, following me around the room.

I think Billco sensed it even before I did, the artist in him coming to the fore.

'You've seen him before, haven't you?' he said quietly.

'Do you? Do you know this guy?' said Maxine, gripping my arm.

'Look at the eyes, Punter, concentrate on the eyes,' said Billco. 'Here, try this.' He ripped a clean sheet of paper from his pad and then tore it in half. Then he placed one end above the eyebrows and the other just below the nostrils, blocking off the rest of the head and face. I locked eyes again with the strapper killer, this time without the jockey cap to distract me.

Something seemed to tug at the strings of a distant memory. A vague recollection of someone I thought I recognised. For just a second his face ghosted around in my mind, teasing me, mocking me in my attempt to try and identify it. I shut my eyes tightly, willing the face to show itself clearly. It lingered for an instant, so tantalisingly close. I had it in my mind's eye. Knew I'd seen him somewhere before. Then the apparition seemed to laugh at me and fade into any one of ten thousand other faces I'd seen around the track over the years. I'd lost him.

19

At Caulfield races the next day, I couldn't help thinking about Billco's sketch. It had triggered some recall, however small, in the back of my mind. I'm pretty good at remembering a horse's head or a human face. I can watch a horse walk into the mounting yard and most times I don't need a formguide to tell me who it is. The same for people. I might not always remember their names, but when I see them hanging out at the track, I file them away and make a mental note to myself that this person or that are players. And Billco's sketch was bugging me because somewhere on a racecourse, I knew I'd seen that face.

I tipped George from the Salvos as I walked in. Put a couple of dollars in his bucket to grease the wheels of luck and keep them turning. He gave me a kind-hearted smile and wished me well like he always does. George has wide, honest eyes. There is not an ounce of badness in his entire face. Not that I remotely suspected George of being the strapper killer, but with Billco's sketch on my mind, I found myself looking at every man I met with renewed interest. I bought a coffee from Daisy in the café and agreed with her that yes, I was a bit on the thin side and would definitely try and make it back at lunchtime for one of her roasts. She's got a set of concerned, motherly eyes. Kind eyes that smiled at me when I tipped her a horse in the third.

I unsuccessfully avoided Trader Bill and his usual spiel about buying a watch. I wondered how Billco would fare, trying to draw his face from my description. Quite easily, I would imagine. Trader's eyes were large and round and mischievous. I never knew a man who could look you in the face and lie continuously without even blinking like Trader could. But Trader's lies and tales of deceit were harmless puffery about his watches. And his eyes were those of a harmless con man, not a killer. I parted Trader's company minus a 'lazy twenty' which he promised to return by the end of the meeting. Kiss that goodbye.

After a couple of races I forgot about Billco and his sketch and slipped back into my normal raceday routine. The day passed uneventfully and in between races I spoke with Big Oakie and swapped notes about who we thought could win today and what price they'd be. I watched the horses in the mounting yard before each race. Some I played, some I passed on. I won a few, lost a few and finished up a little ahead after the first five races with my best selection still to run in the last.

Around three, I made my way down from the grandstand to the café. It was time to join the gang for a sandwich and a drink. I took a couple of steps inside and paused for a moment, looking through the crowd to the usual corner where they hung out. Tiny was there sharing a formguide and a couple of beers with Louise. Got on well, those two, like bread and butter. Kate and Nathan, or Ned; I could never remember which, were talking to them. Ric was propping up a pylon like it would fall over without him. He was nursing a glass of red and was there with Matt and my brother and Myles Perry. Thommo was standing, juggling a plate of sandwiches in one hand and a *Best Bets* in the other. He kept an ear to the conversation and a sharp eye on the crowd collecting bets at the tote window. Sizing them up for a friendly 'bump' later in the day, no doubt. David held his glass up when he saw me and I waved back at him.

I bought a lemon squash at the bar then sidled up to David and Myles. I raised a glass at Tiny and Louise and smiled at Kate. Thommo asked me how the battle was going and I gave him the standard response.

'Hard game the punt, old son.'

I stood next to Ric, who was still leaning against the pylon. He was watching the constant stream of races on the TV monitor, as we all seemed to be doing. Sydney, Adelaide, Brisbane. Didn't matter if you hadn't backed a runner, you were always on the lookout for a good thing beaten.

I was down to the ice cubes in my lemon squash and I twirled them around while watching the TV. Kate and her boyfriend came over and she demanded I mark her card for the rest of the day. I flicked through the pages of her race book, circling a horse here and there while her stupid boyfriend stood right in front of me, blocking my view of the TV. I gave Kate her book back and made some small talk, then offered to buy a round of drinks. I hadn't timed it well. It was rush hour at the bar, a long queue four or five deep waiting to be served. I thought as I'd be waiting a few minutes anyway, I may as well pay a visit to the gents' and come back.

I walked into the toilets, a smallish bathroom with half a dozen cubicles and a stainless steel urinal. The flusher must have been stuck or broken; the water sounded like a tiny waterfall as it washed down the trough and over the citrusy-smelling tablets floating in the urinal. I stood on the metallic grid, the only person there apart from someone in one of the cubicles. I heard it flush and someone came out and started washing their hands. It was Matt.

He flashed a friendly grin at me from the mirror on the wall as I walked over and joined him. I gave him a nod and asked him how he was going.

'Up and down,' he said.

'Yeah, know that feeling.'

I started washing my hands and gave him a smile, catching his face in the mirror. He looked down as he soaped his hands then raised his head again to see me still staring at his reflection. We locked eyes for a moment before he looked away again. I turned off the tap and grabbed a hand towel by the door and gave my hands a quick dry. Then I stood leaning against the door and stared back at him. He pretended not to notice at first; made a show of inspecting his fingers. Holding them out over the basin as if to see if he'd missed anything, then soaping them up and washing them again. Only so many times a man can rinse his hands. I stood and I stared. Took in the back of his head. Noted the shortish carrot-coloured hair. Met his gaze again as his eyes slowly lifted to meet mine in the mirror. His eyes; not so welcoming this time. A flash of annoyance had suddenly crept into them.

It was quiet in that toilet; nobody else there but Matt and I and the sound of the water trickling from the flusher. His eyes hadn't left mine. It was like we were engaged in some kind of staring competition and the first to weaken and turn away would lose.

'They're clean enough, Meggsy,' I said.

He went on washing his hands, holding me in his stare, and I kept on leaning there against the door with my arms folded, looking right back at him. Finally he looked down at the basin and turned off the tap.

'No one's called me that for a long time,' he said.

'Let me guess, not since you were a kid. Back when you used to work for Chas Bannon.'

He turned around slowly and faced me.

'And now you've got another nickname, haven't you? Strapper Killer.'

He gave me the faintest of smiles. 'When did you work out it was me?' he said calmly. 'When did you find out?'

'I recognised your face from a drawing.'

'The police drawing? Bullshit. That stupid thing in the paper didn't look anything like me.'

'No, not that one. I got an artist friend of mine to sketch another one up for Maxine.'

Matt turned around and started lathering up his hands again. Obsessive compulsive; carefully and methodically rubbing the liquid soap into his palms and through his fingers.

'You know, that doesn't surprise me, you doing that. Getting your artist friend involved. Sticking your *fucking* beak in where it's not wanted. You must have been snooping around Chas Bannon's to find out about me.'

His eyes were fixed on mine like magnets now, glued to me from the back of the mirror. Following me around just like they had in Billco's sketch. They'd turned into narrow, angry slits. I could see the anger and hear it in his voice. I stood watching him warily, keeping my distance and blocking the door. It was amazing to see the true Matt emerge from his disguise, like a clever actor discarding his costume. He'd fooled a lot of people, me included, for a long time. All that joviality; the cheerful personality. Good old easygoing Matt. It was all just a facade.

'I didn't recognise you at first,' I said. 'But the new sketch caught your eyes. I knew I'd seen you somewhere, but I only recognised you when I walked in and saw your face in the mirror.'

He rinsed the soap off his hands as carefully as he'd lathered them up. Watered off the inside of his palms, then made sure the backs of his hands and fingers were thoroughly done. Some ritual. Then he shrugged and made a face of resignation at me from the mirror? 'I suppose it's all over then, isn't it?'

I nodded. 'It's over, Matt,'

'What do you suggest we do now, then?' he said.

I pulled out my mobile, watching Matt cautiously as I called up a name. The phone picked up and Beering's voice greeted me.

'It's Punter. I'm with the strapper killer in the members' toilets at the back of the Manikato restaurant.'

A stunned silence for about half a second. Then, 'You're *what?*'

'You better get here. Like, *now.*'

'Are you okay?'

'We're just fine.'

'Don't move! I'll be there straightaway.'

I snapped the mobile shut. Hadn't taken my eyes off Matt the whole time I'd been talking to Beering.

'They're coming to get me, then?' he said. Pattered on as if I'd just called him a cab. Seemed to accept the situation. Perhaps he was glad the game was up.

'Uh-huh.'

'It's probably best that way,' he said. He held his still dripping hands awkwardly up in front of him like he didn't quite know what to do with them, and motioned with his chin to the basket of hand towels by the vase.

'Would you mind passing one over?'

I should have seen it coming from a mile off. I only glanced to where he was looking for a second, but that was all he needed. He charged at me like a runaway horse, except runaway horses don't carry knives. This one did, a menacing glint of steel with my name written on the blade. He ran at me like he was possessed. I was already hard against the door and slammed back into it, managing to get in one decent drop kick against his stomach. I succeeded in shoving him away, but only for a moment, then he came for me again in a swearing, slashing frenzy.

'I should have done a proper job on you the first time,' he growled at me.

I groped desperately for anything I could use as a weapon. Grabbed at a bunch of the hand towels which I instinctively wrapped around my left fist. Matt laughed cruelly at my futile effort to arm myself. He brought his knife up slowly in front of him, teasing me with its point, and slowly advanced. I held my left hand out like some sort of shield. It was a poor substitute, but it wasn't all I had to defend myself with. I reached down with my free hand and unbuckled my belt, ripped it out of its keepers. That drew another laugh from him. I flicked the length of the belt at his face like a stockwhip and he respectfully took a half step back as the heavy buckle hissed past just short of his face. It wouldn't really stop him, but at least it gave him something to watch out for.

'Come on then, you weak prick,' I said. 'Bit harder this, isn't it, than creeping into some sleeping girl's bedroom.'

He didn't like that. A flaring of the nostrils and a narrowing of those angry slits. Billco really had captured those eyes.

'Well, it's true, isn't it?' I taunted. Nothing to lose and it just might buy me some time. Time for Beering to come. *If* he ever came.

'Up against a bloke your own size now. Big difference, isn't there?'

I flicked another roll of the belt at him, put some power into it, and he winced slightly as the buckle barked against his knuckles.

Behind him, a door opened and some punter walked in. I'd forgotten that the toilet had two doors, the far door leading through to another section in the members' betting area. The guy freaked out when he saw us. Matt with the knife and me fending him off like some gladiator with my towelled-up hand and the belt. He ran out the way he'd come in, shouting for police at the top of his voice. Matt picked up the plastic canister of hand wash from the basin and threw it at me. I blocked it easily with my fist but it glanced off and hit me in the forehead, disgorging its soapy liquid into my eyes. Then I heard the crash of the door flung back on its hinges as Matt bolted.

I took off after him, wiping my eyes with the sleeve of my jacket as I ran. Bloody soap stung like crazy and my eyes were watering like a sprinkler. I heard a shout off to one side but didn't stop to find out, just sprinted after Matt as I saw him disappearing through the crowd. He didn't have much of a break on me, thirty metres maybe, but it's hard work trying to push your way through a packed betting ring at a walk, let alone at a gallop. I side-stepped one gambler reading his formguide and elbowed another bloke to his side as I rushed through the gap. Copped a spray off him, but there was no time for apologies. I saw Matt running ahead of me as I raced past Big Oakie White's stand. Caught a glimpse of the big fella watching dumbfounded as I sprinted by. Up ahead, Matt had cannoned into an elderly lady and sent her sprawling. A group clustered around to help her up. Matt ran on towards the members' exit and jumped the turnstiles into the public area.

'Punter! Where's he gone?' yelled Beering. He had two policemen in tow who he must have grabbed on the way through. About bloody time, although to be fair only a few minutes had elapsed since I'd rung him. I stopped for a second and pointed to Matt who we could see running through the terraced area towards the exit gate about a hundred metres away.

'Quick, there he goes,' I said.

We stormed after him as best we could and burst through the old-fashioned exit turnstiles to find ourselves outside the track opposite the railway station. A lone yellow taxi drove off from the rank with Matt grinning at us from the back window. He'd slipped the net.

We reconvened in Beering's office. He was working his phone non-stop, answering calls and making them. One of his calls was to Detective Wells from Homicide and fifteen minutes later, he and his offsider, Tony, arrived.

They'd tracked the taxi down, but it had already dropped off its fare in Malvern.

The driver said he'd let the man out onto the busy shopping strip in Glenferrie Road and that's the last he'd seen of him.

'Shit, he could be anywhere by now,' said Beering.

'Even so, we'll comb the area,' said Wells. 'Right, what else do we know about this guy?'

'We know he's a regular club member,' I said. 'Can't we bring up his details on the database?'

Beering reached for his phone, got hold of the marketing manager.

'. . . I don't care if it was the Queen who won the previous race, let someone else do the presentation and get your arse down here like it was yesterday.'

Annie, the marketing manager, came flouncing into Beering's office in a huff. Complained of not looking after the club's sponsors and so forth. She was in her mid-thirties, dressed for business, and carried plenty of attitude at being pulled away from her corporate entertaining duties. She soon dropped the attitude when Beering told her why he wanted her so urgently. Amazing what effect the words *strapper killer* had around the racecourse. She got to work straightaway on Beering's desktop computer, firing it up and opening up the membership file.

'Okay, we've got nearly nine thousand members, guys. You tell me where to prune it down,' she said.

'His name's Whittle,' I said, 'Matt Whittle.' I spelled it out for her.

Annie keyed in his name and then looked over at us. 'I haven't got any Whittles.'

'What? You *must* have.'

'No, definitely no Whittles,' she said. 'I've got lots of Whites, but no Whittles.'

We all clustered around behind her, staring at the screen, willing it to give up the name. It was as she said, devoid of anyone called Whittle.

'Are you sure that's his surname?' asked Beering.

'It's him all right. It's Col Whittle's stepson. Hang on,' I had a sudden thought. 'Maybe he's not using his stepfather's surname.'

'Makes sense,' said Beering. 'A lot of kids don't always take up a step-parent's name. But if not, then what's his real name?'

'All right,' said Wells, 'so we haven't got his surname for now. Let's run with his first name and see what comes up. Annie, can you try a sort by Matt?'

She typed a few key strokes, highlighted the screen and did a sort by members' first names.

'There're fourteen Matts listed,' she said.

'That's doable,' said Tony. 'We can check those addresses out.'

'Wait,' said Beering. 'How many Matthews you got?'

Annie did another sort and we could all see the whopping list it generated. 'Two hundred and seventy-two Matthews,' she said.

'Plus the fourteen who've registered as Matt, makes nearly three hundred-odd addresses to check out,' said Wells. 'Shit.'

'I know someone who might be able to filter it down,' I said.

They all looked at me expectantly.

'Matt's got a mate here today who might know more about him.'

'A *mate*,' said Beering. 'Wouldn't have thought this creep would have any of those.'

'Maybe that's too nice a word. Drinking buddy is more like

266

it. You want me to see if I can find him and bring him back? He's probably still over in the café.'

'I'll come with you. Let's go,' said Beering, already reaching for his hat.

I pointed out Ric exactly where I'd left him; propping up a pylon with a drink watching the races on the TV monitor. I don't know what Ric must have thought when Beering flashed his badge and told him he needed to ask him some questions about Matt back in his office. I didn't tell him anything on the walk back; I left that for Beering, who broke it to him about as subtly as a golfer hitting off from the tee.

'Now then, what this is about is your mate, Matt. He's been identified as the strapper killer.'

Ric looked incredulous. 'Matt? *Him*, the strapper killer?'

'Yeah, yeah, Matt,' said Beering, impatient to get on with it. 'Do you know where he lives?'

'Shit, I hardly know the bloke. I mean, the only time I ever see him is at the races to have a beer with him. We were only just drinking with him half an hour ago like we normally do every Saturday.'

Wells chipped in. 'Ric, this is really important. Do you have an address for Matt or do you know his surname? Maybe you've got his mobile number?'

Ric shook his head. 'I've never known him by any other name apart from Matt; I only ever see him at the races. We've never swapped numbers. But he lives locally, I dropped him home in a cab one day.'

Beering nearly jumped over his desk. 'You know where he lives?' he thundered. 'Then get over 'ere in front of this computer and pick 'im out.'

Poor Ric looked shell-shocked. Dragged from a pleasant afternoon drink at the races into a full-on police interrogation. Annie pulled over a chair next to her and let Ric sift through the list of Matts and Matthews she had up on the screen.

'Okay, that makes it easier if he's a local,' she said. 'I'll delete all the non-local suburbs from the list.'

Ric looked blankly at the computer. 'Well, I don't know *exactly* where he lives.'

'For God's sake, man, you just said you shared a cab home with him, didn't you?' said Beering.

'Yeah, but I'm not sure where.'

'Well, which suburb is it; Caulfield, Caulfield South, Glen Huntly, Murrumbeena?'

Ric still had the blanks. Wells had to help him out.

'You said you dropped him at his house, right?'

'Not his house.' He frowned as if trying to remember. 'It was one evening we shared a taxi back from the track and he got me to drop him off home. Well, it wasn't home, it was his street, though. He said to the driver to pull up and he could walk the rest of the way 'cause it was just around the corner.'

Wells looked pleased. 'Okay, that's good. Take another look and see if you recognise any streets.'

We waited silently as Ric worked slowly and thoroughly through the list. He didn't get any quicker, even with Beering impatiently pacing the room, hands-behind-back style. But Ric wasn't going to be hurried. He pointed at a name, then another which Annie highlighted. By the time he'd gone through them all, there were eight addresses all around the cusp of Murrumbeena and Carnegie. Beering pulled out a Melways directory from a shelf and spread it open on the desk.

'This help?' he asked. 'Can you recognise any of those from the map?'

Ric peered back and forth between the directory and the computer screen for a moment, before giving a frustrated sigh.

'No. They're just names, I'd only be guessing. But there's a way I could remember. If I took the same route the cab took, I'd know where we dropped him, even though it was dark. We went down Grange or Koornang Road and I dropped him off at an intersection there somewhere, before the taxi drove me home to Beaumaris. There was a milk bar, a little corner shop. If I saw that again, I'd know.'

Over the next forty minutes we cruised up and down Grange and Koornang roads three times. Wells was driving, Ric was in the front with him and Beering and I shared the back. A second unmarked car carrying Tony and two other policemen followed behind us. Ric thought it must have been Grange Road that the taxi driver had gone down, but we trawled up and down and there was no milk bar on any side street. In fact, there wasn't any milk bar full stop. We didn't have any better luck in Koornang Road either. We swept down past a small group of community shops; a greengrocer, newsagent and a florist.

'You sure that's not them?' asked Wells. 'Things always look different in the dark.'

'No, it was just the one corner shop on the left-hand side driving south. I'm sure of that,' said Ric.

We drove all the way down to North Road before Ric made us turn around and go back up again. Wells drove on a little bit further and then pulled over to the side of the road opposite a development site. He turned the engine off and started drumming his fingers on the console.

'Maybe we oughta try the next one up, Murrumbeena Road,' he said to Ric.

Beering, who'd been studying the road directory, agreed. 'There's two or three members' addresses here with streets that criss-cross Murrumbeena and go all the way through to Grange.'

Ric didn't look happy. 'I know I saw it. I'm sure it was in one of these two streets.'

'Yeah, but it don't seem to be there, does it?' said Beering.

'Perhaps it used to be,' I said.

Wells spun around to look at me. I nodded to the empty development block opposite us. It had a bulldozer and a tip truck parked within it's wired-off fence. Outside was a skip bin full of rubble. Sitting on top of the rubbish was an old neon advertising sign cheekily proclaiming: *Peters Ice-cream, the health food of a nation!*

'That could be what's left of the milk bar,' I said.

We all sat looking at where the milk bar had stood before it was demolished. 'Good call,' said Wells to me. 'You reckon this is the spot?' he asked Ric.

Ric nodded confidently back. 'This is it. Corner of Koornang and Leielia.'

Beering rustled around next to me sorting through his list of names. 'But there's no Matthew or Matt registered as living in Leielia Street.'

'You sure?' asked Wells. 'What's the nearest Matt or Matthew on that list to this street?'

Beering shuffled around with the Melways and his list again. He was pretty quick at sorting through them. Helped that he knew the area, I suppose. 'Nearest I've got is listed eight blocks away. A bloke by the name of Matthew Power.'

Wells shook his head. 'I can't see why he'd get a cab to drop him eight blocks from home, no matter how paranoid he might be about revealing his address.' He turned to Ric again. 'You're sure his home was in this street?'

'He said just around the corner.'

I had a thought which I ran past Beering. 'This list is generated from first names, right?'

'Yeah, it's all we've got to work with. Matts and Matthews.'

'But there's none in this street.'

'Which is why I think we've got the wrong street.'

'No,' I said. 'We're asking the database the wrong question. Can you get hold of Annie again?'

'Yeah, why?'

'Call her and ask her to run a sort by members in Leielia Street.'

Beering called her and she gave us the answer almost straight-away.

'There's only one member with an address in that street. Goes by the name of M T Renford.'

I looked at Beering and Wells. 'I'll bet that's him. M for Matt and Renford is probably his mother's maiden name or real father's surname.'

20

Ric and I found ourselves standing by the roadside, staring forlornly at the back of two unmarked police cars as they roared off down the road. As soon as Wells and his team decided to raid Matt's house, we'd both been evicted rather unceremoniously from the car and told in no uncertain terms to stay right away from the area. Wells said he didn't want civilians contaminating evidence or placing ourselves in any unnecessary danger. I thought that was a bit rich, given what I'd been through that afternoon. And so we were left stranded on the corner, the decision ours whether to hoof it back to Caulfield or hail a cab. We ended up walking back, talking as we went. So much for Ric's form as a reluctant conversationalist; now I could hardly shut him up.

'I still can't believe it,' said Ric. 'I wouldn't have picked him in a million years. I mean, the whole thing's crazy. Matt'd be the least likely guy I'd nominate as being the strapper killer. Maybe they've made another mistake and got the wrong guy again?'

'Not this time they haven't. How well did you know him?'

'Matt? As well as the rest of the gang did.'

'No, you knew him better than us. I remember you drinking with him before any of us had met him.'

Ric put his hands in his jacket pockets and walked briskly down the footpath alongside me. He frowned as if trying to remember.

'It was about a year ago. I'm always first to the bar at the races. I camp there the whole afternoon and watch them on the TV, not like you, wanting to walk all around the course. I noticed him drinking on his own, reading a formguide. He'd usually be there at the same place most Saturdays and we ended up sharing a beer talking about the neddies. It just grew from there. I'd nod at him; ask him how he was going. We'd talk racing, have a dig at each other for backing losers. Then he sort of became one of the regular gang by hanging out with me.'

'Did you ever, like, go out socially with him?'

'Never. The only time I've ever been with him outside of a racetrack, is that time I shared a cab on the way back home with him. Other than that, he's always been just good old Matt from the track.'

We stopped to let some cars past on Grange Road then walked quickly across through a gap in the traffic.

'See, that's the thing with him, isn't it?' I said. 'No one really knows anything of substance about him, other than he seemed a nice bloke and was good company.'

'You're right. He joked with all of us about betting and horses and stuff and he and I always took the piss out of each other. I've always thought of him as a regular family man.'

'Maybe he's just been a good actor all this time.'

By the time we reached the car park entrance in Kambrook Road, the races had long since finished and only a sprinkling of cars remained for their owners to collect them. I'd parked my van in the members' area further down, so I said goodbye to Ric by the corrugated iron fence and turned to move on. Ric stood, a bit undecided, fiddling with the car keys in his hand.

'What do you think will happen to him?' he said.

'They'll find him, I guess. Put him away. Sooner rather than later, I hope.'

'What if they don't find him?' He jerked his head at some racetrack graffiti painted on the fence: *Winners keep winning and losers keep on losing.*

'Killers keep killing, don't they?' he said.

I had a stack of missed calls and text messages banked up on my mobile. I scrolled through them as I walked to my van. Most of them were from the gang demanding to know what the hell had gone down that afternoon. All they'd seen was Ric being marched off by Beering, but you could bet news of my run-in with Matt and our chase after him would have spread all over the course. Tiny had rung twice but hadn't left any message. Kate had rung and left a voice message and a text message with a terse, 'Punter, ring me.' She could sniff a story from a mile away, that girl. My brother had called, as had Maxine, who'd left a rather pathetic-sounding cough-cough-I'm-sick message. Said she'd come down with a cold and a headache and would I mind if I skipped her coming over to my place tonight, she was going to take some aspirin and go to bed. I rang her anyway and told her the news about Matt.

'Jesus, you actually knew this guy? Like, he hung out with you and the gang the whole time?' she said incredulously. It came out like an accusation and I think she realised it as soon as she said it. 'I'm sorry, I didn't mean it like that.'

'He's fooled a lot of people for a long time,' I said. 'Ric still can't believe it and he knew him better than most of us.'

'Are you okay? That's the second time you've got into a fight with him.'

'I'm all right.'

She went quiet, then: 'Punter, what do you think he'll do, where do you think he'll go?'

'I can guarantee you one place he won't be next Saturday, and that's at the races.'

'Be serious.'

'I don't know. I honestly don't know. He's been flushed out so he can't go back to his home. The police know exactly who they're looking for now, so he'll have to stay in hiding. But he can't do that indefinitely. You know something, I think that until he's caught you should be extra careful.'

'Don't worry, Dad's penthouse has the max in security. No one comes in or out without getting past the doorman and cameras. Even the elevator needs a security card to get up to the top floor. Besides, he doesn't know my movements or where I live now. I haven't gone near my apartment since he attacked me that night. But maybe you ought to think about taking some extra precautions yourself.'

'Me? I've seen that weak dog's form. All he's got the guts to do is prey on sleeping women. Don't think he'll be stealing into my bedroom any time soon. If he does, fine, bring it on.'

'Even so, Punter, you want to take care.'

'I will. See you tomorrow?'

'I'll see how I feel. I'll call you if I'm feeling better.'

I returned Kate's call next, kept it short and sharp.

'You never got this address from me, right?'

'Got what address?' she replied suspiciously.

'Eighty-four Leielia Street, Murrumbeena. Belongs to an M T Renford. The police are raiding it as we speak.'

'Should I know this person?'

'Kate, it's Matt. Matt from the gang.'

'*Matt*, Ric's buddy?'

'Uh-huh.'

'What are the cops doing there?'

'He's the one, Kate. He's the strapper killer.'

'Are you serious?'

'You want a scoop, get yourself down there. I'll call you later, bye.'

At my flat later that night, I thought through the day's activities over a cold beer and a bad movie. In the ad breaks, they had lots of live news crosses to where the police had cordoned off Matt's place. The media had got onto it fast; all the major networks seemed to have a TV crew outside Leielia Street. When the nine o'clock newsflash came on, there must have been a dozen camera crews parked out the front of the house, their portable spotlights illuminating number eighty-four like a Christmas tree. Neighbours stood at a respectable distance behind the crime-scene tape, trying to guess what all the activity was about.

They didn't have to wait long to find out. This time around, the police didn't hold anything back from the press. After all, they had a killer on the loose and the public had to be warned who he was. They showed an actual photo of Matt which they must have found inside his place. He appeared much younger in the photo than he did now, but he hadn't changed all that much.

I fielded a lot of calls that evening. Beering rang and filled me in with the latest. After Ric and I had been ejected from the car, they'd raided Matt's place, which turned out to be a flat behind the main house. Apparently he owned the house which he rented out. They probably only missed him by an hour or less, which was about the time it had taken us to figure out his address. A young girl from the family in the house said she'd seen him running up the driveway of his flat and then ride off on a bike shortly afterwards. The police were still searching through his household contents, but they'd taken away various items of clothing to the lab for testing as well as his car, which had been impounded. They now had the whole place sealed off and guarded. Beering said he'd call me again in the morning and that Ric and I would have to answer a few more questions. Big Oakie called. He said I'd have won a Newmarket the way he saw me sprinting through the betting ring. I told him that despite my chase, it had been a wasted effort; that Matt had escaped. He said he'd just seen the news and wondered if I was all right. Tiny rang me while the news bulletin was showing, demanding to know what had gone on. He was bouncing at the Tavern in King Street and I spent five minutes explaining to him what had happened. A minute later, David rang up and I went through the whole thing again with him. I felt like I should make a recorded message: *Punter's Saturday night crime beat update.*

During the evening Kate called back twice wanting to check her story. She already had more than enough to be ahead of the other Sunday papers. I knew Beering had always had a soft spot for her, would have given her a couple of good angles. So I figured her story tomorrow would be worth reading.

Next morning Che woke me at five with his usual scratch-the-door-it's-breakfast-time antics. I got up and fed him, then poked my head outside to see what the weather was doing. It was still semi-dark, bloody daylight saving; surfers like me can't stand the stupid idea of being robbed of an hour's prime surfing time at dawn. I could just make out the flag above Scotch College. It hung limp. Not a breath of wind; a beautiful, still morning for a surf. That's what I did all day Sunday. Made an absolute glutton of myself with two long surfing sessions, morning and afternoon. I hit Big Lefts first, paddled out just after seven. There were a couple of longboarders out, but no sign of Billco. Pity, because I wanted to thank him again for the sketch he'd done. I scored some nice waves over a couple of hours, good, clean four- to six-foot faces, with the occasional bigger rogue set rolling through, trying to catch me unawares. When the tide got too fat, I came in and walked back up the cliff-side track and under the pines to where my van was. After I changed, I dropped by Billco's house, but his car wasn't there and no one answered when I knocked on the door. So I drove on to Flinders, bought the Sunday papers and ordered a late breakfast at the bakery.

Matt had made the front pages. The *Herald Sun* had gone with 'Strapper killer identified'. *The Age* had a similar headline: 'Police raid strapper killer's house'. Both of them carried the photo of Matt that I'd seen on the news last night. There were pictures of the police cordon set up around his house and also of Wells and Beering, along with their comments. I was glad that Ric and I had been kicked out when we had, or we would probably have been splashed across the papers as well. Kate's article was very good and she must have burned the midnight oil to get it out on time. But there was another interesting story written by one of her *Age* colleagues which hit on the fact that Kate, as a reporter, had unknowingly mixed socially with Matt at the races.

COFFEE WITH A KILLER

Afternoon tea at the races is something to look forward to. A dabble on the horses, a sociable drink and a chance to meet people. Hardly a place you'd expect to share coffee and cake with a killer. But that's just what happened to *Age* crime reporter, Kate Truscott, who had afternoon tea with alleged killer Matt Renford at Caulfield races yesterday. In an extraordinary turn of events, Ms Truscott revealed that an acquaintance of her regular social group at the races had turned out to be the alleged strapper killer.

'It was quite incredible,' she said. 'One moment we were sharing drinks and swapping hard luck stories like we do every Saturday, then moments later we heard a fight had broken out and the police were chasing Matt through the betting ring. He used to drink with our group every race meeting. He'd be the last person any of us would have thought of as being a killer.'

I trawled through every story in both papers and the consensus was that Matt had escaped after a short struggle and chase. He'd been traced to his address nearby, but it appeared he'd again just eluded police when they'd raided his flat shortly after. It was still too early to get an accurate, detailed background on Matt, given the scant information available. A *Sun* reporter had a go at filling in the gaps. What he lacked in facts, he filled in with horrified comments from neighbours, shocked to find they were living next door to an apparent serial killer. I took another look at his photo in the paper with the caption screaming out: *Have you seen this man?* I still thought Billco's sketch had captured his eyes better.

I don't think the photo looks anything like me. It certainly doesn't resemble my appearance now. Amazing what a pair of sunglasses and a baseball cap worn backwards can do for you. Not to mention the number one haircut I gave myself last night. I look again at the photo of me as a teenager staring back from the newspaper. The police must have taken it from my flat. Taken that and everything else that I have.

The waitress brings my scrambled eggs and caffè latte and deposits them in front of me with an insincere, 'Enjoy.' As soon as I touch the glass I know they've burnt the coffee. Why can't they ever get the temperature right? I think about sending it back but stop short of getting up and making a scene. Fly under the radar, don't draw attention to yourself. Different ball game now that I've been identified. I skim through some of the stories again. They don't know shit. Just making it up as they go along. That Indian family who rent the house off me; asked if they ever suspected I was a killer. Those morons, what a joke. And that stupid bitch reporter friend of Punter's, did you see her nothing article? What about Punter? I notice he neatly avoided any mention. The smug fuck.

I sip at the burnt coffee and pick at the scrambled eggs. Disgusting. If I was at home, I could have fixed my own breakfast rather than pay some disinterested waitress for her slack service and a restaurant's bad food. But the rules have changed, haven't they? I don't actually have a kitchen to fix myself a meal in. 'Home', as of now, is a smelly room in a tatty St Kilda backpacker hostel. They actually asked me if I minded sharing the room. No matter that I paid cash for a single. Obviously booked out and trying to maximise the rooms, the cheap bastards. The place is disgracefully noisy. Travellers; partying to all hours. Talking, laughing, drinking. More than once I was tempted to storm into the room opposite and tell them I'd cut their little backpacker tongues out if they didn't shut up. But I kept to myself, lay on my bed all night staring at the ceiling and thinking.

And now what?

After breakfast I sit on a seat by a path overlooking St Kilda pier thinking about what has happened and what I have to do. Behind me is my bicycle and on the seat beside me is my pack stuffed with the few scant possessions I was able to gather at short notice. A change of clothes, the roll of money from the freezer, my knife and the jockey silks, of course. Because after yesterday's fiasco at the races, Punter's actions have forced me to leave my own home. What an utter debacle. Punter recognising me in the toilets, the scrimmage with him. I was lucky to escape before police or security nabbed me and it will change my situation drastically. It just doesn't seem possible that my fortunes could change so abruptly. Punter's ruined everything. I knew I should have finished him that night at Maxine's. Should have stuck the knife in good and hard and finished the job off properly. Done them both instead of leaving loose ends. That had been a sloppy night's work, which I was paying for now.

It hurts. It really hurts.

It's my property! I live in the flat and I rent out the house. I get four hundred and twenty-five dollars a week from the Indian family I lease it out to. It's mine; my mother left it to me in her will when she died. Mother's death . . . If I had the knowledge and the strength of conviction that I possess now, I would have hastened that disgusting old whore's departure into the next world a lot sooner than the heart attack she died from. She deserved worse, much worse. I should have slit her filthy throat . . .

Where was I? My house . . . Now I daren't show my face at the real estate agent. I will no longer be able to collect an income because the property will be under watch and the police will be waiting for me. Not only that, I can't sell it without the police being notified. Fuck! Punter hasn't just cost me the weekly rent, he's taken away my inheritance as well. What's the place worth? The house is old and in need of repairs, but anything in Murrumbeena fetches six hundred thousand these days. And mine is an extra large block with a flat at the back, just ripe for developers to put up townhouses. Eight, maybe nine hundred thousand. That's what that bastard has done me out of. Punter has cost me my car too. I didn't want to leave it behind, but the police would have traced the registration details and that made it too risky to drive around in. By now the police would have gone right through my flat, my garage, the car and all of my belongings. They'd have seized my computer and the newspaper clippings. Intruded into every part of my personal life, then sorted it away in neat little boxes.

I think about going away, interstate perhaps. Perhaps I could book a plane ticket or hire a car and just go. Except I realise I can't do that now without difficulty. You need a credit card or EFTPOS for that and my card is cactus; they'd have an alert out on it by now. So I sit by the water, a seething rage building about my predicament.

I try to be calm about it, try to think it through rationally. But I've got no home, no income and no car. And by now, my name and description will be on every policeman's lips in Melbourne. It's just so unbelievable, so unjust, that someone can simply come in and take it all away from me in the blink of an eye.

A flock of seagulls begins milling around me, thinking they might scrounge an easy feed off an unwary tourist. I pick up a stone and throw it at them; hit one of them in the chest, and when the pebble falls to the ground the others immediately pounce on it. The stupid birds peck and caw at each other over what they think is a possible food scrap before realising there's nothing to fight over. And I smile for the first time that day. Smile at the sheer stupidity of the birds. They exist as a pack, a follow-the-leader mentality. But I'm not stupid. I don't follow anyone, I make my own rules. So I don't have a permanent roof over my head. No matter, plenty of hostels and caravan parks around where they don't ask any questions. The danger of being recognised? Easy. I've already changed my appearance. I might even get a couple of fake tattoos and really blend in like some of those nitwit backpackers. And money, I have the five-thousand-dollar roll and another twenty-five hundred in my savings account which should be plenty for the moment. Transport? Okay, so I have no car. But nothing wrong with my mountain bike. It has no registration to trace and is particularly good for getting around the city. And I'd be just another of the thousands of cyclists who ride around town every day. Maybe I could pose as a bike courier . . . See, I'm already looking ahead to new possibilities. But there's unfinished business to attend to first. Sloppy work that has to be corrected. And Punter has to be punished, must be punished for what he's done to me.

When I came back from my second surf on Sunday afternoon, I still hadn't heard from Maxine. So much for her promised call. I rang her anyway and left a message. I stopped off at Gino's for dinner on the way home and caught up with Billy over a pizza. He said we'd had an okay week, but that was as far as talking business went. All he wanted to do was talk about Matt being the strapper killer. Billy had lots of theories on why he'd turned out the way he had; I must have heard at least a dozen in the half hour I spent with him. I was secretly glad when it started getting busy and he had to leave me and lend a hand behind the counter. When I got home I still hadn't heard from Maxine. It wasn't too late to call her, but I figured she'd have rung me by now if she was going to. Besides, I was knackered from my two surfing sessions and the drive back from the peninsula, so I took a shower and went straight to bed.

On Monday morning after breakfast, I dropped by Beering's office. He was leaning back in his chair reading the formguide.

'Don't you ever make appointments, Punter?' he grumbled.

'Yeah, I can see you're so busy.'

'Well as it turns out, I'm not. Leastways not after Saturday. Coffee? Help yourself, you know where it is,' he said. Beering put aside his formguide and I poured myself a coffee from the percolator and sat down in the chair in front of his desk.

'It's all out of my hands for the moment,' he explained. 'The police are conducting the search for Renford. Meanwhile, they've gone through his flat, turned it inside out. And his car too.'

'Find anything interesting?'

'They've found enough. DNA from his clothes and bed linen which match the DNA found at the murder scenes. In his flat and car they found plenty of clear prints and a roll of venetian cord, consistent with what he tied his victims up with.'

'What about his wife and kids, where do they all fit into this?'

'There is no wife and kids. At least, none that we've been able to discover.'

'But he told us all he was . . .'

Beering shook his head. 'That's all just part of the fantasy world he created. See, they can be very clever, the way they portray themselves, these people. Making out he was just a regular family guy was part of his devious personality.'

I thought back to when I'd asked Matt about his family. 'He

once spun some yarn about his wife always going shopping on a Saturday afternoon while he was at the races. And his kids; I remember him being a little unsure of school holiday dates. Didn't think anything of it at the time.'

'Why wouldn't you believe him? He played the part so well he probably believed it himself.'

'He told us all he didn't have to work, that he'd been left some property investments by his parents. Is that just make-believe, too?'

'Actually, we're still trying to get all the history from the real estate agent. Wells was talking to them yesterday. But it looks like he was left the house and the flat out the back by his parents. His stepfather was a builder, who built them both. It seems Matt rented out the house and lived in the flat. He survived on the rent, never had to work. So I suppose the property investor part is true.'

I took a sip of my coffee; lukewarm and bitter, been sitting in the jug since early morning. I downed it anyway. 'He had a pretty comfortable life then, didn't he,' I said. 'The house as income. The flat to live in. No boss. Could come and go as he pleased.'

'Yeah, well, he won't be doing that from now on. That lifestyle vanished as of Saturday. He's got you to thank for that, Punter. You and that artist mate of yours.'

'Did they find the silks?'

Beering shook his head. 'Must have taken 'em with him when he shot through. We can't have missed him by much. I reckon he must have high-tailed it back to his place and grabbed what he could. One of the kids in the front house reckons she saw him ride off on his bike. Apparently he was into cycling.'

'Doesn't make him any easier to find.'

'Nope, it doesn't.'

'What do you think he'll do, I mean for money and stuff?'

'We know he withdrew two and a half grand of his savings on Sunday from an ATM in the city. So for the time being he's not short of a quid.'

'You reckon he's hiding out in town somewhere?'

'Could be anywhere. Police are going through all the hotels and motels. Issuing copies of his photo. They got a watch out at the airports and stations. Wells reckons he's probably still close by. He can't use his credit card without leaving a trail, so that cancels out a lot of options for him. It's a game of hide and seek now, but the police are confident they'll flush him out soon.'

In the afternoon, I did some form for tomorrow's Geelong meeting then went down to the garage to put a new set of fins on my wave ski. My plan was to get a morning session in at Torquay Point, then catch the races at Geelong on the way home. I spent the best part of an hour fiddling around in the garage. Che was helping me, of course. Jumping up on the workbench and trying to cram his head into the jars of nuts and bolts. You never know; could be a moth hiding in there that needed pouncing on. The only thing he caught was a scolding from me for getting in the way. I replaced the old fins and was glad I did, because the middle one had a crack running down to the screw and would have split on the very first bottom turn I cranked out on a wave. I tightened the new fibreglass fins in the boxes, then checked the seatbelts and footwells. All good, so I shooed Che outside, locked the garage door and went back upstairs. When I checked my phone, Maxine had left me a text message: *Kinda busy all wk. Maybe Friday night?*

A *text*, for Christ sakes. Couldn't she just call and talk to me? What sort of a stupid message was that anyway? *Kinda busy.* Busy doing what? Work, another art gallery opening? Presumably she still had to eat; not out of the question she could at least share a meal with me. I mean, I could even manage an early-morning breakfast meeting if she managed to fit me into her busy schedule. And what's with the *maybe*? Why not say, 'Meet me at 7.45 pm your place', or the Canary Bar, or wherever. Somewhere, some place you actually make a commitment to. I cracked the top off a Beck's and sat at the kitchen table sulking over the text. I felt like a task that had been reprioritised. Is that what this relationship had really got down to? Me, a chore to be attended to when time allowed?

I ended up sinking another two beers at the table with Che as my drinking partner. Don't laugh; at least he spent quality time with me. By the third round, I'd composed some fantastical, long-winded response in my mind that I was going to send back to Maxine by text. Firstly, I'd question her ruthlessly on just what was keeping her so busy. Raise the issue of her time management skills and work-life-relationship priorities, so forth. Che thought it sounded all right when I recited it to him. Meowed encouragingly at the bit where I said I wasn't going to wait around like a cancelled appointment waiting to be rescheduled. And by the way, where did she think this relationship was headed? The damn thing sounded like a letter in an Agony Aunt column.

'Forget it, Che,' I said, giving him a scratch under the collar. 'It would take me half the night to send by text, anyway.'

No, I'd handle it in my own usual, unsatisfactory manner, the same way I always did with the female of the species. Too proud to communicate my feelings. Too stupid to do anything but mull it over endlessly and say nothing. Stew on it. Let it build up till the whole thing explodes in my face. You're a fucking mug, Punter.

At Torquay Point the next morning, I surfed aggressively. Manoeuvring myself way inside everybody else, clinging to the prime take-off spot like some selfish eighteen-year-old short-boarder with attitude. More than once I called another surfer off my wave with a curt '*Oi!*' as I attacked the wave face and screamed past them. I chased down every swell that came my way, a greedy little wave hog who didn't even look like he was enjoying himself. Nor was I having a good time. That's not my normal surfing style. I usually give away as many waves to others as I catch. But today I was sitting grim-faced on my ski, wanting to take on the whole world.

When I came in from my surf, I ate a chicken wrap at Spooners on the main drag. The guy who served me just wanted to yap and I didn't feel much like talking, so I pretended my phone was ringing and put it to my ear. Pathetic, isn't it, when you have to resort to deceptions like that to make an escape.

Afterwards, I killed some time wandering aimlessly through the surf-second shops looking for something to buy. Couldn't find a single thing I needed. The day had turned to shit and it didn't improve any at the races. My main chance was a late scratching in the third. He'd hurt himself in the float coming down to Geelong, which meant I'd have to wait around until the seventh race before I could do any business. I found myself getting bored and restless and breaking my cardinal rule of having 'play' bets. Even play bets start to add up and I was chasing my tail by the time the seventh eventually came around. The mood I was in, the day I was having, most people would have packed up and called it a day. Not me. John Punter, number one sucker for self-inflicted punishment, decided to stay for a final round. I backed three horses in an eight-horse field. Broke another rule doing that, too. *Small fields, beware.* I took the shorts about the favourite, saved on the other two and then watched in disgust as a bolter stormed down the outside to relegate my horses to second, third and fourth. Score: Punter, zilch. Bookmakers, a big smile on their faces.

I didn't go to the Triangle that night for our regular game of snooker. I was feeling too shitty and I just knew the whole night would be one endless question and answer session about Matt anyway. So I rang David with some excuse and told him I was a no-show.

On Wednesday I hadn't heard any more from Maxine. I debated whether to call her or respond to her text. Decided to do nothing. I went out to Sandown in the afternoon. A better result for me than the previous day; I only played the one race and it won convincingly. Thursday was Bendigo. Although I didn't end up having a bet, the day turned out okay. I spotted a couple of runners worth jotting down in my black book for next time and enjoyed a nice fisherman's pie in a local restaurant on the way back home.

She still hadn't rung.

On Friday I launched into the weekend's form straight after breakfast and tackled it solidly all morning before my phone rang about lunchtime. It was Kate.

'I'm sorry to hear about you and Maxine,' she said.

'*Sorry?*'

'About you and her breaking up.'

'Come again?'

'I just saw the picture in the afternoon *Xpress*, you know, her and that lawyer caught pashing on at the food and wine festival yesterday.'

I'd had a nasty feeling all week. The radar on the back of my neck had been sending signals and yet I'd been ignoring them.

'Punter, you there?'

'Yeah, I'm here. And *thank you very much* for that,' I said as sarcastically as I could. 'Not often a guy gets the heads up from his ex that he's just been dropped. I think I would have preferred to find out first from Maxine.'

I could have heard a pin drop at the other end as Kate realised the huge gaffe she'd just made.

'Oh my god, I'm so sorry. Punter, I didn't realise that she –'

'What, that it might have slipped her mind to tell me?'

'I'm sure she –'

'She'd get around to it?'

Sure she would. If she wasn't so *kinda* fucking busy.

21

I slammed the phone down and tossed it onto the table. Was it true? Was that what Maxine had been up to behind my back? On Saturday night she'd said she was sick and the rest of the week she'd been too busy. Busy all right. Busy with I bet I knew who. I stormed up to the newsagent to get a copy of the afternoon *Xpress* and opened it inside my van. Sure enough, there she was on page four in the *City Confidential* section, kissing that smarmy lawyer, Rodney Ellis. All over him like a rash and he was hardly fighting her off. I forced myself to read the caption, though it just about made me sick: *Girl about town Maxine Henshaw snapped yesterday at the Southbank food and wine festival with prominent QC Rodney Ellis. It appears Ms Henshaw was doing a little tasting of her own when spotted by City Confidential.*

Rodney bloody Ellis. I should have known. Interstate business seminars. Weekend planning sessions. After-hours briefings. What a crock of shit; she'd been out with him the whole time. But why couldn't she just have told me it was over instead of playing games? I tried to think back to other times in my life when a relationship I'd been in had ended. It usually finished after an argument, or someone had gone away or simply hadn't bothered to get back in touch. Sometimes, as with Kate, we'd remained friends and just moved on with our lives. But this was different; I'd been traded, dumped for another. A huge kick in the backside of a man's pride. I felt humiliated, ridiculed. The ego's a fragile thing and mine just wanted to run away, but it's hard to hide when your girlfriend's plastered all over page four with another guy. Rodney *bloody* Ellis.

I drove back home not quite knowing what to do. Then I realised I'd been sitting in my parked van for a good ten minutes and that I should get out, go upstairs and do something. Should I ring her? *No way.* Absolutely not. I had my pride. About the only thing I had left from this relationship. If she wanted to make contact, then fine, so be it. But I wasn't going to call the bitch first.

I don't remember much about the rest of the afternoon. I know I went for a walk by the Yarra. Did a nice slow circuit at the back of Scotch College and followed the river back by the parkland down behind Riversdale Road. But I don't recall seeing anything. I must have been a walking zombie. When I got back, I took a bath; a very long one. Lost myself in the steamy waters and the comforting mask of a hand-towel draped over my face. I stayed until the water got tepid, then I let some out and topped it up again with more hot water. So much for the number four drought restrictions. Yarra Valley Water could go screw itself, and send the bill to Maxine Henshaw while they were at it.

I wasn't going to call her. End of story. How many times do I have to say it, for Christ sake.

I fed Che; he knew something was up. They say animals can sense human emotions; death, sadness. Unfaithful girlfriends? He looked at me with his ears pricked, his head on the side. It didn't stop him eating his dinner, but he ate cautiously, taking little mouthfuls and watching me the whole time as if he knew.

'You never liked her anyway, did you, little fella?' I said to him. 'She was always tripping over you in the hallway, wasn't she?'

I cooked up some stirfry for dinner. It tasted like crap and I had no appetite anyway, so I threw it in the kitchen bin after two mouthfuls. I cracked the top off a Beck's and sat in front of the TV, aimlessly flicking through channels. One beer downed soon became two. I got up to grab another from the fridge, aware that I was starting to get into dangerous territory. The booze was kicking in on an empty stomach. My mobile lay on the kitchen table where I'd left it, as if challenging me not to use it. Mocking me, knowing what a weak bastard I really was. *I've already told you, I'm not going to do it.*

When I called her, she picked up straightaway, almost as if she'd been expecting me. 'Is there anything you want to tell me?' I said.

When I ride past on my bike it's dark, but at least the apartment block's floodlights light up the Glenferrie Road side. There's an entrance there and the letterboxes out the front are numbered one to four, indicating there must be at least another four flats around the other side, because the telephone book said he lives in number eight. I stop for a moment and reach into my shoulder bag. I pull some advertising leaflets out that I stole earlier from the local shopping centre and make a show of inserting them into all the letterboxes, even the ones that say 'No junk mail'. Anyone watching me would see just another pamphlet deliverer. A good disguise, isn't it?

I ride around the corner and into the side road to another collection of letterboxes and a second common entrance. This is where Punter lives, the block of apartments opposite Scotch College, and to be sure, there's his van parked in the driveway. They're nice Art Deco units. Punter owns his. I know that because I've heard him drop it in on conversation once or twice, the conceited bastard. I used to have a flat and a house too. Technically I still own them, but thanks to Punter I can never return. Now then, what to do?

I drove over to meet Maxine, wondering why I was even bothering to go. I'd have been quite happy to end it on the phone with her. After all, there's no rule that says you have to have a face-to-face. I still had the keys to her South Yarra apartment; could have just posted those back to her with a little note saying 'Fun while it lasted'. Didn't even need to do that, really, since she wasn't going anywhere near the place again. But she wanted to talk, to explain what had happened. Would have thought page four of the *Xpress* did a pretty good job of that.

She'd told me on the phone that she was at the Waiter's Bar at the top end of Latrobe Street. Probably there with Rodney Ellis, and she didn't deny it when I put it to her. I told her she was kidding if she thought I'd be coming in to have a drink with her. I wanted to keep this short and to the point, so I suggested we meet outside in my van. When I got there, all the spots were taken and I had to double park outside. I called her on my mobile. She said she'd come out straightaway, and within a couple of minutes I saw her walking out the door. She stood for a moment, looking for me, and I flashed my lights a couple of times at her.

She came to the driver's side and I wound the window halfway down. I kept my eyes dead straight, looking away from her, held up the keys and jangled them in front of her.

'Yours,' I said. 'Don't think I'll be needing them again.'

Bit childish, but I wasn't going to make it easy for her. She took them in her hand, looking at me and trying to read what state I was in.

'Are you going to invite me in, so we can talk?' she said.

'There's nothing to talk about really, is there?'

She was silent a moment, then, 'I just wanted to explain. I never meant to . . . hurt you.'

Someone gave me an angry toot and flashed their lights at me for blocking the lane. 'You can't stay here,' she said. 'Drive us around the corner, somewhere you can find a park.'

I reached across and opened the passenger side door. She walked around and climbed up, sat down, pulled the door shut and fastened her seat belt. Hands tightly clasping her keys, she stared ahead at the dashboard.

'I don't know what to say,' she said.

'Jesus, Maxine, is that the best you can come up with? Did I come over tonight to hear that?'

'I'm sorry. I . . . it just happened.'

'It just happened, huh? For Christ sake, you fucking lied to me. All that bullshit about work and business trips away.'

I heard her sniff and saw her pluck a tissue from her sleeve. Hello, here come the waterworks, all part of the act.

'No! That was all legit. The work and travel just sort of brought Rod and me closer together while you and I were apart.'

'Apart?' I said brutally. 'You go up to the Yarra Valley for what, one weekend, and you can't keep your hands off some jumped-up QC who makes a pass at you? Thought you told me you had a golden rule of never sleeping with your clients?'

Her tears flowed and I'd lost my temper; I guess it was going to be one of those shout-'em-down partings I'd been determined to avoid.

'It just happened,' she said again, sobbing into her tissue. 'It was just one of those things.'

I shook my head. 'That's rich.'

She stopped her crying and dabbed at her eyes. 'I'd like to think we can, like, still be friends.'

'*Friends?*' I said incredulously. 'What, escort you on an endless round of opening nights, or as a fill-in when *Rodney*'s not around? You're nothing but trouble, Maxine, always have been, always will be. Now get out of my van and get out of my life.'

I reached across to open the door for her and suddenly saw her head pull back sharply, unnaturally, as a hand snaked across her mouth. Then I caught the glint of a steel blade held under her chin. Heard a chilling voice we both recognised from the back of the van.

'Come on, Punter, we can all be friends, can't we?'

It was him. The bloody predator had been hiding in the back all the while I'd been driving over to see Maxine. He leant over from behind Maxine's seat, the knife pressed tightly against her throat, and she let out a choked gasp, her eyes wide with terror. I spun around in my seat to try and face him.

'Where did –'

'Shut up!'

I realised I'd stumbled upstairs in a daze after reading about Maxine and Ellis and left the van unlocked all afternoon. That was how he'd got inside.

'What the bloody hell do you want with us?'

'I said shut the fuck up! Not a word from the pair of you. And Punter, you just try one fucking thing and I'll start slicing Maxine's face to ribbons before you can even turn around. You hear me? You know I will.'

'Are you crazy, what do you want, for god's sake?' It struck me how stupid my question was. Crazy? This psycho had written the book on it.

'Didn't you *hear* me?' He'd only uttered a few words but already a note of hysteria had crept into his voice.

'All right, I hear you.'

'Keep both your hands on the steering wheel where I can see them. And look straight ahead.'

I did as he asked, my brain scrambling to think of what I could do.

In the silence that followed, I could hear Maxine's stilted breathing and swallowing. And I felt Matt's eyes on me, burning like a laser right through the side of my head.

'Well now,' he said after a moment. 'This is all very nice; such a friendly little party, isn't it?'

I said nothing. Sneaked a look into the rear-vision mirror and saw a maniacal set of eyes staring back at me. Thought of Billco's sketch; the resemblance was uncanny. I wished to hell the eyes were still in his drawing and not in the back of my kombi van.

He laughed, a taunting, told-you-so snigger. 'Friends, eh? You weren't much of a friend to Punter, were you?' he said to Maxine. 'Playing around like the filthy little silk chaser that you are.'

I could see Maxine's hands quivering with fright out of the corner of my eye.

'I picked it from the moment I saw you in the strapper's competition. And, well, it's quite ironic, isn't it?'

'What are you talking about?' I said.

'Don't you see?' He let out an obsessive-sounding laugh, seemingly eager to make sure that I understood. 'The dirty trollop got exactly what she was after. She dressed for a jockey and scored a silk. But it was a different type of silk, Punter; A *Queen's Counsel*. Not a bad catch as far as silks go. You do see the —'

'Jesus, Matt. Give it up. There's nothing you can do, the police know who you are.'

'Yes, they do. They know who I am and they know where I live. And I can't ever go back there again . . .' He trailed off for a bit. 'And it's all thanks to you, Punter. All your sly prying ways. Always too clever by half, weren't you? You've cost me my house, my flat, all my income, even my car. You've taken away my life.'

'I haven't taken anything from you.'

'Don't try and spin your way out. It's all your fault.'

He leant forward again, readjusting his grip on Maxine. His knife had never left her throat, but this time he let his left hand slip from her mouth and grab a clutch of her hair in his fingers. He knew what he was doing, pulling her head back just enough to make it hurt, the knife blade an ever-present threat if she moved suddenly. He was on her left, so I couldn't make a grab for the knife or swing a punch at him even if I wanted to. I thought wildly if there was anything I might use against him. It certainly wouldn't be a belt this time, not in the confines of the van. There was a tyre lever in the back, along with some screwdrivers I keep for my wave ski repairs. But I couldn't reach them. Fat lot of good they'd be to me. I had no weapons and no hope.

'Drive,' he said.

I turned the key in the ignition, started the van up and switched the lights on. Perhaps if I left them on high beam, or even better, put my flashing warning lights on, it might attract the attention of a passing police car.

'Don't think about using any of your smart-arse tricks, Punter. Any bullshit and I'll cut her. I'll cut her good and fuckin' proper.'

'Please . . .' said Maxine. 'We'll do what you want, just promise you won't hurt me.'

Matt thought that was funny; actually chuckled, the bastard. Something amusing in her plea. I wondered if he'd laughed like that at all the others before he'd killed them.

'The only promise I'll make to you, sweetheart, is that if Punter doesn't do exactly as I say, I'm going to give you a face like a noughts and crosses puzzle.'

I shook my head. 'I'll do what you say. Where to?'

'Caulfield racecourse. You know where that is, Punter, or do you need directions?'

Matt let go of Maxine's hair but kept the knife at her throat, and I heard him zip open a bag or a pack and rustle around as if he was looking for something. I glanced in the rear-vision mirror. He pulled out some venetian cord; situation not looking good. He fastened Maxine's hands, tied them securely in front of her.

'Keep you eyes on the road,' he growled threateningly at me.

I knew that if I drove into the racecourse at this hour, there'd be no one about to see or hear us. It would all be deserted. The parking area in the middle of the course, the stripping sheds, the grandstand, hell, he could take his pick, it would all be empty. No one would hear us scream for mercy as he took his time killing us. He'd probably do Maxine first, make me watch, like the sadist he was. I could see how he'd work it once we got there. Pass me a loop of cord and tie me to the steering wheel. If I didn't, he'd use the knife on Maxine. Whatever scenario I ran through my mind, I couldn't work out how to rush him without him getting to Maxine first.

I did a U-turn on Latrobe and headed back towards King Street. A typical Friday night in the city; full of people. Swarms of them, heading out to clubs or bars. I had to slow down at a set of lights to let one group of young men swagger by. I had right of way with the green light, but they straggled across the road like they owned it. Strength in numbers; it was like watching a David Attenborough animal documentary about pack behaviour. That's what they were, a marauding mob looking to conquer another's territory. One of them stopped and glared at me, his hands clutched around a stubby of beer.

I thought he might do something, actually hoped he would, because it might give us some chance of escaping. But he just stood there holding us up against the lights as if challenging us to do something about it.

'Go. You've got a green light.'

'I can't, the guy's standing in front of us.'

'Then run the little runt down. *Move it!*'

I gave the guy a toot and swerved a little to the side so I wouldn't hit him. Heard the crash of a bottle as he heaved it against the side of the van and the cheering of his mates as they gave us the finger.

'Drunken scum,' said Matt. 'Should be locked away.'

I snuck a quick look at Maxine, but she had her eyes glued to the floor. I drove on, traffic starting to pick up a bit now as we headed towards King Street and the nightclub precinct. Thought about running a red as I approached Russell Street. Maybe a cop would see me and give chase. Where were they when you needed them? Matt, as if reading my mind, gave me another warning. 'You drive nice and steady and make a proper job of it. You understand?'

I shrugged. 'Sure.'

We drove on in silence for a moment. I felt helpless, racking my brains for anything to distract him. All I had was the vague knowledge of his background. So I started to talk to him.

'What was it like working for old Chas Bannon all those years ago?'

No answer. Continued on anyway.

'Because Chas told me about you when I went to see him about the colours.'

'Shut up.'

'I just thought you'd want to know how I pieced it together, that it was you.'

'My working for Chas wouldn't lead you anywhere. You just got lucky.'

'Maybe,' I said nonchalantly, 'but seeing Chas at his stables reminded me of something about you.'

'That silly old fool. He's nothing, a *nobody*.'

'Why? Because he sacked you?' Niggling him, for what it was worth.

'He didn't sack me. I left on my own terms. Anyway . . . he couldn't train a pig to be dirty. Now shut up and drive.'

Ignore. 'I think he knows his trade. I've put money on for him before and he's always done a *proper job*.'

Stole another glance at the mirror and immediately caught the recognition in Matt's eyes. Narrowed, angry slits.

'You used his expression,' I said. 'Must have had it ingrained in you as a kid while you were working there. Whether Chas is describing a jockey's ride or cleaning a saddle, it's always a *proper job*. He uses it every second sentence and it rubbed off on you.'

'You're full of shit, Punter.'

I continued on; at least it was buying some time. 'I couldn't quite work out the connection until I traced the colours back to Chas and your stepfather. Then when Chas said he'd put on Lillian's troubled child . . . I started to figure it out.'

'I wasn't *troubled*!' He'd raised his voice now. Very intense. 'I said I *wasn't* a troubled child.' He'd moved across from Maxine's far side and was propped in the middle between us. He'd let the knife drop from Maxine's throat and out of the corner of my eye I could see him, twitching, holding it only a blade-length away from my neck.

'*Did you hear what I said!*' he shouted. He pointed the tip of the knife into the side of my head, forcing me to turn it sideways to avoid the pain. I felt it break the skin; not very pleasant.

'Yeah, I heard you. Why don't you put that fuckin' thing away before you cause me to crash, because if I do we'll all be in the shit.'

He kept the pressure up for a few more seconds then roughly grabbed hold of the back of my hair like he'd done with Maxine.

'You think you're so fucking smart, don't you. Always got an answer to everything. *Watch out!* You'll get caught in the slow lane. Turn here, turn left.'

I'd dawdled into the stop-start centre lane, but he knew as well as I did that I'd have to swing a left to head out to Caulfield. The King Street clubs were in full swing, punters lining up outside waiting to get in. There seemed to be packs of drugged-up or intoxicated idiots streaming across the road, walking the footpaths, all looking for action. Reminded me of the night out with Maxine when we'd got caught up in the fight. I slowed for a red light; had no choice as the car in front of me had stopped. Matt immediately resumed his hold on Maxine, making sure I wouldn't try anything. As if. A group of three guys walked past a gleaming new Range Rover in front of us. One of them did a drum roll on the bonnet with his fists, then gave a quick finger to the driver. Wisely, he didn't get out. Stayed locked in, head down, too frightened to say anything. Is that what this part of the city had degenerated into? A cesspit, a fight club where you couldn't even drive safely down the main street.

I thought of Tiny, who worked this strip. I didn't fancy his job, trying to keep this mob under control. He'd be on duty tonight, manning the door at the Tavern. That was only a few blocks down. What I'd give to have him with me in the van right now. But even if he was, there was still the insurmountable problem of Matt holding the knife against Maxine. Any attempt to rush him, he'd kill her. Even if it meant going down himself, because he had nothing to lose. We drove on past an obviously drunken group punching on in a laneway. Par for the course in clubland.

'Mates of yours, Matt?'

'They're sick. Animals,' he said, watching the spectacle.

I was glad I'd got a response, something that caught his attention even if it only served as a minor distraction. Because it had given me the ghost of an idea.

'Yeah, but let's face it, Matt, sick as they are, they're never gonna be as troubled as you are.'

'*I'm not troubled!*' he shouted.

I'd drilled right into the nerve like a sloppy dentist doing root canal treatment. A flash of anger that was set to explode. I wanted it to, needed it to, but only just at the right time. Matt began talking in a manically fast dialogue, almost as though he was trying to rationalise his actions, his very being, in front of us both.

'I'm not like them,' he said, waving his knife dismissively at the hordes we drove past. 'Can't you see, *they're* the ones with all the problems!'

I drove on, a bit like a cabbie who's heard it all. 'Sure, Matt, whatever.'

He didn't like my attitude; let me know big time.

'Are you fucking listening to me?'

'Yeah, yeah.'

'You flippant little prick.'

He let go of Maxine again and squatted behind me. Could almost feel the cold of the blade as he held it at the back of my head. Maxine gave me a frightened glance which I pretended not to notice. I focused on the road ahead and the neon sign I was looking for.

'I mean, the difference is, they're just pissheads, out for a night's fun. But you can't really compare them with yourself, can you? I mean, they haven't got your sort of problem, your sort of troubles, have they?'

Goading him. *Risky*, very bloody risky, but I needed to take his attention off my driving. I'd gone past the Lonsdale inter-section and just needed another block to try and do my thing. If it didn't come off, we were both as good as dead anyway, because the crazy bastard was starting to slice his knife blade into the back of my seat, only centimetres away from my shoulder. Short, stabbing thrusts, each time piercing the vinyl and burying the blade to the hilt in the foam underneath.

'Yeah, I've heard about that sort of thing,' I went on, 'where a person can't see they've got issues. It's called denial.'

His eyes were wild, flittering this way and that across the mirror at me. The punishment to the seat continued unabated; stab, thrust, rip, tear. Start over again. Could just about feel him ready to ignite.

I'd crossed Bourke Street and claimed the inside lane and could see the yellow flashing neon sign of the Tavern ahead on my left. I kept glancing at the mirror every few seconds now, important to keep check of when he would strike, because surely it was only a matter of when. The throng of people on the footpath had intensified noticeably down this end of town, where half a dozen clubs stood almost side by side. Lines of clubbers waited to get in, tangled with those wandering about outside on the footpath.

'Yep, that's what you're doing, Matt, isn't it? Denying you have any troubles.'

'I've got no troubles!'

He screeched it out hysterically, and even though I'd been expecting it, it reverberated around in the confines of the van. Then I saw his arm lift higher than before; he'd hacked the seat into an upholsterer's nightmare and the next thrust of the knife wouldn't be for the seat, it would be struck at me.

I swerved into the telephone pole doing sixty, and when I hit it, it sent shards of broken glass and sheered metal against the terrified pedestrians I'd just managed to avoid. Maxine screamed as we collided and I watched the disappearing soles of Matt's runners as he was flung head first through the windscreen. Shows what happens when you don't wear your seatbelt.

I didn't want to hurt my old bus, but it was the only way. I crashed it right into the laneway next to the Tavern night-club and did a 'proper job', as Chas would have said. I'd aimed the van for the middle of the pole and we'd come off second best, embedding ourselves into the pylon with a force I thought would make my seatbelt snap. I yelled out to Maxine, asking if she was all right, and she stammered out a shaken okay, so I told her stay put till the police came. I got out my door; had to kick it open as it was jammed. We were surrounded by shocked onlookers who now started to gather around the crashed van and offer help. I heard somebody say they'd called an ambulance and another said they'd called the police. There were dozens of people pressing forward around the van and another group staring down the laneway towards where Matt must have landed. I stood up on the kickboard and looked over past the telephone pole. Could just make out the shape of a body lying on the cobblestones in the laneway. I had to get to him, but I just couldn't get past the throng of people circling us.

I looked up and down wildly through the crowd and saw two big guys who could only be bouncers come running up from the Tavern. Thank god one of them was Tiny. He's hard to miss; the big sinewy frame standing head and shoulders above everyone else.

'Punter, is that you?' he yelled out, elbowing his way in and surveying my wrecked kombi. 'Ya silly bastard, what've ya done? You all right? Are you hurt?'

Suddenly I saw Matt get up and stagger a couple of steps before he stood, staring at me. Then he turned and ran up the alley.

'Tiny, quick!' I yelled, pointing. 'It's Matt; it's the strapper killer.'

Tiny waded through the crowd just like he must do on the packed dance floors of the clubs he bounces. I was glad to follow in his wake. He announced his intentions clearly enough: '*Comin' through!*' then he did just that, bulldozed his way using his hip and shoulders to force a passage. If you were in his way, well, it was probably like an elephant parting the branches of a tree as it walks through. I followed him around to the passenger side of the car, where we finally got into the laneway.

'Where is he?' said Tiny.

'He got thrown through the window,' I said, pointing to the shattered windscreen, 'but I saw him get up and run off.'

'Let's get after him.'

We set off up the laneway at a sprint. Matt couldn't have been far in front of us and he'd taken a knock, he'd be shaken, and possibly injured from the crash. The laneway continued for a short distance then turned a sharp dog-leg right before looping back out to the main road. We ran past a derelict hunched against a doorway, his empty bottle lying on the ground next to him. We paid him just enough attention to make sure it wasn't Matt, then took off again. It was hard work keeping pace with the big fella's strides. He loped ahead of me, taking two steps to my one. When we reached the end of the laneway and came out at Collins Street, both of us stopped.

'See him?' said Tiny.

There were lots of people on the street. All I could see were seemingly endless groups of young men and woman drifting along the pavement and across the roads. But he couldn't have got far. He only had about ten seconds' head start. I checked the footpath back towards King Street. No sign of him. The other side of the road had more of the same: it seemed like they'd cloned twenty thousand young men and woman and let them all roam around clubland like zombies on a Friday night. The men, all with the 'trendy scruffy hairstyle', their long-sleeved shirts fashionably untucked, and wide-toed shoes. The women in impossibly short skirts and high heels; no wonder they staggered between venues. A darting shadow caught my eye in a landscape where nothing else hurried. Fifty metres away, a furtive shape was running between people. He paused for a moment outside a shop window and looked back our way. I nudged Tiny and pointed discreetly.

'There he is,' I said.

We took off after him again and closed the gap. He seemed to be limping, no doubt as a result of the crash. It was even more crowded on this block and we found ourselves dodging lines of drunken nightclub patrons spread out like grazing cows and blocking our way. In the end we gave up on the footpath and ran down the side of the road, weaving between cars. We chased him into the entrance of yet another laneway and a few strides into that, we'd just about collared him.

'Stop, Matt!' I yelled at him.

A group of girls were walking ahead of us, oblivious of our presence. They turned around as I called out, startled. Matt pounced on one of them. She screamed and tried to fight him off, but he succeeded in grabbing her around the neck and then wheeled her around to face us. He was panting from the run, as we were, and he held his knife unsteadily at the girl's throat, gasping for breath.

'Stop, or I'll kill her! You know I'll do it, Punter.'

'Put the knife down, Matt,' said Tiny. 'Let her go, she's got nothing to do with this.'

'Shut up and stay where you are, all of you.'

We stood still, the other girls falling in behind us as Matt backed away, holding the knife to his victim's throat. As he limped backwards, another group of clubbers headed down the far side of the laneway towards us.

'Run!' I said to the group of girls behind me. 'Go and call the police.'

They didn't need telling twice and took off in a clatter of high heels over the cobblestones. Matt looked wild-eyed at the girls fleeing from us, but kept backing back up the alley with his hostage. We kept following, stepping slowly after him.

'I told you to stay!' he barked at us, like an angry owner to a disobedient dog.

'It's not gonna happen, Matt. Just give it up now,' I said.

The group of clubbers had almost come up behind where Matt was: a pack of six or seven noisy young guys all swigging from beer bottles. A couple were carrying cardboard cartons on their shoulders; the night's additional grog supply, no doubt. They were barely managing to keep a rein on their testosterone levels; you could see it in their aggressive swagger and hear it in their slurred conversation. Every second word was the 'F' word, every sentence a threat against the nightclub they'd just been evicted from. When they reached us, it seemed they'd decided we were the perfect scapegoats for them to vent their frustrations on. Matt spun around when he heard them advancing. The girl, sensing her chance, broke free and ran back past us. There was a stand-off for a moment as the group stood in a semicircle around Matt. Then he held his knife up at them and told them to fuck off.

One of them threw a bottle at him. It missed and smashed loudly against a brick wall. Another was thrown, this time hitting him in the chest and sending up a fountain of foamy beer. Then the bottles rained down on Matt like hailstones on a tin roof. They picked him off without mercy. The bottle that felled him actually came from a guy who smashed it over the back of his head. I saw Matt's knife clatter to the ground and he followed it down a moment later. Then the rain of bottles was replaced with a frenzy of kicks as they lined up to put the boot in.

Tiny leant towards me, spoke in my ear. 'Punter, you want me to bust 'em up?'

He didn't seem overly concerned about the imbalance in the numbers, nor about Matt's fate. I didn't say anything, just watched as they laid into the strapper killer's head, his ribs, his crotch; wherever they could find an unguarded body part.

'Punter? There's seven of 'em,' said Tiny, 'They'll fuckin' kill him, unless we do something.'

The spate of gruesome strapper murders flashed in front of me. The 'strapper killer' headlines which the papers had been running for what had seemed an eternity. I thought about the terror those young girls must have endured when they'd woken up to find him standing over them. And I thought about the night I'd surprised him in Maxine's apartment. Remembered the fight I'd had with him in the members' toilets. The near miss when he'd hidden away and ambushed us in my van tonight. Most of all, I remembered Ric's words as we gazed at the graffiti last Saturday outside the races: 'Killers keep killing'. I watched one of the mob raise a bottle above his head and take aim at Matt lying on the ground. He was only a youth; could picture him innocently tossing burgers at Maccas during the week. But here, in front of his drunken mates, he was a potential killer. Just like Matt.

'Oi!' I yelled out at him. The kid spun around, the bottle still in his hand. 'You're right Tiny, let's break 'em up.'

22

Maxine, Tiny and I spent most of what was left of the night down at the city police station. Detective Wells and his offsider Tony were there and Beering came in about half an hour later. They split us up when we arrived and I went into an interview room with Wells. When Beering got there he joined us as I went over my story once again. I took him through the whole thing and didn't hold anything back, which included my reasons for driving out to meet Maxine and how it was all over between us.

'Sorry to hear it didn't work out, Punter,' said Beering with empathy. I got another sympathetic hearing shortly after, this time from Wells, when I told him how I'd had to crash my van to try to lose Matt when he'd ambushed us.

'Is it a write-off?' he asked.

'Nah, she's tougher than that. It'll be a major job, but it's only the front end. Good thing the motor's in the back of a kombi.'

'That was sharp thinking,' he said. 'Not much else you could have done. If you bailed out, he had Maxine. If you tried to tackle him in the van, he's still got the knife on her. You couldn't win no matter what. And if you did nothing . . . well, that would have been a one-way drive out to Caulfield racecourse.'

During the interview a policeman came in with news for Wells which he discreetly whispered to him in the doorway.

Wells shared it with us anyway as soon as he was told; they'd found the girl who Matt had grabbed in the laneway. She and her friends had reported the attack to police. But of the pack that had laid into Matt there was no sign. They'd vanished into the night; just another drunken mob staggering around in clubland. Good luck to the police if they could find them.

Wells asked me, 'You say the group came down from the other end of the laneway and Matt spun around when he heard them, and then the girl escaped?'

'Uh-huh. She ran past me and Tiny. I guess she found her friends and they took off.'

'And then a fight started between Matt and the group?'

'Words were exchanged, he waved his knife around at them and then it was on.'

'They just about beat him to a pulp. Would have, if you and Tiny hadn't broken it up.'

I thought of Tiny, wading into battle like some giant warrior. He may well have been, too, if he'd been born a few centuries earlier. Could picture him, long sword in one arm, mace in the other. He had no medieval weapons tonight, but his huge fists had chopped a swathe through that pack of hoons just like a knight in battle. He'd decked three of them and thrown another against a wall before they realised they were out of their league. The others had turned and fled when they saw there was a demon amongst them.

'I don't think I contributed much to that,' I said.

'Even so, you two probably saved his life. He's at the hospital under police guard until we get the doctor's all-clear to interview him.'

I answered some more questions for another half hour or so and then I was allowed to go. Beering offered to call me a taxi, but I knew Tiny was waiting to run me back, so I thanked him for everything and said goodnight. Outside, Tiny was sitting at a table sharing a coffee with Maxine in a near-empty squad room. I walked over and joined them, nodding at Maxine. She had a couple of elastoplast bandages on the side of her face and another on her chin. Appeared to be minor cuts and scrapes, nothing serious.

'Sorry about the sudden stop,' I said. 'Only way I could think of to lose him. You all right?'

She nodded back. 'It would have helped if your van had airbags,' she said, clutching her ribs.

'Doubt they were invented in my old bus's day. Still, the seatbelts saved us.'

'The police told me what happened to Matt.'

'Bastard got what he deserved,' said Tiny cheerfully. 'A bloody good kicking. And more importantly, he's been caught.'

Maxine went silent on us and I couldn't read her mood. Didn't know if she was glad or sad. She held her cup in both hands under her chin and gazed straight ahead at the wall.

'So I guess it's all over, then,' I said clumsily.

She shot me a look. Not my best choice of words.

'With Matt, I mean.' *And us, too, you idiot.*

'Yeah, I guess it's over,' she said.

Tiny stood up. 'Can we give you a lift home?' he said to Maxine.

'Um, no thanks. I'm waiting on one now.'

We saw her lift arrive a moment later. He walked up to the front counter as Tiny and I were going out. Maxine followed behind us when she saw him. She acted a little sheepish when he bounded over and gave her an exaggerated, over-affectionate hug and a kiss on the cheek. Definitely didn't want me around seeing that sort of thing. She must have thought she'd be well rid of me by now and here I was, still hanging around getting in her way. She shot me a guilty look and tried to keep it civil.

'Um, Punter, this is Rodney.'

He surveyed me coolly, obviously knew I was the ex. Looked me over like I was the vanquished bull elephant, beaten by the young up-and-comer. Winner takes all, so forth. No effort by either of us to offer a handshake.

'Mmm, you were both very fortunate to get out of that situation,' he said in his wanky lawyer's voice. I could just imagine him, both thumbs in his lapels as he swaggered up and down the courtroom telling the jury that the accused was indeed fortunate to be represented by he, Rodney Ellis QC. The arrogant prick; I so wanted to hit him.

'*Fortunate*, is that what you'd you call it?' I said aggressively.

Tiny could sniff out potential conflict like smoke at a barbeque. He put his giant paw around my arm, stepped between me and Ellis and excused us both. 'We're just leavin',' he said. I stared back at the two of them as Tiny marched me out the door. Maxine stood there returning my stare. A neutral, whatever-will-be-will-be sort of look that seemed to acknowledge our parting. Ellis placed a possessive arm around her shoulders and saw me off with a snooty glare as if defying me to take it further. Yeah, good luck to you, mate; I'll bet you evens you'll be traded in within three months for a new model.

When we got outside Tiny said, 'Mate, I'm sorry about back there, but I could feel a blue comin' on and a cop shop's not the place to start throwing punches.'

'I wasn't going to start anything.'

'Yeah, right.'

'That's a first for me, being evicted from a police station.'

'I'll give you the same advice I give to all the young drunks I throw out at the clubs.'

'What's that?'

'Forget about her, she's not worth worrying about.'

Tiny was right. She was Rodney Ellis' trouble now.

When Tiny dropped me off at my flat it was nearly dawn. Outside I noticed there was a bike leaning up against the side of the letterboxes. Silly place to leave it; would get stolen for sure around here without a lock and chain. I ignored it and went upstairs and hit the sack. Slept the sleep of the dead, and was woken up later that morning by a pitiful-sounding Che, who was sitting on my pillow and meowing so loudly it was a wonder the RSPCA hadn't come to the rescue. I stumbled out of bed and fixed him his breakfast. Then I washed my face and went downstairs to get the papers. Outside, the first thing I noticed was the stupid bike from last night still leaning against the letterboxes. It deserved to get stolen, being left like that. I figured it must belong to someone visiting one of the other apartments. None of my business.

But I made it my business. I had to wheel the bike forward anyway so that I could get my papers out. As I did, the pannikins on the rear pack rack brushed against the letterbox, showing the outline of something stored inside. I felt a little guilty but at the same time curious, so I undid the buckle and folded back the flap to take a peek. Inside there was a white plastic shopping bag with an item of clothing in it. I nearly dropped it straight back into the pannikin, except that I felt the garment's texture through the plastic. Smooth and lightweight, and I could see it was brightly coloured. I shook the bag's contents out and two items fell on top of the bike's pack rack. When I saw what they were, I jumped a step backwards like I'd discovered a big huntsman spider. It was a jockey's cap and vest coloured with red and white horizontal bands. The strapper killer's silks.

Kate dropped around to my place on Monday night after work. She'd just finished a story about the strapper killings which would appear in tomorrow morning's paper. We talked about that for a while, then she said, 'I owe you an apology. About Maxine.'

I shook my head. 'You don't have to say a thing.'

'No, I blurted it out like the nightly news and that was wrong of me.'

'It sure made the news,' I said, thinking about the photo of Maxine kissing Ellis in the paper.

I offered her a glass of chilled dry white and we sat at the kitchen table sharing a drink. Che, as usual, wasted no time in jumping up on her lap and demanding a cuddle. She stroked his ears playfully as we spoke.

'Actually, I've got some bad news myself,' she said. 'About Nathan.'

I raised my eyes sharply. 'Nathan?'

'Yeah,' she nodded. 'Seems like it's a bad week for people breaking up.'

It took me a moment to pick up on what she meant. 'Don't tell me . . .'

'Us too. We've split up. It didn't work out.'

'You poor thing.'

'He said he'd found someone else; someone he knew he could really relate to.'

'I can't believe it. He left *you* for another woman? The fools deserve each other, then. That's all I can say.'

There was a little trickle of tears which she started dabbing at, but she sniffed them away defiantly.

'He didn't leave me for another woman, Punter. The new person in his life is *Richard*.'

She spat out the name like a mouthful of rotten banana, and I nearly choked like I was swallowing one.

'Um, did I just hear you right?'

She sniffed again and patted Che for comfort. 'You did. He's bisexual. Bastard never told me he batted for *both* sides. You'd think I would have known; all that time he spent down at that bloody camp gym he used to work out at. Hanging out with his gay-boy mates every chance he got. I should have seen it coming.'

'Jesus, I don't know what to say.'

'Yeah, well, it doesn't exactly give the ego a boost, I can tell you.'

She took another sip. 'It's not the only bad news I've got.'

'There's more?'

'I've got to vacate my flat. My landlord's moving his teenage daughter in so she can be nearer to uni.'

'No way. You've been there forever.'

'Well, forever runs out in four weeks.'

I cracked open another bottle from the fridge; didn't bother asking her permission as I topped up her glass and sat the bottle down between the jumbled pages of the weekend paper's car guide. She jutted her chin at it.

'See you're still reading through the car section,' she said, changing the subject.

'Got to stay in touch with the latest trends in automotive technology.'

She laughed. 'Oh, of course; I can see why. Given that you've had your old kombi van for about twenty years. I don't know why you bother to read up on it; it's not as if you'll ever buy a new car.'

'Hey, you can talk. You and the movie reviews you pore over. When was the last time you ever actually went and saw a film?'

'You know I can't stand going to the movies. Everyone makes too much noise. I wait till they come out on DVD.'

'Liar, you don't even do that.'

'Doesn't mean I can't read about them.'

'My point exactly.'

I played with my glass a bit; swirled the wine around in it and took a sip.

'You know, if you're stuck, there's always the spare room out the back of my apartment.'

'Thanks, Punter. That's awfully kind, but you know it wouldn't work out.'

'No, I suppose not.'

'We're not really suited to each other. We'd clash; cramp each other's style. We'd end up squabbling over things like the grocery bill.'

'We would?'

'Well, you insist on buying all those upmarket feline dishes for this spoilt creature,' she said, scratching Che behind the ears. 'And I'm not going halves on that when the home brands are just as good.'

'He won't eat the home brands.'

'You don't *buy* the home brands, Punter. Then of course there's the problem of where I'd park my car.'

'That's no problem, there's plenty of off-street parking.'

Kate shook her head and took another mouthful. 'No, I'm not going to park my little MG out in the rain and cold. It simply won't do.'

Che didn't think it would do either. He gave a supportive little chirp; he was taking Kate's side of the argument, the little traitor. Maybe I should take another look at buying the home brand cat food after all.

'You've got a vacant garage.'

'Uh-uh. That's for my van.'

'Don't be ridiculous, Punter, when was the last time you actually parked your van anywhere but the street?'

'All right, but I keep my surfing gear in there.'

'Punter, there's acres of room in that garage. It's like a TARDIS and if you cleaned it up properly some day, it may surprise you to find that it can actually store both.'

I looked at her over the rim of my glass. Impossible woman. Would always beat me with logic and fact. 'You're right,' I said. 'It wouldn't work out, would it?'

'No,' she agreed. 'It wouldn't work.'

I topped up our glasses again and opened the car section. Pretended to read it just to annoy her. Not to be outdone, she foraged around until she found the movie guide. We both absorbed ourselves in silence for a few moments; me looking at cars I was never going to buy and Kate reading about films she had no intention of seeing.

'You can have the room for an even two hundred a week and I'll buy the cat food,' I said, not looking up from the paper.

'A hundred and fifty and I want the garage thrown in,' she said, rustling her pages. Impossible woman.

I got a call from Beering early on Tuesday morning. He brought me up to date on the latest about Matt.

'Now that they know who he is,' said Beering, 'they've been able to correctly match DNA from all those victims directly to him. Going right back to Amanda Kaisha and the other five he killed. And the knife they found on him in the laneway is another nail in his coffin. I'm told police won't have any trouble confirming that as the murder weapon. Oh, by the way, those jockey silks you found on his bike outside your place contain more than enough evidence to put him away.'

I thought about Matt riding by my flat, stalking me. My own bloodstains could very nearly have been added to the others on those silks.

'Jim, have they worked out why he did it?'

'They've only just started questioning him. Took him two days before he could even talk after that bashin' he copped. They'll go over everything with a fine-tooth comb. It'll all come out in the wash.'

'Yeah, I guess. But the silk chaser messages; there's something, I dunno . . . what made him do it, do you think?'

'Son, he's a nutter, a crazy, who knows? Twelve months from now, some psychologist will figure out a theory. Probably write a thesis about it and make up some fancy name for Matt's condition. I'll tell you something for nothin', though, guys like him, once they start, they never stop. They just carry right on until they get caught.'

'Yeah. Killers keep on killing.'

'Exactly.'

'What'll happen with him now?'

'The normal legal process. They'll charge him. He'll eventually go to trial. It's almost a certainty he'll spend the rest of his life behind bars.'

'I guess that's some comfort for the families of the victims.'

After Beering's call I tuned into Russell Henshaw's radio show. Becoming quite a convert, I was, in a perverse sort of a way. I'd be seeing him later that afternoon at the races, when Princess Upstart went around. He'd actually left a couple of messages on my mobile and even called my brother demanding to know about the registration of the ownership papers. Pushy bastard, he could bloody well wait until this afternoon when I was good and ready. Henshaw had one of his regular guests on his show; the police commissioner. That usually made for lively entertainment, so I turned up the radio. Henshaw was on his soapbox talking about one of his favourite topics, violence around the nightclub district. That subject included the strapper killer's bashing and capture last Friday night which had been covered by the media to the point of saturation ever since. In fact, Henshaw'd had Maxine appear exclusively on his show yesterday for an hour to talk about her experience. How's that for a scoop? 'Superstar shock jock interviews daughter victim'. Love to see what ratings they pulled for that. The media angle now seemed to have switched to just how hard the police would actually look for the group who were responsible for Matt's bashing. It raised an intriguing question and one which *The Sun* had put to a readers' poll. Almost every respondent had replied with the predictable: 'Thugs did a good turn for once', or, 'Served him bloody right, but didn't go far enough'.

Henshaw wasn't silly. He was well attuned to the popular opinion of his listeners and how they felt about the fate of the strapper killer. This morning he was giving the police commissioner his usual grilling.

'It does appear these thugs have actually done the public a favour, in this case,' said Henshaw. 'They've stopped the killer and given him a thrashing, which a lot of people would say he thoroughly deserved.'

'We don't condone violence in any shape or form,' said the commissioner with staunch political correctness.

'Right, but putting that aside, some might say they didn't go far enough. Reports indicate that those louts may very well have killed him if they hadn't been disturbed.'

'I'm sorry, your point is?'

'That if they'd taken this killer out, they'd have saved everyone the time and money of an expensive trial that will probably see him spend the rest of his life behind bars anyway.'

'That's just conjecture. I'm not going to hypothesise on what might have happened.'

'Well, we don't have the death penalty in this state anymore, so that's where he'd end up, wouldn't he?'

'I suppose so.'

'And tell me, Commissioner, police won't be exactly falling over themselves to find these thugs who bashed the killer, will they?'

'We'll continue to make inquiries and those responsible will be pursued just as in any other assault case.'

'Of course, of course. You'll do what you can, Commissioner,' Henshaw said affably. 'But the public would understand that the police have only got finite resources.'

'They're your words, not mine.'

'We're going to open up the lines now, and listeners, I want you to ask yourselves this; should the strapper killer bashers be applauded or apprehended?'

I got to Caulfield a little before twelve. It felt funny catching a train in, but the van was at the panel beaters and they hadn't even got around to assessing the damage yet, let alone repairing it. I might have to look at getting a hire car if it dragged on too much longer, but for now I had a zone two met ticket to get me around town. Inside the course I tipped some change into old George's bucket, then grabbed a cup of coffee and a sandwich in the members' bar. I sat down by an empty table opposite a TV monitor and checked my scratchings, went through my prices and looked at some form again for a couple of horses I wasn't quite sure about. Most of the card today was rubbish, a typical bookmaker's picnic which I had no intention of playing. But there was one horse that interested me in the first race of the day.

With twenty minutes to go I walked down to the mounting yard. Only three horses had entered the ring, their strappers parading them around in a circle to a small group of owners and trainers. The others were stringing along slowly up the walkway, ready to join them. The top weight was a dud; even the girl in the cloakroom knew that. Hadn't won since fluking a stakes race on a heavy track a year ago. Pass. O'Reilly's horse, number three, looked well. They always did, but the form was all wrong. Dismiss. Pricey's filly? Maybe as a saver if I got decent odds.

The remaining horses started to trickle in. I could see Princess Upstart being led up the chute. Hard to miss her or her attendant. There was no strapper's prize being awarded today, but Maxine still stood out like a model amongst the other stablehands. She wore the hip-hugging white jodhpurs, the knee-high boots. No outrageous silk-coloured hat on today, thank god. That was replaced by a red checked scarf. I watched her lead the filly around the yard. She gave a flick of her hair and seemed to share her smile with every male aged between fifteen and seventy who stood staring at her over the mounting yard fence, drooling.

Gorgeous? Yes, undeniably.

Desirable? I had once found her so.

She used to be mine, you know.

I flashed my pass at the gateman and went over to join my father and David, who were talking to our jockey. Dad gave me his usual nod and grunt. The original man of few words.

'Oh, hello, *owner*,' said David, ribbing me good-naturedly. 'You sure know when to jump on board. A last start winner and a short-priced favourite today . . . not bad timing to get in on a horse.'

'Got Russell's generosity to thank for that,' I said.

'He's been trying to track you down since last Friday about the registration papers. He's convinced you've cocked them up somehow, made a mistake with the ownership details.'

He opened up his race book and held it up for me to see. 'You want to check it over again? If it's wrong, we'll need to notify the stewards.'

Even Dad joined in with a warning growl. 'I don't want Henshaw mucked about, he's an important client to me.'

I ignored David's race book and brushed off Dad's concern. 'It's all good, trust me.'

'Well, you can tell him yourself. Here he comes now,' said David.

Henshaw came bustling up through the side gate carrying a race book and a pair of binoculars in their case. He had on a grey suit and a loud yellow tie with a matching carnation in his lapel; way over-dressed for a lowly mid-week meeting like today's. He looked around amongst the other trainers and jockeys and when he saw us, he made a beeline straight for me.

'What the devil did you do with those registration papers I gave you?' he demanded.

I gave him a blank stare. 'Sorry, what do you mean?'

He waved the race book in front of me and pointed at Princess Upstart's entry.

'This!' he said by way of explanation. 'All you had to do was fill in your ownership details and lodge the form like I told you. But you've gone and messed it all up.'

I stood next to him and leant over the race book, pretending to make a study of it.

'No, definitely no mistake there, Russell,' I said thoughtfully.

'Well, of course there is! I gave you a half share in the filly, so it should be your name in the race book and mine. So who in hell is this Caff Girls Dreaming Syndicate which appears there?'

'Perhaps you'd better ask them.'

They came pottering through to the mounting yard like a conga line of old teapots, a dozen elderly ladies clutching their handbags and dressed in their best Sunday dresses. Daisy led them proudly along, the matriarch of the clan. I took a step towards her and gave a wave. She saw me, gave a quick little wave back and hurried the rest of her group over to join us; a pack of Dots and Ediths and Merles.

'Hullo, luv,' she said, kissing me like a long-lost nephew. 'It was such a nice thing for you to do. And when you said we were racing it with Russell Henshaw, well, we were all so excited!'

Henshaw looked on, his mouth agape, mystified at this sudden intrusion of pensioners into his inner racing sanctum.

'I'd better introduce you and the girls, Daisy. This is Russell Henshaw, and of course, you know my father and David.'

'Ooh, Mr Henshaw,' Daisy said, grabbing hold of his arm, 'I listen to you every single morning, I do. Haven't missed your

316

show in years. All of us tune in at the café before the races come on, don't we, girls?'

An immediate chorus of agreeable clucking noises.

'Er, that's nice,' said Henshaw, 'but –'

'When Punter told us he had a quarter share in his filly we could race with you, we just about died of excitement!'

'But, it's not . . .'

'We said we couldn't possibly afford it, but Punter kindly offered to deed us half of his share for nothing. Wasn't that lovely of him?'

Henshaw seemed lost for words. At least words that we could hear. His mouth opened and shut and he seemed to be making an effort to talk, but nothing came out. David grinned and a wry smile appeared on Dad's face.

'I said to the rest of the girls that the least we can do to repay Punter is give him a cup of coffee and a sandwich on the house whenever he drops by. And you can too, luv,' said Daisy, taking a firmer hold of Henshaw's arm. 'You feel free to come around the caff any time and me an' the girls will see you right.'

Henshaw looked aghast. I could just see him swapping his permanent raceday booking at the Blue Diamond restaurant to line up in the café queue with the hoi polloi.

When the stewards called for the riders to mount up, David and my father went out into the mounting yard, leaving me and Henshaw with the rest of the ladies. Henshaw was looking to bail, but Daisy still had a hand looped through his arm. Escape wasn't so easy.

'Now then, luv, where do you sit; up in the owners' stand? Me and the girls will follow you up.'

'Er, I really need to check out the betting ring first. In fact, I'd better get a move on. Don't want to miss out on the best price, do we!'

'Of course not, luv. We'll save a seat for you.'

Henshaw extricated himself from Daisy's clutches and scurried off, glaring at me as he pushed past.

Out in the ring, they were giving two seventy about Princess Upstart. Big Oakie had her a tad longer so I claimed him and backed Pricey's horse at the fours as a saver as well. I sat in my usual spot in the grandstand although today, I was perfectly entitled to a seat in the owners' section. I swung my binoculars over to that part of the stand and immediately picked up Henshaw, surrounded by Daisy and her teapots chattering him to death. His face was as red as beetroot and when my father and David walked up into the stand, I saw him waving furiously at them to come and sit beside him. They did join him, but I chuckled to myself because he still couldn't shake off Daisy, who was sticking tighter than a shoe nailed to a hoof.

At the home turn, I was happy I'd backed my saver. She was bowling along in front and Princess Upstart had got caught up behind a wall of horses. But a run came and she poked her nose through the gap and gamely gave chase. She plugged away all the way down the straight and I didn't think she'd get there till her bobbing head just collared the other's right on the post.

'It's close!' said the race caller. 'But give it to Princess Upstart by a whisker . . .'

I walked down to the mounting yard and into a pensioners' party. Daisy and the girls were shrieking and cackling like they'd been on the sherry. Henshaw was caught up in the middle of it and had given up trying to fend off congratulatory kisses from his adoring horde. Several racing reporters and photographers had cottoned on to it pretty quickly and were busy snapping away at Henshaw, encircled by Daisy and the others by the winner's stall. A winner for Henshaw was always good press anyway, but who were these old ducks sharing the occasion?

'He's such a lovely boy, he is,' said Daisy. She had a hand through Henshaw's arm again and was already hijacking the interview. 'Letting us into the horse like that. Me and the girls never miss his radio show, you know . . .'

I sidled up and dug Henshaw good-naturedly in the ribs. Leant across and spoke softly into his ear so that only he could hear.

'Such a *lovely* boy.'

'You really are a bastard, Punter,' he said.

'Told you it was going to be fun racing a horse with you.'

Peter Klein
Punter's Turf

John Punter, professional gambler and amateur private investigator, has seen his fair share of crime and shady dealings, both on the race track and off it. So when the daughter of a bookmaker friend is kidnapped, following hot on the heels of a gruesome murder after an abduction-gone-wrong, Punter's offer of help is gladly accepted.

But then, just when everything seems to be going right, a local trainer strikes an unexplained run of beaten favourites and a young jockey dies under suspicious circumstances. With the help of a journalist friend, Kate, Punter begins to put the pieces together, and finds himself drawn into a tangled web of underworld crimes that are much more sinister than he had anticipated . . .

'Peter is a skilful author and knows his subject well – I know because he and I worked for my Dad, Tommy Smith, in the late seventies, early eighties, where he was T.J.'s "travelling head lad". *Punter's Turf* is an authentic account of the racing world. Well done!'
GAI WATERHOUSE

'*Punter's Turf* is an exceptional novel: it is fast moving, exciting and holds the reader in its grip until the end. Clearly, Peter Klein is Australia's answer to Dick Francis. Francis wrote over 40 books, readers will hope Klein "goes as long!"'
ROB WATERHOUSE

'A good yarn, well told. Should appeal to everybody.'
KEN CALLENDER

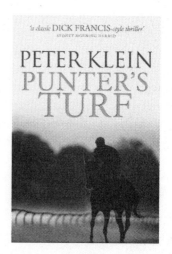

'We may have found Australia's Dick Francis . . . Klein writes with a rare passion and knowledge about the turf . . . for all crime mystery readers.'
BREEDING AND RACING

Katherine Howell
Cold Justice

The past haunts the present . . .

Nineteen years ago teenager Georgie Daniels stumbled across the body of her classmate, Tim Pieters, hidden amongst bushes. His family was devastated and the killer never found.

Now political pressure sees the murder investigation reopened and Detective Ella Marconi assigned to the case. She tracks down Georgie who is now a paramedic. She seems to be telling the truth, so why does Ella receive an anonymous phone call insisting that Georgie knows more? And is it mere coincidence that her ambulance partner, Freya, also went to the same high school?

Meanwhile, Tim's mother suddenly turns her back on the investigation yet his cousin, the MP whose influence reopened the case, can't seem to do enough to help.

The more Ella digs into the past, the more the buried secrets and lies are brought to light. Can she track down the killer before more people are hurt?

Malla Nunn
Let the Dead Lie

DURBAN, SOUTH AFRICA, 1953: Forced to resign from his position of Detective Sergeant and re-classified as 'mixed race' after an incident involving a young black woman, Emmanuel Cooper winds up powerless and alone in the tough coastal city of Durban, mixing labouring with surveillance work for his old boss, Major van Niekerk. Patrolling the freight yards one night, he stumbles upon the body of a young white boy and the detective in him cannot, or will not, walk away. When two more bodies – this time an older English woman and her maid – are discovered at his boarding house, he unwittingly becomes the prime suspect in a triple murder case.

At Major van Niekerk's behest, Cooper is given 48 hours to clear his name and – unofficially – solve the three murders. And so, temporarily back to being a European Detective Sergeant, he descends into Durban's seedy underworld, a viper's nest of prostitution, drugs and violence run by Indian gangsters. To solve the crimes and save his own skin, he must place his trust in a mysterious figure who drives a white De Soto convertible, a Zion Gospel preacher, and the exquisite yet streetwise Lana, who also happens to be Major van Niekerk's mistress …

Suspenseful, compelling and rich with the complexities of life in Apartheid-era South Africa, *Let The Dead Lie* cements Malla Nunn's place as one of Australia's most engaging crime writers.

Kathryn Fox
Blood Born

For pathologist and forensic physician Dr Anya Crichton, the death of a gang rape victim hours before she is due to give evidence at trial is a double tragedy. The violent Harbourn brothers, the girl's accused attackers, now look like they will escape prosecution.

But the Harbourns' trail of destruction doesn't end there. When two sisters are brutally assaulted and one of them is killed, Anya begins working round the clock to catch the Harbourns and nail their ringleader, the deviously clever Gary. With the help of Detective Kate Farrer and the surprise involvement of star litigator Dan Brody, she begins to discover just how twisted this family really is, and what they're capable of.

In Dr Anya Crichton's most difficult case yet, she must piece together the evidence before a killer's attention is turned on her . . .

Sydney Bauer
Matter of Trust

'*It's Marilyn . . . she's missing.*'

It's been a long time since criminal defence attorney David Cavanaugh has heard his childhood friend Chris Kincaid speak of Marilyn Maloney; for hers is a name from their past, from a time when David, Chris, and the third in their gang of three, Mike, vowed never to let a girl get in the way of their friendship.

But now Chris is the 'successful, happily married US Senator for New Jersey', and when he pleads with David to return home to Newark to help him locate the girl he 'used' to love, David reluctantly agrees, leaving his wife and baby daughter behind in Boston.

What starts out as a favour to a friend soon turns into a major homicide investigation when a woman's bruised and battered body is hauled from the freezing waters of the Passaic. Marilyn is dead, Chris is charged with her murder and David faces the harrowing responsibility of defending one childhood friend accused of killing another.

Buried family secrets, devastating lies and a seemingly uncatchable killer plague David as he races toward a trial which appears impossible to win. Worse still, he soon discovers that proving Chris's innocence is linked to an unthinkable mistake . . . made by someone very close to him, many years before . . .